第二期

SINO-AMERICAN JOURNAL *of* COMPARATIVE LITERATURE

中美比较文学

主编 张 华
Paul Allen Miller

中国社会科学出版社

图书在版编目（CIP）数据

中美比较文学. 第二期 / 张华，(美) 米勒（Miller, A. P.）主编 . —北京：中国社会科学出版社，2016.6
ISBN 978-7-5161-8029-7

Ⅰ.①中… Ⅱ.①张… ②米… Ⅲ.①比较文学—文学研究—中国、美国 Ⅳ.①I206 ②I712.06

中国版本图书馆CIP数据核字（2016）第084299号

出 版 人	赵剑英
责任编辑	凌金良　陈　彪
特约编辑	胡国秀
责任校对	冀洪芬
责任印制	张雪娇

出　　版	中国社会科学出版社
社　　址	北京鼓楼西大街甲158号
邮　　编	100720
网　　址	http://www.csspw.cn
发 行 部	010-84083685
门 市 部	010-84029450
经　　销	新华书店及其他书店

印刷装订	北京金瀑印刷有限公司
版　　次	2016年6月第1版
印　　次	2016年6月第1次印刷

开　　本	710×1000　1/16
印　　张	15.75
插　　页	2
字　　数	241千字
定　　价	59.00元

凡购买中国社会科学出版社图书，如有质量问题请与本社营销中心联系调换
电话：010-84083683
版权所有　侵权必究

《中美比较文学》（*Sino-American Journal of Comparative Literature*）为中国北京语言大学与美国南卡罗来纳大学合作项目，由中美比较文学界同仁共同创办和编辑。中方和美方两个编委会分别负责审阅中美学者的来稿，刊物将由中国社会科学出版社出版，中英文双语发行。

　　本刊旨在集中展示中美比较文学界在比较文学与世界文学学科范围内及相关学科的最新研究成果，探讨前沿理论问题，拓展文学批评空间，研究学术焦点现象，以促进比较文学与世界文学研究领域的最平等、最直接、最充分的学术交流。

中方主编：张　华
美方主编：Paul Allen Miller
中方副主编：李丙权　黄　悦
美方副主编：Alexander Beecroft, Zahi Zalloua, Eric Hayot

中方编委会（按姓氏音序）：
黄　悦（北京语言大学）
李丙权（中国人民大学）
宋旭红（中央民族大学）
韦清琦（南京师范大学）
张　华（北京语言大学）
张　甜（华中师范大学）
张喜华（北京第二外国语学院）

美方编委会（按姓氏音序）：
BEECROFT, Alexander（南卡罗来纳大学）
HAYOT, Eric（宾夕法尼亚州立大学）
MILLER, Paul Allen（南卡罗来纳大学）
RAPAPORT, Herman（维克森林大学）
SHANKMAN, Steven（俄勒冈大学）
ZALLOUA, Zahi（惠特曼学院）

Sino-American Journal of Comparative Literature is a joint project between Beijing Language and Culture University, China and the University of South Carolina, the United States. The journal is published by the China Social Sciences Press both in English and in Chinese. The co-founders and editors, as well as the members of the editorial board, as experts in the field of comparative literature in China and the U. S. are responsible for refereeing all submissions. Articles submitted in Chinese are edited by the Chinese editorial board, those in English by the American board.

The journal is designed to be a platform to gather and exhibit the latest research findings in Comparative Literature, World Literature and related disciplines in both countries. Its mission is to explore the latest theoretical issues in both countries and to expand the range of literary criticism available in each. It aims to promote a full and critical dialogue in the field of Comparative Literature and World Literature as well as intercultural comprehension.

Chinese Editor in Chief: ZHANG Hua
U. S. Editor in Chief: Paul Allen Miller
Chinese Deputy Editors: LI Bingquan, HUANG Yue
U. S. Deputy Editors: Alexander Beecroft, Zahi Zalloua, Eric Hayot

China Editorial Board (by surname sequence):
HUANG Yue (Beijing Language and Culture University)
LI Bingquan (Renmin University of China)
SONG Xuhong (Minzu University of China)
WEI Qingqi (Nanjing Normal University)
ZHANG Hua (Beijing Language and Culture University)
ZHANG Tian (Central China Normal University)
ZHANG Xihua (Beijing International Studies University)

U. S. Editorial Board (by surname sequence):

BEECROFT, Alexander (University of South Carolina)

HAYOT, Eric (Penn State University)

MILLER, Paul Allen (University of South Carolina)

RAPAPORT, Herman (Wake Forest University)

SHANKMAN, Steven (University of Oregon)

ZALLOUA, Zahi (Whitman College)

目 录

The Way Chinese Ideology "Entered" the
　　Western Conceptual System ……………… Yang Huilin(1)
The Ecological Adaptability of Greek and
　　Chinese ……………………………… Alexander Beecroft(16)
An Ancient Greek *Journey to the West*: Reading the
　　Odyssey through East-Asian Eyes ………… John T. Kirby(46)
THE *ZHUANGZI*: A Verse Translation ………… Steven Shankman(109)
Extravagant Writing: Of Excess and
　　Frivolity ……………………………… Herman Rapaport(124)
Žižek with Stendhal: Irony and the
　　Death Drive …………………………… Zahi Zalloua(149)

叶维廉与英、美新批评 ……………………………… 于　伟(172)
朗费罗《人生颂》传播到中国的追问与思考 ………… 柳士军(189)
世界文学视野中的性别写作研究：以凌叔华、
　　曼斯菲尔德和伍尔夫为例 ………………… 林晓霞(202)
翻译的"恐怖"以及"恐怖"的翻译：但丁《神
　　曲·地狱篇》翻译三题 …………………… 乐安东(222)

The Way Chinese Ideology "Entered" the Western Conceptual System

Yang Huilin [*]

中文摘要 16、17世纪以来,中外文化交流开启了中西思想往来传播、互相影响的通路。古代中国的经典通过传教士、学者的翻译传入西方,在西方固有的基督教精神和哲学思想中找到了对应共通的智慧。本文以理雅各对儒家的"恕"和道家的"韬光养晦"、"大道无为"的对译——"reciprocity"、"sheathing the light"、"doing nothing with a purpose"为例,分析了传教士在翻译、传播中国思想时是如何从西方人熟习的《圣经》、《约翰福音》等基督教经典中寻找对应的观念的。这实现了中西方经典辨读(Scriptural Reasoning)的互通,成为中西思想跨越界线、积极对话的重要基础。

关键词 基督教;理雅各;忠;恕;文化对话

It is my great pleasure and honor to join the conference and offer the presentation. Please allow me to extend my sincere thanks to our host

---

[*] 杨慧林,哲学博士,中国人民大学文学院教授、博士生导师,原中国比较文学学会会长,主要研究方向为基督教文化与比较文学。

university and those who make everything happen. My appreciation also goes to my colleagues who proposed such a challenging topic for my presentation and sent it to the organizers timely or probably too timely. To be honest, I was more or less surprised to recognize that I would have to argue for the "way" Chinese "ideology" entered the Western conceptual system, which might be an impossible mission for anybody. Anyway, I think the topic in Chinese hermeneutically means something much more humble and positive than it is in English, not so aggressive and quite different with the word-by-word translation. It is probably an instance to show the importance of the conference on *Translating the Ancient Classics* and let us know the necessary "reduction" in understanding the translated resource, beyond the plain sense of a text.

As the matter of fact, what I mean by the proposed topic lies in the concerns of the cultural contact and the mutual understanding between different traditions, particularly demonstrated or embodied in the act of translation. When a greater attention has been paid to introduce our own culture (or so-called core values) to others, as expected everywhere nowadays, it is even more critical and crucial to explore the existed translation and experienced reception of the classics in a foreign context first of all. Taking into account of this, the translations and commentaries of Chinese classics by Christian missionaries could be taken as a typical case, provided a clearer view of the efficiency of the "entry" and ensure a real intelligent dialogue. In this sense, the more adequate topic of my presentation could be revised as "The Nomination and Reception of Chinese Thought in Western Conceptual System", with its focus on the travel of some key terms, "reciprocity" and "sheathing the light" specifically, in the translation of Chinese classics by James Legge.

I. The re-nomination of 恕 in the *Analects* as "reciprocity" and its travel

In many discussions of the translation of Chinese classics by missionaries, the western translators are frequently blamed on "naming Chinese ideas with western concepts". Anyway, it is such re-nomination and re-interpretation that simultaneously and paradoxically brought Chinese ideas into the western conceptual system, in their borrowing the conceptual tools of the West to "name Chinese ideas", which vividly embodied the interaction between the "spreading of Western learning in China" and the "transmission of Chinese learning in the West", and established various possible channels between Christian and Chinese traditions, such as the equivalence with "Dao" in the work of *Laozi* and the "Word" in the Gospel according to John, similarly the relation of "kenosis" in the New Testament and "the Use of Emptiness" in the Daoist writings, the sharing of Golden Rule in Christian Bible and the *Analects*, etc. And so, it seems to be understandable that some commentators remarked on James Legge: in his "translating and explaining the learning of the East to the scholars and the missionaries of the West", "he was actually a missionary to his own people and race first." [1]

Indeed, the major achievement of James Legge during his lifetime was not his spreading of Christianity to Chinese people, but his translation of the Chinese classics into English. Although his Christian standpoint was always apparent, and his aim of evangelism was undoubted, the words engraved on his tombstone approved the balance of his double "identities": "Here Rests

---

[1] Lindsay Ride, "Biographical Note" for the third edition, in James Legge, *The Chinese Classics, with a translation, critical and exegetical notes, prolegomena, and copious indexes* (Taibei: SMC Publishing Inc., 2001), 10.

in God/James Legge/Missionary to China/and First Professor of Chinese/in the University of Oxford. " ①

My question is that if we could really distinguish the James Legge as a missionary from the James Legge as a sinologist, who both steadfastly upheld the Christian faith and thoroughly studied so many Chinese classics. In some sense, James Legge witnessed a kind of vacillation or shift in his identity, or his "moving subject" in phrase of Karl Barth. In other words, the "identity" of James Legge is not only drawn on his direct expression of faith, but also implied in his translations and commentaries left to us.

If we parallel the two prefaces of *The Analects* written by James Legge in 1861 and the revised one in 1893, we may be astonished to read his completely different comments on Confucius. In the earlier edition, he said: "the more I have studies his character and opinions, the less have I regarded him as a great man". And in the later edition, he rephrased his comments just with a few words changed but the whole tone perverse: "the more I have studies his character and opinions, the more highly have I come to regard him. He was a very great man, and his influence has been on the whole a great benefit to the Chinese, while his teachings suggest important lessons to ourselves who profess to belong to the school of Christ. " ②

If there is really some vacillation in the view point and intelligence of Legge, I think it is more obvious and significant in his translation and interpretation of *Dao De Jing* in his later years. And if we could accept the idea of some Continental philosophers, like Alain Badiou, that "the subject is not constitutive but constituted" ③, the consequence of the vacillation is not

---

① Lindsay Ride, "Biographical Note" for the third edition, in James Legge, *The Chinese Classics, with a Translation, Critical and Exegetical Notes, Prolegomena, and Copious Indexes* (Taibei: SMC Publishing Inc. , 2001), 9.

② James Legge, *The Chinese Classics, with a Translation, Critical and Exegetical Notes, Prolegomena, and Copious Indexes*, 111.

③ Alain Badiou, "The Event in Deleuze", translated by Jon Roffe, *Parrhesia*, Number 2, 2007, p. 37.

"contradiction" but "contrariety", because the "subjectivity" of a reader, translator or interpreter has been produced and constituted as a result of this vacillation.

Going back to the case of Reciprocity, it is of course fine to be translated, in the sense of Political Sciences and Economics, as "equally and mutually benefited" based on its Latin root "*reciprocus*". But in Christian tradition, "reciprocity" might first of all remind people of human-God relation and human-neighbor relation. As described in the 15 chapter of John (15: 12 – 14): "My command is this: Love each other as I have loved you. ...If you obey my commandment, you are my friend." In the item of the Catholic Encyclopedia, these verses are stressing the function of reciprocity so that love can be the genuine friendship between human beings and God. Another Christian Theological Lexicon explains "reciprocity" as establishing an "inter-dependent relationship" on the basis of "commutative justice". Interestingly, this theological meaning and the word "reciprocity" is used by James Legge as nothing but the Confucian key term "Shu (恕)".

In the chapter Li Ren of the *Analects*, it is recorded that a disciple of Confucius, Zi Gong, asked his Master: "Is there one word which may serve as a rule of practice for all one's life?" The Master said, "Is not RECIPROCITY such a word? What you do not want done to yourself, do not do to others." Here "reciprocity" is closely related to the "foremost demonstrated principle" *in The Analects*, that is "faithfulness and mutual understanding"(夫子之道忠恕而已矣, or literally, the core principle for Confucius is nothing but loyalty and pardon or forgiveness). The Chinese word "Shu" (恕 pardon or forgiveness) comprises of two parts. The upper part "Ru" (如 same as or compare with) is only phonic and gives the sound of the word, without any concrete meaning; the lower part "Xin" (心 heart) serves as a radical which gives meaning of the word. So it is said in Chinese 从心如声 (taking meaning from the lower part and sound from the upper.) James Legge used "reciprocity" to translate this word, instead of the commonly used terms "forgiveness", "pardon" or "mutual tolerance", and later on, for the convenience of the missionaries and even ordinary Chinese people who do not so care the definition in ancient dictionaries, the word tend to be understood as 如 (same as) plus 心 (heart and feelings), that means to compare your own emotion and feeling with those of others, or judge others as you would like to be judged by others. Seen from a western missionary's eyes, this has more in common with the logic of "correlated other" in the Christian sense. It is probably not exactly equivalent to the traditional interpretation of 恕, but more likely to the theological idea of "commutative correlation".

And then James Legge quoted Zhu Xi's commentary on *Analects* to prove this equivalence. As the most important philosopher and interpreter of Confucius writings in Song Dynasty, Zhu Xi explained that: "doing one's best means 忠 (faithfulness or loyalty); putting oneself in the other's place is 恕 (pardon, forgiveness or reciprocity)." Gradually, even native speakers of Chinese accepted such a "super-sign" and plainly understanding of this term promoted by Legge.

In the year of 2001, a British scholar, or "Marxist scholar", Terry Eagleton took "reciprocity" as a tool in his work to explain Marx's proposal to "escape from binary logic", and proclaimed that "our powers and capacities" should be realized "freely and reciprocally". (Terry Eagleton, "God, the Universe, Art, and Communism", *New Literary History*, 2001, p. 32, note 4) And more interestingly, in September 2010, the EU held a summit on foreign policy concerning the "strategic partnership". There were many disputes but finally for the first time the EU affirmed the importance of "strategic partnership" to EU foreign policy. And the Permanent Chair of EU Council Herman van Rompuy, former Primary of Belgium, made it clear that "In the framework of strategic partnership, the most important concept is reciprocity."

In the travel of "reciprocity", from the text of the *Analects*, to the collected commentaries of Zhu Xi, then the interpretation and translation of James Legge, the widely acceptance of "如心" ("same as" plus "heart and emotion") and the definition of "strategic partnership" by EU leaders, again, what is demonstrated is only a shift or vacillation of a dynamic procedure, and we could hardly say which is constitutive and which is constituted. I think that is the charm and attraction of the act of translation, in which the travel of the ideas makes them "return to their emergence and semantics" [1].

II. "sheathing the light" (韬光养晦) and "doing nothing with a purpose" (大道无为)

Many of you may have heard that Mr. Deng Xiaoping used to quote quite a famous ancient moral teaching and then it was regarded as the principle of Chinese diplomatic policy for many years. That is 韬光养晦, widely translated as "to hide one's capacities and bide one's time." I am not sure if Western scholars and politicians would think of this idiom positively as practical wisdom and temperance, or regard it negatively as being crafty and conspiratorial. Personally, I do believe that this translation would be likely to leave a very skeptical impression. Some of the professional interpreters in the Diplomatic Ministry of China obviously shared the same worry, so they suggested that this should be translated as "to keep low profile" to make it more friendly. But I am afraid many people are so familiar with the story of Liu Bei from the *Romance of Three Kingdoms* (《三国演义》), who pretended to spend all the time on planting vegetables in his garden and not care for the

---

[1] Jacques Derrida, *Acts of Religion*, ed. Gil Anidjar (New York: Routledge, 2002), 48.

future political power, that they could hardly take the new translation as 韬光养晦. (It is even worse that a book in Ming Dynasty, entitled 韬晦术, described the "technique" 术 as "letting others not know your intention even they are your good friends". 虽知己者莫辨其本心. What a danger it is to have friends like this!) On the other hand, it is also quite hard to believe the moral teachings from our sincere and earnest ancestors could be so deceitful. Anyway, in reading the translation and commentaries by James Legge, we would have some confidence that, historically, in the classics in Pre-Qin period, 韬光养晦 had been really understood in another way.

In chapter 7 of the Tao Te Ching, Lao-Tzu compares the sages or the gentlemen of great virtue with the principle of Nature. James Legge's translation is as follows: Heaven is long-enduring and earth continues long. The reason why heaven and earth are able to endure and continue thus long is because they do not live of, or for, themselves. This is how they are able to continue and endure. Therefore the sage puts his own person last, and yet it is found in the foremost place; he treats his person as if it were foreign to him, and yet that person is preserved. Is it not because he has no personal and private ends, that therefore such ends are realized?

The key points are more explicitly explained by a later American sinologist, Robert Henricks, as "The Sage...has no self-interest, that he is therefore able to realize his self-interest" (圣人无私而故能成其私).

Given James Legge's position as a Christian missionary, it might be useful to remind us of some similar sayings in the Bible, which are differently formulated but similar in logic. *The Gospel of Mark* has Jesus saying,

> If one of you wants to be great, he must be the servant of the rest; and if one of you wants to be first, he must be the slave of all. The Son of Man came to serve, not to be served. (Mark 10: 43 – 45)

I suppose James Legg e must have recognized that there is a large space for inter-interpretation between the Chinese classics and the Christian Bible. Accordingly, he made a very important footnote both in English and in Chinese in his translation of chapter 7 of the *Tao Te Ching* to explain further his translation. The English is "sheathing the light," and the Chinese is 韬光.

Why did he parallelize 韬光 with "sheathing the light"? It is because he believes this chapter of *Tao Te Ching* "teaches that one's best good is realized by not thinking of it, or seeking for it." ① That is his understanding of 韬光, which has resonance with "the Heaven and Earth...do not live of, or live for, themselves" quoted above.

What we should pay more attention to are his further explanations with his translation of the classics in other parts. For instance, 上德无为 in chapter 38 of *Tao Te Ching* is normally translated as "the highest virtue takes no action" or "does nothing." ② James Legge, however, adds "with a purpose" in brackets, in order to make it clear what is meant by "doing nothing." ③ Taking this as a clue, we may again read comparatively a passage in the New Testament: "I may give away everything I have and even give up my body to be burnt—but if I have no love, this does me no good" (1 Cor 13: 3) Following the phrase of "give up my body to be burnt," some ancient manuscripts have "in order to boast." I think "doing something in order to boast" is very close to "doing something with a purpose," both of which, according to James Legge and Lao-Tzu, have nothing to do with "the highest virtue."

Furthermore, such an explanation may lead to the Biblical saying "Blessed are the poor in spirit" (Matt 5: 3) and the terminology of

---

① Legge, *Sacred Books of China*, 52.
② Lao-Tzu, *Lao-Tzu Te-Tao Ching: A New Translation Based on the Recently Discovered Ma-wang-tui Texts*, trans. Robert G. Henricks (New York: Ballantine Books, 1989), 7.
③ "(Those who) possessed in the highest degree those attributes did nothing (with a purpose)." See James Legge, *Sacred Books of China*, 80.

"kenosis" (Phil 2: 7) or "self-emptying." ① In his commentary on the *Tao Te Ching*, Legge mentions time and again "The Use of Emptiness," "The Empty Heart," or "there is nothing before the Tao; it might seem to have been before God. And yet there is no demonstration by it of its presence and operation. It is like the emptiness of a vessel". ②

In summary, in the comparison of James Legge's interpretation of Chinese classics and his Biblical framework of pre-understanding, I think 韬光 is almost the same as the phrases "poor in spirit", "kenosis" and "self-emptying".

Therefore, when "doing something" (有所作为) is added as a supplementary aspect of Chinese foreign policy, what a footnote would James Legge leave if he were still alive? I think it might be "doing nothing with a purpose" or "doing something by not thinking of it, or seeking for it" in accordance with the above. In its essential nature, this expression should be considered as the typical form of negative thinking or "weak thought", both in Eastern wisdom and in the Christian Bible and theology. That is a deep impression we could get from James Legge and his inter-cultural translation.

Related case 1: The Tao that can be trodden is not the eternal Tao, the name that can be named is not the eternal name, as Christians cannot have the name of God, whose being cannot be known but can be only embodied. That is the reason why he who does not love does not know God (for God is love). And that is the "essential of the essence" in the inter-interpretation of Chinese classics and Bible.

Related case 2: In the *Principle of Mean*, sincerity and honesty is listed as the ultimate goal that we could never reach. What we could do is to learn to be sincere and learn to be honest, which is basic virtue but not the sincerity

---

① John B. Cobb and Christopher Ives, eds., *The Emptying God*: A Buddhist-Jewish-Christian Conversation (*Maryknoll, N. Y.*: Orbis Books, 1990).

② Legge, *Sacred Books of China*, 49 – 50.

and honesty itself.

Using of the resources of Christian theology seems to be something like to bring coals to New Castle. Anyway, in the past years a lot of coals have been actually imported to New Castle from other places. And whatever resources we use, if properly reinterpreted, we may find something new, something different, and something with more vitality, as what has been done by Alain Badiou, Vattimo or Zizek in the interpretation of St. Paul to reconstruct the foundation of universalism.

The travel of the translated terms in the perspective of SR

Religious dialogue in the framework of "Scriptural Reasoning", promoted by some theologians since 1990s, would probably lead us to some challenging questions, for instance, why people are not so tolerant in talking of tolerance, not so peaceful in searching for peace, and why there are so many quarrels or even conflicts among communities who are supposed to share similar or same values.

In Christianity there has been a long tradition of "exegesis", whose goal is to explore the meaning of the Scriptures through various methods of interpretation, and to establish its authoritative and legitimate values in interpreting the Scriptures.

The "reasoning" in the reading of the Scriptures actually began with the formative process of the Bible. For instance, in the New Testament, only four times was Jesus recorded as using his mother tongue, which means surprisingly that "the words of Jesus, which have come down to us, (whether they are in Hebrew, Greek, English or Chinese) are only translations". Although sometheologians believed that "everywhere behind the Greek text we get glimpses of…Jesus'mother-tongue," they have to admit at the same time that "the task of translating his sayings into Greek … necessarily involved…many changes of meaning."

We also read from Biblical writings that:

> …a letter of Christ… [was] written not with ink but with the Spirit of the living God, not on tablets of stone but on tablets of human hearts…. ; for the letter kills, but the spirit gives life. (2 Cor. 3: 3 – 6)

Based on this proclamation, the exclusive meaning and the explicit interpretation of the biblical texts might never have been existed. Understanding the Christian faith and Christian Scriptures from this perspective has opened a space for "exegesis" or "interpretation" and implicates the possibility of "reasoning" or "debate".

"Reasoning" in the reading of Scriptures has certainly included debates on "orthodoxy" and brutal fights over power. However, once the "Scripture" can be read, interpreted and debated, it must lead to two logical conclusions: 1) When "Scripture" is offered for "reading", it is hard to maintain an "orthodox" or "definitive" meaning; 2) When "Scripture" is the scripture as such, it is expected as something "absolute" exactly in diverse interpretations. Thus, just as the theologians have repeatedly told us: when people attempt to explicate the "absolute truth", they are inevitably "relativized" by the truth; when they hope to "truthfully refer to the ultimate Truth", even the "theological statements" have to "acknowledge their own limitation and relativity as statements", or (otherwise) they can only obtain "a false conception of 'orthodoxy'".

The theme of "reasoning" in the reading of Scriptures has given rise to a contemporary trend known as "Scriptural Reasoning", a practice of reading the Christian Bible alongside with the Jewish Tanakh the Islamic Quran.

Personally, my interest in SR was stimulated in a dialogue organized by Arch Bishop Rowan Williams at Lambeth Palace 6 or 7 years ago, where Prof. David Ford from the University of Cambridge made a very impressive presentation and my job was to give him a response. I found Scriptural Reasoning, described as "a wisdom seeking engagement" by Prof. Ford, and its framework and potentiality could be more than relevant for the studies of humanities in any context, including Chinese context.

Along with some Chinese scholars were involved in the discussions, another rich resource closely related to the westernized sense of "sacred books" has been gradually recognized, that is the Chinese classics translated by Christian missionaries, like James Legge, with detailed and paralleled commentaries in the perspective of Christianity. And it is also in this procedure that Chinese classics, religious or non-religious, were re-interpreted into "The Sacred Books of the East", as the series of publication edited by Max Muller in the late years of 19th century. And an often-quoted dictum became the pre-condition of religious studies and comparative literature, that "He who knows one knows none".

Consequently, in the dialogue as well as argument of Scriptural Reasoning, something both challenging and encouraging has been mutually accepted as follows:

1. Scriptural Reasoning should be a wisdom-seeking engagement, in which the diversely involved voices cannot be integrated into a monologue, and the presence of the similar perfectness might be variously identified. Therefore, it is without authoritative overviews, original texts or native speakers, and nobody exclusively owns the final meaning of the Scripture.

2. "Scripture" is dynamic, but not a noun sitting there waiting for our interpretation. So in the more legitimate talk of "Scripture", we are actually talking about its emergence and the semantics, in its reading, understanding, translation and interpretation. Theologically, it is to find the perfectness where it is not, find the possible in its impossibility.

3. SR will help us gain a better understanding of "others" as well as our own classics and tradition. What is highlighted in the end is the value and ideal that is above any part in dialogue. In one word, SR is an absolute humility, against any attitude of priority, individual, ethnical, cultural, ideological, including religious priority. In this case, tracing back to the tradition of Christian theology, a very interesting phrase is normally introduced in talking of "justice", that is "commutative justice", as mentioned in the translation of "reciprocity". Therefore, "justice" is particularly used in passive voice in New Testament, that is "to be justified" or "to be accounted as justice".

In this sense, "Scriptural Reasoning" not only stimulates the mutual reflection among different traditions but also re-constructs the self-understanding of each tradition; it not only reveals the "similar perfectness" but also de-constructs the "monologues" through "dialogues"; it not only helps us understand "differences" but also witness the "Perfectness" in the differences. It might be the very premise to break down the narrow-minded "identity" position and uncover our common values in a pluralistic context. In this case, I think "Scriptural Reasoning", or "Reasoning" in the reading of Scriptures as such, should be the fundamental spiritual basis for any dialogues.

The western learning brought to China with the missionaries about 400 years ago did stimulate continuous debates and controversies between China and West, while the "East" used to think that Western learning was "nothing new - something that had originated in China anyway", or that the Chinese should make use of "Western learning for the benefit of Chinese learning"; and the "West" also treated Oriental civilization as something that "had not left behind its primitive mode", or as the "projected Other" judged by the West. It is only via communication and dialogue that such gaps can be overcome.

To reflect on the encounter of, and dialogue between, Eastern and

Western ideas over the past 400 years is to understand that whether in the East or the West, people share similar passions; whether in the North or the South, the way of learning has never diverged beyond being able to compare. What is more, in this work we can find a channel to connect East and West, past and present, and can learn the lessons of history and look into the future with the wisdom of the past. As the world influences China, China is responding to the world. Eastern learning and Western learning are destined to forge a mutually open and mutually attractive East and West.

Works Cited:
1. Lao-Tzu, *Lao-Tzu Te-Tao Ching: A New Translation Based on the Recently Discovered Ma-wang-tui Texts*, trans. Robert G. Henricks (New York: Ballantine Books, 1989).
2. John B. Cobb and Christopher Ives, eds., *The Emptying God: A Buddhist-Jewish-Christian Conversation* (Maryknoll, N.Y.: Orbis Books, 1990).
3. Lindsay Ride, "Biographical Note" for the third edition, in James Legge, *The Chinese Classics, with a Translation, Critical and Exegetical Notes, Prolegomena, and Copious Indexes* (Taibei: SMC Publishing Inc., 2001).
4. Jacques Derrida, *Acts of Religion*, ed. Gil Anidjar (New York: Routledge, 2002).
5. Alain Badiou, "The Event in Deleuze", translated by Jon Roffe, *Parrhesia*, Number 2, 2007.
6. Legge, *Sacred Books of China*.

The Ecological Adaptability of Greek and Chinese

Alexander Beecroft *

中文摘要 根据出现的时间顺序，世界文学大致可以划分出六种文学生态系统，第一类是基于小型部落社会的史诗型；第二类是泛希腊化的类型，特征是人们已经形成了一个文化共同体并有基本的文化认同；第三类是帝国类型，其基础是伴随着疆界广阔的大帝国的建立，一种语言在广阔的范围内迅速普及并持续使用；第四类是方言文学，在前述帝国型的内部某些地方性语言的使用积累到一定程度而凝聚出的文学成就，这种文学类型往往和政治势力的崛起相关，但又突破了其限制；第五种是民族文学，这一种生态类型是在方言文学的基础上伴随着民族国家的出现而在欧洲成型的；第六种也是最终的形式就是世界文学，这种类型是伴随着单一的语言特别是英语突破了国族界限被广泛使用而出现的。古希腊文学和中国古典文学是帝国类型文学的代表，与当下的阅读者之间已有隔膜，虽然有强大的回归传统的动力，也仍然会遇到瓶颈，从文学生态的角度来看，这并不是一种缺陷，而是一种特点。辨明文学生态有助于打破古代文学传播发展的瓶颈，是通往世界文学的途径。

---

* 作者为美国比较文学学会秘书长、南卡罗莱纳大学副教授、文学博士，主要研究方向为古典文学与比较文学。

关键词 世界文学；类型学；生态适应性；希腊

In my recent book, *An Ecology of World Literature: From Antiquity to the Present Day* (Verso, 2015), I expand on a typology of literary systems I developed earlier in an article in the *New Left Review*.[1] These literary systems, or ecologies, group literatures across time and space into a collection of six types, based on the kinds of interactions found between a given literature and its cultural, political, economic, etc. environment. These six ecologies I identify as:

1. Epichoric, or local, literary ecologies are the limit case of literary circulation, where verbal art (frequently, though not necessarily, oral) may be transmitted over long periods of time but does not leave the small-scale local community (be it a Greek polis, a Chinese city-state of the Warring States era, or a tribal community among the aboriginal populations of the Americas and the Pacific).

2. Panchoric ecologies are those that form in regions with small-scale polities but where literary and other cultural artifacts circulate more broadly through a space that is self-aware of itself as some kind of cultural unity and that define themselves by the exclusion of other polities that do not share that culture. The paradigmatic example of this ecology is the Panhellenic culture of archaic and classical Greece (and my coinage, "panchoric" is a generalization of the more familiar Panhellenic), though I have attempted to show, here and elsewhere, that the Chinese world of the same era is comparably constituted, and there are a limited number of other possible cases around the world.

3. Cosmopolitan ecologies are found wherever a single literary language is

---

[1] Alexander Beecroft, *An Ecology of World Literature: From Antiquity to the Present Day* (Verso, 2015); Alexander Beecroft, "World Literature Without a Hyphen: Towards a Typology of Literary Systems", *New Left Review*, No. 54 (December 2008): 87 - 100.

used over a large territorial range and through a long period of time. Such languages frequently emerge as the result of a great world-empire (those of Alexander the Great, of the Guptas in India, the Han in China, or the Islamic Caliphate, for example), but the languages and literary cultures they spawn (almost necessarily written) long outlast those more transient political formations.

4. Vernacularecologies emerge (as Pollock describes) out of cosmopolitan ones when sufficient cultural resources accumulate behind some version of a locally spoken language to allow for its use for literary purposes. Vernaculars are often developed in the context of new political formations, though their uses frequently spread beyond the borders of those polities. Since many vernaculars emerge out of a dialect continuum (as, for example, Italian, French and Spanish all do), they are often themselves somewhat abstract languages, generalized from a point on that continuum, rather than simply reflecting the speech habits of any one community (though they may represent themselves as so doing).

5. The national literary ecology emerges out of the vernacular literary ecology of Europe, together with the emergence of nationalism per se, gaining considerable momentum in the aftermath of the French Revolution, Napoleonic Wars, and independence movements of the settler colonies in the Americas and continuing to grow throughout the nineteenth and twentieth centuries. This ecology spreads gradually around the world, as a direct consequence of European imperial expansion during this period.

6. Global literary ecology, my sixth and final category, represents another limit case—the literary circulation that truly knows no borders. As major languages (most obviously, of course, English) escape the bonds of the nation-state, and texts begin to circulate more rapidly around the planet, we may be moving in the direction of just such a borderless world (though linguistic competency will always create barriers of its own).

Although I have listed these ecologies in the chronological order in which they seem to have first appeared, and in a sequence which suggests a general movement from smaller to larger systems of literary circulation, I do not think of the set of ecologies as providing a simple historical narrative, moving only forward. In most phases of human history, more than one ecology has existed simultaneously, and literatures have frequently moved "backwards" through this list, as when (as I argue) Latin moves from being a vernacular language in its early centuries to a cosmopolitan status in Late Antique and Medieval Europe.① Moreover, far from being a series of developmental stages through which all literatures must pass, I believe there is only one literature that could plausibly claim to have participated in all six of my ecologies: Chinese. Even finding literatures which have been through five of the six is difficult: the only plausible candidates, I would suggest, are Greek and (perhaps) Arabic. Spoken by twelve million people today, Greek has little opportunity to participate in a future global literary system, where Chinese, as the world's largest language by any measure, will clearly play some significant role in that system. Leaving aside the more problematic case of Arabic (the timeframe in which Arabic might have moved from epichoric and/or panchoric to cosmopolitan is very, very, brief, and the nature of the culture of that period imperfectly understood; while even as the literary language of twenty-six modern nations, Arabic remains something of a cosmopolitan language), we are left with just two languages which have undergone something like a complete transition through the full range of the literary ecologies I have sketched out. Why would this be so? To be sure, Greece and China are both ancient civilizations: but other regions of the world (Egypt, the Near East, India) have equally ancient civilizations, but do not know the kind of linguistic continuity we find in Greece and in China. That continuity, of course, is partly a question of terminology: both Greek and Chinese have changed substantially over the millennia, and students in modern Athens or Beijing can only read the epics of Homer, or

---

① Beecroft, *An Ecology of World Literature: From Antiquity to the Present Day*, 157.

the poems of the Shi Jing, with special training. Many linguists would identify Homeric Greek and modern Greek, or the Chinese of the *Shi Jing* and modern spoken Mandarin, as distinct languages, and by the standard of mutual intelligibility, they are correct.

That said, there is an incredible tenacity to the identification with tradition in the cases of both Greek and Chinese. While vernacular elements had been a feature of many literary texts in China since at least the Tang dynasty (and earlier than that in some genres), and while entire genres such as drama and prose fiction relied heavily on vernacular forms and diction, it was only in the 1920's that Chinese intellectuals began to imagine the need for a rupture with the past tradition, calling for the equivalent of a Dante or a Luther to complete the vernacular revolution. Set expressions from the classical language remain a key element of educated spoken and written literary style to this day. Similarly in the case of Greek, colloquial and literary registers of the language co-existed for a considerable time, with the latter (known as Katharevousa, or "purified" language) remaining the standard in education and for official purposes until 1976. Since then, the colloquial register of the language, Dimotiki, has become almost completely ascendant. Compare this late adoption of a completely vernacular language with the almost complete replacement of Latin by Western European vernacular languages in almost every register of intellectual and cultural life by the end of the seventeenth century,[1] and the roughly contemporaneous replacement of Sansrkit by Indian vernaculars.[2] (Compare it, too, to the relationship between classical and vernacular language in Arabic, where the literary standard based on the classical language remains the sole form with official recognition, and where vernacular forms are used in only a limited

---

[1] Francoise Waquet, *Latin or The Empire of a Sign: From the Sixteenth to the Twentieth Centuries* (Verso, 2003), 80 – 83.

[2] Sheldon Pollock, "The Death of Sanskrit", *Comparative Studies in Society and History* 43 (2001): 392 – 426.

range of literary genres).

The question of why Greek and Chinese have endured so long, when speakers of Ancient Egyptian gave way to Arabic; those of Akkadian and Sumerian to Aramaic, Greek, and Arabic; those of Sanskrit to Hindi, Bengali, Marathi, and other languages: this is not a question to be answered simply or briefly. In this article, I would like to suggest a couple of preliminary reasons. One (which I explore in more detail in my first book, *Authorship and Cultural Identity in Early Greece and China*) is that both Greek and Chinese literatures began as media for interaction between small and rivalrous polities sharing a literary language, and that, as a result, the texts in those traditions proved particularly adaptable to new and different ecological contexts.[①] My second argument is that both Greek and Chinese, unlike a number of other cosmopolitan languages, were successful both at integrating vernacular elements into the existing tradition, and at becoming the languages of specific nation-states. Throughout each of these phases, Greek and Chinese have alike shown a remarkable ability to adapt to new environments, where other languages have struggled. In particular, they have both made two particularly difficult transitions, each on its own made by few languages; the two together, by fewer still: from epichoric and panchoric to cosmopolitan; the second, from cosmopolitan to vernacular and national. Chinese may be in the process of continuing this last transition onwards to global status.

The First Bottleneck: From Epichoric and Panchoric to Cosmopolitan

As I have suggested above, both Greek and Chinese began their long

---

[①] Beecroft, *Authorship and Cultural Identity in Early Greece and China: Patterns of Literary Circulation*, 1st ed. (Cambridge University Press, 2010).

lives as the shared language of a collection of small polities, frequently at war with one another, but with a slowly emergent sense of a culture they shared with each other, but not with all of their neighbors. This is precisely the literary ecology I call "panchoric", though as I explore in some detail elsewhere, it is mostly in the context of the panchoric that we actually encounter epichoric readings of literary texts. We only know that we are reading locally when we have some other kind of reading against which we can compare the local. ① Early Greek and Chinese texts are frequently available to be read in two ways: epichoric and panchoric; in other words, as both the products of specific local cultures, and as the synthesis of those local traditions in a larger cultural context.

While these reading practices can be identified with a great range of texts, there are certain points within each tradition where the two patterns are particularly apparent, particularly in Homeric epic and in the Shi Jing, or *Canon of Songs*.② In particular, through the devices of catalogues and anthologies—specifically, the *Catalogue of the Ships* in the *Iliad* and the section of the *Canon of Songs* titled the *Guofeng* 國風, *or Airs of the States* - we see at work both the presentation of individual local traditions, and a Panhellenic or "Panhuaxia", respectively, tradition designed to integrate the local. Both of these texts produce the effect of geographically comprehensive listings of the constituent polities forming the larger cultural order: the cities and kingdoms of the Hellenic world and the regional states of the Western Zhou and Spring and Autumn eras. And yet in both cases the geography is glaringly flawed; important places are omitted, comparatively minor places are given strange prominence, the same territories are identified by more than one name, and polities that did not exist contemporaneously are

---

① Beecroft, *An Ecology of World Literature: From Antiquity to the Present Day*, 86 - 87.
② What follows is a somewhat abridged and altered version of the discussion at ibid., 115 - 126.

anachronistically brought together. I would argue that this is a feature, not a flaw, of the panchoric system, that the system benefits from this very geographic imprecision in that it puts the device to work in the service of a panchorism where the component parts are rendered uniform by a centralizing textual authority. Devices like catalogues and anthologies literalize and literarize this notion of culture by aggregation, but completeness and accuracy are clearly not essential to the effectiveness of the system. Indeed, I will go so far as to argue that both the Greek and Chinese panchoric ecologies thrived in full awareness of, and in part *because* of, this imprecise aggregation, which allowed the whole to represent itself as greater and other than the sum of its parts by making the listing of those parts always somewhat arbitrary and incomplete.

A case in point is the *Catalogue of Ships* in book two of the *Iliad*, a listing (with occasional geographic detail and mythological ornament) of twenty-nine lands (and many of the cities located within them) that have sent their troops to the fight at Troy, naming also the forty-six heroes leading the soldiers of those lands and enumerating how many of the 1,186 ships deployed they commanded. The total passage, 266 lines in length, tends to have a somewhat soporific effect on modern readers of the *Iliad*, unused to such catalogues and unfamiliar with many of the locations and heroes mentioned.

To an ancient Greek audience, of course, this material was of much greater potential interest, potentially linking the audience member's own community to the great Panhellenic charter-myth of the Trojan War, and we know that the *Catalogue* was frequently cited in ancient times. There are a number of geographic and chronological difficulties with the Catalogue, which I will only briefly indicate here. Many of the places mentioned in the *Catalogue* (not merely the minor cities mentioned but even some of the regional kingdoms) are obscure in the extreme, and there is little to no evidence for their existence in Mycenean or Archaic times; others seem to have existed *only* in the earliest of times and to have disappeared by the

Classical era. Conversely, some quite important and long-established cities, such as Megara, are omitted altogether, as are almost all of the Aegean islands. The kingdoms of several of the important heroes, including those of Agamemnon, Ajax, Diomedes, Odysseus, and Achilles are strangely configured in the *Catalogue*.① Political arguments have been adduced to account for these discrepancies,② but the very abundance of geographic problems with the *Catalogue* suggests also the argument that inconsistency might have had the positive value of rendering the text relatively ineffectual as a tool for local propaganda of this kind.

The *Catalogue* also lavishes minor attention on certain figures while dismissing in very brief terms much more significant figures. At the same time, however, a closer examination of many of these detailed descriptions of minor figures reveals more significance than might be apparent on a casual reading. As an example, the first sixteen lines of the *Catalogue* are devoted to Boeotia and its leaders, five grandsons of the little-known Itonus. Of these five, three (Arcesilaus, Prothoenor, and Clonius) are mentioned only once more in the *Iliad*—at their deaths; one (Peneleus), is also killed during the action of the poem but is additionally mentioned three other times (once when exhorted by Poseidon and twice when he kills Trojan heroes); the only one to survive the poem (Leitus), is mentioned three times (once to be exhorted by Poseidon in the same passage as his brother, once when he kills a Trojan, and once when wounded in the wrist by Hector). At first glance, these figures seem like nothing more than the archaic equivalent of cannon fodder, faceless figures

---

① A still useful summary of the geographic complexities of the *Catalogue* is T. W. Allen, *The Homeric Catalogue of Ships*, Oxford: Oxford University Press, 1921, which offers the interpretation, contested by many, that Pelasgian Argos is a synonym for Thessaly. Peter Loptson, "Pelasgikon Argos in the Catalogue of Ships (681)", *Mnemosyne* 34 (1/2), Fourth Series, 1981: 136 - 8.

② See, e. g., Margalit Finkelberg, "Ajax's Entry in the Hesiodic Catalogue of Women", *The Classical Quarterly* 38 (1), New Series, 1988: 31 - 41. Finkelberg 1988 for the possible interests that Athens, Argos and Corinth might have had in representing Agamemon's kingdom in the way Homer does.

remembered only because they are among the thousands who die at Troy.

A closer examination, however, illuminates something about the *Catalogue's* role as a work of Panhellenic synthesis. These "Boeotian Five" heroes are part of the Hellenic genealogy as are certain other obscure figures in the Catalogue, like the leaders from Arcadia and Phocis. There are also some indications that the Boeotian Five may have been the object of hero-cult in Boeotia itself (see, e.g., Pausanias 9.39.3 on the tomb of Leitus). Further, the decision to emphasize the Boeotian Five seems deliberately to exclude Thersander, the son of Polyneices, and heir to the Theban throne in the Theban cycle of myth. According to the Cypria, indeed, Thersander was the original leader of the Boeotian troops at Troy, but died at the hands of Herakles' son Tlepolemus, during the Greek siege of Mysia, mistaken for Troy during an early phase of the war. The Iliad ignores Thersander's role, part, I would suggest, of a general downplaying of the Theban cycle in the Homeric epic, a phenomenon seen also at *Iliad* 4.370 – 410, when Agamemnon refers to the Theban war as part of an exhortation to Diomedes, in language which seems to diminish the earlier conflict by comparison with that at Troy.

The choice of the "Boeotian Five" as leaders of the Boeotian contingent in the Catalogue of Ships, then, represents not merely a pedantic listing of invented names, nor simplythe assemblage of a collection of heroes rich in local tradition to create a whole greater than the sum of its parts. While these five heroes do seem to have been a part of Boeotian epichoric tradition and were likely the object of hero-cult, their selection also has the effect of sidelining figures from another mythic tradition centered in Boeotia, one with its own Panhellenic circulation: the Theban Cycle. [1] As such, and in line

---

[1] Although "Boeotian" and "Theban" mythology often seem to exist in separate universes, so much so that a recent and very thoughtful study of Boeotian mythology and the construction of local identity does not once mention the Theban Cycle or its contents. See Larson 2007. Stephanie L. Larson, Tales of Epic Ancestry: Boiotian Collective Identity in the Late Archaic and Early Classical Periods, Bilingual, Franz Steiner Verlag Wiesbaden GmbH, 2007.

with the discussion earlier in the chapter, I would argue that the *Catalogue's* choice of the Boeotian Five as the leaders of their contingent, rather than Thersander, is less a question of choosing the local over the Panhellenic than of deciding what sort of local can be represented in a Panhellenic context, with the selected option chosen because it de-emphasizes local traditions not relevant to Panhellenic narrative.

Similarly, the first section of the *Canon of Songs*, the Chinese collection of ancient poetry traditionally attributed to Confucius, is the *Airs of the States*, a collection of some 160 relatively short poems, many of which are dominated by imagery of the natural and agricultural world, and frequently interpreted in modern times as popular in origin. The *Airs of the States* is divided in the orthodox Mao-school edition (of the last few centuries BC) into fifteen sections based on a notional geography of the states into which China was divided during the Spring and Autumn period, which covered the early part of the second half of the Zhou Dynasty (771 – 476 BC) and was named after an annalistic history also said to be edited by Confucius. As I have already noted in *Authorship and Cultural Identity*, this geography is notional rather than real; there is no historical moment at which all fifteen states represented in the collection existed simultaneously, some states overlap in geography, and some may never have existed at all[①]: The *Airs of Qin*, the *Airs of Zheng*, and the *Airs of the Royal Domain* (Wang), for example, were associated with the late Western Zhou and early Spring and Autumn Period. Bin, however, is a polity always associated with the pre-dynastic stage of the Zhou, while the *Airs* of Zhounan, Shaonan, Bei, Yong, and Tang all seem to reflect, if anything, the political terminology of the early Western Zhou. There is thus no century, much less year, within which all the states represented in the *Airs of the States* might have coexisted.

As with the *Catalogue of Ships*, there are also strikingly wide disparities

---

① Beecroft, *Authorship and Cultural Identity*, 202 – 204.

in power and significance among the states. The *Zuozhuan* tells us of twenty-six states established by Kings Wen and Wu and by the Duke of Zhou; of these, only three (Wei, Cao and Jin) are directly represented in the *Airs of the States* (*Zuozhuan* Xi 24; p. 47). Of a fairly standard list of the fifteen major states of the Spring and Autumn era, ostensibly the time of composition of most of the *Songs*,① only seven (Qi, Jin, Qin, Cao, Zheng, Chen, Wei) are represented in the *Airs*. Three more (Chu 楚, Wu 吴 and Yue 越) are excluded as still on the southern borders of the ethnically Huaxia world before about the sixth century BC, after the presumed closing of the canon of the *Songs*,② while Lu and Yan, are represented through genealogical metonymy; Lu through its connections to the Duke of Zhou (and thus to the *Airs of Zhounan*) and Yan through its associations with the Duke of Shao (and thus to the *Airs of Shaonan*). Lu and Song are additionally represented in the *Hymns* section of the *Songs* through, respectively, the *Lu Hymns* and the *Shang Hymns* (since the state of Song was understood as ruled by the heirs of the Shang). The reasons for the exclusion of Cai 蔡 and Xu 许 are more obscure.

When looked at from a geographic perspective, the states represented do at least provide a fairly broad degree of coverage of the two capital regions and of points east and west along the major river valleys. Four of the states (Wei, Tang, Qin, and Bin) can be associated with the areas to the west of the old Western Zhou capitals near modern Xi'an, while two (Zhounan and Shaonan) have a connection to the region as well as to points east; to the extent that the *Airs of Qin* reflect the Spring and Autumn period, they, too, can be connected to the Western Zhou capital regions. No fewer than five

---

① Hsu (1999) 547.

② For a discussion of the cultural integration of these states into the Huaxia sphere, see Falkenhausen, *Chinese Society in the Age of Confucius*, (2006) 262 – 283. The state of Chu will, in due course, be connected to its own poetic anthology, the *Songs of the South*, 《楚辞》, dating from roughly the fourth century BC onwards.

(Bei, Yong, Wei, the Royal Domains, and Zheng) relate to the general area around Luoyang. Finally, four relate to areas east of Luoyang: Chen and Kuai to modern Henan; Qi and Cao to modern Shandong. Viewed within the sequence of our text, the move is broadly from core to periphery, with the Western Zhou capital region first, then the Luoyang region, then a move east to Qi, then west to the Qin and those associated with it, then the relatively minor states of Chen, Kuai, and Cao. The collection concludes with Bin, a move that brings us to the far west geographically but, temporally, back to origins. The collection's movement is thus both geographic and chronological, as David Schaberg has noticed.[①] Within the geographic structure of representing the music of different regional polities, we find encoded a narrative of the rise and fall of the Zhou Dynasty, with those states associated with the pre-dynastic and early Western Zhou understood as embodying the virtues of idealized rule and those associated with later times representing decadence and decline. With the exception of the final section, the *Airs of Bin*, which as noted returns us to origins, the general movement of the collection thus mirrors the general movement of Western Zhou history as understood by the Ruist tradition, from triumphant foundation to decadence. This structure of historical decline is then reproduced within each of the state collections, as read by the Mao preface.

But whose thinking does this arrangement reflect? We cannot be certain when exactly the division of the *Airs of the States* assumed its final form. The recovered *Confucius' Discussion of the Songs*, dating from the fourth century BC, identifies songs as coming from the *Airs of the States* but at no point identifies which state any given song comes from; the local, here as so many times, is generic rather than genuine. Likewise, and for the most part, citations of the *Airs of the States* in the historical text the *Zuozhuan* (also likely

---

[①] David Schaberg, A Patterned Past: Form and Thought in Early Chinese Historiography, Cambridge, MA: Harvard University Asian Center, 2001, 89.

from the fourth century BC) make no mention of the association of particular poems with particular states; indeed, such citations frequently take place in a performance context of interstate negotiation in which fragments of the poem are deployed without regard for the sense of the poem as a whole, let alone any imagined originary compositional context. The Shuanggudui manuscript, excavated from a tomb sealed in 165 BC, does identify and (in some cases) discuss the divisions of the *Airs of the States* into essentially the same states as the Mao tradition, in spite of its very considerable manuscript variations from that tradition; we may, perhaps, thus assume that the collection had assumed something like its current organization by at least that date. While it is possible that the poems were already associated with specific states by the early fourth century, it is striking that almost no text that might date from that period identifies them in this way; it is as if the *Airs of the States* are generically regional (as opposed to Panhuaxia), without any specific regional associations. ①

With both the *Catalogue of Ships* and the *Airs of the States*, then, we can see that a text that appears on the surface to offer a panchorism in which the best of the local traditions is combined into a notional whole, is in fact much more complicated. In neither case is there a possible historical moment in which all of the parts in question could have coexisted, nor is there any definition of the limits of the cultural world that would encompass all of the parts, and nothing further. These anachronisms and inconsistencies, I would argue, do their own work within the tradition, insisting on the panchoric culture as the sum of parts, while simultaneously reshaping those parts and detaching them from any specific local context. These texts, therefore, both represent their respective cultures as built out of a collection of local

---

① For more on this subject, see also Alexander Beecroft, "Authorship in the *Canon of Songs* (Shi Jing)", in *That Wonderful Composite Called Author: Authorship in East Asian Literatures from the Beginnings to the Seventeenth Century*, ed. Christian Schwermann and Raji C. Steineck (Leiden; Boston: Brill Academic Pub, 2014).

traditions, while at the same time insisting that it is the supra-local, the panchoric, that authenticates and legitimates local tradition.

The brilliance with which both traditions simultaneously represent and suppress the local is, as I have argued extensively elsewhere,① a significant part of why and how both Greek and Chinese eventually became cosmopolitan languages. Greek spread rapidly as the language of power and of culture in the wake of the conquests of Alexander the Great, reaching around the Mediterranean World, through the Near East, and having an enduring presence as far east as modern Pakistan. Chinese likewise spread rapidly with the growth of the Han empire, and then spread further still with the adoption of classical Chinese as a literary standard in the states of what would become Japan, Korea, Vietnam, and elsewhere. The cosmopolitan spread of classical Chinese is in particular a spectacular example of literary cosmopolitanism as understood by Sheldon Pollock—the spread of a language as a tool for the aesthetic self-representation of power, achieved not through conquest, conversion, colonization, or even through trade, but rather through the charismatic force of the language and of the texts composed in it. Few languages were ever able to make it through the bottleneck from local or panchoric to cosmopolitan status; the peculiar adaptability of both Greek and Chinese to new contexts, even in their earlier stages, may help account for why they were able to do so.

The Second Bottleneck: From Cosmopolitan to National and Global?

Cosmopolitan literary languages have proved to be extraordinarily durable. Each of the relatively small number of such languages that can be

---

① Beecroft, *Authorship and Cultural Identity in Early Greece and China: Patterns of Literary Circulation.*

identified (e. g. Akkadian, Sumerian, Greek, Latin, Arabic, Persian, Sanskrit, classical Chinese) endured for at least a thousand years, and sometimes much longer. In the process, most long outlived their status as living spoken languages, if that they ever were. Certainly, it is unlikely that anyone ever spoke in the classical Chinese of Confucius or Mencius in daily life, and scholars have argued that Sanskrit,[1] and Akkadian and Sumerian,[2] may never have really been everyday spoken languages, either. Certainly, each cosmopolitan language was used by many individuals whose native spoken language will have been quite different. These languages were used over thousands of miles as well as thousands of years, and...while many (unlike Sanskrit) were originally spread through conquest or other forcible means, all long outlasted the political formations that were their original champions.

Nonetheless, in nearly every case (Arabic remains a partial exception) these cosmopolitan languages gradually gave way to literatures in vernaculars, languages which did not claim universal status, but which instead claimed to speak to a more focused community. The earliest vernaculars, I would argue, are languages such as Hittite and Ugaritic, written in the mid-second millennium BC in regional outposts of the Ancient Near East, alongside cosmopolitan languages. Latin, too, as I have already suggested, is best understood as beginning as a vernacular competing with Greek. Nonetheless, there was across Eurasia an astonishing burgeoning of vernacular literatures beginning in the middle of the first millennium AD. From Old Irish and Anglo-Saxon to Japanese and Javanese, from Armenian and Coptic to Kannada and Tamil, vernacular languages flourished across the continents. Many of these early vernaculars began in part because the spoken languages of their communities were extremely divergent from the written literary standard: Japanese has no linguistic

---

[1] Sheldon Pollock, *The Language of the Gods in the World of Men: Sanskrit, Culture, and Power in Premodern India* (Univerisity of California Press, 2009), 49.

[2] P. Michalowski, "The Lives of the Sumerian Language," in *Margins of Writing, Origins of Culture*, ed. S. L. Sanders (Chicago: University of Chicago Press, 2006) .

relationship to Chinese; nor does Javanese to Sanskrit. Anglo-Saxon and Old Irish are genetically related to Latin, but at sufficient distance that Latin would have been a learned language for anyone speaking an early Germanic or Celtic tongue. It is perhaps unsurprising that intellectual elites in such regions established literary traditions in the vernacular—not supplanting cosmopolitan languages, but providing a more accessible alternative.

Other literary vernaculars emerged later, particularly those which were more closely related to the cosmopolitan language, as the Romance languages were to Latin, or the Indo-Aryan languages of North India were to Sanskrit. In many such cases, the challenge in creating a vernacular was not simply breaking free of the prestige of the cosmopolitan tradition, but also deciding on which point on an extensive continuum of spoken dialects to build a literary language. The spoken dialects of Romance Europe, or North India (or indeed the Arab world or China) each merge imperceptibly into each other, from city to city, and region to region, and the decision of which of these languages to standardize and use for literature was never easy. In Italy, Dante's *De vulgari eloquentia* ("On Eloquence in the Vulgar Tongue") explored the possibilities of the various Italian spoken dialects, without being entirely satisfied with any of them (though Dante's use of his native Florentine in his vernacular literary writings would end up resolving the question for Italian), but similar debates raged across all the regions mentioned. The choice was obviously a politically loaded one (and capital cities and/or regions of economic power tended to win), but at the same time there were always tradeoffs. For the speaker of a dialect far removed from the vernacular standard, learning the new vernacular might be as difficult (or even more difficult) than mastering the classical, cosmopolitan language, while devoting one's energies to mastering a difficult vernacular risked cutting oneself off from the great mass of the cosmopolitan tradition. Little wonder that in such regions cosmopolitan languages tended to last longer.

These regions did gradually adopt vernaculars, but in the meantime texts in a range of regional forms, and in a variety of registers of language, from heavily classicizing to highly colloquial, were written and transmitted. These divergent linguistic forms tended to be subsumed under a narrative of progressive vernacularization, where the (necessarily constructed) vernacular language is taken as the natural*telos* for all vernacular registers and forms, and where those vernaculars which cannot be explained as ancestors to the modern standard are instead explained as "dialects" of the then-current stage of what would become the modern standard vernacular. Thus, in Italy, Venetian, Neapolitan, Piedmontese—all are seen in traditional scholarship as "dialects" of Italian (i. e. of the modern standard language), and historical versions of those "dialects" are likewise dialects of earlier equivalents to standard Italian, although contemporary linguistics would tend to see Venetian and so on as distinct languages, related to the spoken language of Tuscany at some distant time, but undergoing a separate history of development since[①]. All vernacular traditions of Italy, from courtly poetry of the thirteenth-century Sicilian school, to the Venetian comedies of Goldoni in the eighteenth century, are subsumed in the history of a single, "Italian" vernacular literature.

We see something quite similar at work in the narration of literary history we find in the work of May Fourth era Chinese intellectuals such as in Hu Shi 胡适 (1891 – 1962) 's famous essay "A tentative discussion of literary reform" 文学改良刍议, published in January 1917 in the journal *New Youth* 新青年, a crucial document of the so-called May Fourth Movement:

I take only Shi Nai'an, Cao Xueqin and Wu Woyao to be the main literary lineage, which is why I say "don't avoid common characters and common language." ... Actually, spoken and written language have been running apart from each other for a long time. Since Buddhist scriptures were imported into China, and translators found the literary language (*wenyan*) insufficient to convey their ideas; accordingly, for ease of translation, they

---

[①] Arturo Tosi, "The Language Situation in Italy", *Current Issues in Language Planning* 5, No. 3 (2004): 247.

used a form approaching the vernacular (*baihua*). Later, a great many Buddhist conversations and explications used *baihua* as well. This was the origin of the "conversational" style. Song dynasty intellectuals used *baihua* for their *Conversations, and this became the standard style for intellectual discussion. (Ming scholars followed them in this)*. *By this time*, *baihua* had already entered rhymed prose genres, as can be seen from an examination of Tang and Song *shi* and *ci* poetry in *baihua*. By the time of the Yuan dynasty, the northern part of China had already been ruled by alien nations under the Liao, Jin and Yuan. During these three hundred years, China developed a sort of popular literature: in prose, there were works like *The Water Margin*, *The Journey to the West* and *The Romance of the Three Kingdoms*; in drama, an incalculable number of works... From the perspective of modern times, Chinese literature should consider the Yuan to be its acme; the number of works that will last was without a doubt greatest in the Yuan. At this time, Chinese literature was closest to the spoken language, which almost became the literary language. Had this tendency not been checked, a living literature might have developed in China, and the achievements of a Dante or Luther would have taken place in our land. [In the European Middle Ages, each nation had its own vulgar tongue (*liyu* 俚语), and Latin was the *wenyan*, *and all authors wrote their works in Latin, just as in our country they all wrote in* wenyan. *Later, the Italian literary giant Dante began to write in his own* liyu, *and national languages (*guoyu*) began to replace Latin. The religious reformer Luther began to use German to translate the Old and New Testaments, and thereby began German literature. English and French followed a similar pattern; the normal Bible translation in English today was written in 1611, only three hundred years ago. Accordingly, the literatures of all of the European nations use their own* liyu. *Literary giants began to emerge, living literatures began to replace a dead literature in Latin, and with a living literature came a* guoyu *which merged speech and writing)*].
This tendency, then, was unexpectedly checked in the Ming, when the

"eight-legged" essay style was used to select civil servants, and when contemporary literati like the Seven Ming Masters such as He Jingming 何景明（1483-1521） and Li Mengyang 李梦阳（1473-1530） contentiously elevated "returning to antiquity"; the once-in-a-millennium opportunity to merge writing and speech was prematurely killed off half-way there. However, from the perspective of recent historical evolution, it can be asserted that *baihua* literature is the main lineage of Chinese literature, and that future literature must use this medium (this assertion is the author's own; those today who support his position may not be numerous). For these reasons, I believe that today's writers of poetry and prose should use common characters and words. Using dead words from three thousand years ago is not as good as using living words of the twentieth century, and using language of the Qin, Han and Six Dynasties, which can be neither widespread nor universal, is not as good as using the language of *The Water Margin* and *The Journey to the West*". ①

---

① 吾惟以施耐庵、曹雪芹、吴趼人为文学正宗，故有"不避俗字俗语"之论也。（参看上文第二条下。）盖吾国言文之背驰久矣。自佛书之输入，译者以文言不足以达意，故以浅近之文译之，其体已近白话。其后佛氏讲义语录尤多用白话为之者，是为语录体之原始。及宋人讲学以白话为语录，此体遂成讲学正体。（明人因之。）当是时，白话已久入韵文，观唐、宋人白话之诗词可见也。及至元时，中国北部已在异族之下三百余年矣（辽、金、元）。此三百年中，中国乃发生一种通俗行远之文学。文则有"水浒"、"西游"、"三国"……之类，戏曲则尤不可胜计…. 今世眼光观之，则中国文学当以元代为最盛；可传世不朽之作，当以元代为最多。此可无疑也。当是时，中国之文学最 近言文合一，白话几成文学的语言矣。使此趋势不受阻遏，则中国几有一"活文学"出现，而但丁、路得之伟业，（欧洲中古时，各国皆有俚语，而以拉丁文为文言，凡著作书籍皆用之，如吾国之以文言著书也。其后义大利有但丁〔Dante〕诸文豪，始以其国俚语著作，诸国踵兴，国语亦代起。路得〔Luther〕创新教，始以德文译"旧约"、"新约"，遂开德文学之先。英、法诸国亦复如是。今世通用之英文"新旧约"乃 1611 年译本，距今才三百年耳。故今日欧洲诸国之文学，在当日皆为俚语。追诸文豪兴，始以"活文学"代拉丁之死文学；有活文学而后有言文合一之国语也。）几发生于神州。不意此趋势骤为明代所阻，政府既以八股取士，而当时文人如何、李七子之徒，又争以复古为高，于是此千年难遇言文合一之机会，遂中道夭折矣。然以今世历史进化的眼光观之，则白话文学之为中国文学之正宗，又为将来文学必用之利器，可断言也。（此"断言"乃自作者言之，赞成此说者今日未必甚多也。）以此之故，吾主张今日作文作诗，宜采用俗语俗字。与其三千年前之死字（如"于铄国会，遵晦时休"之类），不如用 20 世纪之活字；与其作不能行远、不能普及之秦、汉、六朝文字，不如作家喻户晓之"水浒"、"西游"文字也。

Hu Shih thus develops a narrative of Chinese literary history in which the driving force over the past fifteen hundred years or more has been the emergence and development of writing in the vernacular. [1] What I wish to draw attention to here is the degree to which the vernacular becomes a continuous tradition: Buddhist homilies of the Six Dynasties era, Yuan-era novels such as *The Water Margin*, and contemporary spoken language, seem like they may be the same language. Certainly, the parallelism of the last sentence implies a strong connection between, if not the actual identity of, "living words of the twentieth century" and "the language of *The Water Margin* and *The Journey to the West*." To the extent that all vernaculars in this text are not in fact identical, they certainly seem linked through evolutionary development, as different phases in a continuous process of development, rather than as fragments of quasi-spoken language preserved in a range of different texts, created in different eras and regions for different audiences. The teleology of the vernacular in Hu Shih's account appears seamless.

In fact, as Zhang Zhongxing has shown, the situation is far more complex. [2] Some genres are clearly more vernacular than others, but even the most vernacular of pre-modern genres include occasional quotations of poetry or the classics, while the most classicizing of genres include snatches of vernacular dialogue. Moreover, while some phrases and constructions can be identified as either vernacular or classical, others are at home in both registers, and resist easy classification. Classical and vernacular language in pre-modern Chinese texts thus exist in a complex form of diglossia. Perhaps better, we might borrow Sheldon Pollock's term "hyperglossia," for the situation where speakers think in terms of a single language, but where in

---

[1] Beecroft, *An Ecology of World Literature: From Antiquity to the Present Day*, 264.

[2] Zhongxing Zhang, Wen Yan He Bai Hua, Di 1 ban (Ha'erbin: Heilongjiang ren min chu ban she, 1988). (张忠行:《文言和白话》,黑龙江人民出版社 1988 年第 1 版。)

reality there is what Pollock calls "a situation of extreme superposition between two languages". ① The brilliance (and enduring success) of Hu Shih's intervention was his inversion of this hyperglossia, privileging the linguistic elements which had previously been undervalued, and replacing the ideology of timelessness of the classical language with that of an eternal, but eternally-evolving, vernacular.

Something similar operated in Greek over the long history of Byzantine and Modern Greek. The literary history of the Byzantine era, down to the fall of Constantinople in 1453, was punctuated by returns to classicizing style (which is to say that the language of these texts was continually in danger of slipping away from that style), and as vernacularizing texts begin to emerge in the tenth century AD and onward (particularly in poetic romances), it is often difficult to distinguish between "vernacular" and "classical" uses of a word. ② Later, as Greek nationalism was emerging in the late eighteenth and nineteenth centuries, intellectuals (like those in China a century later) debated the form of the Greek language most appropriate to the new nation. Some, like the philologist Adamantinos Korais (1748 - 1833), sought to bring the modern language as close to the ancient standard as possible, "correcting" usage by reintroducing ancient syntax, conjugation and declension, and creating vocabulary for new ideas on the basis of the ancient lexicon. ③ The version of Greek he promoted is referred to④ as

---

① Sheldon Pollock, *The Language of the Gods in the World of Men: Sanskrit, Culture, and Power in Premodern India*, 50.

② Karl Krumbacher, *Geschichte Der Byzantinischen Litteratur* (München: Beck, 1891), 795 - 6.

③ Peter Mackridge, "Korais and the Greek Language Question", in *Adamantios Korais and the European Enlightenment*, ed. Paschalis M. Kitromilides (Oxford: Voltaire Foundation, n. d.).

④ Though not by Korais himself. See Roderick Beaton, "Korais and the Second Sophistic: The Hellenistic Novel as Paradigm for a Modern Literary Langauge", in *Standard Languages and Language Standards: Greek, Past and Present*, by Alexandra Georgakopoulou and M. S Silk (Farnham, England; Burlington, VT: Ashgate Publ. Co., 2009), 342.

katharevousa, or "purifying", Greek – the term itself, participial in form, suggesting that the purification of language is an ongoing process, a transformation of some more natural linguistic formation. Others, like the later Ioannis Psycharis (1854 – 1929), himself the coiner of the term *diglossia*, argued instead for the use of "Demotic" Greek, freeing schoolchildren and the people generally from both the drudgery of having to learn artificial forms for writing, and from the shame of thinking their spoken language to be vulgar and embarrassing.[1] Even Psycharis, however, does not insist on using only the modern spoken language of the people as the basis for literary language, arguing for instance that Ancient Greek words, if borrowed into the modern language, should adapt to the forms of the spoken language – not that they should never be used at all.

Both Psycharis and Hu Shih see this diglossia or hyperglossia as a bad thing, as an impediment to mass education and to literature composed in a natural language of the people. These concerns carry real weight. Why, then, did the movements they promoted face resistance, powerful and enduring resistance especially in the Greek case? In part, as I have suggested, this is because the challenge of imposing a working vernacular literary language on a broad dialect continuum is harder than it seems at first, and the resulting language further from the everyday speech of the streets than its promoters would claim. There is another reason, however, of great significance: there is a certain sadness inherent in the transformation of a cosmopolitan language, used across the known world, into a national language, fit for a specific people.[2]

As the western concept of the nation-state emerged in China, it was introduced into Chinese (and other East Asian languages) using the ancient

---

[1] Pernot Ioannis Psicharis, *The Language Question in Greece: Three Essays* (Printed at the BaptistMission Press, 1902).

[2] For the similar case of modern Turkish, see Nergis Erturk, *Grammatology and Literary Modernity in Turkey* (Oxford University Press, USA, 2011).

term *guo* 国, originally used to refer to the regional states of the Spring and Autumn and Warring States eras. A key early theorist of China as a nation was the late Qing and early republican scholar and writer Liang Qichao (1873 – 1929):

> 仅淬厉固有而遂足乎？曰：不然！今之世非昔之世，今之人非昔之人。昔者吾中国有部民而无国民，非不能为国民也，势使然也。吾国凤巍然屹立于大东，环列皆小蛮夷。与他方大国，未一交通，故我民常视其国为天下。耳目所接触，脑筋所濡染，圣哲所训示，祖宗所遗传，皆使之有可以为一箇人之资格，有可以为一家人之资格，有可以为一乡一族人之资格，有可以为天下人之资格；而独无可以为一国国民之资格。夫国民之资格，虽未必有以远优于此数者，而以今日列国并立，弱肉强食，优胜劣败之时代，苟缺此资格，则决无以自立于天壤。（新民说。第三节　释新民之义）(1906)

Is it enough to hone the things we already have? I say, not at all! Our world is not the world of the past; our men are not the men of the past. In the past our China had townsfolk (*bimin*), not citizens (*guomin*). It's not that China was not capable of creating citizens, but simply because of circumstances. Our nation once stood majestically in the great East, surrounded on all sides by *man* and *yi* (barbarians). We had no communication with other great nations (*guo*), so our people frequently saw their nation (*guo*) as all under heaven (*tianxia*). Everything that reached our eyes and ears, everything which tinged our brains and muscles, all that our sages and philosophers taught us, everything our ancestors passed down to us – all of this served as the qualities we needed to become individuals, to become people in families, to become people in villages or clans, and to become people in "all under heaven" (*tianxia*); it was insufficient only for becoming the citizens (*guomin*) of a nation. Now the qualities sufficient for being citizens, need not be far superior to these other qualities, but today, with the various nations (*lieguo*) existing side by side, where the strong exploit the weak, in this era where the excellent profit and the inferior lose out, if we lack these qualities of citizenship, then surely we will lack the means to position ourselves between heaven and earth. (*Discourses on the New Citizen*. Chapter 3: Explaining the meaning of the "New Citizen".) (1906)

    Particularly interesting, in my view, is Liang's claim that the qualities possessed by traditional Chinese civilization were sufficient to found strong families, villages, and clans, and to create a universalizing civilization – but not to found a nation-state. The usefulness of the cosmopolitan classical Chinese tradition is demonstrated, as we have seen, by its applicability to a variety of other regional polities, in Korea, Japan, Vietnam and the northern steppes, each of which in its own way was able to appropriate the universal claims of traditional Chinese culture as a marker of its own distinctive community. This very reproducibility of the properties of Chinese civilization, however, was what, at least for Liang Qichao and others, made this civilization inadequate as a response to the pressures of nation-state formation in the early twentieth century. What was needed was a sense of culture and history which was not reproducible, which could be applied to the Chinese people, and to them only. The development of a standard written and spoken vernacular, of course, would prove invaluable in supplying that sense.

    The situation of the Greeks was of course quite different. While in the seventeenth and eighteenth centuries both China and Greece were under the control of great empires whose rulers were not native speakers of the cosmopolitan language (the Manchu-speaking Qing and the Turkish-speaking Ottomans, respectively), the position of those cosmopolitan languages was very different. As the Qing and the Ottomans collapsed within a few years of each other in the early twentieth century, the Ottoman successor-state of Turkey developed a vernacularized and nationalized version of Turkish as its national language; the native Manchu of the Qing was, by this time, almost extinct as an everyday spoken language in its homeland. [1] Greek nationalism, facilitated by a weakening Ottoman empire, by sympathetic Western Europeans, and in a sense by the peripheral position of Greece within the Ottoman world, also began a full century earlier than Chinese nationalism (in the modern, Western, sense). Moreover, while China, as it became a modern nation-state, is a vast and multilingual space which contains within its borders most of the world's indigenous speakers of Chinese dialects, the Greek nation-state as it emerged in the nineteenth century excluded many regions with large numbers of Greek-speakers, including portions of Asia Minor where Greek had been spoken for more than two thousand years. [2] These substantial ecological conditions aside, language was certainly an important element in Greek nationalism as it was in Chinese, even though the transition from cosmopolitan to national language played a complex role in both cultures. To return to Adamantios Korais, he described the Greek language as "the possession of the whole nation, and a sacred one". [3] Time alone, Korais says, and not rulers, can change the language of the nation— though "the nation's men of learning" as legislators for the republic of language, have an obligation to "correct" flaws in the language. This language must reflect the spoken idiom, but elevate and clarify it, in a typically progressive vision of nation-building not dissimilar to that found in Hu Shih. With the help of "legislators" such as Korais and Hu, both Greek and

---

[1]　Gertraude Roth Li, *Manchu: A Textbook for Reading Documents* (Natl Foreign Lg Resource Ctr, 2010), 14.

[2]　For statistics on the Greek population of Ottoman Antatolia before the First World War, see Dimitri Pentzopoulos, *The Balkan Exchange of Minorities and Its Impact on Greece* (Hurst, 2002), 29 - 30 Some regions, notably Smyrna, may have had a Greek majority.

[3]　Cited at Beaton, "Korais and the Second Sophistic: The Hellenistic Novel as Paradigm for a Modern Literary Langauge", 343 - 44.

Chinese are able to make the perilous journey from cosmopolitan to national language, a journey Arabic, for example, has yet to complete.

And thus both Greek and Chinese make it through a second ecological bottleneck. One of the consequences of long-term diglossia is that it provides a mechanism for bridging the vast linguistic changes natural over several millennia, imposing a sense of continuity where otherwise it might not be felt. When Dante speaks of the language of Italy, he sometimes calls it the "language of *si*", and sometimes "vulgar Latin". That he can still refer to Italian as Latin is a function of the extent to which the vernacular is still in a state of diglossia for him. By the time the expression *linguaggio italiano* "the Italian language" exists (it is first attested in a letter from Leonardo da Vinci to Pope Leo X, c. 1513 – 16), that diglossia has reached a stage where the two languages, Italian and Latin, are found in discrete texts, rarely intermingled on the same page. The earlier emergence of *frances* (c. 1100) and *castellana* and *espannol* (1254 and 1284, respectively) as language names points, perhaps, to Italy's greater attachment to Latin as a "local" language, a claim central to Dante's *De vulgari eloquentia*.[①] The fact that the separation of vernacular and classical language into discrete corpora of texts happens so late in both Greek and Chinese contributes, I would argue, to the fact that English still uses the same name for ancient and modern languages in both cases, modifying them with adjectives as needed, and, more broadly, to the sense of cultural and linguistic continuity which is important in both cultures today. The terms used within these languages to refer to classical and vernacular likewise hint at continuity rather than rupture. In Greek, the ancient and modern languages are called αρχαια ελληνικη and νεα ελληνικά; as in English, distinguishing the two only through a qualifying adjective. In Chinese, the generally used terms, *wenyan* 文言 and *baihua* 白话 (respectively, "literary language" and "everyday

---

[①] Beecroft, *An Ecology of World Literature: From Antiquity to the Present Day*, 222.

speech") are in no way ethnonyms, and are designed to indicate linguistic registers rather than distinct languages. These distinctive language names, designed to emphasize continuity rather than change, attest to the profound sense of connection with the linguistic past shared by Greek and Chinese speakers, in contrast to the speakers of many other modern national languages.

Given the small size of the Greek nation today, it is difficult to imagine a strong future for the Greek language as part of the global literary ecology. It is likely to remain a national language for the foreseeable future. Chinese is another matter. Across its regional forms, Chinese has by far the most native speakers of any language: more than the next five languages (Spanish, English, Arabic, Hindi, Bengali) put together. While geographically and politically concentrated to a smaller region and to a single-nation state (as compared in particular with Spanish, English, Arabic, and also French), the sheer vastness of the Chinese-speaking population, together with the depth and richness of the literary tradition it represents, make Chinese what I have called a "regional world-language"; that is, a language that constitutes a world unto itself. [1] As such (and even though it is also the language of one of the world's largest diasporas, present on every continent), Chinese does not need the lingua franca status of English, or the multi-continental reach of French or Spanish, to thrive as a major literary language in the still-hypothetical global literary marketplace of the future. While the infrastructure of translation today continues to restrict access to Chinese literature for non-Chinese speakers (Chinese has historically been the source language for fewer translations than Norwegian), [2] there are signs this is slowly beginning to change. This literary language which once served a small elite population in a handful of cities on the Yellow River has gone through

---

[1] Beecroft, *An Ecology of World Literature: From Antiquity to the Present Day*, 375 – 80.
[2] Beecroft, *An Ecology of World Literature: From Antiquity to the Present Day*, 357 – 60.

many adventures over a long period (and the Greek which began as a shared literary language for a collection of tiny city-states in the Aegean has journeyed almost as far), adapting at each stage to the unique and challenging ecological contexts in which they have found themselves.

Works Cited:

1. Allen, T. W.. *The Homeric Catalogue of Ships.* Oxford: Oxford University Press, 1921.
2. Beaton, Roderick. "Korais and the Second Sophistic: The Hellenistic Novel as Paradigm for a Modern Literary Langauge." In *Standard Languages and Language Standards: Greek, Past and Present*, by Alexandra Georgakopoulou and M. S Silk, 341 - 53. Farnham, England; Burlington, VT: Ashgate Publ. Co., 2009.
3. Beecroft, Alexander. *An Ecology of World Literature: From Antiquity to the Present Day.* Verso, 2015.
4. *Authorship and Cultural Identity in Early Greece and China: Patterns of Literary Circulation.* Cambridge: Cambridge University Press, 2010.
5. "Authorship in the *Canon of Songs* (Shi Jing)". In *That Wonderful Composite Called Author: Authorship in East Asian Literatures from the Beginnings to the Seventeenth Century*, edited by Christian Schwermann and Raji C. Steineck. Leiden, Boston: Brill Academic Pub, 2014.
6. "World Literature Without a Hyphen: Towards a Typology of Literary Systems", *New Left Review*, No. 54 (December 2008): 87 - 100.
7. Erturk, Nergis. *Grammatology and Literary Modernity in Turkey.* Oxford University Press, USA, 2011.
8. Finkelberg, Margalit. "Ajax's Entry in the Hesiodic Catalogue of Women." *The Classical Quarterly*, New Series, 38, No. 1 (January 1, 1988): 31 - 41.
9. Ioannis Psicharis, Pernot. *The Language Question in Greece: Three Essays.* Printed at the Baptist Mission Press, 1902.
10. Krumbacher, Karl. *Geschichte Der Byzantinischen Litteratur.* München: Beck, 1891.
11. Larson, Stephanie L.. *Tales of Epic Ancestry: Boiotian Collective Identity in the Late Archaic and Early Classical Periods.* Bilingual. Franz Steiner Verlag Wiesbaden GmbH, 2007.
12. Li, Gertraude Roth. *Manchu: A Textbook for Reading Documents.* Natl Foreign Lg

Resource Ctr, 2010.

13. Loptson, Peter. "Pelasgikon Argos in the Catalogue of Ships (681)." *Mnemosyne*, Fourth Series, 34, No. 1/2 (January 1, 1981): 136 - 38.

14. Mackridge, Peter. "Korais and the Greek Language Question." In *Adamantios Korais and the European Enlightenment*, edited by Paschalis M. Kitromilides. Oxford: Voltaire Foundation, n. d.

15. Michalowski, P.. "The Lives of the Sumerian Language." In *Margins of Writing, Origins of Culture*, edited by S. L. Sanders. Chicago: University Of Chicago Press, 2006.

16. Pentzopoulos, Dimitri. *The Balkan Exchange of Minorities and Its Impact on Greece*. Hurst, 2002.

17. Pollock, Sheldon. "The Death of Sanskrit." *Comparative Studies in Society and History* 43 (2001): 392 - 426.

18. Sheldon Pollock. *The Language of the Gods in the World of Men: Sanskrit, Culture, and Power in Premodern India*. University of California Press, 2009.

19. Tosi, Arturo. "The Language Situation in Italy." *Current Issues in Language Planning* 5, No. 3 (2004): 247.

20. Waquet, Francoise. *Latin Or the Empire of a Sign: From the Sixteenth to the Twentieth Centuries*. Verso, 2003.

21. Zhang, Zhongxing. *Wen Yan He Bai Hua*. Di 1 ban. Ha'erbin: Heilongjiang ren min chu ban she, 1988.

An Ancient Greek *Journey to the West*: Reading the *Odyssey* through East-Asian Eyes

John T. Kirby [*]

中文摘要 对于古代经典进行比较研究势必会遇到文化隔阂的障碍，但回归到经典的标准和定义就会发现，经典具有三个特点，第一，是同类作品中最好的；第二，它经过了时间的检验；第三，它接近阐释的文化的神话式的价值。坎贝尔《千面英雄》里提出的单一神话模式认为英雄历险的传奇是全世界神话的共同结构，其中包括了英雄的旅程、不可能的任务，《奥德赛》与《西游记》中都具有相似的结构模式。通过分析古希腊英雄的"西游记"我们可以发现，英雄神话重要的两个特点——即神话固有的特点以及读者对其进行阐释所表现出的特点。在东方视野下对西方经典《奥德赛》的研究与理解进一步证明经典的意义就在于使人们更加尊重与重视不同的文化。

关键词 经典；文化交流；单一神话；《奥德赛》；《西游记》

---

[*] 作者为美国迈阿密大学古典文学与比较文学教授，文学博士。

I

As soon as one proposes to engage in the study of "comparative classics" one is confronted by challenges and obstacles that may seem daunting or even insurmountable. My own work entails the comparative study of so-called "classic texts" from both the Western heritage and the pre-modern Chinese tradition (and by this I mean, principally, *verbal* texts, though there is no reason why we could not include "texts" of other genres and formats, including visual or sonic artefacts). The obstacles in this case include not only the predicament of Kipling's famous maxim "East is East, and West is West, and never the twain shall meet", but also the difficulty of gaining clarity around such terms as "classic", "classical" and-particularly important for understanding the other two— "classicizing". As soon as we attempt to define these latter terms, the challenges become even steeper, as we shall not escape confrontation by other related issues, such as what a literary canon is, how such things are formed, and whether indeed they should exist.[①] But the project of *comparative* classics, I maintain, is not only defensible but vitally important: if we are to hope for peace and harmony in the global culture that is already taking shape, we would do well to discover what common ground we share-in our cultures, in our aesthetics, in our hopes and fears, and in the overall goals we set for ourselves.

Much has been made in recent decades, in the West, of the notion of "cultural literacy" —by which is meant, a Westerner's familiarity with her own cultural heritage. This concept, as popularized by E. D. Hirsch in

---

[①] On the matter of canons and canon formation see Kirby 1998: xvii-xxv, Kirby (2012): 277 - 279, and especially O'Sullivan (1997). On defining "classics" and "the classical", see Kirby (2000): 111 - 113, 133 - 136. On the relation of the oral to the written in the formation of canons, both in ancient China and in the Greek-speaking world, see Beecroft (2010): 47-52.

connection with his books on the topic, ① appears to take the term "literacy" in both a figurative and a literal meaning: figuratively, in the general sense of "competence in a body of knowledge, and ability to articulate that competence"; and literally, in that such a competence is reached by means of the ability to read verbal texts, to comprehend them, and to retain what one reads. Either way, the notion presupposes and relies upon a body of data acknowledged to be important to the thorough understanding of a culture, and a set of resources-above all, verbal texts (beginning with books such as Hirsch's) —that themselves set forth and/or constitute a canon.

Without interrogating the validity of Hirsch's own criteria for inclusion or exclusion—and the promulgation of any canon involves both—we can say at once that the process itself does imply both inclusion and exclusion. These are characterized by the tension between two opposing tendencies that I have elsewhere called the *aggregative* and the *selective*. ② The act of aggregation is what leads to the very compiling of data (and is best represented, perhaps, by the production of encyclopaedias); the act of selection, by contrast, is an exclusionary process that assigns value to individual items in the aggregated set, and privileges those deemed to be of the highest value. These aggregative and selective gestures are themselves attended upon by a number of interactive phenomena, including what I have called *judgment*, *preservation*, and *reproduction*. Judgment, in this sense, is the evaluation of whether an item— in the case of literary canons, a specific text—is worth particular attention, and its selection on that basis for inclusion in the canon. By preservation, I mean the decision to retain a selected text for re-reading. By reproduction I mean the publication and dissemination of texts that have been preserved in the sense just explained.

What mobilizes these tendencies, and their attendant interactive phenomena, is—most fundamentally—love. Lest the word seem too mawkishly

---

① See e. g. Hirsch (1987, 1988).
② Kirby (2012): 277-279.

sentimental, let me point out that the *phil*—in "philology" —thought by some to be the driest of disciplines—expresses a kind of love, in fact a love very closely related to what I have in mind here. [1] Philology is, or should be, at the core of the humanist enterprise: certainly at the core of any work in comparative literature. And love, I submit, is in turn at the core of philology: a cherishing or prizing, and a careful study, of the texts-verbal or visual or in any other medium—that those assessing these texts deem to be of particular value.

We have, as it happens, eloquent testimony on the subject of love from one of the greatest poets (some would say, *the* greatest) of the ancient Greek-speaking world: Sappho. In a famous priamel [2] she begins by saying:

> Some claim that the loveliest thing on earth is a troop of horsemen;
> Others, a company of foot – soldiers; still others, a flotilla of ships.
> But to me, the fairest thing on earth
> Is whatever one loves. [3]

We may cast the logic of these lines in more prosaic terms: because you love ×, you will consider × the loveliest thing on earth. But from the next lines of the extant text of the poem, it seems clear that the psychology underlying this opening assertion actually moves in the opposite direction: because you consider × the loveliest thing on earth, you will love ×.

> So easy to make this understood by anyone:
> For she who far surpassed all humankind
> In beauty-Helen-abandoned
> Her noble husband,

---

[1] The word itself is being newly reclaimed by those who live very close to it, see e. g. Pollock 2015.

[2] On the priamel in this poem, and its rhetorical mechanism, see Kirby 1984.

[3] Sappho, fragment 16 (L-P), lines 1 – 4. My translation (as also for the following eight lines).

>   And sailed to Troy. She gave no thought at all
>   To her child nor to her dear parents,
>   But what led her astray was …
>   [line missing here in the papyrus fragment]

In other words, it is easy to demonstrate that Helen loved Paris: it was, it had to be, because she considered him the loveliest thing on earth. This suggests the possibility of a circular (or perhaps spiral) motion of valuation: loving × as one does, one is repeatedly convinced anew, reinforced in one's conviction, that × is indeed the loveliest thing on earth— which, in turn, reinforces anew one's love for ×.

I think that this is what motivates interpretive communities to consider a work of art a "classic", and moreover what motivates them to create (and cherish) canons of such classics. If we truly understand and appreciate these motivations, we are finally in a position to respect and even to value cultures other than our own. I realize I am largely preaching to the choir in this essay; those likeliest to be reading it are probably doing so because they do love Western or East-Asian cultures, or both. But if the guild of scholars can carry this message beyond the academy and to our own society at large, we may actually—in the long run—help to promote the kind of mutual understanding that brings down barriers between cultures.

To this end, I would like to consider how the *Odyssey* of Homer[①] might resonate with someone who is well-versed in East-Asian culture, particularly in that of traditional China, but who is not so familiar with the

---

[①] To provide an accurate, uncontested date for the *floruit* of Homer—or even to prove that he existed as the ancient tradition presents him—is impossible; and indeed those questions are the sites of many a bloody scholarly battle. But if we were to take the ancient tradition at its face value, we might infer that he was active in the 8th or 7th century BCE (i.e. the middle of the Zhou Dynasty 周朝).

Western heritage. Because there is arguably no author more historically canonical to the latter than Homer, we may also profit from continuing our discussion of the notion of canons and canonicity—in both East and West.

II

The concept of literary canons in the ancient Mediterranean world, if not the use of the Greek word *kanôn* in this sense, goes back to antiquity itself: already in ancient times, Alexandrian critics such as Aristophanes of Byzantium and Aristarchus were already assembling lists of ' best ' authors in a given genre —the three comic poets, the five epic poets, the three iambic poets, the ten Attic orators, and so on. ①Aristophanes was head of the famous Library of Alexandria at around the turn of the second century BCE, as too was Aristarchus around the middle of that century, so their list—making activity may have had something specific to do with their work as librarians, perhaps in terms of cataloguing the holdings of the Library. Even if so, it will for that very reason be a sign that the tendencies discussed above—the aggregative and the selective—were at work already in the ancient world. ②Such lists were not immutable, even in

---

① That is, if we accept the testimony of Quintilian 10.1.54 – 55; on which see (*inter alia*) Zetzel 1983.

② The massive *Pinakes* of Callimachus, which included a complete catalogue of the Library at Alexandria, was apparently an outstanding example of the aggregative tendency. If the work were still extant, we might be able to say with more certainty whether it also evinced the selective. What we can say is that the very assembling of a library, to the extent that this is done by intention and not by happenstance, is itself a selective activity; but Callimachus was presumably cataloguing what was in the Library—not stocking it. In any case, Callimachus was several decades older than Aristophanes of Byzantium, so his own work will have preceded the canon-making activities of Aristophanes and Aristarchus. (For more on Callimachus, see e.g. chapter III of Pfeiffer 1968; for more on Aristophanes and Aristarchus, ibid. chapters V and VI respectively, and chapter 4 of Sandys 1915. On libraries in the ancient world, see Casson 2001.)

ancient times;① nonetheless they demonstrate that the notion of "bestness" in literature, and the kudos attendant upon that, were alive and well, even before the Common Era. But the act of reading, not to mention the process of canon-making, entails a competence known (too ambiguously) as "literacy", which necessarily impinges upon our discussion here.

The available evidence ② suggests that the ability to read and write in the ancient Mediterranean world was extremely limited: probably less than 10% of the population were fully literate at most times and places, and perhaps fewer than that. ③ Thus direct access to first-hand enjoyment of literature was, for all intents and purposes, limited to the elite. (We may perhaps include in this even those elites who could not read but who could and would have a slave read to them for their enjoyment.) To the extent that that is so, it implies another kind of "bestness" as well: those members of society considered the *aristoi*, the "best" in the sense of the word "aristocracy". Social groups have their own mechanisms of aggregation and selection—whether by lineage, by wealth, by political power, or other such modes of evaluation. The costliness of books in the ancient world, the free time needed to read them, and the education required to have the literacy to do so, were all barriers to the enjoyment of literary texts that limited this to the perquisite of the elite.

It seems likely that the same held true in ancient China, though it will be at least as difficult in this case to arrive at any sort of metric that could yield worthwhile data—not only because of our tremendous distance from the period under scrutiny, but also because, while both Chinese (at least in its

---

① A point well made by O'Sullivan (1997).
② Carefully organized and presented by Harris 1989. See also Johnson and Parker (2009), Johnson (2010).
③ In this connection, see the discussions in Beecroft (2010): 101-102 and Beecroft (2011) of whether Homer could read and write.

putonghua and *guangdonghua* manifestations) ① is, like ancient Greek, spoken with pitch – accent,② the script (s) used in writing the different forms of Chinese are not fully phonetic representations of the spoken sounds,③ and one of the factors that needs to be taken into account will be the question of whether a non-phonetic writing system made literacy even more difficult to achieve in ancient times. That said, I would not be at all surprised to learn that literacy rates were generally not higher in ancient China than in the ancient Greek-speaking world. ④

And in view of the foregoing, it is worth mentioning that the word "literacy" itself is a contested site: what constitutes literacy?⑤ Surely some account must be taken of a spectrum of competences, ranging from the most rudimentary ability to the most sophisticated levels of interaction. At a minimum, rudimentary literacy must involve the ability to [a] perceive written signs, [b] recognize them cognitively, and [c] understand what the

---

① We must set aside for the moment the vexed question of what, as regards Chinese, constitutes a "dialect", a "language", or a "language group". The hanzi that might give us some clue—traditional 話 or 語, simplified 话-as in 官話 *guānhuà*, 普通話 *pǔtōnghuà*, 廣東話 *guǎngdōnghuà*—is variously translated in English as "language", "dialect", or even just "speech" —and thus begs the question. The Taiwanese term for what is called *pǔtōnghuà* on the Mainland, namely 國語 *Guóyǔ*, is likewise tantalizing in that the word 語 *yǔ*—clearly related in its written form to 話/語 *huà* — also covers a fairly broad semantic field including "language" or "words". For a point of entry into the linguistic controversy, one might begin with Ramsey 1987.

② Another contested issue is the putative distinction between "pitch" and "tone" —which, again, we must for now set aside.

③ On the other hand, it is interesting to note that Greek during the Classical period, while written in a phonetic script, was not written with pitch accents. These were apparently developed at some point in the post-Classical period, though exactly when is not securely known; see Laum 1928 and the extremely cautious discussion in Pfeiffer 1968: 180.

④ Johnson (1985b) offers a nine-part matrix of literacy categories (along axes of "education/literacy" and "dominance") plus some circumspect quantitative estimates of literacy levels for Ming- and Qing-era China. His work draws somewhat on Rawski 1979. It seems reasonable to surmise that as one looks further back in time—as the historical and material-culture records become more exiguous—it will become correspondingly more difficult to make such estimates with accuracy.

⑤ An attempt to define the word "literacy" is made in Harris 1989: 3 – 5.

written text signifies, and perhaps also [d] phonate the text aloud. ① Above and beyond this, there is what is known as "functional literacy" —yet another highly contentious term—but presumably meant to indicate that the reader can read at a basic level, but may not be able to understand difficult texts such as legal or technical documents, or sophisticated literature (in the sense of *belles lettres*). Even in the upper levels of competence we may distinguish gradations: is one "fully literate" if one can read Dostoevsky in English translation, but not in the original Russian? If one can read a modern Beijing newspaper in simplified hanzi, but not the *Madman's Diary* ② of Lu Xun in traditional *hanzi*? and so on. Such gradations, for ancient China as for the ancient Greek-speaking world, may be impossible to assess.

In any case, the notion of something like a canon—if not yet a word for it—was already in place in China by the third century BCE—that is, right around the same time that Callimachus was active in Alexandria. In China as in the ancient Mediterranean, what was included in such canonical lists also seems to have undergone some variation and adjustment, as did the actual content of individual texts. ③ But the first and principal canonical list of those ancient Chinese texts that eventually came to be called 經 *jīng* (of which more in a moment) was what is known as the 五經 *Wǔjīng* or "Five Classics". ④

---

① By "perceive written signs" I mean to interact with the text visually (as in the ordinary ocular sense of reading) or manually (if the text is in Braille or some other tactible format). By "cognitive recognition" I mean what Saussurean semiologists would call the connection of the signifier and the referent via the signified, or what Peircean semioticians would call the connection of the representamen and the object via the interpretant. By "understand" I mean the process of thinking about the data gained via "cognitive recognition". And by "perhaps also phonate the text aloud" I mean to acknowledge that reading may be done quite silently, or "for the inner ear", or actually with the involvement of vocal production.

② *Kuángrén Rìjì*, 狂人日記 or 狂人日记 (published in 1918).

③ Beecroft 2010: 23, citing Ma 2001 and Nylan 2001.

④ Beecroft 2010: 22 (with n. 36) points out that before this period, the texts that came to be known as the 五經 "Five Classics" were not yet referred to by that title, nor individually by the term 經 *jīng*. For more on canons in ancient China, see e. g. Henderson 1991, Nylan 2009.

These were the 詩經 Shījīng "Book of Songs", the 書經 Shūjīng "Book of [Historical] Documents", the 禮記 Lǐjì "Record of Rites", the 易經 Yìjīng "Book of Changes", and the 春秋 Chūnqiū "Spring and Autumn Annals". ①
The Wǔjīng as a group is typically associated with Confucianism, but early versions of the oldest of these texts may long antedate the lifetime of Confucius himself (traditionally 551 – 479 BCE); portions of the Yìjīng (better known in its Wade-Giles transliteration as the *I Ching*) may go back to the second millennium BCE.

What we see in the ancient Mediterranean world, and arguably also in ancient China, is a process of retrospection whereby certain texts gain respect, esteem, even reverence. This seems to be one of the ways in which texts become thought of as "classics" in a given culture. I have elsewhere ② defined "classic" by the following three criteria:

1. a classic is the best of its kind;
2. a classic has withstood the test of time;
3. a classic taps into the mythic values of its culture.

The notion "best of its kind" is fairly self-evident. Indeed our word "classic" comes from the Latin noun *classis*, which in early Latin had referred to "classes" or categories of citizenry; by the time of Seneca the Younger (ca. 3 BCE to 65 CE) it could refer to "types" of people as categorized by their progress in gaining wisdom (*Epistulae morales* 75. 8 ff., where the word is used as a synonym of Lat. *genus*, "kind"). By the second century CE, an author such as Aulus Gellius could use the term *scriptores* classici to denote

---

① There may have been a sixth book, the 樂經 Yuèjīng "Book of Music", but legend has it that this was lost in the horrific "Fires of Qin", the 焚書坑儒 fénshū kēngrú "Burning of Books, Burial [alive] of Scholars" under 秦始皇帝 Qín Shǐ Huáng Dì, the first Qin Emperor, in 213 210 BCE. It is possible, however, that the Yuèjīng was actually just a selection from the 詩經 Shījīng or Classic of Songs, one of the extant Five Classics, and not a sixth distinct work.

② Kirby 2000: 133 – 134; cf. Kirby 2012: 278 – 279.

writers whose prose style was of the highest quality. ① Gellius, citing Marcus Cornelius Fronto (ca 100 – 170 CE) in this passage, does not make explicit reference to canonical lists of *classici* or "classical authors" here, though such canons did exist long before Gellius or Fronto (see above on Aristophanes of Byzantium). ② So the word "classic" in its earliest usage seems to have been applied to *persons* rather than to their literary works *perse*; to designate a *text* a classic comes by virtue of a kind of metonymy, or what is sometimes known as a "transferred epithet". This detail is perhaps important when thinking about the meaning of the word "classic" and its application in the creation of *canons*. Moreover, the act of making such lists is a conscious acknowledgment that the creative period entailed is already over; indeed, by the Alexandrian period, we have left the classical era proper, and have already entered what we might call a *classicizing* era—a nostalgic (Schiller might say "sentimental") ③ attempt to recapture the pristine power and grandeur of the classical. We should perhaps contemplate how much the process of classicizing is in fact crucial

---

① See Gellius, *Noctes atticae* 19.8.15, *idest classicus adsiduusque aliquis scriptor, non proletarius*. The word *adsiduus* here may be in explicit antithesis to *proletarius*, and as such may be an index not just of classicism but of classism—the strong inference being that writers coming from a higher socioeconomic class are likely to exhibit better Latinity. But the notion of superior literary style being an inevitable factor of class is negated in the classical period itself by the exaltation of the works of e.g. Plautus, who was said to have worked as a manual laborer, and of Terence, who was brought to Rome as a slave, and appears to have been born to a mother who was a slave. (It may be no coincidence that the stock character of the "clever slave" figures prominently in the plays of Plautus.) Going back further still in time, and pushing the concept to a greater extreme: the notion of superior intellectual capacity not being a factor of socioeconomic class is illustrated vividly in Plato's *Meno*, in which Socrates questions one of Meno's slave-boys.

② This Aristophanes is not to be confused, of course, with the comic playwright Aristophanes of Athens, who lived in the 5th century BCE, and who in fact figures as one of the six canonical playwrights of Attic Old Comedy in the Alexandrian librarians' list. Even so, Aristophanes of Byzantium died around three hundred years before the birth of Aulus Gellius.

③ Schiller 1795.

to the notion of the "classic" and the creation of canons. ①

This leads me to my next point, which is that a classic has "withstood the test of time." But: how much time? A year? A century? A millennium? This is not immediately obvious, and moreover may differ from genre to genre, or from culture to culture. We can see an implicit valorization of, say, Homer in the careful and detailed discussions of the Homeric poems in the dialogues of Plato, which were composed in the 4th century BCE. This is part of the process of retrospection just mentioned. It is not to imply that there was no process of evaluation or adjudication in the Archaic period itself; if the ancient tradition is to be believed, the archaic *aoidoi* (bards) engaged in performance contests, as Hesiod describes in the *Works and Days* (650 – 659), and there is even a tradition that Homer and Hesiod met and competed against one another. ② Certainly by the fifth century BCE in Athens, the annual play-writing competitions at the Great Dionysia very specifically reified the ranked evaluation of each year's submissions to the contest, and (cumulatively) led to ranked evaluations of the playwrights competing. ③ So the elements of canon-making, if not the instantaneous evaluation of "classic" status, can begin to manifest themselves immediately upon a first reading (or performance, which as Alexander Beecroft reminds us was integrally linked to the notion of authorship in the ancient world). ④ But for the the concept of "classic" in its richest sense, per my criterion No. 2 above, there will still need to be an element of elapsed time; how much time is "enough" to satisfy this criterion is perhaps more of an open question. It is not impossible that at

---

① For more on classicizing, under the heading of what I there call the "Age of the Scholar", see Kirby 2009: 21 – 24.

② This is the premise of the *Contest of Homer and Hesiod* (conveniently collected in West 2003: 318 – 353). See also West 1967 and (more generally) Griffith 1990.

③ For what can be known about the so – called "Victors" Lists, our epigraphic sources for information about the winners year by year in the Dionysia and Lenaea, see chapter 4 of Millis and Olson 2012.

④ Beecroft 2010.

least one generation must pass first before any given group of people can themselves authoritatively recognize a classic coming into being in their own midst. ① Yet another question that must be frankly faced here is whether, at a certain point, a work of art ceases to withstand the test of time—and how this would be recognized. Is it at that moment no longer a classic? This, in turn, leads to my third criterion.

A classic taps into the "mythic values" of its interpretive community:

>...part of what gives us a sense that a work of art is a classic is that it seems to give access to what Joseph Campbell has felicitously termed the "Power of Myth": the ideas, or the tropes, or the very mode of execution of such a work, have a power to them that transcends mere innovation or cleverness or piquancy. Rather, they inspire, they instruct, they give hope. And that is, ultimately, the source of their enduring value. For as long as the fabric of a given culture remains unrent, the same symbolic values will continue to hold their power for that culture. ②

These three criteria, then, are how I would go about defining what is a "classic" in the verbal or visual arts, and what constitutes the "classical" in such designations. When I arrived at these criteria, I was thinking consciously about the Western heritage as it stems from the ancient Greek and Roman civilizations. But can they also be applied to the "classical tradition" of East Asia? Let us focus this inquiry on Chinese

---

① To the extent that I am right about the need for elapsed time, the notion of an "instant classic" will be not so much paradoxical as nonsensical: those who use the phrase probably intend either "succèsd" estime´ or "popular favorite". In any case I am not aware of any ancient source that refers to "instant classics".

② Kirby 2000: 133 - 134. I have borrowed the term "intepretive community" from Stanley Fish, in his famous formulation of "reader-response" theory (see, par excellence, Fish 1982).

culture.

We must now turn our attention to the Chinese word 經, which is pronounced *jīng* in modern *putonghua*. This variously translated as "canonical text", "classic", or even "scripture". ① The character in its traditional form is composed of a compressed form of 糸 *mì*, one of the words for "silk", plus a graph that seems to depict the warp threads on a loom (Figure 1).

Figure 1. Left: Zhou-period seal-script character for jīng, showing the vertical threadsor "warp" on a standing loom. Center: the (traditional) hanzi for same. Right: an illustration of woven cloth, showing its warp and weft threads. (Illustration courtesy of the author.)

The simplified *hanzi* (经), though pronounced in putonghua the same way as the the traditional, does not illustrate the notion as clearly. But from this ideographic etymology we can make the connection with *weaving a fabric*.② And indeed one meaning of 經 *jīng*, as a verb, is "to pass through", which is surely also associated with this imagery of weaving.

---

① Beecroft 2010: 22, prefers to translate 經 *jīng* as "canon". The point is well taken, for reasons explained in his text. If I do not unambiguously adopt this translation, it is in order to keep clear the distinction we have been making here between "classic" and "canon". Nylan 2009: 721 N. 1 finds that … "scripture" —suitable in some contexts, as when we speak of liturgies based on the Classics—is highly unsuitable in most Qin and Han contexts where the religious dimension of the Classics is not to taken to be the reason for their elevation to *jing* status.

② Much of my etymological discussion here is indebted to conversations with Victor Mair, who also includes some of this material in Mair 1990.

Interestingly, the Indo-European languages also make similar connections. 經 *jīng* is the standard Chinese translation for the Sanskrit term सूत्र *sūtra*, which is defined by Monier—Williams as follows:

> Sūtra, n. [...] a thread, yarn, string, line, cord, wire [....] that which like a thread runs through or holds together everything, rule, direction ... a short sentence of aphoristic rule, and any work or manual consisting of strings of such rules hanging together like threads (theseSūtra works form manuals of teaching in ritual, philosophy, grammar & c [....]) ①

The noun *sūtra* is apparently deverbal from सिव् √*siv* "to sew" or "stitch"; our English words "sew" and "suture" are, in fact, cognate with √*siv*. (Latin, too, has a verb *texo*, *texere*, *texui*, *textus*, which means to "weave"; our word "text" comes from this, as do the Italian *tessere* "weave", *tessuto* "[woven] cloth", and *testo* "text".) These words for weaving and stitching—and indeed silk—bring to mind some extremely ancient artefacts from China: first, the 简牍 *jiǎndú* or writing strips of bamboo that, already in the second millennium BCE, were being used to make books. These narrow strips were typically wide enough for a single vertical column of characters; to make a "book" of such strips, they had to be *stitched together* with thread. Another important connection between text and textile was made when a magnificent trove of texts was discovered, in 1973, in tomb number 3 at Mawangdui —*texts inscribed on silk cloth* (Figure 2).

Moreover, this interpretation of *jīng* has a very direct connection with the Greek word κανών (*kanôn*), which meant a "straight rod" or a bar of some sort that was used to maintain straightness. Those who write about the literary canon are fond of pointing out that such rods were often used for *measuring*,

---

① Monier-Williams 1899: 1241 *sub uoc.*

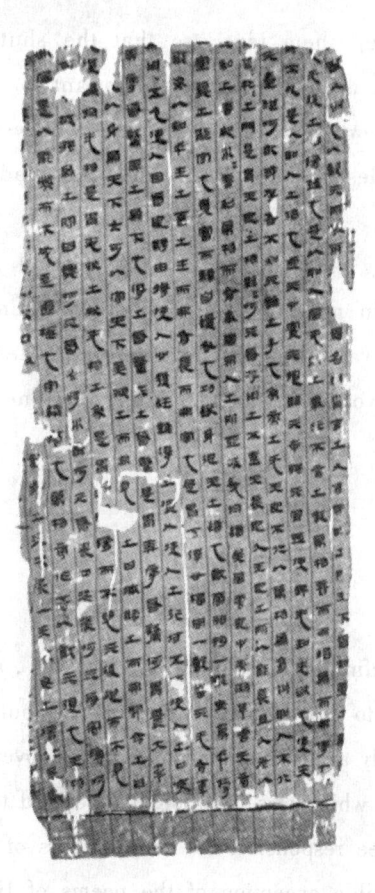

Figure 2. Daoist manuscript discovered in tomb no. 3, Mawangdui. Ink on silk; 2nd century BCE. (Source: public domain)

such that the word "canon" might be taken as metaphoric for a *standard* of quality in the literary arts. The word doubtless early had this meaning in some contexts; but we should note that *kanôn* could also refer to a "weaver's" rod or "warp beam"① —the rod to which the warp threads of the loom were

---

① So too Beecroft 2010: 22: both *jing*, which refers to the warp thread, and *canôn*, which refers in Greek to the rod that guides the shuttle, are weaving terms for the system that guides the production of cloth.

tied in order to keep them taut, so that the shuttle could be passed through.① A *kanôn* is thus integrally important to the creation of woven textile; and it is worth pondering whether whoever first employed the *kanôn* metaphor in describing literary works also had the image of fabric-weaving in mind.

Words like *jīng* and *sūtra* serve to remind us of the laborious handwork entailed in making a book in ancient times. That, in turn, bears witness to the value placed upon the kind of text that would merit so much labor: a text worth cherishing. A text that one loves. Perhaps, one might say, a classic.

III

Whatever our definition of "classic" or "canon", and regardless of when those terms began to be employed as the vocabulary of an evaluative aesthetics, it is hardly an exaggeration to say that, over time, the *Odyssey*—along with the *Iliad*, which was traditionally ascribed to the same poet—was to a significant degree responsible for the contours of the Western tradition itself. With the possible exception of the poems of Hesiod,② they are the oldest narrative texts in the Western tradition. Now terms like "East" and "West" are tendentious and arbitrary designations; there is no magic boundary that visibly demarcates the distinction. Indeed, despite the profound cultural influence of ancient Greek culture on Western Europe and its colonies, Westerners visiting present-day Greece are likely to be struck by

---

① The word occurs with this meaning in e.g. *Iliad* 23.761; Aristophanes's *Thesmophoriazusae* 822 and *Wealth* 2.156b; and Nonnus's *Dionysiaca* 37.631 (all verse, ranging from 7th or 8th century BCE to 5th century CE), as well as in Plutarch's *Banquet of the Seven Sages* 156B (prose, circa 100 CE?).

② West 1966: 46 – 47 would place the *Theogony* earlier.

how exotic it feels to them—how (one might say) "non-Western" the culture seems. Was the traditional distinction misguided? Have the boundaries shifted? Has Greece itself changed over the centuries? Regardless of the answer, many observers today will be likelier to underscore the distinctiveness of Greek culture, its difference from their own, than to say, with Shelley, "We are all Greeks". ①

If one does decide to reassign or redraw cultural boundaries, at least as far as ancient Mesopotamia, then the "oldest narrative text in the Western tradition" would be, not the poems of Homer or Hesiod, but the *Epic of Gilgamesh*, of which the Sumerian texts appear to date from the third millennium BCE. ② But setting the *Gilgamesh* aside for our current purposes, and returning to what is ordinarily regarded as the Western canon: it is difficult to give non-Westerners-or, for that matter, to give even non-specialist Western readers these days—any adequate sense of the massive importance that the *Iliad* and *Odyssey* have carried in Western culture for almost three thousand years. They were seen even by the ancients as the foundation of Hellenic (and thus also of Roman) culture. They have been compared to the Judeo-Christian Bible for their treatment of the interaction between the human and the divine; they have been characterized as an "oral encyclopaedia" of Greek culture; they were rapturously and endlessly revered by later writers in the ancient world; they inspired countless later works of verbal and visual art—in ancient Greek, in Latin, and in more modern languages. Taken together as the record of a more or less unified *legendarium*, they are undeniably one of the most important sources for classical Greek myth.

But first and foremost, they are memorable as tales of extraordinary

---

① On the aptness or otherwise of this *aperçu*, see e. g. Kirby 2000: xi-xii.

② The Akkadian version appears to date from the early second millennium BCE. For editions of the *Gilgamesh* in English, see Kovacs 1990, or Foster 2001 (which will include some useful secondary materials as well).

beauty and significance. Those whose cultural exposure is principally Chinese will perhaps grasp something of this beauty and significance if I say that they combine the magnetic narrative power of the *Romance of Three Kingdoms* (三国演义 *Sanguo Yanyi*) with the astute character psychology (and sometimes the elegant melancholy) of *Dream of Red Mansions* (红楼梦 *Hong Lou Meng*). Their scope is grand, their narrative arcs are masterfully crafted, their gifts of description and character development are unforgettable. They are surpassed by nothing in subsequent Western literature, and they have few rivals in any culture, ancient or modern.

As soon as we begin to look more closely at the *Odyssey*, we discover that the field of Homeric studies is not only vast and unimaginably complex, but also a site of endless contestation, even where the most fundamental questions are concerned. Who is the author of this work? Is the epic in fact the work of a single poet? When was it composed? Was it composed in writing, or at first generated orally and only subsequently recorded in written form? If the latter, then when and by whom? and so on, and on. It is enough to deter some scholars entirely from specialization in the subdiscipline. That is unfortunate, because those who forge ahead undaunted will find the Homeric poems[1] to be works of arresting, captivating, unforgettable.

In attempting to categorize these long narrative poems, we almost immediately run aground on the rocky shoals of terminology. The commonly-used term—I have already used it myself—is "epic". But what exactly is an "epic"? Must it be a notably long narrative? Must it be composed in verse? Must the narrative be played out on the divine as well as the human level?

---

[1] I have in mind principally the *Iliad* and *Odyssey*. The so-called *Homeric Hymns*, though important for many reasons and worthwhile in their own right, do not seem to have been composed by Homer, nor even to partake of the same antiquity as the *Iliad* and *Odyssey*.

Must it have a "hero" as its central or focal character?① And if our answer to all these questions is Yes, then what about prose texts? What about movies that, like *Gone with the Wind* or *Nicholas and Alexandra*, are referred to as "epic films"? There are pitfalls at every turn, and some (at least) of these concerns must be shelved, at least temporarily.

One provisional solution to the problem of nomenclature, when speaking of Homer at least, is to use the term that the ancient Greeks themselves used in referring to this genre: *epos* (plural *epê*). In addition to its cultural proximity to the Homeric poems, this has the virtue of a direct etymological relation to our modern word "epic". The main problem is that the ancients themselves seem to have delineated the genre with reference to specifically metrical concerns, rather than according to subject-matter. ② But no label is likely to be perfect, and the very "foreignness" of the Greek term should serve at least to help demarcate the genre as a particular category.

Moving gingerly forward, then, we may say that the *Odyssey* (as we now have it) is a poem of just over 12,000 lines of hexameter verse; it appears to have been composed orally, in the "Dark Age" between the Mycenaean ③ and the Classical periods of Hellenic culture, and originally to have been, not recited, but *sung* to the accompaniment of a lyre. Ancient tradition, as well as some scholars, have attributed its composition (substantially if not entirely) to a single artist (whom for convenience if nothing else) we may call Homer, also revered as the composer of the

---

① And if so, what is our definition of "hero"? Must this be someone in the public sphere, or is the notion of a "private hero" as valid? Must s/he serve, or be able to serve, as a role model for others in their community? Must s/he be someone entirely admirable, or are the so-called "anti-hero" and "dark hero" suitable stand-ins for the moral paragon? Need the hero (like the main character in an Aristotelian tragedy) undergo a peripety or fundamental reversal of fortune? And so on, and on.
② Kirby 1989.
③ Mycenaean culture flourished in the second half of the second millennium BCE—at the same time, that is, as China's Shang Dynasty 商朝.

Iliad, to which the *Odyssey* is in some senses a sequel. ① The language of the text is *sui generis* in ancient Greek; we may say it is "semiotically marked" in that it is not a natural language, but rather a synthetic Greek amalgamated from elements of numerous natural dialects. It seems to have been developed specifically for the oral composition of *epos*. As in the case of the *Iliad*, and of a number of other *epē* that have not survived the wrack of time, the narrative material for the *Odyssey* is drawn from the legendarium of the Trojan War and its aftermath. It is worth our saying some more about this.

Interestingly for the title of this essay, the first-recorded voyage in the Greek tradition was actually a journey to the *East*: the massive armada of the Achaeans, under the leadership of Agamemnon their high king, sailed from the Hellenic peninsula to the northwest coast of Asia Minor, in order to rescue Agamemnon's sister-in-law, Helen, from Troy. How she got there in the first place was a matter of dispute in ancient times: was she abducted by main force? Was she bewitched by the power of amorous passion? Did she perhaps herself make the decision to leave her husband, Menelaus king of Sparta, and go with Paris② to his father's high-walled citadel in Troy?③ Regardless of the cause of her departure from Sparta, it was deemed to be

---

① Additional thorny questions: Did Homer exist? If so, when and where did he live? Was he, as the ancient tradition has it, blind? Did the same poet, as ancient tradition again has it, compose both the *Iliad* and the *Odyssey*? If these poems were originally generated orally, how and under what circumstances did they get written down? My reader can perhaps begin to see what I mean by "site of endless contestation". For some (seriously divergent) opinions on these and other issues related to the so-called Homeric Question, the reader is encouraged to begin by consulting e. g. Kirk 1962, Parry 1971, Lord 1981, Janko 1982, Foley 1991 and 2005, Nagy 1996, and West 2011 (to name only a very few).

② Known in the Homeric texts as "Alexandros".

③ Yet another ancient tradition holds that the "Helen" of Troy was never the corporeal Helen at all, but rather an *eidôlon* ("image"—we might today say "hologram") of the actual woman, who in fact spent the duration of the war in Egypt. On the Helen tradition see e. g. Suzuki 1989, Austin 1994, Hughes 2007, Blondell 2013—and, of course, the Sappho poem cited above.

a true *casus belli* by Menelaus and the entire vassalage of his brother Agamemnon, who besieged Troy in order to take her back. The *Iliad* proper narrates some of the events that occur toward the end of this disastrous ten-year conflict.

The *Odyssey*, on the other hand, relates the long postwar journey of Odysseus, one of the great princes fighting for the Achaean side, from Troy back to his native Ithaca, an island off the west coast of the Hellenic peninsula. Told in an intricate narrative style, in which the events of the tale are recounted at different narratological levels (and sometimes out of chronological sequence), the *Odyssey* also affords us some details about the course of the Trojan War itself that are not included in the *Iliad*. Moreover, the *nostos* (homecoming) of Odysseus offers a poignant foil to that of Agamemnon: Odysseus's journey takes ten more years after the end of the war, but he arrives home to find his wife Penelope still waiting faithfully for him, whereas Agamemnon reaches his own home speedily-only to be murdered by his wife, Clytemnestra, and her lover Aigisthus.

The sea voyage from Troy to Ithaca should only have taken a few days" time—a couple of weeks, perhaps, allowing for a bit of inclement weather and some stops along the way. Instead, it takes Odysseus another decade *after* the war to reach home. This has a number of advantages for the storyteller: among others, the very scope of the duration allows the poet to expatiate at generous length upon the numerous and various adventures that befall Odysseus. Too, a time – lapse of this length means that his son, Telemachus, is by the climax of the story about twenty years old—just on the brink of manhood and of social/political autonomy. This latter detail has some extremely significant implications for the shape of the narrative, both for his own sake and for that of his parents.

IV

Asked what he himself considered his greatest scholarly achievement, Joseph Campbell would probably have named his massive four-volume compendium of world mythology, *The Masks of God*.[1] But the work for which he is surely best remembered is his formulation of a narrative pattern that he termed the Monomyth.[2] This was first propounded in his 1949 book, *The Hero with a Thousand Faces*, where it is limned in somewhat recondite terms, drawing on a number of disparate ancient sources.[3] Campbell's work was, however, made far more accessible to a broad audience when he had the good fortune to be interviewed by Bill Moyers for a six-episode television series called *The Power of Myth*.[4] The transcript of these enduringly popular programs was itself turned into a book of the same name, and this has been often republished, sometimes as a coffee-table book with lavish illustrations.[5] The notion has been picked up and elaborated by many other scholars since Campbell's first articulation of it.[6]

The Monomyth is an extraordinarily important narrative template; its ability to affect, impress, and move readers and audiences is perhaps unlike that of any other. By no means every tale is an instantiation of the Monomyth;

---

[1] Campbell 1959.

[2] He did not, however, coin the term himself; its first known appearance is in James Joyce's *Finnegan's Wake*. Campbell's own schema is also not entirely original; he seems to have digested, and been influenced by, the work of Lord Raglan (Raglan 1936), to name only one predecessor.

[3] Campbell 1949.

[4] On the PBS television series, see online e. g. at http: //www. imdb. com/title/tt0296362/. The entire documentary is available on DVD: http: //www. shoppbs. org/product/index. jsp?productId = 18274906.

[5] Campbell 1991.

[6] For just one example of this, see Leeming 1998.

but those that are, tend to be unusually memorable. Such is its power, in fact, that we may decide it is one of the essential components of the epic genre. ① In order both to present the Monomyth in the clearest possible terms, and to make it applicable in the widest variety of instances (both diegetic and mimetic, including cinema), I offer here a substantially modified formulation of the schema. I present this under ten headings; eight of these may be termed "intrinsic" to the very material of the narrative, and two of them "extrinsic", having rather to do with aspects of the composition of the narrative and the way the reader/audience assesses the work. Herewith, then, my own version of the Monomyth.

First, the "intrinsic" elements:

1. THE HERO ON A JOURNEY. What constitutes a "hero" is, as already noted, a subtle problem. Classically the Monomyth Hero was a male youth on the threshold of manhood;② he may be of aristocratic or even divine lineage, and there may be extraordinary or miraculous events that surround and semiotically mark his birth. In any case, the nature and strength of his character will emerge over the course of the narrative. The journey he embarks upon is typically a literal one, though (particularly in later literatures) it may be a metaphoric "journey" that traces a process of personal development.

2. THE "IMPOSSIBLE" TASK. The Hero sets out on his journey in order to complete a task that is impossible, or seems so at the outset. Elements of this are *danger* and *conflict*, two particularly exciting aspects of narrative for most readers/audiences. The narrative function of such a task is of course to test the mettle of the Hero and to demonstrate his moral

---

① If not necessarily of the epos as that was conceived in antiquity.

② This predicament is also the source of the *Bildungsroman*. But in fact some of the best Monomyth narratives center on *female* heroes. That said, I shall use masculine pronouns in this description in order to insist upon the androcentric nature of ancient Mediterranean cultures—and their literatures.

superiority in some capacity. It may be the determinative quest that serves as his *rite de passage* from youth to manhood. In some cases the Hero may be set this task in an attempt to get rid of him permanently: thus Heracles is despatched to bring back Cerberus from the land of Hades; thus Dorothy is sent to bring back the broom of the Wicked Witch of the West; thus Beren is commanded to fetch a Silmaril from the very Iron Crown of Morgoth.

3. THE FAITHFUL COMPANION. Rarely, especially in elaborate narratives, does the Monomyth Hero go it alone. Instead, he is accompanied by a faithful "sidekick" who accompanies him on his journey. The Faithful Companion is typically somehow "less than" the Hero: less nobly born, less handsome, less intelligent, less serious-minded, less powerful. But without his assistance at crucial moments, the Hero would not be able to complete the impossible task.

4. THE WISE COUNSELOR. Often the Hero will be apprenticed to a mentor who helps him develop in ways crucial to the successful completion of the Impossible Task. Sometimes their interaction is limited to a single, pivotal encounter. But whether the interaction is limited or extensive, the Wise Counselor tends to be somehow "more than" the Hero: older, stronger, wiser, more experienced, more powerful. For this reason, the Wise Counselor is typically limited to cameo appearances in the narrative as actually presented to the reader/audience: otherwise, he risks upstaging the Hero. His narrative function is usually to provide the Hero with some material object (on which see below) or some information vital to the successful completion of the impossible task.

5. THE TALISMAN. There is no reason why a Talisman could not be some non-material object, such as a word or idea; but classically the Talisman is an item presented to the Hero (and typically by the Wise Counselor) in order to equip him to complete the Impossible Task. Popular examples of this are a magic sword, helmet, or ring, though it may be a live animal of some sort (like Pegasus), an incantation, or some other piece of

vital information. Odysseus receives both material and non- material Talismans in the *Odyssey*: the *môlu* root from the god Hermes, the life-saving sash from the goddess Leucothea (on all of which, see below); and, in the Underworld, the three pieces of vital information from Elpenor, Tiresias, and Anticleia.

6. THE ADVERSARY. At first I was inclined to call this element the "villain"; but over time I came to see that the distinctions of good and evil in this character are not always so simple. In some cases it is the Adversary who actually sets the Hero his Impossible Task. For instance, if the Impossible Task is to rescue a princess who has been imprisoned or held captive, the Hero will sometimes find that the task has been set for him by the princess's father, who wants to test the Hero and see if he is worthy of the hand of the princess in marriage (and perhaps also the inheritance of her father's kingdom). But the simplest type of Adversary, in narrative terms, is one who embodies Evil in specular opposition to the Good embodied by the Hero himself. In such cases he is a foe to be vanquished, which might itself be the impossible task.

7. KATABASIS. There is arguably no other element of the Hero's journey more constitutive of, or essential to, the Monomyth than this one. The word *katabasis* is ancient Greek for "descent", and the Katabasis of the Monomyth Hero marks his descent into the underworld. Again, this may be literal (the Hero may die temporarily, or may take it upon himself to visit the land of the dead -so Gilgamesh, Odysseus, Aeneas, Heracles, Gandalf, Aragorn) or metaphorical (so Theseus, who must descend into the labyrinth to slay the Minotaur; so Beowulf, whose Katabasis is underwater, where he fights and slays the mother of Grendel); but whichever is the case, the Hero comes back transfigured. From that moment onward he is profoundly different. He may have been reborn; he may have undergone such a drastic transformation that his life is for all intents and purposes new. But in one way or another, the Katabasis is central to the Monomyth narrative, and to the

completion of the Impossible Task. In some cases, indeed, the completion of the Katabasis *is* the Impossible task-as in the case of Heracles or Orpheus.

8. VICTORY & REWARD. Perhaps it is possible for the Monomyth Hero to attempt the Impossible Task-and to fail.① But the expected formulation is that he will succeed, against incalculable odds, and return (unimaginably altered) to his original situation in order to be fêted and celebrated- perhaps made king. If the Impossible Task was to rescue the beautiful princess from her distress, the reward for the victorious Hero might be to claim her hand in marriage.②

My two "extrinsic" elements are as follows:

9. SPLINTERING. [a] It is not uncommon for one of the above – listed elements to be proliferated: there may be more than one Faithful Companion, more than one Talisman, more than one Wise Counselor, even (as in Tolkien's *Lord of the Rings*) more than one Monomyth Hero. I call this phenomenon "Splintering". Among other things, it allows for the creation of a more complex, nuanced, or multifarious narrative. [b] A special case of Splintering involves what we may term "Trebling"③ -that is, Splintering into three. The Hero may be granted three wishes; a family may have three daughters; the achievement of the impossible task may require three attempts; and so forth. But for whatever reason, the number Three seems to exert a special narrative fascination, particularly in traditional or folkloric contexts.

---

① In both *Gilgamesh* and *Beowulf*, there is Trebling (element 9b) of the Impossible Task (element 2). In both cases, the Hero succeeds in completing the first two, and fails in the third. For both, poignantly, that failure leads to death-for Gilgamesh, indirectly; for Beowulf, directly.

② An interesting variant or, as it were, "allomorph" of the "Wise Counselor" element occurs when the Wise Counselor is, in fact, the princess herself-a variant known as the "helpful princess" theme (de Luce 1997). Examples of this in classical legend would include Ariadne (who helps Theseus), Medea (who helps Jason), and Dido (who helps Aeneas) —all, however, to their own eventual chagrin.

③ Borrowing the term from Propp 1958, who recognizes the phenomenon as an element of traditional folktale, but (too modestly) does not extend its implications beyond that genre.

So pervasive, in fact, is this privileging of the number Three, that it is worth following this rule of thumb whenever Splintering is found in a tale: Where there are Two, look for Three.

10. IDENTIFICATION. Why is it that we love the Monomyth so much? What is the source of its incomparable power? I think this has to do with the fact that the reader/audience is invited to identify with the Hero in some significant way.[1] It may be that we use the Hero as a sort of screen onto which we project our selves, in the cinema of the psyche. But whatever the mechanism, a Monomyth tale is particularly effective because we feel that the story of the Hero is, somehow, *our own* story. This is what I mean by "identification". Other narrative forms besides the Monomyth may well afford the reader/audience an opportunity for identification with the main character; and that may indeed be a source of their power as well.[2] But because "Life is a journey" is one of the most fundamental "conceptual metaphors" of human thought,[3] the Monomyth is ready-made for applicability to one's own life journey. Our deepest and most cherished goals may often seem impossible of realization; and living through the cataclysmic events that on occasion beset our lives may cause us to feel as though we have indeed died and come back from the dead. Small wonder, then, that the elements of the Monomyth make it the most gripping of narrative formats.

V

By now it should be clear that the *Odyssey* of Homer is the quintessential Monomyth. Like many other tales from Greek antiquity-Oedipus and the

---

[1] On this (though not in explicit connection with the Monomyth *per se*) see Jauss 1974.

[2] A good example of this would be Shakespeare's *Romeo and Juliet*, surely one of the most powerful tales in all of dramatic literature—but not a Monomyth.

[3] So assert Lakoff and Johnson 1980, and I think rightly so.

Sphinx, Apollo and the Python, the labors of Heracles, the adventures of Theseus and of Perseus, to name but a few— it follows in minute detail the pattern I have elaborated above. Odysseus's Impossible Task, of course, is the journey itself: he must try, despite the focused animosity of his Adversary, to get home to Ithaca. That Adversary is no less an opponent than the mighty sea-god Poseidon, whom he has offended by blinding Poseidon's son, the Cyclops. His Faithful Companions are the men on his ship, and (later) his own son Telemachus. He has quite a literal Katabasis in book 11 - a journey to the Land of the Dead, in order to gain vital information. He has a number of Wise Counselors, including Teiresias and the ghost of his mother in the underworld and, above all, the goddess Athene (who often serves this narrative function in Greek legend-for Achilles, Heracles, Theseus, Perseus, and Telemachus, to name a few others besides Odysseus). His Talismans include the magic sash given him by the goddess Leucothea (*Odyssey* 5. 333 - 353), the *môlu* root given him by Hermes (*Odyssey* 10. 286 - 306), and the mighty bow of Iphitus (*Odyssey* 21. 11 - 41), which none of Penelope's suitors could string, and which-when Odysseus himself has strung it-becomes the weapon of mass destruction by which he achieves final victory under his own roof. The beautiful princess is, of course, already married to him; the astonishing thing is that, even after twenty years, she has never given up hope that he would return to her. But there is some Splintering of this element, in that Odysseus could have remained on the island of the Phaeacians and married another (much younger) beautiful princess, Nausicaa. [1] We find an extraordinary example of Trebling in the trio of tests that Penelope sets him, in order to test his identity: first, the description of the Odysseus" clothing (*Odyssey* 19. 215 - 250); second, the contest of the bow (21. 404 - 430); and third, the test of the marriage - bed (23. 173 -

---

[1] Where there are Two, look for Three: is the third "beautiful princess" the goddess Calypso, who keeps him on her island for seven years (*Odyssey* 7. 259), in a perverse caricature of marital bliss?

206).

We should consider the possibility that the role of the Hero itself has been trebled in the *Odyssey*. Certainly Telemachus fits the typical profile of the youth-on-the-brink-of-manhood; and he himself goes on a (relatively short) journey of his own, in the so-called Telemachy (books 1 – 4 of the *Odyssey*), and succeeds—or "would have succeeded"—at the Impossible Task of stringing the bow (*Odyssey* 21. 124 – 130). ① If, however, we have a second Hero in the *Odyssey*, then—following the principle of "Where there are Two, look for Three"—who is the third? One fascinating possible answer is: Penelope herself. ② Her journey is, of course, a metaphoric one, as we never see her leave the palace precincts; but her Impossible Task is as daunting as any in the narrative: fend off the suitors until such time as Odysseus (whom she has no assurance is even still alive) should return home.

Regardless of how we construe the role of Hero in the *Odyssey*, it seems certain that this tale was one of the prime examples from antiquity that

---

① Homer tells us that after the trebled failed attempts he "would have strung" it (καί νύ κε δή ρ' ἐτάνυσσε βίῃ τὸ τέταρτον ἀνέλκων, 128) but that-at a surreptitious signal from Odysseus-he purposely pretends to be unequal to the task. Narratively speaking, of course, this is mandatory, as the "prize" for stringing the bow is the hand of the beautiful princess in marriage — but the princess, in this case, is his own mother, Penelope. In this regard, as likewise in his not needing to best his father, Telemachus may be regarded in Freudian terms as the narrative opposite to Oedipus (whose legend was known, in some form, already in the time of Homer; see *Odyssey* 11: 271 –280).

② Monomyth Hero or not, Penelope has been provocatively suggested as the pivotal character in the story (Butler 1897). Certainly she is the narrative lynch-pin to which the journeys both of Odysseus and of Telemachus are fastened: the father, whose goal is to return home; and the son, whose goal is (in some sense) to leave home—or at least to cut the apron-strings. How to do so without outraging the Greek reverence for what the Chinese would call 孝 *xiào*—on which more anon—is part of the task that confronts Telemachus in this. Apropos, three proverbs come to mind: 百善孝為先 *bǎi shàn xiào wéi xiān* ("of the hundred virtues, *xiào* is the foremost"); 虎父無犬子 *hǔfù wú quǎnzǐ* ("a tiger father does not have a dog son", roughly equivalent to "like father, like son"); and 大樹底下長不出好草 *dà shù dǐxia zhǎng bù chū hǎo cǎo* ("grass cannot grow well under a big tree": the son must come out from under the shadow of his parents, and become a man in full).

suggested the contours of the Monomyth to Joseph Campbell; and the fact that it is such a perfect Monomyth tale goes a long way toward explaining its perennial appeal.

VI

One way of looking at the *Odyssey* through East-Asian eyes will be to read it comparatively, against a Chinese narrative with which it may be said to share some salient characteristics. For this I would like to skip forward a couple of millennia, to the 16th century CE, in fact. For it is in this period, during the late Ming dynasty, that one of the most remarkable and deeply-beloved works of Chinese literature was composed.

Journey to the West (西遊記 *Xi You Ji*) is known as one of the Four Great Classics of premodern Chinese fiction. ① As such, its compositional date is much more recent than that of the *Odyssey*. The dramatic date of at least some of the narrative is set in the Tang dynasty; indeed the Tang emperor 太宗 *Tàizōng* (r. 628 – 649 CE) figures as one of the characters in the tale. The breadth and resilience of its popular appeal is evinced by the many retellings and adaptations-in narrative text, in stage-play, in cinema and television, even in video games-that it has spawned and continues to spawn. ② Its sheer narrative exuberance and rhetorical plenitude set it apart

---

① The other three are *The Water Margin* (水滸傳 *Shuihu Zhuan*), *The Romance of Three Kingdoms* (三國演義 *Sanguo Yanyi*), and *The Dream of Red Mansions* (紅樓夢 *Hong Lou Meng*). These so-called 四大名著 *si da ming zhu* or "four high-rank writings" date from both the Ming and Qing periods (the character 名 *ming* here refers not to the Ming Dynasty (for which the *hanzi* is 明) but to "rank" or "position"). Taken as a group like this, we may also note that these four works form a canon of their own, though of course a much more recent one than the earliest such lists in Chinese literature, such as the 五經 *Wǔjīng*.

② For an extensive, though probably not exhaustive) list, see online at http: //tinyurl.com/xiyouji-media (accessed February 2015).

even from other rollicking adventure narratives; it is a "cracking good yarn" like few others in any literary tradition. ①

As with Homer and the *Odyssey*, we have the name of the putative author of *Journey to the West*: the work was very early on attributed to one Wu Cheng‐en (吴承恩), though not all scholars accept that attribution. In any case there are numerous elements of the narrative that have traditional (folkloric) antecedents. But above and beyond this, it has at least some roots in the soil of history: Xuanzang② was a real person who actually lived in the Tang Dynasty, and whose life's work can truly be said to have had a massive impact on the history of the world. For it was Xuanzang who decided that his monastic life in China was insufficiently informed by the primary documents of Buddhism, and that it was incumbent upon him to learn Sanskrit, to go to India himself, to obtain as many Sanskrit texts on Buddhism as he could, and then to bring these back to China and translate them into Chinese. He was neither the first to do this, nor the last; but few would dispute that he is the most revered for it. The diachronic effects of the project could hardly be overstated—for Buddhism in China (from the Tang Dynasty to the present day), for the spread of Zen in Japan (and thence worldwide), and indeed for

---

① What may be called the standard edition in English is that of Yu 1983 (in four volumes), with extensive introduction and notes. There is also a six-volume bilingual edition, with facing pages in English and (simplified) *hanzi* (Jenner 2010).

② Born 陈祎 Chén Wěi, he came to be known as 玄奘 Xuánzàng, i.e. "Mysterious and Powerful"; in chapter 9 of the fictional version, it is the abbot at the Temple of Gold Mountain that gives him this 法名 *fǎmíng* or religious name. Perhaps as a paronomasia on Xuanzang, though the *hanzi* (and one of the tones) are completely different, he receives in chapter 12 the courtesy name of 三藏 Sānzàng, i.e. "Three Containers" —a reference to the *Tripiṭaka* or "three baskets" originally used to sort into categories the scrolls of the Pāli Canon of Theravadan Buddhism (*Tripiṭaka* is the Sanskrit for which the Pāli term is *Tripiṭaka*), though in chapter 12 Guanyin refers to a *Tripiṭaka* of Mahayana Buddhism. The English version of Yu 1983 frequently refers to Xuanzang as "Tripitaka" where the Chinese text has 三藏 Sānzàng. (Yet another paronomasia for Xuanzang is 唐僧 Tángsēng, "Tang-era monk" [僧 sēng < Sanskrit सङ्घ *saṅgha*, an "assemblage", in this case, a Buddhist community; 僧 can be an individual monk or a member of a *saṅgha*]).

the survival of the tradition, whose importance in India itself subsequently waned dramatically. The lasting heritage of Xuanzang's efforts may be measured not only by the effects just mentioned, but also by the fact that some of the core Buddhist texts are still read by readers of Chinese in the very translations made by Xuanzang.

The journey of the historical Xuanzang from China to India and back is a thrilling (and lengthy) adventure in itself. (The distance, there and back again, has been calculated at between 10,000 and 16,500 miles.) ① It has been the subject of several recent books;② but—more relevant to the topic at hand—it was the basis for *Journey to the West*, or at least for the portion of that text's one hundred chapters beginning with chapter eight. ③ The primary source for information on this journey is Xuanzang's own 大唐西域記 *Dà Táng Xīyù Jì* (*Great Tang Dynasty Record of the Western Regions*), which gives the event a notable vividness, even after almost fourteen centuries. ④

I shall eventually have much more to say about Xuanzang-the historical figure, the fictionalized character in *Journey to the West*, and the relation between the two-but first I would like to examine the question of unity (or lack thereof) in the narrative of Journey to the West, as this problem impacts our understanding of the role of Xuanzang in it.

It would be well to begin by interrogating a very widespread aesthetic principle: is unity of concept and execution, an overall sense of "wholeness", a paramount value for works of art? If a work appears to lack

---

① Wriggins 1996 [2004]: 265 n. 1. Google Maps (maps.google.com) in 2015 calculates the time to travel by airplane from Luoyang (in Henan Province) to Bodhgaya (in Bihar, eastern India) at 17 hours, 45 minutes.

② See e.g. Wriggins 1996 [2004], Bernstein 2001, Saran 2005, and Chandra and Banerjee 2008.

③ It is possible that the narrative as we have it, complete in one hundred chapters, is a conflation of two earlier separate narratives.

④ For a modern English translation of the 大唐西域記 *Dà Táng Xīyù Jì* see Li 1996.

unity or wholeness of this sort, do we judge it to be inferior? My sense is that for most of human history, this has been the case. There are notable exceptions: for example, one of the most vital characteristics of the postmodernist moment[1] has been the privileging or prizing of fragmentation, disunity, and deferral over wholeness, unity, and presence. But the very development of such a moment in philosophy and culture was as a conscious and considered gesture of protest, of resistance, of demurral. Such a gesture in itself underscores the ascendancy, in general, of what we might term the "unity principle", at least in Western aesthetics. It was repeatedly articulated in the Greek and Roman traditions by their most eminent theorists, beginning in discussions of rhetoric and poetics. Plato, for example, has Socrates opine in the *Phaedrus* that the several parts of an oration ought to cohere as a single unified whole, the way the various limbs of a living organism compose a single being.[2] Horace, in his enormously influential *Ars poetica*, coined the oft-quoted phrase *simplex ... et unum*.[3] This is surely not the place to adjudicate the case; the verdict, at any rate, is likely to be *non liquet*. But I do want my reader to ponder the problem, for how each of us feels about this is going to affect how we feel about the unity (or otherwise) of *Journey to the West*.[4]

In any case, the text of *Journey to the West*, as we have it now, is a single long narrative that traces the adventures, first of 孫悟空 *Sūn Wùkōng*-

---

[1] I say "vital characteristics", not "fundamental principles", because postmodernism strikes me as anti-fundamentalist in every sense.

[2] Plato, *Phaedrus* 264C. The irony of this is that the *Phaedrus* has itself been criticized for lack of conceptual or thematic unity.

[3] Horace, *Epistles* 2.3.23. (The sobriquet "Ars poetica" was apparently given to the work by Quintilian (cf. his *Institutio oratoria* 8.3.60).

[4] For that matter, the *Odyssey* itself has long been the subject of just such discussions, being as it is the topic of dissent between so-called "unitarians", who assert that the poem was conceived and composed as a unified work, and "analysts", who hold instead that our text of the *Odyssey* is the compilation of a number of shorter "lays" —perhaps by several different poets—that was eventually assembled by a later redactor.

the Monkey King-and then of the Sun Wukong and Xuanzang as they journey together to India. In a sense this companionship is itself the source of the confusion, because while the quest for the Mahayana Sutra is obviously (and specifically) Xuanzang's, the character who is present throughout the narrative-and, for most readers, the most charismatic-is the Monkey King. [1] For this reason each of them, in his own way, might claim to be the central figure of the narrative. To the extent that one discerns a Monomyth as a structuring principle of the tale, one will perhaps favor Xuanzang as Hero, with Sun Wukong as Faithful Companion; but to the extent that Sun Wukong is seen as unifying the collected episodes, the centrality could be said rather to be his.

In view of this complex and confusing juxtaposition, it is possible that the tale as we have it is a conflation of two distinct, originally independent narratives that were subsequently brought together as one-perhaps for the first time by Wu Cheng-en himself, as a single overarching trajectory for this hundred-chapter narrative, though the conflation might well have occurred much earlier in the tradition. Indeed it may be that Sun Wukong is the narrative transmogrification, the fantastical reimagining, of another historical character—another Buddhist monk, in fact, who like Xuanzang traveled from China to India and back. But of this, more anon.

It will be clear to all readers of *Journey to the West* that, like the *Odyssey*, the Gilgamesh, and so many other tales from the ancient world, its several narrative elements fit very comfortably into the Monomyth template as I have sketched it out above.

The Hero on a Journey—the eponymous Journey to the Thunderclap Monastery, at least—is, of course, Xuanzang; Certainly there are

---

[1] Indeed Arthur Waley's popular adaptation of the work (Waley 1942) is called *Monkey: A Folk-Tale of China*, and that has made sense to its innumerable readers.

miraculous elements surrounding his birth, as recounted in chapter 9. Sun Wukong may seem at first blush to be more of a picaresque hero in general, a trickster figure,① and/or a comic foil to the more serious Xuanzang; but there is much more to be said about Sun, and we shall touch upon them below. Meanwhile we should note that he, like Xuanzang, goes on the journey to complete the Impossible Task; he too has extraordinary circumstances surrounding his birth, and a Katabasis; he too reaps the Reward of Victory-indeed the same Reward as Xuanzang himself. ②

The Impossible Task, for Xuanzang, is to fetch the Mahayana Sutra from the Thunderclap Monastery, far away in India of the Great Western Heaven (chapter 12) —the eponymous *"journey to the West"* of the work's title. Sun Wukong has a number of Impossible Tasks of his own, including— notoriously—the theft of the Peaches of Immortality from the fabulous garden of the goddess 西王母 Xīwángmǔ, Queen Mother of the West,③ which are lusciously described in chapter 5.④ These, and the attendant task, are remininscent of the Apples of the Hesperides, the fetching of which was one of the twelve Impossible Tasks of Heracles; but the cultural symbol and literary motif of the peach are themselves suggestive, and we shall return to them shortly.

Taking Xuanzang as the Hero, his Faithful Companions are several: Sun Wukong, of course (see chaper 14); Zhu Bajie (see chapters 18-19); and

---

① On Sun Wukong as a "pointedly metic character", see e. g. chapter 7 of Raphals 1992 (and on *mêtis* itself see, famously, Detienne and Vernant 1974).
② Raphals 1992: 168 takes Sun Wukong as unambiguously the "hero" of *Journey to the West*.
③ Also known as 王母娘娘 Wángmǔ Niángniáng, "royal mother empress". On Xiwangmu see Cahill 1993.
④ On the aesthetics of Chinese gardens in the time of Wu Cheng-en, see e. g. Clunas 1996.

Sha Wujing (see chapter 22). ①

Xuanzang's Wise Counselor is without a doubt the bodhisattva Guanyin, who serves in the narrative as his tutelary divinity, much as Athena does for Greek Monomyth Heroes. The emperor Taizong may also be counted as a Wise Counselor, in that he gives Xuanzang some important Talismans.

Xuanzang's Talismans in the story (chapter 12) include, from Taizong, a safe-conduct document stamped with the imperial seal; a golden bowl, and a drink of wine with a pinch of dust "from home" in it. From Guanyin, Xuanzang receives a cassock and nine-ring monk's staff (the 錫杖 *xīzhàng* or "tin staff" adorned with rings that jingle as he walks). ② Sun Wukong had already received his Talismans in chapter 3 from 敖廣 Aoguang, the Dragon King of the Eastern Ocean, and his three brothers: the marvelous 如意金箍棒 *rúyì jīngū bàng* or "wish-fulfilling gold-ringed cudgel", a magical rod of iron that changes size at his command and indeed makes him invincible, plus some magical clothing of his own: shoes, chain-mail, and a cap. These are in narrative terms the specular counterparts of the cassock and staff of Xuanzang himself, though they equip the two travelers in fundamentally different ways.

The Adversaries come thick and fast in this story; to name only two, we

---

① It is difficult to decide whether to include 玉龍三太子 *Yùlóngsāntàizǐ*—the Jade Dragon, Third Crown Prince of King Aorun (see chapter 15)—as a fourth Faithful Companion. He serves as Xuanzang's steed—what in Hindu thought would be referred to as his वाहन *vāhana* or "vehicle". In the Indic tradition the *vāhana* is a complex figure, sometimes functioning as a totem of the god, sometimes as a full companion. In some instances they are revered as gods themselves. But of course *Journey to the West*, though certainly profoundly indebted to the Indic tradition, would not be obligated to replicate all its cultural details—and if it did, those details would more likely be Buddhist than Hindu. In any case, it is interesting that the narrator refers in chapter 100 to "the elder, his three disciples, and the white horse"—setting the Faithful Companions, as a group of three, apart from the dragon-horse.

② 錫杖 *xīzhàng* is the Chinese name for the Sanskrit खक्खर *khakkara* or monk's staff. The bodhisattva tells the provenance and magical qualities of the cassock and staff in chapter 12 (see Yu 1983 [vol. 1] 281 – 283 for the narrative.

Figure 3. A 錫杖 xīzhàng or Buddhist monk's staff, adorned with bell-like rings that will jingle as he walks, announcing his approach. The xizhang had different numbers of rings depending on the bearer's status. (Source: public domain)

might single out the bandit Liu Hong in chapter 9—beginning even before the moment of Xuanzang's birth—and the Demon King in chapter 13. Ironically, the historical Taizong emperor was himself an Adversary, at least at first, in that his prohibition against foreign travel meant that Xuanzang's surreptitious departure could have won him the death penalty; it was only when Xuanzang prepared to return to China that he obtained an official pardon from the emperor. ① In *Journey to the West*, by contrast, it is Taizong who (in chapter 12) actually sends Xuanzang on his way. This too, as we noted earlier, is one of the narrative functions of the Adversary in the Monomyth.

---

① Yu 1983 (vol. 1): 4.

Sun Wukong has a spectactular Katabasis, in that he is imprisoned by the Tathāgata (in chapter 7) under the Five-Phases Mountain[①] for five hundred years, as punishment for his rebelliousness and insolence. Only when visited by the compassionate Guanyin, in chapter 8, is his Buddha mind made manifest, and enlightenment attained—the necessary precursor to his release when rescued by Xuanzang in chapter 14. Interestingly, the Taizong emperor himself has a very prominent Katabasis in chapters 10-11, where he dies, tours the underworld, and returns to the land of the living. And Xuanzang has a memorable Katabasis of his own, when in chapter 72 he is lured by seven monster-spirits, like demonic spiders with the temptation to violate his monastic vows, and imprisoned in their cave when he proposes to leave. He is

---

① 五行山 wǔxíngshān, the "Mountain of Five Phases" —the latter being the "five elements" of Chinese cosmology: Wood (木 mù), Fire (火 huǒ), Earth (土 tǔ), Metal (金 jīn), and Water (水 shuǐ). These may be called "phases" because, in Chinese astrology, they cycle through the calendar-one "phase" per year-against a concurrent cycle of the twelve zodiacal signs. By this mechanism there will be a convergence of phase and sign only once every sixty years. The year in which I write this, for instance—2015 CE —is the year of the 木 羊 mùyáng (Wood Sheep); the last previous Wood Sheep year was 1955.

We may also note that this mountain, or chain of mountains (山 shān can mean a mountain-range as well as a single peak) is of course a magical one, manifested or transformed from the fingers of the Tathāgata's hand. Given the exuberantly fantastical nature of the *Journey to the West*, it may not be too fanciful to see in this hand movement, and the magical transformation it brings about, a *hastamudrā* or "hand gesture" of the kind traditionally depicted in iconography of the Hindu gods, or of the Buddha and bodhisattvas. Each of these gestures has a ritual semiotic value, and when properly (per) formed they are thought to possess a supernatural efficacy. If I am right about this, the original mudrā (when Sun Wukong is in the palm of the Tathāgata's hand) may have been the पद्मकोश मुद्रा *padmakośa mudrā*, the "lotus-calyx gesture", i.e. the fifteenth of the twenty-eight single-hand mudras listed in the *Abhinaya Darpana* ("Mirror of Gesture") of Nandike? vara (2nd century CE). When the gigantic hand is in this position, the five fingers look (to Sun Wukong) not like the petals of a lotus-symbol of enlightenment—but like "five flesh-pink pillars". When the Tathāgata flips his hand upside down, the fingers become five connected mountains—under which the benighted Monkey is imprisoned. As the visual reverse of the *padmakośa mudrā*, the mountain made by the Tathāgata's hand, imprisoning Sun Wukong, may symbolize his lack of—and need for—enlightenment. (For more on the mudrā see e.g. Saunders 1960, Bunce 2005, and Carroll and Carroll 2012.)

trussed in their web like a fly, and only the devotion and determination of his Faithful Companions enables them to rescue him. As with Sun Wukong and the mountain, this Katabasis has specifically to do with the question of devotion to the life of Buddhism.

The Victory and Reward of the two pilgrims—Xuanzang and Sun Wukong—is as absolute as it is inevitable given the Monomyth structure: both eventually attain Buddhahood.

As noted above, Sun Wukong is not only far and away the most beloved character of the tale: he is that Hero who is present from start to finish. Moreover, he is the most complex figure in the narrative: he figures not only as a Hero but also as a Faithful Companion. There is something endearing about "dressed animal" figures in a story-we know this from *The Wind in the Willows* and *Winnie-the-Pooh*-and there is something of that appeal to the Monkey King. But he is more than simply a dressed animal. I mentioned earlier that Xuanzang was not the last Chinese Buddhist monk to travel to India; the last was, in fact, a man named ... Wukong.① This monk was in India for forty years-much longer than Xuanzang's own sojourn there, in fact-and returned to China in 789 CE. Thus his period of activity was fully a century later than Xuanzang's, and consequently closer to the time of Wu Cheng-en. It may be that Wu was trying to find a way to spin a tale about both monks and their shared enterprise. Why he should make one of them a monkey is more mysterious.

The answer may lie partly in a proverbial Chinese expression, 心猿意馬 *xīnyuányì mǎ*, "the heart/mind is a monkey; the will is a horse".② (A poem is cited in chapter 7 of the narrative that includes the line 馬猿合作心和意 *mǎyuán hézuò xīn hé yì*, "horse and ape together compose mind and thought".) For Buddhist practitioners, ध्यान *dhyāna* (contemplation,

---

① Yu 1983 (vol. 1) p. 1 and n. 2.
② On the concept and the proverb, see (*in extenso*) Carr 1993.

meditation) is the kind of focused concentration that can lead to समाधि *samādhi*, the pinnacle of reflective absorption that is the final goal of yogic practice. (Indeed the standard Chinese translation of *dhyāna* is 禅 *chán*- the word that gives its name to an entire tradition of Buddhism.)① The "monkey mind" is that all-too-familiar flitting, easily distracted consciousness that is disruptive to the kind of focused concentration that practitioners of meditation seek. The 空 *kong* of Wukong— "empty, hollow" —is the Chinese translation of the Sanskrit शून्यता *'sūnyatā* "emptiness", a complex and vital concept in Buddhist thought, related in some contexts to the peaceful serenity of *dhyāna* and *samādhi*. So it may be that Sun Wukong is a specular counterpart of Xuanzang on his pilgrimage toward enlightenment-a reification of his "monkey mind" that must, like the rest of him, attain self-mastery, the fullness that is emptiness. ②

Too, we may find a clue in the peaches of immortality that Sun steals in chapter 5 of the *Journey to the West*. Insofar as he succeeds in stealing and eating them—thereby gaining immortality—he may be said to serve, in narrative terms, as guarantor of the survival (and eventual Buddhahood) of Xuanzang.

Another highly attractive possibility is that Sun Wukong finds his origin, or part of it, in a much earlier Monomyth narrative from India: the *Rāmāyaṇa* of Valmiki. ③ In this epic tale, Hanuman is a god with the face of a monkey who is ardently devoted to Rāma, the Hero of his eponymous tale. In that narrative, Hanuman is Rāma's Faithful Companion on his journey and indeed

---

① *Chan*, which in Japan becomes 禅 Zen. On all this see (among countless others) Watts 1957, Schlütter 2008. *Samādhi*, on the other hand, is simply rendered by words of similar sound: 三昧 *sānmèi*.

② For the *Journey to the West* as an allegory—a "manual for self-cultivation" in the *sanjiao*, an "allegory of the process of enlightenment", and so on—see chapter 7 of Raphals 1992.

③ For this idea, see Mair 1989, Yu 1983 (vol. 1) 13 - 15, Walker 1998. On Hanuman generally, ranging from the *Rāmāyaṇa* material to Indian religious culture of today, see the very thorough treatment in Lutgendorf 2007.

is of crucial assistance in the completion of the Impossible Task—the rescue of Rāma's wife Sītā and the defeat of Rāvaṇa king of Lanka. As with Sun Wukong, the iconography of Hanuman includes a metal rod or mace (see Figure 4); also like Sun Wukong, Hanuman is capable of tremendous feats-himself completing several Impossible Tasks worthy of any Monomyth Hero.

Figure 4. Hanuman bringing Mount Dunagiri to Lanka. Color print, Ravi Varma Press, circa 1910. (Source: public domain)

If the Hanuman tradition were known—even in some garbled form-in China by the time of Wu Cheng-en, this might explain the simian form of Xuanzang's fellow pilgrim, as well as some the latter's attributes in the narrative.

VII

So far I have attempted to illuminate the gross formative structure of the Odyssey by pointing out the distinctive elements of the Monomyth-elements that it shares in common with a celebrated Chinese tale, *the Journey to the*

West. Another way might be to point to the endless abundance of cultural production that the Odyssey has spawned over the centuries since its composition, and that—again like *Journey to the West*—it continues to spawn even to this day. ① Yet a third way, perhaps, to see the Odyssey through East-Asian eyes is to focus on some key words from the text of the *Odyssey* itself—to try and elucidate their semantic import for Homer's ancient Greek audience—and to look at a particular scene in the *Odyssey* that, as a motif, shares some profound characteristics with a similar motif in Chinese literature and culture. ② Let us begin, then, with two words that are of paramount importance in the ancient Greek-speaking world as we see it portrayed in Homer, and attempt to explain them in ways that will resonate with comparable aspects of traditional Chinese culture. These will, in turn, prepare us to examine the motif in a similar way.

The Ocean

Our English word "ocean" comes from the Greek *Ôkeanos*. Like most phenomena in nature, and indeed many abstract concepts as well, bodies of water were held by the ancients to be full of gods—indeed to *be* gods—and Ôkeanos is no exception. The word is itself the name of a god, ③ physically constituted as a divine river that (in the ancients flat-earth notion of cartography) encircled the entire central land-mass that they thought of as

---

① To list only a few literary adaptations of Homer from just the twentieth and twenty-first centuries, written in English (and excluding actual translations): Pound 1924; Walcott 1992; Frazier 1997; Logue 2003; Simmons 2003; Atwood 2005; Malouf 2009; and of course Joyce 1922. For a few films, again mostly in English: Godard 1964; Coen 2000; Minghella 2003; Petersen 2004. Operatic adaptations range (mostly not in English) from Monteverdi's *Il ritorno d'Ulisse in patria* (1629) to Tippett's *King Priam* (1962), in a list far too massive to summarize here. As a source of subject-matter for visual artists in the Western tradition, the Homeric material looms perhaps even larger.

② Some of the following material appears, in somewhat different form, in Kirby 2012b.

③ Technically, a Titan (see e.g. Hesiod, *Theogony* 133), son of Ouranos and Gaia, the hypostatized Heaven and Earth.

"earth". ① In the Archaic period Ôkeanos is also seen as the source of all other waters upon the earth, salt or sweet:

> There is a great river [*potamos...megas*] beside you right now,
> If he is capable of helping, but no one fights Zeus,
> Not even the great Achelous, not even Ôkeanos,
> From whose deeps every river [*pantes potamoi*] and sea [*pasa thalassa*],
> Every spring [*pasai krênai*] and well [*phreiata*] flows. Even Ôkeanos fears
> The lightning of Zeus and his crackling thunder. (*Iliad* 21. 192 – 199) ②

Ôkeanos too is important in terms of his offspring. His daughters include the Oceanids, sea-nymphs that, according to Hesiod, number three thousand (*Theogony* 364).

Even to venture into the closest waters of Ôkeanos would be held an act of tremendous boldness, perhaps also as a kind of rashness that borders on madness—for it is madness to tempt the gods with our safety. To understand the dimensions of this madness it is important to bear in mind three related aspects of ancient cultures the world over: first, boats had to be made by hand, with tools that were themselves made by hand—there was no advanced technology to increase convenience or enhance safety. Second, because of this resulting inevitably rustic level of shipbuilding, each and every venture

---

① See e. g. Iliad 18. 399, *Odyssey* 20. 65 where it is called *apsoroos Ôkeanos*, "Ocean that flows back into itself [as it circles the earth]". This and other citations from Homer are adapted from the translation by Stanley Lombardo (Lombardo 2000).

② Achelous is the eponymous god of the river Achelous, the largest in the Hellenic peninsula. Because of its size he is held to be an especially important and powerful river-god (hence "not even the great Achelous" in this passage).

onto the waters of sea or ocean was fraught with peril. You literally risked your life every time you decided to do it. And while you could beseech various sea gods to help you travel safely and return home successfully, there was no guarantee that they would be coaxed into complying. And this is the third cultural detail one must bear in mind: one of the main differences between the loving reverence held for Guānyīn 觀音 or Māzǔ（媽祖, also called Tiānhòu 天后, "Empress of Heaven") in East Asian cultures, on the one hand, and gods like Poseidon in Greek culture, on the other, is this very deep and warm affection that Guanyin's followers hold for her. And indeed as 菩薩 pú sà, the Bodhisattva of Great Compassion, *Dabei Guanshiyin* 大悲觀世音 hears the cries of all suffering beings, and lifts her thousand arms to help them. Not surprisingly, then, Guanyin and especially Tianhou are particularly beloved of east Asian sailors, who for centuries have prayed to them for protection from storms, shipwreck, and sea monsters. ①

The relationship of the ancient Greeks to their gods, by stark contrast, was frankly (even coldly) contractual. The ancient Roman formula that expressed the nature of this system was *do ut des*: one gave in order to be given to in return. Pragmatically speaking, this is the very point of sacrifice; it is a form of barter: goods for services. The goods, to be brought by the person asking for the god's help, must be as fine and as costly as he can afford. The services, as we learn from ancient modes of prayer, are seen as a form of recompense for the goods offered; they foster, one might say in Chinese terms, a very practical and ongoing system of 關係 *guanxi* between the supplicant and the god. ② But nothing could be further from the notion of

---

① For more on Tianhou, see Watson 1985.

② 關係 or 關系 guānxi, "relation (ship)" is a complex dynamic of Chinese social relations based on networking. Among other things, having guānxi with someone can suddenly make what was previously "impossible" possible. It would be simplistic to reduce it to the ancient Mediterranean notion of do ut des, but that is certainly a part of it. For more on the nature of guānxi see e. g. Gold 2002.

Christianity—that God is our Father, who loves us and watches over us like a family-than the ancient Greek notion of the relation between human and god. One will often hear modern-day Christians speak of a "close personal relationship" with Jesus; nothing could be more alien to the ancient Greek mind than this. To an ancient Greek, a good day was one in which the gods did not notice you even once. A whole week of such days? Even better. One only approached the gods when it was absolutely unavoidable. (For heroes it was different: they had, and could survive, intimate contact with the gods, as we see in the case of Achilles in the *Iliad* and Odysseus in the *Odyssey*. But for humans who did not live their lives on this grand scale, an epiphanic experience of the manifest presence of one of the great Olympian divinities was invariably disastrous-even fatal, as we see in the case of such poor mortals as Semele or Hyacinthus. Ordinary folk instead lived by the proverb *lathe biôsas*: live unobtrusively. ①This pertained first and foremost to the realm of the divine.)

In Greek myth and legend no less than in Chinese-very likely in the archetypal thinking of all humankind-the ocean has an incalculably great significance. In the *Journey to the West* alone we meet 敖廣 Aoguang, 敖欽 Aoqin, 敖順 Aoshun, and 敖閏 Aorun, the four Dragon Kings of the Eastern, Southern, Northern, and Western Oceans respectively. These are sea-gods, shape-shifters comparable in the Greek tradition to Nereus or Proteus. Homer refers to the latter as ὁ γέρων ἅλιος, the Old Man of the Sea, and tells (*Odyssey* 4. 382 - 570) how Menelaus wrestled him into submission and coerced him to recount the fortunes of the other Achaeans after the Trojan War. The Old Man, classic Wise Counselor that he is, tells Menelaus about three (n. b. !) men in particular: two of them—Ajax and Agamemnon—have died, but the third is still alive; and that third is of

---

① A proverb associated principally with Epicurus, who may have coined the actual phrase himself.

course Odysseus. Menelaus, a Wise Counselor in his turn, offers this crucial information as a Talisman to Telemachus in book 4. The Dragon Kings are linked to the Homeric Old Man of the Sea, not only in that they are sea-gods, not only in that they are shape-shifters, and not only in that they serve as Wise Counselors who furnish Sun Wukong with Talismans, but because they do the latter only under duress, just as the Old Man would never have yielded up his crucial information about Odysseus if Menelaus had not forced him.

This is but one example, of which hundreds could doubtless be given. In any case, *Ôkeanos* has a deeply mystical valence in Greek myth. It represents the uttermost limits of human existence, and the threshold between us and the unknown, the infinite. Its origin in Greek traditional culture probably comes from some vague awareness that beyond the Pillars of Heracles lay an impossibly vast and dangerous body of water: the Atlantic Ocean itself. And this is a detail to which we shall soon return.

The City

The disposition of the city of Troy was not dissimilar to what one might find on the mainland of Greece, at a place like, say, the Mycenae of Agamemnon himself: an *akropolis*, or citadel, built on a hill or small mountain as inaccessible as possible, to protect against the attack of potential assailants, and walled about with a stone curtain wall as high and as thick as they could make it. The citadel's vertical height, and its lofty position at a high elevation, not only served as protection, but also to emphasize the nature of the people who occupied it: these were the royalty and the aristocracy of the kingdom. In the lowland territories surrounding the citadel dwelt the agrarian lower classes, the people who grew the crops and raised the livestock that nourished the nobly-born families living inside the *akropolis*. And indeed these lowland territories-relatively flat, with access to river and spring water- were where those crops and livestock were raised. They were also comparatively much more open to attack and plunder, both because of the open nature of the landscape and because these people were not themselves members of the elite warrior class. Those were concentrated, in time of war, within the confines of the citadel. It does seem that Homer sometimes uses the wordpolis (or its variants *ptolis and ptoliethron*) to refer to the citadel or acropolis itself, though they can also refer to these combined areas—the citadel and its outlying lowlands—to mean a "city" or even, in some collective sense, a city/state; his word *astu* refers sometimes to the specifically to the buildings—the structural and architectural elements—of the *polis*, as distinct from the people who live in it. [1]

We should probably bear in mind that for us today, the word "city" may bring with it modern industrial connotations that would have been quite unimaginable for Homer and his original audiences (and, for that matter, equally unimaginable for Wu Cheng-en and his readers throughout the Ming and Qing eras). Particularly in the case of the lower socioeconomic classes of that time, an urban environment as we conceive of that would be completely outside the realm of their daily experience; their lives were probably focused around farms and villages, and the ancients had a word for this less dense, more agrarian kind of living environment: the *dêmos* or "deme", which term also came to refer to the people living in such an area.

If there is anything in Bronze-Age culture that can in any way accommodate the notion of an "urban" environment, it is probably the life within the citadel itself. But to grasp this with any degree of historical accuracy, we must adjust our notion of scale, and envision at this period a (peace-time) community that would have been measured in hundreds of people rather than thousands or hundreds of thousands. (In war time the habitation density of the *akropolis* doubtless increased dramatically, as people from the outlying demes came to take refuge in, and help defend, the fortified citadel.

---

[1] E. g. *Iliad* 17. 144. The meanings of all these words shift some according to time and place; in later writers such as Herodotus and Thucydides, for example, *astu* is used to mean the lower part of the town as distinct from the citadel.

But the historical walled city of Troy, at its largest dimensions in pre-classical times, cannot ordinarily have held more than a few thousand people at most.)

From a military standpoint, the weak link in a structure like these Bronze-Age citadels was the gates, which more or less had to be made of wood; it behooved the inhabitants of any *akropolis*, if they wanted it to be safe, to add the minimum possible number of gates; to make them as thick and sturdy as possible; and then to guard them aggressively and at all times. The fact that the Trojan citadel is said to have had several gates is a tribute not only to its impressive circumference, but also to the power of the king who ruled it: he could afford to man all these gates constantly with fierce guards. ①And indeed in the Trojan legend the Achaeans find it remarkably difficult to sack the city: despite the quantity and quality of their massed troops, it takes them ten years to storm the citadel and take back Helen for Menelaos. Even then this is achieved not by main force, but by a clever ruse devised by Odysseus himself: none other than the famous "Trojan Horse". The Achaeans trick the Trojans into thinking they have sailed back home, leaving behind this enormous wooden horse as if it were some sort of votive offering to the gods. Though the Achaeans are only hiding a small distance down the coast, the Trojans, falling for the ruse, haul the horse inside the gates of the citadel, unaware that it is full of enemy soldiers who will lay the citadel open to attack by their fellow Achaeans.

This part of the story is actually not told in the Iliad itself, which culminates before the end of the Trojan War. To hear this tale, you must go to Book 8 of the *Odyssey*, ② in an episode where Odysseus is the guest of the

---

① The imposing Lion Gate at the entrance to the *akropolis* of Mycenae, still extant after thousands of years, has—just inside its entrance, on the right side as you go in—a stone pillbox from which a guard could observe (and attack) any intruder who managed to force his way inside the huge gates.

② The incident is also mentioned in *Odyssey* 4. 265 – 289, in a reminiscence by Menelaus himself. In some ways the most famous account of the Trojan Horse is to be found, not in Homer, but in Vergil's *Aeneid*, at the beginning of book 2.

Phaeacians, denizens of a fabulous utopian kingdom on the island of Scheria. Here Demodocus, the bard of Alcinous king of the Phaeacians, sings the story of the Trojan Horse, accompanying himself on the lyre as he sings. As Odysseus is in disguise, and has presented the Phaeacians with a false identity, no one in the audience realizes that the mastermind behind the Trojan Horse is sitting in their very midst-not, that is, until Odysseus, unable to restrain his overwhelming flow of emotion, bursts into tears at hearing the tale (*Odyssey* 8. 485 – 534) . Alcinous the king, ever the thoughtful and generous host, notices the grief that Odysseus is suffering, and quickly stops Demodocus from singing any more that evening. But he soon also discovers Odysseus's true identity, and offers to send a ship, laden with gifts, to transport Odysseus safely home to Ithaca.

Scheria, the island of the Phaeacians, is no ordinary place. It is in fact as close as the ancients could come to imagining an actual earthly paradise, an idyllic land where life was more beautiful and peaceful than anything they could encounter in their own reality:

...One day
Great Nausithous led his people
Off to Scheria, a remote island,
Where he walled off a city [*polis*] built houses
And shrines, and parceled out fields.
After he died and went to the world below,
Alcinous ruled, wise in the gods' ways. [*Odyssey* 6. 10 – 12]

It is not, however, a completely Golden-Age magic kingdom; despite the life of tremendous ease lived by the Phaeacians, there is nonetheless work that must be done. Nausicaa, the king's daughter, must wash her clothes in river pools outside the citadel ("The laundry pools are a long way from the city", 6. 40) and near the seashore (6. 94 – 95), and her mother sits by her hearth spinning yarn (6.51 – 53). Meals do not spontaneously appear on the table; they must be cooked (7.13). Ships do not row themselves (6.268 – 272), though they do have some extraordinary, even magical characteristics, as we shall see.

But overall, the life on Scheria is undeniably pleasant and easy. Indeed it has some of the delights of the island of Penglai (蓬萊仙島 *penglai xiandao*)① or of the community living by the Peach Blossom Spring ([世外]桃花源 [*shi wai*] *tao hua yuan*)② as described in Chinese legend and lore. In Penglai, the astute reader will remember, the wine cups refill themselves magically, and the rice bowls are never empty; but also, Penglai is where a host of supernatural fruit trees grow. Like the denizens of Penglai, the villagers living near the Peach Blossom Spring are described as "carefree and happy",③ dwelling in a lush and fertile landscape. So idealized is the life of these people, in fact, that the very phrase *tao hua yuan* (*or shi wai tao hua yuan*, peach-blossom spring beyond the world) has become a modern Chinese colloquialism for a land of bliss and bounty.④

The fruit of tree and vine grows on the island of the Phaeacians with an ease and effortlessness that would be beyond the dreams of any gardener:

---

① See e.g. the description in *Shan Hai Jing* (山海經, *The Classic of Mountains and Seas*), a substantial and valuable sourcebook of culture and legend. It is of uncertain date, but appears to have been compiled over time during the Warring States, Qin, and Han periods.

② Known first and foremost from the *Tao Hua Yuan Ji* (桃花源記, *The Record of the Peach Blossom Spring*), a poem, with prose preface, by Tao Qian 陶潛 (also known as Tao Yuan-Ming 陶淵明, 365 – 427 CE). Paradoxically, the prose text is more celebrated than the poem itself, which "is usually taken to be little more than a perfunctory versification of the story" (Hightower in Mair 1994: 578). For the likely literary antecedents of Tao's work, and their Daoist elements, see Bokenkamp 1986.

③ Citations from the *Tao Hua Yuan Ji* in this essay are from the translation by Hightower.

④ "Spring" in this sense (源 *yuán*) refers to a source of water, not the season. That is, it is a synonym of 泉 *quán*, not of 春 *chūn*. To add still more confusion to this context, *yuán* is also the *putonghua* vocalization of the *hanzi* for garden or "orchard" (園); and the pinyin for 桃 *táo* "peach" invites confusion with the Wade-Giles transliteration of 道 *dào* "way".

> ...Outside the courtyard,
> Just beyond the doors, are four acres of orchard
> Surrounded by a hedge. The trees there grow tall,
> Blossoming pear trees and pomegranates,
> Apple trees with bright, shiny fruit, sweet figs
> And luxuriant olives. The fruit of these trees
> Never perishes nor fails, summer or winter—
> It lasts year round, and the West Wind's breath
> Continually ripens apple after apple, pear upon pear,
> Fig after fig, and one bunch of grapes after another.
> The fruitful vineyard is planted there, too. [*Odyssey* 7. 112 – 122]

Readers of the *Tao Hua Yuan Ji* will recall that the entrance to the magical region is marked by a grove of peach trees, whence the title of the work; the peach, in traditional Chinese iconography, is an important symbol of 壽 *shou*, or longevity. Once the fisherman who discovers the region passes through the cave under the mountain to reach the magical village, he also discovers "mulberry, bamboo, and other trees and plants" growing there. The peach grove also brings to mind the wondrous Garden of Immortal Peaches in chapter 5 of the *Journey to the West*.

Homer's Scheria is at once both remote and luxurious. This paradox is both odd and clearly explained in a comment made by Nausicaa herself:

> There is no man on earth, nor will there ever be,
> Slippery enough to invade the land of the Phaeacians,
> For we are very dear to the immortal gods,
> And we live far out in the surging sea,
> At the world's frontier, out of all human contact.
> [*Odyssey* 6. 201 – 205]

It is odd to think that there should be such ease and comfort on an island, far from all other humans; but that oddness underscores the fact that their paradisical existence[①] is a gift from the gods. So too at the Tao Hua Yuan, the villagers are—and prefer to be—completely isolated from the rest of humanity: "As he [sc. the fisherman] was about to go away, the people said, 'There's no need to mention our existence to outsiders'." Apart from the magnificent peach grove itself, however—which is (perhaps significantly) situated *outside* the cave passing under the mountain, and thus separated from the village proper—their crops do not appear to grow unbidden; the workers are described as "coming and going about their work in the fields".

In the *Odyssey*, Nausicaa describes to Odysseus the *ptoliethron* of her father, and her description reminds us that this is a place where city life and maritime living blend into one single existence—a life where the city indeed meets the ocean, and no one lives without a boat:

> …It has a high wall
> Around it, and a harbor on each side.
> The isthmus gets narrow, and the upswept hulls of the ships
> Are drawn up to the road. Every citizen
> Has his own private boatslip. The market's there, too,
> Surrounding Poseidon's beautiful temple

---

① Chiang 2009 underscores the technical distinction, made by specialists in utopian studies, between "utopia" and "paradise", the former being "primarily a sociopolitical vision, which usually involves an ideal community, social structure, economic system, and/or political philosophy", whereas the latter is "primarily a religious or mythical vision of happiness, which promises immortality, everlasting youth, supernatural power, …and/or other heavenly bliss and earthly pleasures" (97). Chiang, however, concludes that "'Peach Blossom Spring' is both a utopia and a paradise in that it is at once a human society and a mystical state of mind" (117). By these same parameters, a similar conclusion might be drawn about Homer's depiction of Skheria.

And bounded by stones set deep into the earth.
[*Odyssey* 6. 262 – 267]

Even their ships have no need of steering:

For Phaeacian ships do not have pilots,
Nor rudders, as other ships have.
They know on their own their passengers' thoughts,
And know all the cities and rich fields in the world,
And they cross the great gulfs with the greatest speed,
Hidden in mist and fog, with never a fear
Of damage or shipwreck. [*Odyssey* 8. 557 – 563]

And when the Phaeacians take Odysseus to Ithaca, the ship travels with supernatural speed:

And as four yoked stallions spring all together
Beneath the lash, leaping high,
And then eat up the dusty road on the plain,
So lifted the keel of that ship, and in her wake
An indigo wave hissed and roiled
As she ran straight ahead. Not even a falcon,
Lord of the skies, could have matched her pace,
So light her course as she cut through the waves...
[*Odyssey* 13. 81 – 87]

The location of Scheria, the land of the Phaeacians, was disputed even in antiquity. Some would place it in the eastern Mediterranean; others identified it with the island of Corcyra (modern Corfu), off the west coast of Greece.[①] But the ancient writers Strabo and Plutarch located it in the Atlantic Ocean. Here once again we run up against the possible distinction—or lack of distinction—between the Atlantic as *Ôkeanos*, and the "open sea" on which Odysseus and his men have their adventures. Perhaps the best way to cope with this problem of location is not even to try to find a place for the island on our modern-day maps: its narrative function is as a magical place filled with splendor and abundance, where life is rich and delightful, and where maritime life blends intimately and imperceptibly into the rhythms of life in the city. It is a notable detail of this that, although the standard of living in the palace of Alcinous is gorgeous, it is not starkly different from that of his subjects. All live in peace and plenty.

The island to which Odysseus is transported from Scheria is that of his own kingdom, Ithaca. He has an impressive palace of his own, with many servants inside and out, and store-rooms chocked with treasure and weapons. The description of his palace in the *Odyssey* suggests that Homer envisions a fairly typical Bronze-Age complex including a walled courtyard with interior portico, and a *megaron* or great hall with a central circular hearth (Figure 5).

Odysseus's aged father, Laertes, lives not (as we might expect) in this palace, but in a sort of rural retirement, on a farm with a house and a row of huts for the field hands (*Odyssey* 24.205 - 210). His relegation to this farmhouse is another result of the domestic upheaval that issues from Odysseus's long absence This shameful disregard for the eldest surviving member of the royal family was doubtless as shocking to Homer's original audience as it would be to Chinese listeners or readers today, steeped in centuries of the Confucian tradition of 孝 (*xiào*, filial devotion to

---

① As it happens, there is similar dispute over the location of Ithaca, Odysseus's own home. For the latest ingenuity on the latter topic, see Bittlestone 2005. On Homer's landscapes more generally, Luce 1998.

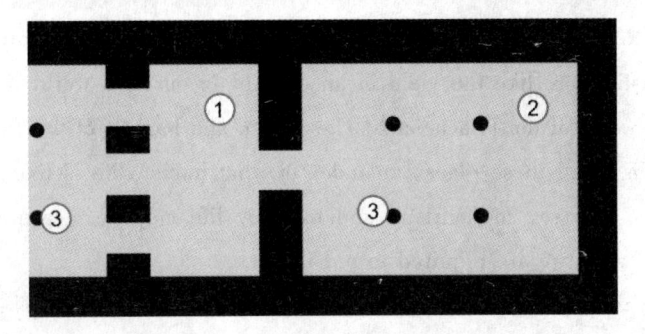

Figure 5. Plan of the typical Mycenaean *megaron*. ①Antechamber. ②Hall (main room) . ③Columns in Porch and Hall. The circular hearth was customarily located in the center of the Hall, and vented through an *oculus* or open hole in the roof. (Illustration: Messer Woland; used by permission.)

elders), and is one of the wrongs that Odysseus is coming home to redress. ①

Like the Phaeacians, Laertes has an orchard of his own; but he must work hard to keep the crops growing. And he had given Odysseus an orchard and a vineyard as a boy:

> You gave me thirteen pear trees, ten apple trees,
> Forty fig trees, and fifty vine rows
> That ripened one by one as the season went on
> With heavy clusters of all sorts of grapes. [*Odyssey* 24. 340 – 344]

---

① The 孝經 (*Xiao Jing* or *Classic of Filial Piety*, usually dated ca 470 BCE-thus around the time Aeschylus was beginning his career as a playwright in classical Athens) is our main source for the early Confucian formulation of this doctrine. A much later but also important document for the study of 孝 xiao is the 家禮 (*Jia Li or Family Rituals*) of the Neo-Confucian writer 朱熹 Zhu Xi (1130—1200 CE); for a translation of and commentary on the latter see Ebrey 1991. Baker 1979: 98 identifies respect for the family as perhaps the most commonly-shared element in the (in other ways often broadly divergent) religious systems of Chinese culture.

But here as well the processes of growth and harvest seem more real and less fantastic-more like the yield of an orchard in our own world than in the fairy-tale world of the Phaeacians. The growth and harvest of the fruit of tree and vine is in all these places an index of what human life is like: what we must do to survive, to flourish, and to enjoy life may be measured by the amount of work we are required to put into it.

So while the land of the Phaeacians is not quite Penglai, it is still (like the Tao Hua Yuan) a refuge of luxury and plenty. Had he remained with the Phaeacians, Odysseus could have married the king's daughter, succeeded eventually to that throne, and lived a life of ease and relaxation. By comparison, the island of Ithaca—Odysseus's own home and kingdom, to which he yearns for twenty years to return—is a world more like the one we inhabit: a place where one must work hard, where one encounters obstacles (and sometimes violence and death, as we see when Odysseus battles the huge band of suitors who have crowded the palace in competition for his wife's hand in marriage). And yet Odysseus is somehow willing to leave behind the luxury and splendor of the one city to return to the other—crossing the sea and risking life and limb in order to do so—for the sake of his throne, his family, and the life he had left behind before the war. Indeed he leaves two great cities behind—mighty Troy, whose magnificent towers he helps to destroy; and delightful Scheria, land of ease and pleasure—in order to achieve his nostos, the homecoming he desires above all things. In this he reminds us of the treasured proverb[①]落葉歸根 *luòyè guīgēn*: No place like home. [②] There is perhaps no greater story of love and dedication than this

---

① I. e. 成語 *chéngyǔ* "fixed expression", the traditional format for brief aphorisms, typically constructed of four *hanzi*.

② Literally, "falling leaf returns to the roots" —said generally of all things returning to their source, but more specifically of a person who has traveled far and yearns to return to his "old home" (老家 *lǎojiā*) —the place where he was born.

earliest Journey to the West, at the very beginning of Western literature. ①

Works Cited:

Atwood, Margaret. 2005. *The Penelopiad*. Toronto.

Austin, Norman. 1994. *Helen of Troy and Her Shameless Phantom*. Ithaca NY.

Baker, Hugh D. R. 1979. *Chinese Family and Kinship*. New York.

Beecroft, Alexander. 2010. *Authorship and Cultural Identity in Early Greece and China*. Cambridge.

—— 2011. Blindness and Literacy in the Lives of Homer. *Classical Quarterly* 61: 1 - 18.

Bernstein, Richard. 2001. *Ultimate Journey: Retracing the Path of an Ancient Buddhist Monk Who Crossed Asia in Search of Enlightenment*. New York.

Bittlestone, Robert. 2005. With James Diggle and John Underhill. *Odysseus Unbound: The Search for Homer's Ithaca*. Cambridge.

Blondell, Ruby. 2013. *Helen of Troy: Beauty, Myth, Devastation*. Oxford.

Bokenkamp, Stephen R. 1986. The Peach Flower Font and the Grotto Passage. *Journal of the American Oriental Society* 106: 65 - 77.

Bunce, Frederick W. 2005. *Mudrās in Buddhist and Hindu Practices: An Iconographic Consideration*. New Delhi.

Butler, Samuel. 1897. The *Authoress of the Odyssey*. London. Second edition 1922 (repr. Chicago 1967).

Cahill, Suzanne E. 1993. *Transcendence & Divine Passion: The Queen Mother of the West in Medieval China*. Stanford.

Campbell, Joseph. 1949. *The Hero with a Thousand Faces*. Princeton.

—— 1959. *The Masks of God*. Four volumes, 1959 - 1968. New York.

——1991. *The Power of Myth*. With Bill Moyers. Ed. Betty Sue Flowers. New York.

Carr, Michael. 1993. "Mind-Monkey" Metaphors in Chinese and Japanese Dictionaries. *International Journal of Lexicography* 6.3: 149 - 180.

Carroll, Cain, and Revital Carroll. 2012. *Mudras of India*. London.

---

① Without implicating them in any of my opinions—or errors—I owe a profound debt of thanks to Stephen R. Halsey, P. Allen Miller, Steven Owyoung, Rebekah Smith, and Robert Wright for their encouragement and assistance in the process of composing this essay, 非常感謝.

Casson, Lionel. 2001. *Libraries in the Ancient World*. New Haven.

Chandra, Lokesh, and Radha Banerjee (2008) eds. *Xuanzang and the Silk Route*. New Delhi.

Chiang, Sing-Chen Lydia. 2009. Visions of Happiness: Daoist Utopias and Grotto Paradises in Early and Medieval Chinese Tales. *Utopian Studies* 20: 97 – 120.

Clunas, Craig. 1996. *Fruitful Sites: Garden Culture in Ming Dynasty China*. Durham NC.

Coen, Joel (dir.) 2000. *O Brother, Where Art Thou?* Touchstone/Universal.

de Luce, Judith. 1997. Reading and Re-reading the Helpful Princess. pp. 25 – 37 in Hallett, Judith, and Thomas Van Nortwick (eds.), *Compromising Traditions: The Personal Voice in Classical Scholarship*. London.

Detienne, Marcel, and Jean-Pierre Vernant. 1974. *Les ruses de l'intelligence: La mètis des Grecs*. Paris. Translated as *Cunning Intelligence in Greek Culture and Society*. (Branch Line 1977, Chicago 1991).

Ebrey, Patricia (transl) 1991. *Chu Hsi's Family Rituals: A Twelfth-Century Chinese Manual for the Performance of Cappings, Weddings, Funerals, and Ancestral Rites*. Princeton.

Fish, Stanley. 1982. *Is there a Text in this Class? The Authority of Interpretive Communities*. Cambridge MA.

Foley, John Miles. 1991. *The Theory of Oral Composition*. Bloomington.

—— 2005 ed. *A Companion to Ancient Epic*. Oxford.

Foster, Benjamin R. 2001 (ed.) *The Epic of Gilgamesh*. Norton Critical Editions. New York: W. W Norton.

Frazier, Charles. 1997. *Cold Mountain*. New York.

Godard, Jean-Luc (dir.) 1964. *Le mépris*. Embassy Pictures.

Gold, Thomas, et al. 2002. *Social Connections in China: Institutions, Culture and the Changing Nature of Guanxi*. Cambridge.

Griffith, Mark. 1990. Contest and Contradiction in Early Greek Poetry. pp. 185 – 207 of *Cabinet of the Muses: essays on classical and comparative literature in honor of Thomas G. Rosenmeyer*, eds. Mark Griffith and Donald J. Mastronarde. Atlanta.

Harris, W. V. 1989. *Ancient Literacy*. Cambridge MA.

Havelock, Eric A. 1978. *The Greek Concept of Justice: From Its Shadow in Homer to Its Substance in Plato*. Cambridge MA.

Henderson, John B. 1991. *Scripture, Canon, and Commentary: A Comparison of*

Confucian and Western Exegesis. Princeton.

Hightower, James Robert. 1970. *The Poetry of T'ao Ch'ien*. Oxford.

Hirsch, E. D. Jr. 1987. *Cultural Literacy: What Every American Needs to Know*. Boston.

—— et al. 1988. *The New Dictionary of Cultural Literacy*. 3rd edition 2002. Boston.

Hughes, Bettany. 2007. *Helen of Troy: The Story Behind the Most Beautiful Woman in the World*. New York.

Janko, Richard. 1982. *Homer, Hesiod and the Hymns: Diachronic Development in Epic Diction*. Cambridge.

Jauss, Hans Robert. 1974. Levels of Identification of Hero and Audience. *New Literary History* 5: 283–317.

Jenner, W. J. F. 2010. *Journey to the West*. Library of Chinese and English Classics. 6 volumes. Beijing.

Johnson, David (1985) et al. (eds.). *Popular Culture in Late Imperial China*. Berkeley.

Johnson, David (1985b). Communication, Class, and Consciousness in Late Imperial China. pp. 34–72 in Johnson 1985.

Johnson, William A. 2010. *Readers and Reading Culture in the High Roman Empire: A Study of Elite Communities*. Oxford.

Johnson, William A., and Holt N. Parker (eds.) 2009. *Ancient Literacies: The Culture of Reading in Greece and Rome*. Oxford.

Joyce, James. 1922. *Ulysses*. Paris.

Kirby, John T. 1984. Toward a General Theory of the Priamel. *Classical Journal* 80: 142–144.

——1989. Humor and the Unity of Ovid's *Metamorphoses*: A Narratological Assessment. pp. 233–251 + plate in Carl Deroux, ed., *Studies in Latin Literature and Roman History*, V (Collection Latomus No. 206). Brussels.

—— 1998 (ed.) *The Comparative Reader. A Handlist of Basic Reading in Comparative Literature*. New Haven.

—— 2000. *Secret of the Muses Retold. Classical Influences on Italian Authors of the Twentieth Century*. Chicago.

—— 2009. The Notion of Comparing and the Meeting of Fragments. pp. 14–29 in Lisa Block de Behar et al., eds. *Comparative Literature: Sharing Knowledges for Preserving Cultural Diversity*. Volume 1. Oxford. Also in digital format as Entry 6.87.1.2 in the Encyclopedia of Human Sciences and Humanities (a part of the

Encyclopedia of Life Support Systems [EOLSS] published by UNESCO; accessed online at www.eolss.net).

—— 2012. The Great Books. pp. 273–282 in Theo D'haen et al., eds., *The Routledge Companion to World Literature*. London and New York.

—— 2012b. Odysseus and the Phaeacians: The City and the Ocean at the Beginning of Western Literature. pp. 24–41 in Jonathan White and Wang I-Chun, eds., *The City and the Ocean*. Newcastle.

Kirk, Geoffrey S. 1962. *The Songs of Homer*. Cambridge.

Kovacs, Maureen Gallery, 1990 (ed.) *The Epic of Gilgamesh*. Stanford.

Lakoff, George, and Mark Johnson. 1980. *Metaphors We Live By*. Chicago.

Laum, B. 1928. Das alexandrinische Akzentuationssystem. *Studien zur Geschichte und Kultur des Altertums*, 4. Erg. Bd. 99–124 and 452. 1.

Leeming, David Adams. 1998. *Mythology: The Voyage of the Hero*. New York.

Li, Rongxi. 1996 (trans.) *The Great Tang Dynasty Record of the Western Regions*. Honolulu.

Logue, Christopher. 2003. *War Music: An Account of Books 1–4 and 16–19 of Homer's Iliad*. Chicago.

Lord, A. B. 1981. The Singer of Tales. Cambridge MA.

Lombardo, Stanley. 2000. *Homer: Odyssey*. Indianapolis.

Luce, J. V. 1998. *Celebrating Homer's Landscapes: Troy and Ithaca Revisited*. New Haven.

Lutgendorf, Philip. 2007. *Hanuman's Tale: The Messages of a Divine Monkey*. Oxford.

Ma Chengyuan (馬承源). 2001. (ed.)《上海博物館藏戰國楚竹書》(*Shanghai Bowuguan Cang Zhanguo Chu Zhushu, i.e. the Shanghai Museum Collections: Bamboo Books from Chu during the Warring-States Period*). Shanghai.

Mair, Victor H. 1989. Suen Wu-kung = Hanumat?: The Progress of a Scholarly Debate. *Proceedings of the Second International Conference on Sinology*. Taipei.

—— 1990. *Tao Te Ching: The Classic Book of Integrity and the Way*. NY.

——1994 (ed). *The Columbia Anthology of Traditional Chinese Literature*. New York.

Malouf, David. 2009. *Ransom*. London.

Millis, Benjamin W. (2012) and Douglas Olson, eds. *Inscriptional Records for the Dramatic Festivals in Athens: IG II2 2318–2325 and Related Texts*. Leiden.

Minghella, Anthony (dir.) 2003. *Cold Mountain*. Miramax.

Monier-Williams, Sir Monier. 1899. *A Sanskrit-English Dictionary* (New Edition; eds. E. Leumann et al. Oxford.

Nagy, Gregory. 1996. *Homeric Questions*. Austin.

Nylan, Michael. 2001. *The Five "Confucian" Classics*. New Haven.

—— 2009. Classics without Canonization: Learning and Authority in Qin and Han. pp. 721 - 776 in John Lagerwey and Marc Kalinowski, eds., *Early Chinese Religion*. Part One: Shang through Han (1250 BC - 220 AD). Leiden.

O Sullivan, Neil. 1997. Caecilius, the "Canons" of Writers, and the Origins of Atticism. pp. 32 - 49 in W. J. Dominik, ed., *Roman Eloquence: Rhetoric and Society in Literature*. London.

Parry, Adam (ed.) 1971. *The Making of Homeric Verse: The Collected Papers of Milman Parry*. Oxford.

Petersen, Wolfgang (dir.) 2004. *Troy*. Warner Brothers.

Pfeiffer, Rudolf. 1968. *History of Classical Scholarship. From the Beginnings to the End of the Hellenistic Age*. Oxford.

Plaks, Andrew H. 1987. *The Four Masterworks of the Ming Novel: Ssu ta chǐ-shu* 四大名著. Princeton.

Pollock, Sheldon (2015) et al. (eds.) *World Philology*. Cambridge MA.

Pound, Ezra. 1924. *A Draft of XVI Cantos*. Paris.

Propp, Vladimir. 1958. *Morphology of the Folktale*. Trans. Laurence Scott. Second edition 1968. Austin.

Raglan, Lord (FitzRoy Richard Somerset, 4th Baron Raglan). 1936. *The Hero: A study in Tradition, Myth, and Dreams*. London.

Ramsey, S. Robert. 1987. *The Languages of China*. Princeton.

Raphals, Lisa. 1992. *Knowing Words: Wisdom and Cunning in the Classical Traditions of China and Greece*. Ithaca NY.

Rawski, Evelyn S. 1979. *Education and Popular Literacy in Chǐng China*. Ann Arbor.

Sandys, John Edwin. 1915. *A Short History of Classical Scholarship from the Sixth Century B. C. to the Present Day*. Cambridge.

Saran, Mishi. 2005. *Chasing the Monk's Shadow: A Journey in the Footsteps of Xuanzang*. New Delhi.

Saunders, E. Dale. 1960. *Mudrā: A Study of Symbolic Gestures in Japanese Buddhist Sculpture*. Princeton.

Schlütter, Morten. 2008. *How Zen Became Zen: The Dispute over Enlightenment and the Formation of Chan Buddhism in Song-Dynasty China*. Honolulu.

Simmons, Dan. 2003. *Ilium*. New York.

Schiller, Friedrich. 1795. über naive und sentimentalische Dichtung. *Die Horen* 11: 43 – 76, 12: 1 – 55, 12: 75 – 122.

Suzuki, Mihoko. 1989. *Metamorphoses of Helen: Authority, Difference, and the Epic*. Ithaca NY.

Tian, Xiaofei. *Tao Yuanming & Manuscript Culture: The Record of a Dusty Table*. Seattle.

Walcott, Derek. 1992. *Omeros*. New York.

Waley, Arthur. 1942. *Monkey: A Folk-Tale of China*. London (repr. New York 1994).

Walker, Hera S. 1998. Indigenous or Foreign? A Look at the Origins of the Monkey Hero Sun Wukong. *Sino-Platonic* Papers 81. Accessed online at http://sino-platonic.org/complete/spp081_monkey_sun_wukong.pdf.

Watson, James L. 1985. Standardizing the Gods: The Promotion of T'ien Hou ("Empress of Heaven") Along the South China Coast, 960 – 1960. pp. 292 – 324 in Johnson 1985.

Watts, Alan W. 1957. *The Way of Zen*. New York.

West, M. L. 1966. *Hesiod: Theogony. Edited with Prolegomena and Commentary*. Oxford.

—— 1967. The Contest of Homer and Hesiod. *Classical Quarterly* 17: 433 – 450.

——2003 (ed. and trans.) *Homeric Hymns, Homeric Apocrypha, Lives of Homer*. Loeb Classical Library No. 496. Cambridge MA.

—— 2011. *The Making of the Iliad. Disquisition and Analytical Commentary*. Oxford.

Wriggins, Sally Hovey. 1996. *Xuanzang: A Buddhist Pilgrim on the Silk Road*. Boulder. (Revised 2004 as *The Silk Road Journey with Xuanzang*.)

Yu, Anthony (1983), trans. and ed. *The Journey to the West*. 4 volumes. Revised edition 2012. Chicago.

Zetzel, James E. G. 1983. Re-creating the Canon: Augustan Poetry and the Alexandrian Past. *Critical Inquiry* 10: 83 – 105.

THE *ZHUANGZI*: A Verse Translation

Steven Shankman[*]

中文摘要 《庄子》虽用散文体写就，却因其整齐的节奏而近似诗体。已有的《庄子》英译本多以散文体翻译，虽然其中有片段是以英式传统五步抑扬格译成的，却往往还是会丢失唤起读者共鸣的美感。目前尚没有全以诗体译就的《庄子》英译本，因此作者试图以英文诗体重译《庄子》，意在将庄子简洁幽默、随心所欲的文学风格在英语世界重现，以更好地让读者体会庄子的主观认知思想和道家万物同一、清静无为的哲学观念。

关键词 道家；《庄子》；翻译研究；格律

INTRODUCTION

Zhuangzi（369？－286？）and his predecessor Laozi are the two great daoist philosophers of early China. Laozi, the purported author of the famous *Dao de jing*（"The Way/Power Classic"）, is the more well known of the

---

[*] 作者为俄勒冈大学杰出教授，哲学博士，主要研究领域为跨文化研究与宗教间对话。

two, and the more frequently translated. Laozi is poetic and austere. Zhuangzi is poetic and playful. In fact, reading Zhuangzi is one of the great pleasures of Chinese literature.

I have attempted to recreate, in English verse, the terseness of Zhuangzi's ancient Chinese as well as his humor and whimsy. The translation is composed mainly in free verse, though there are moments of transition into iambic pentameter—iambic verse being the most conversational of traditional Western meters, the meter that has been thought best for conveying the rhythms of actual, natural conversation. And that, after all, is consonant with Zhuangzi's message: that everything, no matter how strange, how other, is simply what it is. Problems begin when we try desperately to constrict reality so as to fit it within our preconceived, artificial mental categories.

Zhuangzi writesin prose, but his is a prose that is sometimes indistinguishable from poetry. The first chapter of the *Zhuangzi* starts off with what sound like two four-character/four-syllable lines (*bei ming you yu/qi ming wei kun* [in the northern deep there is a fish/its name is roe]) that are reminiscent of the verse of the earliest collection of Chinese poetry, the *Shijing* (or "*Classic of Poetry*"). These are the kinds of effects that are lost—that are in fact impossible to evoke — in translations of the *Zhuangzi* into prose. Some of these poetic effects will be found in the following translation of the *Zhuangzi* into English verse. The second and third lines of this verse translation are composed as two such four-character/four-syllable lines:

In the northern deep there is this fish.
Its name is Roe.
Roe's size? **Don't know**
How many thousand *li*!

In his acceptance of what is, Zhuangzi often presents paradoxes. We encounter one such paradox almost immediately in these opening lines, which describe a huge fish whose name just happens, paradoxically, to be Roe (beginning the word "Roe", in English translation, with a dignified upper-case letter is meant to emphasize this paradox). This huge fish, paradoxically, has the name of something very tiny. Zhuangzi's point is that everything I perceive is relative to what some contemporary philosophers refer to as my "subject position" as well as to the positions of other subjects and other things around us, near and far. What I perceive, I perceive from a particular spot at a particular moment in a vast and varied universe. What I perceive as huge, when compared with something infinitely larger, suddenly seems tiny.

Zhuangzi's perspectivism doesn't, however, induce a nihilistic, horrifying, vertiginous relativism and skepticism of the sort we might associate with a Western thinker like Nietzsche. One senses a confidence and even a comfort, in Zhuangzi, in his calm acceptance of the strange way things are, for I and everything else are—unless we force the issue—at home in, and are inextricable parts of, the great oneness that is the Dao.

Chapter 1

In the northern deep there is this fish.
Its name is Roe.
Roe's size? Don't know
how many thousand li !
Changes and is a bird.
Its name is Peng.
Peng's back? Don't know

how many thousand li !
It gets worked up, flies off,
its wings like the hovering sky's clouds.
This bird: when the sea stirs, it's about to rise
toward the southern deep.
The southern deep: Heaven's Lake.

Qi Jokes : "Stories of the Strange."
Jokes' speaking says,
"When Peng soars toward the southern deep,
Waters thrash three thousand li ,
whips up a cyclone, lifts
ninety-thousand li ,
soaring on six months of stored breath."
Wild horse mists, dust: creatures born of
reciprocally blown breath.
Heaven's blue blue: its true
Color? Or
Distance that cannot reach its outer edge?
Peng's gaze down, too: same blue—
Like depths and that is all.

Water's mass not thick?
Then as for big-boat-bearing: no way!
Kick over a cup of water onto a floor groove?
Then mustard seeds will seem as big as boats.
Plop down a bowl there? Logjam, since
Water's shallow and boat's big.

Wind's mass not thick?
Then as for big-wing-bearing: no way!
Up ninety-thousand li , the wind below!
Then and then only bank on wind.
When Peng's back bears blue sky
and there is nothing to obstruct its flight,
then and then only will it map its southing.

Cicada and Turtle-Dove snicker at it, saying:
"We bust our butts to rise and fly,
then bump up against elm and sandalwood and stop.
Sometimes we just can't get nowhere:
Up, up then THUD! That's that!
Now what's all this about ninety-thousand li ?"

The man who travels to the woods:
Eats three meals and returns,
Stomach still full.
The man who travels a hundred li
pounds grain the night before.
The man who travels a thousand li
culls grain three months.

Those two critters—what do they know?
Nitwits can't reach big wits.
Few years can't reach light years.
How do we know
This to be so?

The morning mushroom doesn't know

the old moon or the new.
The cricket doesn't know
spring and fall.
Their span is brief.

Deep-Sea-Spirit Turtle lives south of Chu,
takes five hundred years for spring;
for fall, five hundred years.
Since high antiquity
the great Chun tree
takes eight thousand years for spring;
for fall, eight thousand years.
Their span is long.

Mr. Peng Zu's famed today
for his longevity, but when hordes
are Peng Zu wannabes, is this not sad?

Tang's asking Ji: like this.
There is, in the bald north, a deep sea:
Heaven's Lake.
In that lake, a fish,
its width several thousand li .
Who can know its length?
Its name is Roe.
In that lake, a bird.
Its name is Peng,
back like Mount Tai,
wings like hovering sky's clouds.
Whips up a cyclone, ram horns, lifts

ninety thousand li , breaks free
of clouds, flies
bearing blue sky—only then
does it maps its southing,
go to the southern deep.

Little Quail snickers at Big Peng; denounces
him, saying: " Dat guy—
where do
he tink he's goin'?
I leap, jump, den lift off
at least several yards, den dip
and soar 'mid brambles.
Dis, too, flight's finish.
Ergo,
where do
dat guy tink
he's goin'?"

Just so differs small from big.

Thus those whose knowledge consists in
efficient handling of a single office,
acting in the interests of a single region,
possessing the power to soothe a single prince,
resulting in a knack for managing a single state—

the self-regard of these recalls
our puffed-up, snickering Little Quail.

At such Song Rongzi snickers,
finds them amusing.
Should the whole world praise him,
it would not flatter his self-regard.
Should the whole world boo him,
it would not bog him down.
Decisiveness in regard
to the clear demarcation between inside and out,
Discernment in regard
to the boundary between honor and disgrace:
in these he excelled, but he went no further.
Let the world think what it would of him—
he remained unflappable,
but he did not plant the firmest root.

Liezi rides the wind, so goes,
waftingly expert,
for fifteen days and, afterwards, returns.
Song Rongzi did not feather his own nest;
he remained unflappable.
Although Liezi did not have to walk,
he still relied on something.
But as for the one who goes
with the flow of heaven and earth and who
mounts, thus, the changes of the six breaths
to wander aimlessly the limitless—
ah, is there anything on which he relies?
Thus it is said:
"Perfect person: selfless.
Spirit person: badgeless.

Sage person: nameless."

Yao begged to resign to Xu Yu
the Underheaven:
"When nature's light is luminous
and you do not snuff out the candles,
if brightness is your aim,
is this not, after all, a waste of effort?
When rain, in its due season, falls
and you persist in watering the fields,
if watering is your aim,
is this, not, after all, a waste of labor?
With you in charge, Sir,
the Underheaven is in order. I see my failings.
I beg you, take control!"

Xu Yu replied:
"The Underheaven is governed well already.
So why should I replace you? For a name?
Names are but guests beholden to true substance.
Why be a guest, incurring obligation?
Wrens nest in dense forests;
need but a branch.
Moles drink from the river;
need but a bellyful.
Return, content, to lording!
I have no use for ruling the Underheaven.
If the cook at a funeral
does not run his kitchen well,
would corpse-mime and priest presume to leap

over wine vessels, sacrificial

carving stands and usurp him, thus?"

Qian Wu asks Lian Shu, saying:
"I heard Qie Yu's chatter.
Big talk, not right;
way-out, no way back.
I shutter at his words—
Just like the Milky Way,
there is no end to them.
Big talk—too much! —
veering from the human."
Lian Shu asked,
"What in the world did he say?"
He said,
"On Mt. Miao Gu Shi
lives a demonic man:
flesh like ice, like snow;
gentle as a virgin.
He shuns the five grains,
breathes wind, drinks dew;
rides the clouds' steam,
drives winged dragons
and roams beyond the bounds of all four seas;
spirit focused, body
plague-proof. Each year
his grains bear fruit."

I took this for madness
and wasn't persuaded.

Lian Shu said,
"Just so the blind: do they respond
to the sight of patterned beauty?
Just so the deaf: do they respond
to the sound of bells and drums?
Are blindness, deafness
restricted but to bodies?
Knowing can also be both deaf and blind—
of this your words are ample proof. But
this man,
this force
embraces
the all-embracing ten thousand things
to make them one.
People push their agendas: hence chaos.
Who, in his right mind, would fuss
over the Underheaven, take it seriously?
This man:
the world can't harm him.
Big flood stretches to
heaven
but he won't drown.
Big drought melts metals, rocks,
scorches the earth and the peaks
yet he's unscorched.
The dust and siftings of his remains
are quite enough to mould a Yao or Shun.
Who would—dis tractedly
dis sipating his energies—
imagine pushing things around is serious business?"

A man from Sung sold fancy hats
then traveled down to Yue
where men had crew-cuts and tatoos
and no use for his hats.

Yao governed the people of the Underheaven,
brought peaceful rule to all within the seas.
He went to seek an audience with the four masters
to far Mt. Gu-She's sunny northern bank.
Dazed, he forgot the Underheaven there.

Huizi called to Zhuangzi, said:
"King Wei gave me seeds from a big gourd.
I planted them, then harvested
a gourd stuffed with five bushels of moist seeds;
I filled it up with water, wine; its strength
couldn't support its weight.
So, I sliced it in
two for ladles, but the scoops
once filled, just top-
pled, could not hold their con tents.
It's not that it wasn't big; it was big, all right.
But thinking it useless, I smashed it all to bits!"

Zhuangzi said,
"When it comes to using big things, you're no good!
Among the Sung there was a man expert
at making potions for chapped hands, his kin
for generations silk-bleachers by trade.

A stranger heard about him, asked to buy
the patent for a hundred coins of gold.
He gathered the clan
and counseled them, saying:
"For generations we've been bleaching silk
but never netting more than a few coins.
Now, in one morning, we can net a hundred.
I humbly advise we sell it to the stranger."
The stranger bought it,
took it to the King of Wu and sung its praises.
The Yue were threatening.
King Wu put the stranger in charge.
In winter they fought the Yue at sea.
The Yue were crushed,
the land was divvied up,
the stranger enfiefed.
The art of preventing the chapping of hands is one.
Of its practitioners, some are enfiefed,
others will not escape bleaching of silk.
The art is one; its uses, users differ.
Just now you had a gourd
with space enough for five bushels of things.
Why didn't you
think to tie it to
your waist, then float through
the Yangtze River—lakes, too?
But instead you
fretted that the gourd was just too
huge to use for storage. Your head is made of straw!"

Huizi hailed Zhuangzi, said:
"I have a big tree.
Men called it Chu Tree.
Its BIG TRUNK,
gnarled and bumpy,
resists conforming to the inked
measuring line,
its curling crooked
branches resist conforming
to square or compass.
It stands by the road side;
carpenters ignore it.
Now your words, sir,
are BIG and useless. Just so,
many might shoo Chu-like you."

Zhuangzi replied,
"Haven't you ever stopped to observe
wild cats and weasels?
Crouching, they hide
and stalk their idle prey.
Westward
Eastward
They leap up and
quickly scurry about,
not shunning high or low,
right into a trap,
they perish, or in a net.
Your YAK, in contrast:
ITS BULK, LIKE BIG CLOUDS, HANGS DOWN FROM THE SKY.

THIS CREATURE MAY, WITH JUSTICE, BE CALLED BIG—
but can it catch a mouse?
You have a big tree, worry that it's useless.
Why not plant it in Nowhereland,
in the wilderness of Broad Nothing?
Wandering, pondering
by inaction's side,
Rambling, ambling,
lie down to sleep beneath it,

spared a young death
from the axe's blade,
unharmed and useless.
Can that be bad?

Extravagant Writing: Of Excess and Frivolity

Herman Rapaport[*]

中文摘要 相当一部分文学作品在其文字特点上表现出了过剩与贫乏，原因在于文字中极度的复杂性和作者狂热的语言实验意图。从托马斯·品钦的长篇小说、詹姆斯·乔伊斯的《芬尼根守灵夜》及《尤利西斯》到萨德侯爵的《索多玛120天》等众多作品，都可因匪夷所思的多余桥段并导致了信息过剩而被当作研究的样本。如果不立足于意义的发掘，那么这些作品很容易给人以轻浮思考的印象。如果我们对草率玩弄遣词造句的游戏只表现出平庸的感觉，那么这种特点将被当成是文学的特征而非写作的过失。雅克·德里达把在早期的启蒙文学中出现的这种现象叫作草率的遗产，在雅克·德里达的观点上，文章在更广的文学和文化范畴与重要的作品中讨论了有关多余的定义、范围、成因及具体体现等相关问题。

关键词 文学批评；过剩；雅克·德里达

---

[*] 作者为美国维克森林大学英语系教授，文学博士，主要研究领域为批评理论、哲学、精神分析和美学。

Extravagant Writing: Of Excess and Frivolity / 125

You have to get hold of eloquence and twist its head off.
——Paul Verlaine

There are numerous literary texts that would qualify as examples of surplus and excess. Given their extreme complexity and aggressive experimentation with language, any of Thomas Pynchon's longer novels would certainly qualify, as would James Joyce's *Finnegans Wake* or *Ulysses*, Ron Silliman's *The Alphabet*, Bruce Andrews' *Lip Service*, Charles Olson's *Maximus*, Gertrude Stein's *Tender Buttons*, Ezra Pound's *Cantos*, Walt Whitman's *Leaves of Grass*, Marcel Proust's *Remembrance of Things Past*, Herman Melville's *Moby Dick*, and, in earlier periods, the Marquis de Sade's 120 *Days of Sodom*, Laurence Sterne's *Tristram Shandy*, Cervantes' *Don Quixote*, Rabelais' *Gargantuan and Pantagruel*, and the *Old* and *New Arcadias* by Sir Philip Sidney. Most of these works would easily qualify as examples of even grotesque excess that raise questions about surplus, if not frivolous undertakings, that reflect an over-production if not stock piling of signification. Indeed, once one begins listing works that one might consider excessive in this way, it may well occur to one that perhaps excess, if not the commonplace sense of a frivolous playing with words, might even be a distinguishing feature of literature per se and not the aberration of writing that we might imagine. Before considering excess in early enlightenment literature in terms of what Jacques Derrida once called an archaeology of the frivolous (one that, in fact, he never quite undertook and that I want to explore on my own), I want to discuss excess more generally in terms of literature and culture that is much closer to us in historical time. [1]

Many critics are in agreement that gross excess in especially contemporary literature and the arts corresponds to what Thorsten Veblen

---

[1] Jacques Derrida, "l'Archaeologie du frivole", preface to Condillac, *Essai sur l'origine des connaissances humaines* (Paris : Galilée, 1973).

called material accumulation and conspicuous waste—the logical consequence of capitalist industrialization. ① Certainly, art movements allied to Pop Culture (most recently, J-Pop, K-Pop) and Postmodernism reflect the material conditions of what Veblen called the leisure class, something that one sees writ large in the paintings of David Salle, Eric Fishyl, Robert Rauschenberg, James Rosenquist, and Roy Lichtenstein. The latter's well known raster dot paintings even call attention to themselves as monumentalized trash (disposable cartoons), though it has to be said that Lichtenstein's contemporary, Rauschenberg, actually worked with trash in his famous combines. Currently in Japan, Takaski Murakami and Yoshitomo Nara are emphasizing the environmental ubiquity of highly commodified and trendy trash culture whose inclination towards the decorative courts a gluttonous taste for regressed sentimentality. Here the fact that there is surplus has to strike one as transparently mimetic of consumer glut in a way that self-consciously prettifies (airbrushes) and reinforces the delicacy and frivolity of commodity fetishism.

In earlier periods such as the Renaissance in Europe, material accumulation is not yet the obverse of conspicuous waste. After all, Lorenzo de Medici and the Borgias didn't confuse art with trash. And yet, Renaissance popes and potentates were besotted with material glut, which spoke to what Jean Starobinski called largesse (surplus). ② In an autocratic, aristocratic world, surplus insures that one has a trickle down economy in which the wealth of a potentate will be distributed by means of "altruistic" largesse. Feudalism proscribed that local potentates would find it in their self-interest if they arbitrarily lavished money on their subjects in huge displays of generosity, something that in democratic societies has lost its mystique in the

---

① Thorstein Veblen, *Theory of the Leisure Class* (Boston: Houghton Mifflin, 1899/1973).
② Jean Starobinski, *Largesse*, trans. J. M. Todd (Chicago : University of Chicago Press, 1994/1997). " Springs and treasures have in common the characteristic of plenty. Both overflow. "

form of rationalized welfare programs. ① Of course, in the Renaissance largesse wasn't rational but miraculous: sporadic, arbitrary, and unreliable. This means that even patrons of artists could be quite fickle. That art is itself a matter of largesse—that of the largesse of genius—did occur to artists in the Renaissance. Certainly, people could see that Michaelangelo's frescos in the Sistine Chapel dovetailed with the largesse of the church. Moreover, such largesse is associated not only with grandiose excesses, but a trickle down goodness (e. g. moral uplift, educational mission, etc.) . Indeed, the massive outputs of many artists speak to a surplus of work that over time trickles down to the masses, however many centuries that may take. Consider not only Homer, but Virgil, Dante, Shakespeare, Milton, Rembrandt, or Wagner, for that matter.

Formalistically, excess has always been a major topic in the arts. One cannot study the formal features of the symphonies of Anton Bruckner or Gustav Mahler and not discuss excess in terms of length and sheer orchestral size, just as one cannot seriously consider Baroque style in the absence of realizing the extent to which excess characterizes, say, its architecture. In literature, which will be our privileged topic, one will have to consider semantic excesses (of vocabulary, word play, tropes, idiom), excesses of content (emotional excess in, say, the laughter released by comedy; extreme brutality in the content of de Sade; excessive emphasis upon action in Ian Fleming, etc.), excesses of form (minimalist excess in the haiku; excess of plotting in the Victorian novel; excess of fragmentation in avant garde poetry, etc.), and syntactic excesses at the phrase and sentence level, whether simplified, as in the case of Hemingway, or elaborated, as

---

① Welfare, of course, is a vast topic extending back, at least, to the poor laws of the Renaissance whereby in countries such as England local parishes were responsible for taking care of the poor and the indigent for fear that otherwise they would become a criminally destabilizing force. Eventually this surplus population would be shipped out to colonies. Nevertheless, the pomp and circumstance of aristocratic largesse still held sway in the social imaginary.

in the case of Proust. In addition to excesses of saying, there are also excesses of not saying, as in the poetry of Stéphane Mallarmé or Paul Celan. Particularly it is the avant garde movements that are subject to excess. The emphasis upon the visual in lettrism, upon irrational juxtaposition in surrealism, upon the materiality of language in conceptual poetry and language-poetry would be typical examples. No doubt, a key point to be kept in mind about avant garde art is that it is generally quite serious, even when it is being funny. Stuart Davis' abstract paintings are a case in point, though one could cite the surrealists, Max Ernst and René Magritte, as well. Perhaps where one does see more frivolity than not is in some of the poetry of John Ashbery and much of the poetry of Charles Bernstein, though even in those cases there is an underlying sense of aesthetic sobriety reminding us that, in fact, we are apprehending a sophisticated form of abstract art, after all.

Of course, the moment one speaks of excess, someone will immediately want to know: "in excess of what?" That is, by what norms is excess to be measured? What justifies the sense or knowledge that something is "too much"? Educationally speaking, these are important questions insofar as our undergraduate students sometimes remark that whatever is assigned on the reading syllabus is somehow so excessive that they cannot relate to it. What they mean, of course, is that authors such as John Donne, Henry James, Franz Kafka, Gabriel Marquez, or Nate Mackey don't conform to the students' normative expectations of how lived experience is represented, in large part, because literary language isn't what they know to be ordinary language. Of course, this presupposes one might easily be able to identify what "ordinary" or "commonplace" uses of language might be, or what normative lived experience is supposed to be.

One way to challenge such assumptions is to consider Andy Warhol's novel *A*, which is composed entirely of literal transcriptions of ordinary language spoken by Ondine and friends who are talking to one another at

Warhol's New York atelier.

> ***Ondine***: Any old amour ahh mour aaghh
> mour huh huh. A little stale but
> so whaaat? Homosexuals have the right huuh heh—don't they...
> Little sticky around the I don't
> care I don't care. I'll waltz if one
> to the thing awright? Oh, I—I—I
> hope he's home. He's beautiful
> ih wi①

However odd the text may sound to us, it*is* precisely the sort of thing that socio-linguists record: unadulterated ordinary language spoken by social subjects who, for all their differences, are typical of a sizable social milieu. And yet, who would consider the following to be normative? "Octavio? I don't know. What is Octavio? Oh, you mean Oxydol. She stopped by there and he wasn't there."② No doubt, one of the difficulties in negotiating a transcription of ordinary language is a lack of explicit reference, given that the speakers inherently know what they are referring to, whereas by definition we cannot. Whereas Ondine refers, we infer. This means listening to such ordinary language is like listening to a telephone conversation in which we only get the input of only one of the two speakers. In fact, at times even the speakers lose track of the content, as in the case of mixing up Octavio with Oxydol. This mix up even exposes a certain tropological literary effect in the fact that the letter O sutures a metonymical, narcissistic string: Ondine, Octavio, Oxydol, and elsewhere, OOLeeoh [Oleo?]③ In

---

① Andy Warhol, *A* (New York: Grove Press, 1968), 407a.
② Andy Warhol, *A* (New York: Grove Press, 1968), 406.
③ Andy Warhol, *A* (New York: Grove Press, 1968), 407.

Lacanian terms, the letter O is the master signifier by means of which everyone is brought into group relation as a social set. Of course, we don't generally assume that ordinary language might be sutured by means of master signifiers that just flippantly turn up.

Throughout Warhol's "novel" there is an obvious excess of talk, a perseveration, most of it trivial and much of it venal (Ondine's anti-Semitism is a case in point). The whole novel, in fact, is the performance of a certain frivolity born of insouciance and arrogance that engage with an immediacy of impressions, amusements, and desires. Warhol's *frivole* (I'm perverting the French by making a substantive of this word) is, in fact, playing the role of diva in a way reminiscent of American Reality TV shows today in which the jealous narcissism of female chatter is put on display by talentless, empty people whose sense of self-importance is grossly out of whack with reality. What Warhol perceived long before today is that this sort of everyday reality (behavior) puts a damper on normativity. And yet, if Warhol's novel shows that it is hard to establish normativity in even the most literal and ordinary uses of language, it is not as if we don't still require or at least imagine norms, if only because everyone would like to predict what to expect in terms of what is reasonable and manageable. For example, it's not unreasonable for one to expect that in the United States people will generally be able to converse in either standard English or something close enough to it in order to be understood. Obviously Warhol was testing that assumption the way that in his society Marcel Proust tested assumptions about sentence length when he wrote page long sentences, or the way James Joyce tested assumptions about semantics when he wrote in Finnegans-Wake-ese. That is, they all were challenging norms by means of extravagant writing.

Of course, there is another way of thinking about excess. Long ago, Erich Auerbach noticed that the excesses of literary writing actually function in the service of representing society to itself according to principles compatible with class interests. [1] For all of Warhol's crazy and unreadable transcriptions, his novel is about the upward mobility of wanna-bes. Ondine and the others are typical, desperate narcissists who are frivolously trying their luck in some aspect of the entertainment business (namely, Warhol's films) that has been dressed up to look like art. Behind all of this stands a rags to riches cliché mediated by Calvinism: that one is destined to be elect. James Joyce's *Finnegans Wake*, for all its linguistic madness, also supports a fairly pedestrian bourgeois norm, which is the nuclear family. Basically, *Finnegans Wake* is a soap opera like East Enders in the U. K. about a profligate father. Kafka's fictions, extremely bizarre as they may seem, are largely about the normative Jewish condition of statelessness in eastern twentieth-century Europe. Kafka's K in *The Castle* is simply a man *sans papiers*. The excessiveness of Kafka's novel may draw one away from the norm, but it confirms and elaborates on the norm, too, by deepening its contradictions. In antiquity one sees something rather similar in Aeschylus' *Oresteia*. These plays adapt myths that are excessively bloody and vengeful, but all of that excess works in the service of establishing legal norms that dispense with revenge as a means of achieving justice and construct, in their place, an ordinary person. In the last play of the trilogy, Orestes is entirely detached and freed from the excesses of his family's past. He is normalized and turned into a judicial social subject who is stripped of the obligation and right to take revenge. Many more of these examples can be given, but the point is that in literature excess and normativity work hand in glove. Even in the Marquis de Sade, virulent excess leads to proper rules of engagement. Sadists, it turns out, are very methodical and proper in their activities.

 The lesson to be learned here is that excess is and isn't outside or beyond

---

[1] Erich Auerbach, *Mimesis*, trans. W. Trask (Princeton: Princeton University Press, 1946/2003).

normativity: it is both an affirmation of as well as a departure from norms. If I have mentioned de Sade, it is because he comes at the end of a lengthy period, stretching back to the middle of the European seventeenth century at least, in which one can see the emergence of a culture of frivolity or surplus and disorder that is indistinguishable from a normative culture of manners (rules of social engagement, methodological behavior). There can be no doubt that this culture of frivolity expresses aristocracy in terms of means, which concerns immense surplus wealth, and in terms of mode, which preserves the absolute and arbitrary right to act however one pleases. Yet, in the case of frivolity all of this is expressed demotically, if not with an air of self-abnegation (indulgent self-destruction and dissolution). In addition, frivolity has a bourgeois aspect that concerns an overproduction of goods, or what the French call*luxe*. Frivolity not only speaks to an excess of wasteful if not dissolute activity, but to an over-abundance or surplus of pleasurable luxuries that are there for whimsical, carefree consumption. Objects of delight become mere playthings randomly engaged. In de Sade, of course, all of this is sexualized, personified, and objectified for perverse sadistic delectation, which is predicated on a class interest (or norm) of old: aristocratic arbitrary right.

  De Sade was, in fact, a practitioner of frivolity. His excesses happened to be perverse both in terms of transgressing norms and a certain compulsion to repeat whereby an over-accumulation or surplus of representations, at once visual and verbal, function in the service of satisfying a drive that is insatiable. As de Sade's work clearly reveals, frivolity bears witness against itself by publically revealing the extremes to which it must go, extremes that challenge credulity even as they insist upon their extravagance. Whereas in the modern world, as Herbert Marcuse noted, the sexual instinct is transformed into the sort of work in which everyone can find their own dreams and fantasies,[1] in the eighteenth century, and particularly in that movement known as the rococo, the sexual instinct was being transformed into frivolous behavior that transgressed the sort of work whose function is to embody shared fantasies and dreams, in part, by means of the over-investment in and over-accumulation of objects that fail to consummate the drive, a failure that in de Sade leads to his wish to brutally punish or break the object for the sake of a surplus pleasure, a pleasure in excess of what isn't realized otherwise. That de Sade was writing fiction was itself an act of frivolity from which whole catalogues of objects were produced in the name of an absolute right to pleasure that refused to recognize any limit or law that might inhibit its freedom. However, this comes at a cost. According to Jacques Lacan, de Sade's work "never presents us with a successful seduction in which his fantasy would nevertheless find its crowning glory—that is, a seduction in which the victim, even if she were at her last gasp, would consent to her tormentor's intention, or even join his side in the fervor of her consent".[2] This speaks to alienation and what Lacan calls "the freedom to desire in vain".[3]

If sadism can be frivolous, frivolity isn't necessarily sadistic, though one might not be wrong in suspecting that cruelty or insensitivity might be a constitutive element. This relates to surplus, because having too much in the way of wealth and opulence commonly means access to an unbridled right to pleasure, a right that surplus wealth stores up within itself. Not only that, but such surplus enables the freedom to desire in vain, that is, to desire frivolously and even perversely, which, as Lacan tells us, is self-defeating. The aesthetic dimension of this freedom to desire in vain can be seen in French rococo interiors in which there is a decorative profusion of

---

[1] See Herbert Marcuse, *Eros and Civilization* (Boston: Beacon, 1955/1974).
[2] Jacques Lacan, *Ecrits*, trans. Bruce Fink (New York: Norton, 1966/2006), 665.
[3] Jacques Lacan, *Ecrits*, trans. Bruce Fink (New York: Norton, 1966/2006), 661.

unidentifiable figures (the anonymous, pornographic object of the Sadist's attention is already prefigured here) that are caught up in dynamic forms typified by flourishes that have the appearance of shells, froth, or flames that are undulating sinuously, as if the whole world were a continuous insubstantial extravagance of erotically changing forms en masse. In terms of rococo design, this puts considerable stress on the spectacle of *luxe* as a dynamic process of libidinal overproduction and stockpiling (surplus) whose eroticization is aesthetically reflected by means of feminine curves and botanical twists, as if there were a connection between production (of objects) and reproduction (of life). If the rococo quickly became identified with a style, however decoratively abusive in its excesses, that style represented the establishment of formalized norms. Another way of putting this would be to say that the norm is the result of a repetition of the drive to *jouissance* in excess, even to the point where that *jouissance* is to be always already expected as the outcome of an automatic process whose features and practices are to be counted upon as reliable. [1]

Frivolously meddling with the delight of such a world in vain was de Sade's concern, though it was the concern of libertines and cavaliers before him, generally. If we take a look at the poetry of John Wilmot, 2nd Earl of Rochester, who was active in the 1670s and 80s, we will note that well before de Sade and the rise of the rococo, there was an interest in the break down of the automatic process that would necessarily lead to erotic pleasure. Both writers, it is fair to say, saw that an excess of sexual excitation may well depend upon the frustration of the sexual act so that what one has instead are endless elaborations of the most frivolous sorts that have a comical dimension. Rochester famously wrote a poem in which he chided his

---

[1] Jouissance or pleasure is a sexualized term in French and was used extensively as a psychoanalytic concept by Jacques Lacan in his many seminars. See Jean-Marie Jadin et Marcel Ritter, *La jouissance au fil de l'enseignement de Lacan* (Toulouse : Éditions érès, 2009).

phallus for losing altitude at the very moment when its penetrative energy was most needed. In speaking to his phallus thus, Rochester proved the Lacanian observation that the phallus seemingly has a will of its own, which is precisely what puzzles Rochester with respect to his erection. It's not entirely his to control, but something alien. Moreover, its function isn't merely that of the object, but as Lacan specifies, that of a signifier. What is it the phallus is signifying in Rochester but its autonomy as a slave to love making that has gone on strike in order to rebel against its masters, Rochester and his female companion? The phallus is therefore in *excess* of the masters' will insofar as it exceeds their demand that it perform its job. In our world, we have Viagra to override man's rebellious member, to force it to labor, to make it do what one wants. But the very act of taking Viagra already testifies to the rebelliousness of the phallus, its unreliability, its status as slave. De Sade would have understood this, given that in his writings not only the phallus but everything else is treated as if it were merely a slave to the sexual act. The familiar whips, chains, and other devices of the sadist are the signifiers of enslavement or, to put it another way, the realization that sexuality is in essence a condition that requires the enslavement of not just the phallus but the orifices that it penetrates. What one has in sadism—and not just there, of course—is a surplus of slaves enlisted in the act of sexual penetration, something that has been visually developed at some length in the art of a contemporary and controversial African-American artist, Kara Walker. Throughout her installations, it is the depiction of sexual slavery, in eighteenth and nineteenth century garb, that is heavily overdetermined in the context of what can only be called an obscene frivolity in which the phallus is shown to be both oppressor and oppressed. In Rochester's libertine poetry, it is the insatiability of lust that causes both men and women to abuse themselves sexually as if they were slaves to the act of coition. As an obscene frivolity, Rochester berates his phallus, not just in order to dominate it, but in order to continue giving it the beating he thinks it requires. In the flagrantly obscene poem "A Ramble in St James's Park" (1672/3), it is the woman's sex that is berated ("salt-swoln cunt"), again for the purpose of having intercourse with it by other means—here by means of *écriture* in which the pen is operative as "fucking post". Given that in Rochester's poetry sexuality is excess by definition (the same would be true for Walker, but also for rococo artists), there is always a surplus of sexual partners, intrigues, and activities that won't allow for monogamy, let alone morality, a surplus associated with the fact that in Rochester's world sexual activities will exceed ordinary human capacity and accede to the vain, the frivolous, and the superficial, provided that lovers convince one another they are living a quasi-mythical existence as beautiful people reminiscent of bucolic maidens and shepherds of Latin poetry. For Rochester, however, the jaded reality that "Fair Chloris in a pigsty lay" offsets the female masquerade of dissembling appearances that dresses up lust. "Beauty's no more but the dead soil which Love / Manures, and does by wise commerce improve" and "as with Indians we / Get gold and jewels for our trumpery, / So to each other, for their useless toys, / Lovers afford whole magazines of joys". [1]

Of course, Rochester was a man of experience: a wit, a cynic, and a rogue who lived what he wrote, so much so, that he was eventually expelled from the court of Charles II. Antecedent to him was the still chaste John Milton, writing in the 1630s, who drew from an excess of classical learning as opposed to dissolute experience at court. Milton, too, had some idea of a culture of the frivolous in "L'Allegro" when he praises the Nymph of mirth. Here, of course, a less jaded sensibility comes to light.

Haste thee, Nymph, and bring with thee
Jest, and youthful Jollity,
Quips and cranks and wanton wiles,

---

[1] "The Advice" in *The Complete Poems of John Wilmot Earl of Rochester*, ed. David M. Vieth (New Haven: Yale University Press, 1962), 18.

> Nods and becks and wreathed smiles
> Such as hang on Hebe's cheek,
> And love to live in dimple sleek;
> Sport that wrinkled Care derides,
> And Laughter holding both his sides. [1]

Mirth is asked to lead "The mountain-nymph, sweet Liberty", which is our hint that Milton is explicitly thinking about libertinage in the context of an overflowing of happiness whose effects are those of wreathing, wrinkling, and twisting: a distortion and contortion of bodies besides themselves with laughter and its slightly sadistic relation, mockery. By way of Liberty, whom she leads, Mirth dissolves the forms by freeing the joy that such forms enclose. This, in turn, eroticizes the bodies by dissipating their boundaries, something that anticipates a rococo aesthetic. Of course, Milton isn't supporting a culture of the frivolous, if only because for him the classical references, however rampantly excessive in these poems, have seriousness of purpose and aren't merely decorative excuses with which to usher in orgiastic fun. And yet certain characteristics of a culture of frivolity are to be glimpsed: arbitrary power, an excess of refinement (education), an emphasis on pleasure for pleasure's sake, laughter (persiflage), and a certain amount of irreligion. Moreover, both "L'Allegro" and its companion poem "Il Penseroso" speak to an accumulation of wealth, which has to do with the poet's taking in of all the natural and cultural riches that he sees and imagines. In other words, these are poems of accumulation, inventory, delectation, and of the ephemerality (the expenditure) of pleasure. As in the case of the French rococo, which Milton obviously couldn't have known about, there is already a *fureur d'amusement* in "L'Allegro" and, too, in

---

[1] Lines 25 – 32. *Complete Poetry and Essential Prose of John Milton*, ed. W. Kerrigan et al. (New York: Random House, 2007), p. 42.

"Il Penseroso," a wayward tendency to distraction and *divertissement* that is dependent on there being so much bounty or surplus. Admittedly, Milton's dalliance with frivolity was but very brief and even went so far as to introduce that key device of the rococo known as the mirror that allowed the gaze to slide (*glissement* is the operative eighteenth-century term) from one view or perspective to another ("L'Allegro" and "Il Penseroso" are mirror poems), enabling thereby an excessive movement between formal coherence and uncontrolled variety, bounded and unbounded experience, measure and surplus. Oddly, Milton is even in advance of Rochester to the extent that Milton has a capacity for taking in a panoramic view of multitudinous play and dalliance, whereas Rochester is rather too focused on the sexual act per se and woman as his possession, if not his instrument of delight. Milton therefore appears to be quite liberated in comparison to Rochester, who by his own admission is a slave to his sexual appetite. Both writers, of course, are actually too serious to be considered proper agents of frivolity, given that Milton is soberly meditating on the relation of poetry to mental states and Rochester, at the end of the day, is a moralizer who distinguishes between appearance and reality, dupery and honesty. And yet, to some extent, both the libertine and the Puritan are capable of hiding under the veil of frivolity: a surplus of exchanges, accumulated wealth, over-refinement, the ephemerality of pleasures and, in Rochester's case particularly, *l'esprit courtesan*.

Generally speaking, frivolity in the late seventeenth and early eighteenth centuries was the joining up of extreme refinement with the lightness of a charming but casual abandon that is distracted and inconsistent: *une vie amoureuse déréglée*. All seriousness is suspended in a hail of *bon mots* and brief moments of scintillating excitement and laughter, in a surplus of joy that stems from an amusement with ever passing tastes that come and go like clouds in the sky. Hence the practice of reason is bypassed for an excess of civilized refinement that superficially wields an arbitrary power that sides with the immediacy of impressions over considered ideas. What a culture of frivolity favors is the establishment of infinite delicacies and amusements mediated by the disguises and illusions of one's own persona as in, for example, Marivaux's charming play, *The Game of Love and Chance* (1730). In such instances, the intimate self is disguised, giving way to the social self that conducts itself as a representation of fleeting desires and wants, sincere or not, presented as social play and dalliance. In Marivaux, however, erotic play and dalliance occurs discreetly and openly in public, whereas the private self does, in fact, genuinely fall in love. In contrast, the most pure type of *frivole* lives a life of allure and enviable happiness, a felicitous order of things that privilege superficial engagements for the sake of commitments that can be broken with indifference. One could even say that frivolity is to importance what atheism is to God, because for the frivolous importance has no authority or agency, since that would put the brakes on what is essentially a style of expenditure that won't tolerate or heed limits. In other words, frivolity assumes an endless surplus of means whereby it can perpetuate itself without any thought to matters of significance. In terms of de Sade this relates to the endless supply of sexual partners without any thought to what might happen to them. That amorality, if this is the right word, underscores that aspect of the *frivole* who is indifferent to the point of amoral behavior. Whereas the *frivole* stops short of any intended criminal behavior, as that would detract from pleasure, he or she pursues an indifference to others that is remarkably callous and objectionable. One sees this, for example, in, of all places, Anton Chekhov's *The Cherry Orchard* (1904) whose protagonist is a frivolous woman. Her self-indulgence has been so massive that she is not only entirely incapable of heeding matters of importance, much like a young child might be, but entirely blind to her class identity as a parasitical aristocrat. In Checkhov's play, the *frivole* is foolish and pathetic, though a certain nobility of style and grace is still to be witnessed more or less as a historical artifact of a by gone age. In fact, when we meet Madame Ranevskaya, she has just returned from a lengthy stay in Paris where she has run through most of her money only to face foreclosure of her estate in Russia. Frivolity, in Chekhov's play, is a behavior that has been handed down more or less as an entitlement, and once it is exposed for what it is, we discover that in fact the *frivole* is quite self-conscious of herself as a social type, almost tragically so. But this comes very late in the history of a social frivolity that has become unsustainable and therefore threadbare. In Chekhov, frivolity is to the rich what alcoholism is to the poor: an understandable vice that however morally fallen stems from an inability to face reality.

That frivolity is an escape from the real concerns my last examples taken from, once more, the English Restoration or thereabouts. We know that members of the court of Charles II were familiar with the court of Louis XIV and that during the late seventeenth century both cultures were immersing themselves in extravagant behavior that broke with rules of ordinary social propriety, so much so that at court there seemed to be two worlds in force, an authoritarian public façade in which a rigid symbolic order was presented for everyone to obey and, behind closed doors, a deregulated private world of sexual intrigues and general roguery. That is, the courts of late seventeenth-century England and France had a certain theatrical dimension in which everyone was acting, whether in public or private. This is very observable in Rochester, to return to him for a moment, because in his poetry there seems to be no question that all social relations are inherently supposed to be masked in classical literary garb, however explicitly superficial and anachronistic. This masking is a *divertissement* that enables one to live in a perpetual state of pretense, a progress of successive mystifications.

Of course, *divertissement* didn't just suddenly appear in the Restoration. It occurs too in poems such as Andrew Marvell's "Upon Appleton House," which was written during the Interregnum, a poem that intentionally dresses up reality in what Jean Rousset, in the context of

Baroque writing of the seventeenth century in France, once called "a new aesthetic":

> In fact, there is consonance between a hero treated as a toy and as a transformed being, if not with a dislocated composition that is open and organized around various centers; the action multiplies itself, time slows down, lines of flight break, threads interlace, the actors are displaced, the dramatic material expands, giving an impression of movement, of complication, and of excess. [1]

If "Upon Appleton House" is a sort of flamboyant disaggregated masque in which everything is transformed into a marvelous shifting paysage of illusion and illusionism, it is actually a rather serious poem consisting of displaced materials, in the Freudian sense, that refer to the traumas of the English civil wars. What appears to be flippant or frivolous in Marvell is, in fact, a distorted reproduction of physical destruction. If Lord Fairfax, his estate, and his family lineage are treated as toys with which the poet can frivolously play by dressing everything up however he wishes with a certain mystifying abandon, displacing centers, perversely interlacing narrative threads, distorting perspectives, and even implausibly deifying Fairfax's teenage daughter, that mayhem has sources in the general's military exploits and victories. Too, that everything in the poem is so aggressively illusory if not baffling introduces a critical, satirical dimension that calls attention to the inappropriateness of the artifice in terms of what Eliot once called a dissociation of sensibility, one that in Marvell's poem most likely has its source in the horror of civil wars in which nearly a million people died. [2]

---

[1] Jean Rousset, *La littérature de l'âge baroque en France* (Paris: José Corti, 1954), 74.
[2] Diane Perkiss, *The English Civil War* (New York: Basic Books, 2007).

If one turns to John Dryden during the Restoration itself, though, one encounters a poet who had to mind the Act of Indemnity and Oblivion of 1660, which made it illegal to refer to the bad old days of Cromwell and the civil wars. This was an age of amnesty and active forgetting that repressed collective trauma, even if various social actors wrote memoirs that wrote and rewrote the past. Dryden, as it happens, was aggressively forgetful and selective and therefore the perfect propagandist for Charles II. He negotiated the king's if not his court's imposture by means of praise (glorification) and revised the past (for example, Shakespeare's plays) to suit the present. Unlike Rochester, who was a sort of court jester with a rakish demeanor, Dryden had a key role in governance as spin doctor, however informal his relation to king and court. Dryden offered the king what we today would call cultural capital. The normative classical and Biblical dressing up of state politics, however illusory, was intended to clarify the structure of human behavior as well as to proscribe how people should act. Normative principles of conduct defined in terms of static oppositions between wisdom and folly, foresight and blindness, genius and dullness favored the sort of moralization appropriate for the construction of maxims and *bon mots* that had the force of a consistent practical philosophy of life derived, mainly, from the secular experience of social and political affairs of men in which one can see obvious relations between behavioral causes/ effects. That is, literature in the late seventeenth century, both in England and France, was eager to chastise extremist tendencies on practical grounds, whether given by way of nature or culture. This was quite evident, for example, in the plays of Molière, though one sees this too in the Restoration drama of Wycherley and others for whom something as vagrant, epicurean, and amoral as frivolity is to be mocked and excoriated because it represents an instance of bad governance in terms of how one conducts one's life.

Considering how alert Dryden was to behavioral norms, how could he be considered to be connected with a culture of frivolity? In his study *The Just and the Lively*, Michael Gelber notes that as a dramatist Dryden had a strong interest in Ariosto's *Orlando Furioso*, which he took as the implausible model for the writing of heroic drama. Dryden appreciated Ariosto's "bewildering profusion of episodes, its sudden jumps from one narrative line to another, its long digressions". ① Citing C. S. Lewis, Gelber notes that in Ariosto every stanza is filled with something new. "Battles in all their detail, strange lands with their laws, customs, history and geography, storm and sunshine, mountains, islands, rivers, monsters, anecdotes, conversations—there seems no end to it." ② There is so much action, we are told, that "we must abandon any hope of keeping the unfolding pattern in our memory". While there are centers around which actions are clustered and to which they refer, it is not easy to recall much except "local effects". Moreover, "As Ariosto refuses to impose on his work the orderly structure of the traditional epic, so Dryden, as he imitates the *Furioso*, abandons of structural principles of conventional drama". ③ Dryden's excessive intricacies in *The Conquest of Granada* "unfold with pomp and circumstance, with spectacle and grandiloquence and with intricacies that approach the labyrinthine". ④ However we consider this, it is not what a classically inspired writer would call good governance. Rather, fancy and wit are allowed to run wild with considerable extravagance and grandiloquence. Apparently, the *Conquest* is a play overrun with sub-plots "centered on petty lusts and intrigues, ignoble aspirations and defeats..." In a word, the play is largely decentered and disaggregated. In line with what Rousset called the "new aesthetic", the plot

---

① Michael Worth Gelber, *The Just and the Lively* (Manchester: Manchester/St. Martins, 1999), p. 135.
② Ibid.
③ Ibid.
④ Michael Worth Gelber, *The Just and the Lively* (Manchester: Manchester/St. Martins, 1999), p. 136.

lines are broken and verges on the anarchic, the major action is implausible, and no practical moral lessons are to be seen. Unlike Ariosto, Dryden avoids the interlace in which various stories are kept going concurrently, leaping instead among the different stories in a discontinuous back and forth movement. Moreover, as Gelber points out, in Dryden's plays "the ending is tacked on merely to bring the curtain down and is in no way required by the previous action". [1]

The apparent lack of pattern and direction in Dryden's heroic plays has occasioned much confusion. Stabilizing elements are present, to be sure: individual episodes are immediately understandable and are governed by the unities of action, place and time; the minor actions which centre on lust and intrigue, though they may be kept going indefinitely, always move towards climax and resolution. But if demands for order are not ignored, the plays remain bewildering. They are centered in the episodic and the discordant, the improbable and the marvelous. Hence it may be argued that Dryden's heroic drama is a total failure. So at least contemporary audiences frequently complained, and so too have scholars and critics complained for the past two or three hundred years. [2]

If scholars have complained aboutDryden's heroic drama, it is because they have failed to grasp the presence of a certain frivolity in Dryden's writings in which excess leads to a surplus of what Gelber calls the episodic and the discordant, the improbable and the marvelous. This surplus shouldn't surprise us, given that Dryden was living in a period of the Baroque which was well on its way to rococo excess on the Continent. Rather, what should surprise us is that all this excess cannot be disentangled from the Restoration's need to establish civil norms and right order.

---

[1] Michael Worth Gelber, *The Just and the Lively* (Manchester: Manchester/St. Martins, 1999), p. 137.
[2] Ibid.

It wouldn't be hard to find more examples of accumulated distraction, lack of pattern, and arbitrary rhetorical largesse in Dryden, though it would be mistaken to imagine that such writing wasn't also functioning in the service of formalized norms. Although comparing the political crisis surrounding succession and the Duke of Monmouth to the biblical story of Absalom and Achitophel was clearly an outrageous *divertissement* intended to amuse, on the one hand, and impugn, on the other, as a political satire the poem "Absalom and Achitophel" nevertheless was formally cogent, its decorative abusiveness having had the aim of judging political actors in light of moral norms. In fact, what one cannot help but notice in much of Dryden's writings is a certain Puritanism carried over from his upbringing—he died a Catholic—in which the frivolous, the decorative, and the ephemeral are not purposed for the sake of happiness but, rather, for sobriety, something that in the context of the rococo is quite unFrench. In fact, Dryden is some sort of middle class *frivole*, a man of Restoration who sees a prosperous future of excess and frivolity (what we might call "partying") made possible by good governance, typified by moderation and commonsense in most everyday affairs. Alexander Pope, in the following century, will be the inheritor of this sort of frivolity, one that is in the service of pragmatism or what Derrida, in the context of his reading of Condillac's *Essai sur l'origine des connaissances humaines*, calls *besoin* (need).

Inturning, finally, to Derrida's "The Archaeology of the Frivolous", which is the subtext of my paper, of importance is that Derrida saw in Condillac a dual understanding of linguistic reference, the one presupposing the identity of the referent to itself, and the other presupposing the referent's non-self-identity or internal difference. That is manifestly obvious in the case of the pun, if not to any word that has multiple definitions (*amorce*: beginning; detonator, bait, etc.). Frivolousness in this context refers to what Ferdinand de Saussure called the arbitrary, something Condillac perceived as well in noting that a French word such as *amorce* is not only assigned arbitrarily to its referents but that these referents are, as a set, arbitrarily related. That is, there is something frivolous (ad hoc, insouciant, perhaps even flippantly happenstantial) about assigning meanings to words, *that frivolity of assignation being the archaic instantiation of language*. Hence there is no a priori identity to which words belong, as Hermogenes imagines in Plato's *The Cratylus*, but only arbitrarily assigned meanings that have their source in *arbitrary right*, if not even a *fureur d'amusement*. Not only the identity of meanings and their supposed ostensive objects, but the things one says are motivated by *needs* and desires that are, according to Condillac, frivolous: whimsical, flippant, and inconsistent, never mind how utilitarian. What we perceive as linguistic over-production has to do with pleasurable, frivolous behavior that evades the "proper", as Derrida puts it. The production of language, then, is seen in its very origin to be a frivolous but also a very sovereign activity reminiscent of Percy Bysshe Shelly's famous remark about the poet being a legislator. By means of writing, the poet posits the world; however, this positing, Derrida notices by way of Condillac, is different in everyone's case and follows the dictates of prejudices, whims, tastes, and wishes that have a will to power in terms of assignation. Shelley's inference that the poet is the only true legislator is, from Derrida's perspective, itself frivolously authoritarian and egotistical in its arbitrary assignation. To recall Dryden and Pope in this context, we should not forget that even when they wrote in highly structured poetic forms, which inherently disavow a certain arbitrariness or casualness, that their satirical judgments are nevertheless typical of what Condillac, as described by Derrida, saw as largely frivolous behavior in which one observes the ad hoc assignation of judgments whose legislation is essentially driven by a need to impose one's capricious individual sovereignty as influential public figure over others who are thought to threaten the norms of one's world. One can see this too in Warhol's novel in which the flippant, arbitrariness of everyday conversation reveals an authoritarian performativity of one-up-man-ship that bends language however it wants. This suggests that not just the poet but everyone (including Warhol's transgender acquaintances) is an unacknowledged legislator of the world, one who is authoritarian and arbitrary, a point that de Sade would have agreed. That we are not necessarily put in check by others, which is to say, that Ondine can say anti-Semitic things with impunity, or that, more typically, we can choose whatever words we want in order to say something, opens up opportunities for self-expression typified by *a right to pleasure* that is arbitrary and therefore inherently frivolous, according to Condillac. When scientists dub their atomic bombs "fat man" and "little boy" we can see a fundamental relationship between what we call literary and ordinary language, as both have their origin in a will to power that draws from a vast surplus of possible verbal choices and, as such, is sovereign in its playful extravagance. As we have seen, and as Derrida has indicated, the frivolous is a constitutive dimension of the performativity of language (its speech acts) in general and striates centuries of literary history, so much so that we should be encouraged to look at literature outside the confines of a stylistic historical period that would assign frivolity to merely a short time-span within the eighteenth century. As Derrida has indicated, frivolity is endemic to the very act of linguistic positing. As such, that positing is by its very nature excessive and extravagant, always a bit too much for a norm to swallow.

Works Cited:

1. Thorstein Veblen, *Theory of the Leisure Class* (Boston: Houghton Mifflin, 1899/1973).
2. Erich Auerbach, *Mimesis*, trans. W. Trask (Princeton: Princeton University Press, 1946/2003).
3. Jean Rousset, *La littérature de l'âge baroque en France* (Paris : José Corti, 1954).
4. Herbert Marcuse, *Eros and Civilization* (Boston: Beacon, 1955/1974).
5. Jacques Lacan, *Ecrits*, trans. Bruce Fink (New York: Norton, 1966/2006)
6. Andy Warhol, *A* (New York: Grove Press, 1968).
7. Jacques Derrida, "L'Archaeologie du frivole", preface to Condillac, *Essai sur l'origine*

des connaissances humaines (Paris: Galilée, 1973).

8. Jean Starobinski, *Largesse*, trans. J. M. Todd (Chicago: University of Chicago Press, 1994/1997).
9. Michael Worth Gelber, *The Just and the Lively* (Manchester: Manchester/St. Martins, 1999).
10. Diane Perkiss, *The English Civil War* (New York: Basic Books, 2007).
11. Jean-Marie Jadin et Marcel Ritter, *La jouissance au fil de l'enseignement de Lacan* (Toulouse: Éditions érès, 2009).

Žižek with Stendhal: Irony and the Death Drive

Zahi Zalloua[*]

中文摘要 死亡驱动是弗洛伊德首创的理论，指的是每个人身上超越快乐原则的过度力量。这一理论打破了被视为贯穿所有心理活动的快乐原则，因而在心理治疗领域引发了争论，但作为一种文化哲学在阐释学范畴内具有很强的生命力。拉康及其追随者淡化了弗洛伊德理论的生物性意义，转而注重其文化符号方面的内涵。齐泽克在整体上赞同拉康式的框架，推进了弗洛伊德的观点。齐泽克认为弗洛伊德分离出一个通往变化的开放空间，其中过度的能量既有可能是建设性的，也可以是完全破坏性的，精神分析学派的任务只是初步指出何以会有这种鸿沟。齐泽克认为弗洛伊德的死亡驱动指向一种人的主体性，使得人可以不完全从属于实际的生活对个人的要求。19世纪司汤达的小说《红与黑》中的主人公于连身上就以反讽的方式体现了这种死亡驱动所带来的困惑。于连的死亡驱动使得他无法安享社会阶层上升所带来的成果，只有独自在监狱中，他才寻找到了不用为社会塑造和伪装的自我，而这个自我是他对抗社会的堡垒。齐泽克指出，死亡驱动就是生命对自我的反叛。最终被推上断头台的于连以反讽的方式实现了他主体性的幸福

---

[*] 作者为美国惠特曼学院教授，文学博士，主要研究领域包括法国文学、文学理论、跨学科研究和性别研究等。

状态，这种终极的和谐摆脱了来自社会、经济、情绪的干扰，超越了未抵达的领域，也超越了人的自然存在。于连设想出来的幸福显然是不可能达到的，但它体现了一种对于逝去的和谐的乡愁，一种渴望回归前语言状态的幻想。这种回归的终极目的是回到"前俄狄浦斯"状态，即与母亲合二为一。于连在追求爱情和名利的过程中过度的力量正是使得一切脱离原来轨道的动力，他追求的是没有欲望的状态，但没有欲望之后生命也就不成其为生命了。死亡驱动是推动人朝向与自己的利益相反方向的力量，它是一种不合逻辑的逻辑。

关键词 齐泽克；死亡驱动；《红与黑》；精神分析；拉康

From its inception, the psychoanalytic concept of the "death drive" (*Todestrieb*) has generated controversy. Freud first introduced it in his 1920 *Beyond the Pleasure Principle*, describing the death drive metaphorically as a yearning to return to an inorganic state, to a peaceful state, that is, to a state without excitation. This led Freud to famously identify the death drive with the "Nirvana principle":

> The dominating tendency of mental life, and perhaps of nervous life in general, is the effort to reduce, to keep constant or to remove internal tension due to stimuli (the "Nirvana principle" …) — atendency which finds expression in the pleasure principle; and our recognition of that fact is one of our strongest reasons for believing in the existence of death instincts. (Freud *Beyond the Pleasure Principle*, 67)

Intimately connected to the death drive is what Freud calls the "repetition compulsion", the compulsion of the human psyche to repeat *traumatic events over and over again.* ① The repetition compulsion transgresses what Freud had understood as a guiding principle of psychic life: the "pleasure principle". In the opening line of *Beyond the Pleasure Principle*, Freud states: "In the theory of psycho-analysis we have no hesitation in assuming that the course taken by mental events is automatically regulated by the pleasure principle." (Freud *Beyond the Pleasure Principle*, 3) He defines the pleasure principle as that which regulates all mental processes, compelling human beings to seek pleasure and avoid pain (or unpleasure), to control levels of excitation, maintaining homeostasis. The repetition compulsion, however, gestures to a *beyond* of the pleasure principle, pointing to the latter's hermeneutic deficiencies, since it offers only a partial explication for human behavior.

Freud's discovery of the existence of ineradicable self-destructive impulses in individuals painted a tragic, if not nihilistic, vision of human existence. For this reason, *Beyond the Pleasure Principle*, in the words of Jean Laplanche, "remains the most fascinating and baffling text in the entire Freudian *corpus*" (Laplanche 106). Many readers of Freud found the death drive difficult to accept. They saw it as excessively speculative, an aberration in thought, or, most importantly, dangerous in its ethico-political implications. William Reich's reaction is representative. For Reich, a psychoanalysis informed by the death drive is at odds with itself. It makes futile any hope of a psychoanalytic "cure". Rather than providing what was needed, that is, a "*sociology* of human suffering", Freud's theory

---

① For Derrida, the compulsion to repetition "remains... indissociable from the death drive" (Derrida *Archive Fever*, 11-12). Similarly, Todd McGowan points out that "Freud makes no explicit distinction between repetition compulsion and the death drive even as he shifts from one to the other. In light of this structure, one can see the concept of the death drive as Freud's way of theorizing repetition compulsion rather than as an altogether new concept. If one doesn't read it this way, the death drive seems to emerge out of thin air, since none of the examples with which Freud begins the book involve seeking out death itself" (McGowan 295n. 26). For a sustained engagement with Freud's *Beyond the Pleasure Principle*, see also Derrida's *Post Card*.

of the death drive proposed a "cultural philosophy of human suffering", a pessimistic diagnosis of an incurable social illness, because it "traced the psychic conflict back to inner elements and more and more eclipsed the supreme role of the frustrating and punishing outer world" (Reich 232-33). ① If aggression comes primarily from within—that is, if its cause is located in unchanging human nature—then psychoanalysis's therapeutic work is rendered ineffectual. ②

Freud's death drive has, however, had a long hermeneutic shelf life. Other social theorists found explanatory value in the death drive by reading it as a social force rather than an individual drive. In *Eros and Civilization*, for example, Herbert Marcuse highlights society's Thanatos, its suicidal tendencies toward aggression, and calls for a stronger expression of Eros, or our sexual drives: "Eros, freed from surplus-repression, would be strengthened, and the strengthened Eros would, as it were, absorb the objective of the death instinct" (Marcuse *Eros and Civilization*, 235). ③

---

① Heinz Hartmann considered it of limited value, since it was based on "biological speculation" (Hartmann *Ego Psychology and the Problem of Adaptation* [1939], 11), while Eric Fromm deemed Freud's account unbalanced and totalizing: "The assumption of the death-instinct is satisfactory inasmuch as it takes into consideration the full weight of destructive tendencies, which had been neglected in Freud's earlier theories. But it is not satisfactory inasmuch as it resorts to a biological explanation that fails to take account sufficiently of the fact that the amount of destructiveness varies enormously among individuals and social groups" (Fromm 180 – 1). Fromm did not see the death drive as an implacable reality but as something that could be neutralized, if not overcome, by the life drive.

② In "A Critique of the Death Instinct", Otto Fenichel also objected to the biological reductionism implicit in the death drive: "Such an interpretation would mean a total elimination of the social factor from the etiology of neuroses, and would amount to a complete biologization of neurosis" (Fenichel 370 – 1). This contrasts with the understanding of neuroses as being "generated by disturbances in human relationships", as Karen Horney argues (12).

③ Marcuse can be seen as historicizing the eternal antagonism between Eros and Thanatos that Freud suggests in the ending to *Civilization and Its Discontents*: "And now it is to be expected that the other of the two "Heavenly Powers", eternal Eros, will make an effort to assert himself in the struggle with his equally immortal adversary. But who can foresee with what success and with what result" (Freud *Civilization and Its Discontents*, 112).

Increasing erotic satisfaction—and thus reducing surplus-repression—does not eradicate the presence of Thanatos but regulates it, keeping it somewhat contained, at bay. ①

Later psychoanalysts, especially those following Lacan's interpretive lead, have effectively downplayed Freud's so-called biologism, and re-interpreted the death drive in relation to the symbolic order and the emergence of subjectivity as such. ② Lacan leaves no doubt about the importance of Freud's notion of the death drive to a psychoanalytic approach: "To ignore the death instinct in his [Freud's] doctrine is to misunderstand that doctrine entirely" (Lacan, *Écrits* 301). For Lacanians, the death drive comes to name an ontological lack, a desire for plenitude, a yearning to return to a state of complete enjoyment, to what has been lost as a result of one's entry into language, one's symbolic castration. ③ Fantasmatically speaking, the goal is to attain the mysterious, transcendent object (*das Ding*) — "to reproduce the initial state, to find *das Ding*, the object" (Lacan *The Ethics of Psychoanalysis*, 53) —that would fully satisfy desire and thus put an end to one's alienation and the suffering one feels faced with

---

① As Todd McGowan observes, "by eliminating the repression of eros, a society lessens the aggression that subjects experience because much of this aggression arises in response to a lack of erotic satisfaction, though this aggression would not disappear altogether" (McGowan 12).

② The English translation of Freud's *Todestrieb* as "death instinct" undoubtedly overstressed the concept's biologism. But, as Jean-Michel Rabaté points out, Lacan was adamant that "one should not talk of a 'death instinct' but of a 'death drive'. His philological precision differentiating Freud's *Trieb* from his lingering Darwinism had a critical agenda. It attacked the second generation Freudians who had dropped the idea of a 'death drive', who had blamed it on what they took as Freud's innate pessimism, his tragic view of life" (Rabaté 129).

③ As Adrian Johnson puts it, the death drive does not entail "literal fixations upon death per se, but the insistent demand for an absolute enjoyment, a demand without consideration for the welfare of either the ego or the physical organism housing these drives" (Johnson *Time Driven*, 238).

one's mortality.① In the words of Martin Hägglund, "the aim of desire is to *not desire*" (*Hägglund* 132). On this account, the therapeutic work of psychoanalysis consists in demystifying the object of desire.② In exposing its illusory character (in showing that the object is not a timeless or immortal being), psychoanalysis hopes to "traverse" this human fantasy of wholeness.

While generally sympathetic to this larger Lacanian framing of the death drive, Žižek gives the Freudian notion still a different twist, highlighting, or better yet harnessing the drive's unruly excess and its self-sabotaging or short-circuiting ways. Two passages illustrate Žižek's position particularly well:

I think that Freud, to put it in fashionable terms, isolates a

---

① The ontological status of *das Ding* is a slippery issue. Lacan asserts the existence of a primordial *jouissance*, a scene of unity and plenitude. In the beginning, prior to any subject/object distinction, the child is said to experience the mother directly (in the fusion of the child and the mother's breast) as a pure satisfaction. After the formation of subjectivity such an experience becomes unrepeatable: all we have access to are partial objects, with partial satisfaction. For Žižek and others, however, matters look more complicated after the entry into the Symbolic, "*after* the letter," as Bruce Fink puts it (Fink 27). Žižek cautions against "substantializing" *das Ding*, and foregrounds the role of language in our conceptualization of *das Ding*, seeing it thus as an *effect* or fiction of the Symbolic: "What we experience as 'reality' discloses itself against the background of the lack, of the absence of it, of the Thing, of the mythical object whose encounter would bring about the full satisfaction of the drive. This lack of the Thing constitutive of 'reality' is therefore, in its fundamental dimension, not epistemological, but rather pertains to the paradoxical logic of desire—the paradox being that this Thing is retroactively produced by the very process of symbolization, i. e. that it emerges from the very gesture of its loss. In other (Hegel's) words, there is nothing—no positive substantial entity—behind the phenomenal curtain, only the gaze whose phantasmagorias assume different shapes of the Thing" (Žižek *Tarrying with the Negative*, 37). William Egginton and Yannis Stavrakakis also make a similar point: "*Das Ding* is... the product of a retroactive abstraction from the phenomenal world" (Egginton 42) and "no doubt, it is common sense to think that something was there before exclusion, otherwise exclusion would make no sense at all; the only problem is that we can't really know what it was. To think that it [the Thing] was a state of fullness is a retroactively produced fiction" (Stavrakakis 43-4).

② "[W]hat is supposed to be found cannot be found again. [...] It is to be found at the most as something missed. One doesn't find it, but only its pleasurable associations" (Lacan *The Ethics of Psychoanalysis*, 53).

certain excess. He calls it death drive, a certain excess of destructability that is, as it were, undermining, destabilizing the social order, an excess that is ambiguous in the sense that it can be a source of constructive energy or it can be purely destructive. The idea is that Freud isolates this space of excess, which then, of course, opens up the space for possible change. I think Freud's basic answer would have been: psychoanalysis just does this elementary job of showing how there is a gap, a failure, a nonfunctioning excess in society. (Žižek "Unbehagen and the Subject: An Interview with Slavoj Žižek", 422)

The Freudian notion of "death drive" points precisely toward a dimension of human subjectivity that resists its full immersion into its life-world: it designates a blind insistence that follows its course with utter disregard for the requirements of our concrete life-world. (Žižek "The Rhetorics of Power", 98)

For Žižek, then, who rejects its identification with the "Nirvana Principle", the death drive is clearly not about "the craving for self-annihilation" (Žižek *The Parallax View*, 62). It is in fact quite at odds with the biological desire for self-destruction: "The ultimate lesson of psychoanalysis is that human life is never "just life": humans are not simply alive, they are possessed by the strange drive to enjoy life in excess, passionately attached to a surplus which sticks out and derails the ordinary run of things" (Žižek *The Parallax View*, 62). Rereading the death drive as "a "natural' glitch in human nature" (Johnston *Žižek's Ontology*, 183) and a hunger for immortality counterintuitively foregrounds the unruly "inhuman" at the core of the human.

In what follows, I want to look at Stendhal's nineteenth-century novel *The Red and The Black* (*Le Rouge et le noir*), which stages, through irony, the perplexities of the death drive of its young hero Julien Sorel. *The Red and the Black* revolves around ambition and excessive desire as it tells the tale of Julien's unlikely rise from provincial peasant and fervent admirer of Napoleon to ennobled member of reactionary Paris society. Julien's trajectory—which ends in his imprisonment and execution—is marked by encounters with a series of prominent figures of power, each embodying the various socio-political milieus of Bourbon Restoration France. ① Under the watchful gaze of Lacan's big Other, Julien traverses these divergent social fields as a subject both formed and self-forming, coerced, constrained, or inhibited by power, and yet not locked into any of his socially given subject-positions. His ontologically precarious and strategically shifting positions in such adversarial relations—his power relations with figures of authority—render problematic any facile determination of his identity. His mutations also highlight the pervasive workings of desire and drive. If, upon "arriving" in Paris high society, Julien asserts that his "novel is finished" (359, translation modified) ("mon roman est fini" [491])—suggesting his desires are absolutely satisfied when he finally becomes who he always was and was meant to be—his drive ironically exceeds the novel plot and the symbolic

---

① For instance, when Julien becomes tutor to the Rênals' children he is exposed to new strategies of normalization, to different disciplining or regulating practices. In sharp opposition to his father's habitual beatings, we discover that M. de Rênal exercises his power over Julien quite differently. He does not manifest it through physical force. Rather, M. de Rênal invites all to address Julien with complete respect: "By my orders everyone here will address you as 'sir'" (25) ("d'après mes ordres tout le monde ici va vous appeler Monsieur" [53]). However, his attitude towards Julien quickly transforms when the latter does not perform according to expectations. The morning after his seduction of Mme de Rênal, Julien—who is waiting to confess his love to her—encounters first her angry husband, "who arrived two hours ago from Verrières, and made no effort to hide his displeasure that Julien had spent an entire morning without paying attention to the children" (45) ("qui, arrivé depuis deux heures de Verrières, ne cachait pas son mécontentement de ce que Julien passait toute la matinée sans s'occuper des enfants" [79]). M. de Rênal reminds Julien of the haves and have nots, of the asymmetrical character of their power relation. The modification of Julien's behavior is not found in coercion but experienced through humiliation.

identity that it confers on its protagonist. ① Julien's drive prevents him from enjoying the fruits of his social climbing and the plenitude of his new identity; rather than achieving novelistic resolution in this climax, he can never fully satisfy his desire for recognition and acceptance (his desire to no longer feel or be seen as a "monster" [360/493]). This drive produces hermeneutic tensions, troubling any hope of narrative and ideological closure, and even contaminating Julien's alleged discovery of his "authentic" self in his prison cell.

So let me begin with the novel's ending. In the solitude of his cell in a Gothic tower at Besan ? on, where he has been jailed for shooting and wounding his mistress, Mme de Rênal, Julien appears to attain full self-transparency, an ultimate sense of his inner self. While meditating on his memories, he experiences a profound sense of happiness about the time he had spent with Mme de Rênal:

> Ambition was dead within his heart; another passion rose from its ashes; he called it remorse for having tried to kill Mme. de Rênal. As a matter of fact, he was madly in love with her. He found an extraordinary happiness when, in absolute solitude, and without any fear of interruption, he could devote himself entirely to memories of the happy days he had spent at Verrières or Vergy. (379)

---

① Julien's transmutation from a poor peasant to a prestigious member of the nobility is not instantaneous but takes place in several stages. First, Julien's duel with the chevalier de Beauvoisis puts into motion the drastic transformation of Julien's identity. In an attempt to protect his aristocratic status—since he cannot be interpreted has having dueled with a mere commoner—the chevalier of Beauvoisis reconfigures the paternal origins of Julien. Likewise, the Marquis de La Mole helps in the (re) *making* of Julien's identity when he offers him the symbolic blue uniform of the aristocracy. His transformation reaches its apogee when the Marquis de la Mole confers a new identity on Julien by renaming him "M. le chevalier Julien Sorel de la Vernaye" (490) in what amounts to a bewildering onomastic metamorphosis: "The change in name struck him with wonder" (359) ("Le changement de nom le frappait d'étonnement" [491]).

L'ambition était morte en son cœur, une autre passion y était sortie de ses cendres; il l'appelait le remords d'avoir assassiné Mme de Rênal. Dans le fait, il en était éperdument amoureux. Il trouvait un bonheur singulier quand, laissé absolument seul et sans crainte d'être interrompu, il pouvait se livrer tout entier au souvenir des journées heureuses qu'il avait passées jadis à Verrières ou à Vergy. (517)

Having relinquished mastery and freed himself from his desire for worldly success, immune, as it were, to the tyrannical gaze of society, he can now enjoy the full presence of the moment: "I have been ambitious [...] *I was acting in those days according to the code of the times. Now* I am living from day to day" (406, emphasis added) ["J'ai été ambitieux [...] alors, *j'ai agi suivant les convenances du temps. Maintenant*, je vis au jour le jour" (553 - 4, emphasis added)]. Yet Julien's account of self should give us critical pause. Although Julien's project has now radically changed, it is problematic to assume that up until his quasi-revelation in the prison, he was merely following the "code of the times". Even a cursory reading of the novel reveals that Julien's protean identity was never a mere *effect* of the "code of the times" but was simultaneously formed and self-forming as a result of his complex encounters with authoritative figures of power. Julien overstates the matter, then. He does not simply abandon a previously "fake" or "inauthentic" identity for a "true" or "authentic" identity that was *always already* there. But critics almost unanimously uphold the veracity of Julien's epiphanic self-discovery. As one put it, "only when Julien's impulses triumph over his will is he *truly himself*" (Tenenbaum 11). For another, Julien's prison is the site where "the ultimate descent into the self takes place", rendering possible "[Julien's] fundamental discovery [...] of identity" (Brombert 97, 98). In this "happy prison", Julien finds a self or identity no longer needing to be socially performed ("Julien stops performing and starts living" because "it simply is" [Petrey 128]). This reading posits a clear teleological arc, leading to a return to an authentic, self-enclosed, and unmediated identity—recuperating, in turn, the romantic notion of identity, or "identity as a fortress against society" (Petrey 129). ①

To be sure, the novel does evoke the romantic dimensions of the character of Julien on numerous occasions. We can see it in Julien's emotional sensitivity, which is contrasted with the brutishness his father displays when, for example, he knocks a book from Julien's hands: "[Julien's] eyes were full of tears, less from physical pain than for the loss of his book, which he worshipped" (13) ("Il avait les larmes aux yeux, moins à cause de la douleur physique que pour la perte de son livre qu'il adorait" [38]). The kind of "spiritual" pain Julien feels at the loss of his "sacred" text (Napoleon's *Memorial of Saint Helena*) is emblematic of Julien's "romantic" sensibility. His antagonistic relation to society, represented by his father, also hints at a Rousseauistic quality: "an unhappy man at war with his whole society" (263) ("l'homme malheureux en guerre avec toute la société" [364]).

When critics evoke Julien's rediscovery of his true identity—his self minus the ideologies and corruptions of social life—they thus seem merely to reaffirm the narrator's own account: "Julien felt himself strong and resolute, like a man who has seen clearly into his own soul" (403) ["Julien se sentait fort et résolu comme l'homme qui voit clair dans son ? me" (450)]. There is arguably nothing controversial about the teleological reading of this ending. Yet from the perspective of the death drive things become less self-evident. Julien's death drive—which functions as a constitutive ironic excess,

---

① Contrary to Petrey, I do not divide Julien's relation to identity into three different phases: 1. Julien the hypocrite (a master performer, one who effectively manipulates the signs around him—Julien at the Seminary); 2. Julien the interpellated subject of aristocracy—Julien as the Chevalier de La Vernaye; 3. Julien *as* he is—Julien in his cell (Petrey). The dynamics of the death drive complicates such a division while still allowing for the radical fluctuations in Julien's identity.

as that which "sticks out and derails the ordinary run of things" (Žižek *The Parallax View*, 62) —both authorizes and thwarts such a reading. The narrator's qualification "Like a man..." in the statement "Julien felt himself strong and resolute, *like a man who has seen clearly into his own soul*", hints at this irreducible difference between the *ego* (his actual, ambivalent self) and *imago* (his idealized or reified image of self, a self immune from the social gaze). As Žižek puts it, "The "death-drive" means that life itself rebels against the ego: the true representative of death is ego itself, as the petrified *imago* which interrupts the flow of life" (Žižek *Tarrying with the Negative*, 179). In this light, rather than bridging the ironic gap separating the two selves, let's look more closely at the type of power relationship and state of being envisaged by Julien as constituting his "ideal" of happiness.

Why Mme de Rênal? Or more importantly, why Mme de Rênal now? The rediscovery and intensification of Julien's old love is primarily motivated by a negation of the type of amorous relationship he had since struck up with Mathilde, the daughter of the Marquis de La Mole. Prior to his "conversion", the Parisian Mathilde is nothing short of an *alter ego* for Julien, sharing many of his characteristics. She is, for example, both nostalgic for the past and highly calculating. On this last point, her contrast with the more *instinctive* Mme de Rênal is quite revealing: "Mme. de Rênal always found reasons to do what her heart dictated; this high-society girl [Mathilde] lets her heart be moved only when she has found proofs based upon good logic that it ought to be moved" (340) ["Madame de Rênal trouvait des raisons pour faire ce que son cœur lui dictait: cette fille du grand monde ne laisse son cœur s'émouvoir que lorsqu'elle s'est prouvé par bonnes raisons qu'il doit être ému" (467)]. It is Mme de Rênal's provincial character which ultimately triumphs in the eyes of Julien.

Julien's seemingly categorical withdrawal[1] (both physical and spiritual) from the Symbolic at the end of the novel is juxtaposed with Mathilde's excessive concerns with the external world: "Mathilde's lofty soul always had to be conscious of a public and *other people*" (378) ["Il fallait toujours l'idée d'un public et *des autres* à l'âme hautaine de Mathilde" (516)] . Himself "tired of heroics" (378) ["fatigué d'héroâme" (516)], Julien is disillusioned about the *good* of the Parisian lifestyle; he breaks with it and refigures happiness precisely as the exclusion of the desire to govern or direct the behavior and actions of the other (or others) . Resistance or conformity to the demands of the various social codes is no longer an issue. Faced with his imminent execution by guillotine, Julien "now" conceives of happiness as a state of *being*: a state of homeostasis and plenitude excluding the possibility of any change or disruption—social, economic, emotional, and so on. He situates his "happy self" outside the process of subjectivization, beyond the realm of *becoming* and the flux of human existence. Julien's *imagined* happiness is clearly unattainable in the here and now of social life; it expresses his nostalgia for a lost harmony (a state anterior to power), a yearning to return to the pre-linguistic Imaginary. This latent manifestation of the death drive, that is, a desire to return to the pre-Oedipal fusion with the maternal Other, the figure of Mme de Rênal, makes his earlier observation— "Mme. de Rênal had been like a mother to me" (387) (Mme de Rênal avait été pour

---

[1] From a Lacanian perspective, Julien's withdrawal must be qualified, since to be fully withdrawn from the Symbolic, to deny or "foreclose" the Name-of-the-Father entails psychosis (see Lacan, *The Psychoses*) . This is clearly not the case with Julien. Julien is not psychotic; he remains quite lucid and cognizant of his surroundings in the prison cell. Nevertheless, Julien does come to question the authority of the Symbolic, lessening its pull on him. As Christopher Prendergast observes, "the prison represents above all a withdrawal from the Other [...], a withdrawal from the communicative situation and hence from the language of social exchange [a move away from the Symbolic]" (138) . Prendergast speculates further about "the implications of that withdrawal for Julien's attitude to language itself" (138), and suggests that "the refusal of the world is also in part refusal of the word [a return to the Imaginary]" (Prendergast, *The Order of Mimesis* 138) .

moi comme une mère" [530]) —all the more truthful and revealing. ① Julien's idealized memory of his love for Mme de Rênal is subject to irony's corrosive effects. This idealized memory represents less a discovery of "true happiness" (the classic romantic ending) than a fear of power, a *kratophobia*. His fetishized memory expresses a hidden desire to transcend power, to eschew the exhaustive demands of the Other, to suppress the *potential* for displacement and reversibility constitutive of power relations.

In short, on this account, Julien desires *not* to desire. Life after desire is indeed no life at all. Julien succumbs to the death drive, to the fantasy of resolution—stasis and wholeness. This, however, is not the only reading of the Freudian death drive that the novel proposes or stages. Stendhal's novel also provides a more radical and unsettling image of the death drive, one that insists on the irreducible gap between *ego* and *imago*, between thinking and being. If a romantic reading privileged the *imago* of Julien, an identification with an ambition-free Julien, an alternative reading of the death drive foregrounds the ways in which all investments into selves, into the *imago*, are subject to disruption and revision. This is how Derrida describes his concept of "autoimmunity" as "a certain death drive against the *autos* itself, against the ipseity that any suicide worthy of its name still presupposes" (Derrida *Rogues*, 123). Julien's death drive is not merely a yearning for an untenable Imaginary, but involves a self-sabotaging impulse that can be traced throughout the novel. Julien's success in the novel lies in his capacity to fashion himself in a way that meets the desire of the Other—understood in Lacanian terms as "desire for the Other, desire to be desired by the Other, and especially desire for what the Other desires" (Žižek, *Violence* 87). The death drive sabotages this capacity. It is an illogical logic,

---

① In *The Ethics of Psychoanalysis*, Lacan links the figure of the mother to *das Ding*: "the maternal thing, of the mother, insofar as she occupies the place of that thing, of *das Ding*" (Lacan *The Ethics of Psychoanalysis*, 67).

a "true evil", according to Žižek, since it "makes us act *against* our own interests" (Žižek *Violence*, 87). An obvious example is Julien's excessive reaction to Mme de Rênal's letter denouncing him as a hypocrite and seducer of women. Rather than shooting her, he could have managed the situation more rationally, in keeping with his calculating ways.

The self-sabotaging logic of the death drive manifests itself in an earlier episode of the novel as well. During his stay in the theological seminary at Besançon, the atheist Julien adopts a new self that will act in "accordance" with the seminary model. As the narrator puts it, "His task was to create for himself a whole new character" (144) ["Il s'agissait de se dessiner un caractère de nouveau" (210)]. Julien's ideal of self-fashioning is tested when he fails to perform his new self appropriately—or more to the point, when he fails to act in accord with his self-interests. "At a dinner of clerics to whom the old priest had presented him as a prodigious scholar: he found himself babbling frantic praises of Napoleon. He strapped his right arm to his chest, pretended that he had dislocated it while shifting a tree trunk, and carried it in this painful position for two months" (20) ["à un dîner de prêtres auquel le bon curé l'avait présenté comme un prodige d'instruction, il lui arriva de louer Napoléon avec fureur. Il se lia le bras droit contre la poitrine, prétendit s'être disloqué le bras en remuant un tronc de sapin, et le porta pendant deux mois dans cette position gênante" (46)]. This self-imposed violence to the body serves as a corrective to his unruliness, to his libidinal investment in Napoleonic ideals. [1]

Julien's practices of self-discipline can be seen as an expression of Julien's life drive, meant to counter, if not tame, the death drive. They exemplify

---

[1] Julien's unruly emotions ironically can momentarily transform Julien the atheist into a fervent soldier of God. After having been moved by the display of religious conviction in a church, the narrator discloses Julien's inner thoughts: "At that moment he would have fought for the Inquisition, and *with full conviction*" (86, *emphasis added*) ["*En cet instant il se fût battu pour l'inquisition, et* de bonne foi" (134)]. Julien's affective dispositions—the unpredictability of his psychic attachments—threaten to disrupt the ideal of homeostasis.

what Foucault means by "ascetic practice", "an exercise of the self on the self by which one attempts to develop and transform oneself, and to attain to a certain mode of being" ("The Ethics of the Concern for the Self", 282). For Julien, the project of self-mastery—controlling and adequately channeling his energy—is a necessary condition for worldly success. This project of self-fashioning is indeed clearly indebted to Napoleon. Napoleonic liberalism endlessly fueled Julien's imagination. With his emphasis on meritocracy, Napoleon jolted the symbolic order of the aristocracy. He disclosed "the inconsistency and/or non-existence of the big Other—of the fact that there is no Other of the Other, no ultimate guarantee of the field of meaning" (Žižek *The Metastases of Enjoyment*, 200). Napoleon introduced contingency into history: one's social status was no longer determined by one's class rank or lineage: *one's (noble) birth was not destiny*. Julien believed that he could heroically overcome or transcend his socially given position. And he did.

But Julien's enthusiastic identification with Napoleon's will to power both follows and exceeds the dictates of the pleasure principle. Adopting a Napoleonic ethos gives Julien purpose, a way of navigating his social obstacles: the decision to seduce Mathilde is a case in point. Julien's successful seduction and sexual conquest of Mathilde both fulfills the pleasure principle and helps to secure for him a privileged place within the symbolic order, which, in turn, increases his opportunities to satisfy his drive for pleasure.① But, as the novel reveals, this same drive for pleasure can

---

① Julien's pleasure principle—in this case, the pleasure of (aristocratic) identity—ironically even overrides, at least momentarily, his attachment to Napoleon. After his genealogy has been "corrected" so that Julien's birth can be deemed noble, after the abbey Pirard hermeneutically reframes the function of old Sorel, repositioning old Sorel within the social order as someone who *merely* took care of Julien, Julien turns inward for evidence of his aristocratic selfhood: "Is it actually possible, he asked himself, that I might be the natural son of some aristocrat exiled among our mountains by *the terrible Napoleon*?" (360, emphasis added) ["Serait-il bien possible, se disait-il, que je fusse le fils naturel de quelque grand seigneur exilé dans nos montagnes par *le terrible Napoléon*?" (493)].

quickly metamorphose into a death drive. A cost-benefit outlook gives ways to erratic behavior and irrational outbursts. Julien's unruliness and the self-destructiveness that it unleashes point to the antagonistic logic of the death drive (*in him what is more than him*). Simply stated, there is *more* to Julien than his calculating self.

Julien's *kratophilia*, his love of power, is, as we have seen, indebted to the fantasmatic figure of Napoleon, which, in turn, be must contrasted with Julien's *kratophobia*, the fatigue from power that he experienced in his prison cell. I prefer the terms *kratophobia/kratophilia* to Hägglund's own dyadic formulation *chronophobia/chronophilia*, a theorization intended to displace the death drive. For Hägglund, "the co-implication of *chronophobia* and *chronophilia*" means that "the fear of time and death does not stem from a metaphysical desire to transcend temporal life. On the contrary, it is generated by the investment in a life that can be lost. It is because one is attached to a temporal being (*chronophilia*) that one fears losing it (*chronophobia*)" (Hägglund 9). The hermeneutic focus on the fear/love of time—Hägglund's subtle analysis of the self's ambivalent relation to temporal existence—purports to counter the Lacanian account of the death drive insofar as it questions not only the reality of wholeness (a return to *das Ding*) but the very desire for wholeness:

> The Lacanian reading stops short...of questioning the *structure* of the traditional narrative of desire. The fullness of pure joy or immortality is deemed to be an illusion, but the *desire* for such fullness is itself taken to be self-evident. Even while debunking the promise of fulfillment, the Lacanian account thus conforms to the conception of desire that has been handed down to us from the Platonic tradition: we are temporal, restless beings but desire to repose in the fullness/emptiness of timeless being. (Hägglund 152)

Yet Hägglund's dyad *chronophobia/chronophilia* does not adequately account for the question of power, for its lure and sublime negativity. It neglects power's intrinsic potential to repress *and* produce identities, as Foucault taught us,① and how this unruliness of power correlates with the operations of the death drive.

By contrast, whereasHägglund brackets power from his analysis, Jacques Rancière, who recently proposed his own "political" account of the novel in *Aisthesis*, brackets the vicissitudes of temporality, ignoring the ways *The Red and the Black* foregrounds what we might call a "politics of temporality", the way it makes power—and an ironic ambivalence toward it—constitutive of the structure of time itself. Rancière also turns to the ending of the novel, but draws out a radically different meaning, one that minimizes an engagement with its protagonist's death drive. In the solitude of his prison cell, Julian is no longer obsessed with transcendence; he becomes quite attentive to the present, beginning to associate happiness, "the sole happiness of feeling, the sentiment of existence alone", with idleness, "the pure enjoyment of reverie that subtracts him from time" (Rancière, *Aisthesis* 44). This form of idleness or *otium* is not laziness (the passivity of doing nothing) but a *willful* mode of resistance to the status quo, a withdrawal from the economy of ends and means and a relief from the restless gaze of Lacan's big Other.② For Rancière, Julien's moment of reverie short-circuits the logic

---

① As Foucault famously put it, "We must cease once and for all to describe the effects of power in negative terms: it "excludes", it "represses", it "censors", it "abstracts", it "masks", it "conceals". In fact, power produces reality; it produces domains of objects and rituals of truth" (Foucault *Discipline and Punish*, 194).

② "Such happiness can be summarized in a simple formula: to enjoy the quality of sensible experience that one reaches when one stops calculating, wanting and waiting, as soon as one resolves to do nothing" (Rancière *Aisthesis*, 44).

of plot, the narrative of cause and effect. ① It draws attention to moments of a-significations that are pregnant with alternative meanings (Tanke 136). In its depiction of this scene of happiness, Stendhal's novel reconfigures his readers' pre-existing horizons of intelligibility, disrupting the rigid order of things under the Bourbon Restoration. This process of reconfiguration defines for Rancière politics as such, politics as the struggle for "a new landscape of the possible" (Rancière *The Emancipated Spectator*, 103), as the unsettling of "the order of the visible and the sayable," as the questioning of the given "distribution of places and roles" (Rancière *Disagreement*, 29, 28). The novel's image of idleness—enjoying the simple pleasure of existence—reworks and expands our relation to the world, or what Rancière names "*le partage du sensible*", "the distribution/partition/sharing of the sensible" (Rancière *The Politics of Aesthetics*). For Rancière, the peaceful moment in the prison abolishes "the hierarchy of occupations" (Rancière *Aisthesis*, 48), reflecting a respite from the tiresome narrative of everyday existence, from what had structured and determined the meaning of every instance of Julien's life. But this does not mean that the politics of aesthetics that Rancière witnesses in Stendhal's novel is reducible to the individual, to Julien's happy state of solitude. Quite the contrary, it is not the self freed from society (a romantic cliché) that attracts Rancière, but the scene's universal appeal, its fundamental promise of shareability (with Mme de Rênal, with the reader, etc.). In other words, what *The Red and the Black* values is the idea of *a sensible moment beyond calculation, a sensation, in principle, open to all.* Its politics is one of equality: "Julien triumphs the moment he stops fighting, when he simply shares the pure equality of an emotion, crying at Madame de Rênal's knees" (Rancière *Aisthesis*, 44).

---

① "*Otium* is specifically the time when one is expecting nothing, precisely the kind of time that is forbidden to the plebeian, whom the anxiety of emerging from his condition always condemns to waiting for the effect of chance or intrigue" (Rancière *Aisthesis*, 46).

While Rancière is surely right to underscore the ways Julien's idleness troubles his society's hierarchies, its *partage du sensible*, his reading ignores the novel's ironic staging of its protagonist's epiphany. By diagnosing Julien's problem as fundamentally an external one, Rancière also downplays the complexities of Julien's subjectivity. The problem is thus: it is society's values and its logic of conquest that make Julien unhappy. So once Stendhal's Romantic hero recognizes what happiness truly is in the solitude of his prison cell, he becomes open to a different economy of enjoyment, one that makes equality axiomatic. But as Joseph Tanke points out, Rancière effectively minimizes the tragic outcome of Julien's epiphanic recognition: "His attainment of happiness is bound to extinction, in much the way that aesthetic happiness is purchased with the dissolution of the subject" (Tanke 140). Our reading pushes further the link between happiness and extinction by foregrounding Julien's *kratophobia*. His problem is not only without, it is also within. This is why readings of the novel that interpret Julien's refusal to fight at his trial, his choice to give up on his life of ambition, as constituting a self-destructive or suicidal act downplay the role of fantasy in the novel's ending. ① In its psychoanalytic sense, fantasy is more than a distortion of reality. It functions, as Alenka Zupančič puts it, as "a screen that covers up the fact that the discursive reality is itself leaking, contradictory, and entangled with the Real as its irreducible other side" (Zupančič 33). The authentic Julien who is preserved by the suicide is the fantasy that covers up the Real of Julien, his unruly excess. Again, reading the novel with an eye for irony, Julien's retroactive idealization of his moment with Mme de Rênal appears less a privileging of shareability and/as equality than a desire to contain his identity, to return to a past devoid of power, immune to the

---

① For Georg Lukács, Julien, lacking a political solution to his alienation, chooses suicide; he preserves his "mental and moral integrity from the taint of [his] time by escaping from life" (Lukács 73). Cf. Žižek *The Metastases of Enjoyment*, 200.

dynamic play of power—to the possibility of loss and corruptibility. Indeed, as Rancière himself suggests, equality is never affirmed in abstraction; this affirmation presupposes the presence of power, the asymmetrical and hierarchical structures of power.

At the same time, the death drive exacerbates this ambivalence toward power. *Kratophobia* and *kratophilia* are ironically intertwined in *The Red and the Black*, constituting two readings of the death drive; indeed, the novel dialecticizes the death drive, disclosing its creative and destructive facets. The negativity of its irony complicates any straightforward hermeneutic application of this drive. *Kratophobia* explains Julien's fatigue in playing the game of desire, and his misguided yearning for a state beyond power, a state of powerlessness. *Kratophilia* attests to the excess of Julien's unruly identity; it helps overcome his historical givenness but this excess always risks self-destruction, the sabotaging his interests. In both cases, Julien's symbolic self/selves are jeopardized. *Kratophobia* dreams of a return to the plenitude and comfort of the Imaginary, whereas *kratophilia* insists for its part on the productivity of power and on the unruliness of the Real.

Works Cited:

1. Brombert, Victor. *The Romantic Prison: The French Tradition*. Princeton: Princeton University Press, 1978.
2. Derrida, Jacques. *Archive Fever: A Freudian Impression*. Trans. Eric Prenowitz. Chicago: University of Chicago Press, 1996.
3. Derrida, Jacques. *The Post Card: From Socrates to Freud and Beyond*. Trans. Alan Bass. Chicago: University of Chicago Press, 1987.
4. Derrida, Jacques. *Rogues: Two Essays on Reason*. Trans. Pascale-Anne Brault and Michael Naas. Stanford: Stanford University Press, 2005.
5. Egginton, William. *Perversity and Ethics*. Stanford: Stanford University Press, 2005.
6. Fenichel, Otto. "A Critique of the Death Instinct." *The Collected Papers of Otto Fenichel: First Series*. New York: Norton. 1953. 363 – 72.
7. Foucault, Michel. *Discipline and Punish: The Birth of the Prison*. Trans. Alan

Sheridan. New York: Vintage Books, 1977.

8. Foucault, Michel. "The Ethics of the Concern for the Self as a Practice of Freedom." *Ethics: Subjectivity and Truth*. Ed. Paul Rabinow. New York: New Press, 1997. 281–301.

9. Freud, Sigmund. *Beyond the Pleasure Principle*. Trans. James Strachey. New York: Norton, 1961.

10. Freud, Sigmund. *Civilizations and Its Discontents*. Trans. James Strachey. New York: Norton, 1961.

11. Fromm, Eric. *Escape from Freedom*. New York: Henry Holt, 1969.

12. Fink, Bruce. *The Lacanian Subject: Between Language and Jouissance*. Princeton: Princeton University Press, 1995.

13. Hägglund, Martin. *Dying for Time: Proust, Woolf, Nabokov*. Cambridge: Harvard University Press, 2012.

14. Horney, Karen. *Our Inner Conflicts: A Constructive Theory of Neurosis*. New York: Norton, 1945.

15. Johnston, Adrian. *Time Driven: Metapsychology and the Splitting of the Drive*. Evanston: Northwestern University Press, 2005.

16. Johnston, Adrian. *Zizek's Ontology: A Transcendental Materialist Theory of Subjectivity*. Evanston: Northwestern University Press, 2008.

17. Lacan, Jacques. *Écrits: A Selection*. Trans. Alan Sheridan. New York: Norton, 1977.

18. Lacan, Jacques. *The Ethics of Psychoanalysis, 1959–1960, The Seminar of Jacques Lacan, Book VII*. Ed. Jacques-Alain Miller. Trans. Dennis Porter. New York: Norton, 1992.

19. Lacan, Jacques. *The Psychoses, 1955–1956, The Seminar of Jacques Lacan, Book III*. Ed. Jacques-Alain Miller. Trans. Russell Grigg. New York: Norton, 1993.

20. Laplanche, Jean. *Life and Death in Psychoanalysis*. Trans. Jeffrey Mehlman. Baltimore: Johns Hopkins University Press, 1976.

21. Lukács, Georg, *Studies in European Realism*. New York: Grosset & Dunlap, 1964.

22. Marcuse, Herbert. *Eros and Civilization: A Philosophical Inquiry into Freud*. Boston: Beacon Press, 1955.

23. McGowan, Todd. *Enjoying What We Don't Have: The Political Project of Psychoanalysis*. Lincoln: University of Nebraska Press, 2013.

24. Petrey, Sandy. "Julienned Identities." *Approaches to Teaching Stendhal's The Red and the Black*. Eds. Dean de la Motte and Stirling Haig. New York: MLA, 1999. 121–29.

25. Prendergast, Christopher. *The Order of Mimesis: Balzac, Stendhal, Nerval, Flaubert*. New York: Cambridge University Press, 1986.
26. Rabaté, Jean-Michel. *Crimes of the Future: Theory and its Global Reproduction*. New York: Bloomsbury, 2014.
27. Rancière, Jacques. *Aisthesis: Scenes from the Aesthetic Regime of Art*. Trans. Zakir Paul. New York: Verso, 2013.
28. Rancière, Jacques. *The Emancipated Spectator*. Trans. Gregory Elliott. New York: Verso, 2009.
29. Rancière, Jacques. *Disagreement: Politics and Philosophy*. Trans. Julie Rose. Minneapolis: University of Minnesota Press, 1999.
30. Rancière, Jacques. *The Politics of Aesthetics: Distribution of the Sensible*. Trans. Gabriel Rockhill. New York: Continuum, 2004.
31. Reich, Wilhelm. *Character Analysis*. New York: Farrar, Straus and Giroux, 1972.
32. Stendhal. *Red and Black*. Trans. Robert M. Adams. New York, Norton, 1969.
33. Stendhal. *Le Rouge et le noir*. Paris: Flammarion, 1964.
34. Stavrakakis, Yannis. *Lacan and the Political*. New York: Routledge, 1999.
35. Tanke, Joseph J. "Why Julien Sorel Had to Be Killed." In *Rancière Now: Current Perspectives on Jacques Rancière*. Ed. Oliver Davis. Cambridge: Polity, 2013. 123 – 42.
36. Tenenbaum, Elizabeth Brody. *The Problematic Self: Approaches to Identity in Stendhal, D. H. Lawrence, and Malraux*. Cambridge: Harvard University Press, 1977.
37. Žižek, Slavoj. *The Metastases of Enjoyment: Six Essays on Women and Causality*. New York: Verso, 1994.
38. Žižek, Slavoj. *The Parallax View*. Cambridge: The MIT Press, 2006.
39. Žižek, Slavoj. "The Rhetorics of Power." *Diacritics* 31, 1 (2001): 91 – 104.
40. Žižek, Slavoj. *Tarrying with the Negative: Kant, Hegel, and the Critique of Ideology*. Durham: Duke University Press, 1993.
41. Žižek, Slavoj. "Unbehagen and the Subject: An Interview with Slavoj Žižek." *Psychoanalysis, Culture & Society* 15 (2010): 418 – 28.
42. Žižek, Slavoj. *Violence*. New York: Picador, 2008.
43. Zupančič, Alenka. "Realism in Psychoanalysis." *Jep European Journal of Psychoanalysis* 32 (2011): 29 – 48.

叶维廉与英、美新批评

于 伟[*]

Abstract　The new criticism in Britain and United States is one of the modern western literary critical theories that Wai-lim Yip contacted earlier, and had deepest influence on his poetics theory construction. When Wai-lim Yip lived in Hong Kong, he initially knew the new criticism by reading poetry and poetic works of 1930s and 1940s; During the study in Taiwan, under the guidance of Tsi-an Hsia, he studied on the new criticism meticulously and translated some poetics of the representatives of new criticism such as Eliot, etc. In the meantime, he recognized the defects of the new criticism methodology and criticized them, and by combining the new criticism with Chinese traditional poetry criticism he put forward his own poetics proposition, then achieved the development of new criticism theory. The New criticism profoundly affected the literary criticism and poetics studies of Wai-lim Yip, and his poetic theories brightly reveal the new criticism traits .
Keywords　New Criticism ; Wai-lim Yip's Poetics; Tsi-an Hsia; perfect critics

---

[*] 于伟，中国人民大学比较文学与世界文学专业博士研究生。

英、美新批评与中国现代文学、诗学渊源颇深：一方面是新批评的重要人物如艾·阿·瑞恰慈（Ivor Armstrong Richards）、威廉·燕卜荪（William Empson）等数次到清华大学、北京大学、西南联合大学等中国高校讲学，一方面是中国知识分子如朱自清、曹葆华、叶公超、钱锺书、卞之琳等人的介绍、翻译新批评理论，并将之运用到诗歌研究与诗学建构之中。在英、美新批评影响下形成的中国现代文学与诗学的精神，虽然由于政治风云的变幻，在大陆被中断了，但其火种却被为数不多的诗人与学者以及大量的三、四十年代诗歌作品传播带到了港台地区，并再度获得了生机与发展。叶维廉在香港与台湾的文学活动、诗歌创作以及诗学研究，就是在这样的氛围中进行的。叶维廉与英、美新批评派理论的关系，代表了港台一批学者成长的心路历程，值得探究。

一 叶维廉与新批评的接触

叶维廉出生于1937年的广东中山，此时的中国风雨飘摇，此时的中国大学正为躲避战火纷纷内迁、重组，此时的瑞恰慈已经完成他在清华大学的教学，在平津地区开始基本语的工作；此时的燕卜荪乘火车刚刚来到中国，到长沙临时大学报到，并随校迁往云南昆明，任教西南联合大学，靠记忆背出莎士比亚剧作作为学生教材，讲授英国文学；此时的翻译家曹葆华选译的《现代诗论》[①] 与伊人翻译的《科学与诗》[②] 已经出版并广为流传。瑞恰慈与燕卜荪播撒下的新批评的种子，几年间便在中华大地上开枝散叶，培养出了一大批优秀的诗人和学者，并结出累累硕果。此时的叶维廉虽尚年幼，但当其长大成人，在香港如饥似渴地读诗、在台湾接受本科及研究生教育时，手之所触，目之所及，几乎都

---

① 曹葆华选译的《现代诗论》，收录了四个曹葆华认为是划时代的批评家的文章，这个人分别是梵乐希（今译瓦雷里）、瑞恰慈、艾略特、墨雷（John Middleton Murray）。
② 伊人翻译的《科学与诗》，是瑞恰慈的重要作品。

是新批评理论影响之下的作品与成果。

叶维廉在《我与三四十年代的血缘关系》一文中，详细记下来他与三四十年代诗歌作品的接触：

> 我猛读"五四"以来的作品，在十五六岁便开始，我从贫穷的农村流落到香港，忧国思家，那些书最能给我安慰……当时读到的作品，使我作为一个新文学作家的血缘未曾中断，在感受上、语言上、思潮上有一种持续的意识，这是我的幸运。但我那时很穷，书买不起，只有猛抄，抄了五大本；五大本中抄得最多的诗人包括冯至、卞之琳、何其芳、王辛笛、穆旦、梁文星、杜运燮、袁可嘉、艾青、臧克家、梁遇春、曹葆华、戴望舒、废名、陈敬容、殷夫、蒲风、罗大刚、袁水拍等。①

在这串长长的中国现代诗人的名单里，我们发现了太多新批评的精神苗裔。他们内化了新批评理论与精神的诗歌作品，深刻影响了叶维廉的诗歌创作与诗学追求，"这些人对我的语态、意象、构思都曾有过相当的影响，我在日记里写诗的时期，曾多方实验过他们的句法"②，并且王辛笛对诗歌"气氛的掌握"、冯至"依着自然事物出现的弧线捕捉其在现象中的意义"、卞之琳"保持事物的现在发生性"以及艾青、穆旦"以戏剧场景代替散文直述"的诗歌写作技巧，更是成了叶维廉日后批评诗歌的重要标准与诗学建构的重要概念。

不仅如此，叶维廉不止一次地告诉我们："李健吾、朱自清、曹葆华、李广田通过现代理论对诗的肌理及文字艺术的剖析"③，为其提供了后来中西比较诗学研究的"新理论实验的果实，让我们后来者沉思"：

---

① 叶维廉：《我与三四十年代的血缘关系》，《中外文学》1977年第12期。
② 同上。
③ 叶维廉：《比较诗学序》，《叶维廉文集》（第1卷），安徽教育出版社2003年版，第22页。

李广田的《诗的艺术》、刘西渭的《咀华集》及朱自清的《新诗杂谈》，他们对于文字的艺术，真可谓是一丝不苟地耐心追问，对文字、意象、意义全盘地推敲，就以他们对卞之琳的《白螺壳》的反复讨论，那种用完全开放的心胸以求诗的意义得以全面的放射，好细的玄思，好深刻的同情，又在拥抱冯至十四行所开放的平凡而深寓哲理的世界时，是我们觉得情感的凝练，而我那时顿觉狂涛之外还有缓缓溢出的动人的丰满。①

朱自清先生等人的诗论作品，是在新批评的影响下写成的，作品中所运用的"解诗"、"论诗"的方法和理论，都是这些学者们在传统诗文批评的理论基础上，借鉴吸收新批评的理论资源而苦心建构起来的。朱自清等前辈学者融合现代西方新批评与传统解诗方法而来的解诗学理论，对叶维廉后来的比较诗学与中国诗学研究，产生了极大的影响。

叶维廉于1955年离开香港，来到台湾，先后进入台湾大学外文系、台湾师范大学英语研究所学习。从时间上看，直到1963年离开台港赴美深造，叶维廉在台湾生活、学习长达8年之久。在台湾的学习与生活，创作与研究，既成就了叶维廉诗人的美名，也为叶维廉日后的诗学研究打下了坚实的基础。在叶维廉台湾求学期间，故事很多，但对其在文学创作与研究方面产生了重大影响的，是夏济安先生对他的指引与教导：

今天我特别要突出一位把我从香港开始对文学的、诗的、理论的、美学的追寻的诸种意绪拨引至一种明澈向度的老师，夏济安老师。②

夏济安曾任教于西南联合大学外语系，1950年经香港辗转到台湾，

---

① 叶维廉：《我与三四十年代的血缘关系》，《中外文学》1977年第12期。
② 叶维廉：《回忆那些克难而丰满的日子——怀念夏济安老师》，载柯庆明主编《台大八十，我的青春梦》，台湾大学出版中心2008年版。

1959 年赴美，在台湾大学外语系任教将近 10 年。然而，在这短短的不到 10 年的时间里，夏济安却"成就了'近人无出其右'的文化志业，对于战后台湾的文学研究和创作，产生深远影响"。[①] 概而言之，夏济安的成就有二，一是将大陆新批评运动的火种带到了台湾，并通过创办《文学杂志》、引进台大课堂、举办文学沙龙等形式广为传播，使得台湾的文学创作与学术研究为之面貌一新；二是为台湾文坛发掘培养了一大批优秀的青年作家与学者，诸如白先勇、朱乃长、刘绍铭、王文兴、陈若曦、李欧梵、叶维廉等人，"无不受过他的启发而努力开拓文学艺术、批评精神的领域"[②]。

关于夏济安对他成长的影响，叶维廉回忆说：

> 说夏济安是个好老师是不够的。他当时教我们"英国文学史"，他驰骋纵横于西方文学的空间，令人神往……他教的小说是小班，他每页都挑出"用字问题"，一步一步带我们品尝"风格"形成的过程，对一个创作者而言，最为有用……他在《学生英语文摘》上的名著选读分析，往往在用字上提供几种不同的写法，并说明每种写法所代表的语态与风格……他对文字的准确性的认识和写作风格与方法的确定，后来通过《文学杂志》来推广，不遗余力，影响至巨。其中两篇文章：《两首坏诗》和《一则故事、两种写法》最脍炙人口。

> 但我个人得益最多的还不是在教室内，而是在温州街他那书堆积如山到没有坐立地步而不到十方尺的斗室。他对我们这些求知欲强的学生真是另眼相看，来者不拒，与我们聊，不停地把他收到的新书（包括当时美国正在盛行的 The Well-Wrought Urn——新批评

[①] 梅家玲：《夏济安、〈文学杂志〉与台湾大学——兼论台湾"学院派"文学杂志及其与"文化场域"和"教育空间"的互涉》，《当代作家评论》2007 年第 2 期。

[②] 叶维廉：《回忆那些克难而丰满的日子——怀念夏济安老师》，载柯庆明主编《台大八十，我的青春梦》，台湾大学出版中心 2008 年版。

代表作品）——从桌上桌下床上床下翻出来给我们看。①

正是在夏济安先生的影响下，叶维廉选定了新批评为其文学批评与翻译事业的起点，他将自己文学批评与文学翻译的目标，瞄准在 T. S. 艾略特这一英美新批评的灵魂性人物及其《荒原》上，并以 The Poetic Method of T. S. Eliot 为题目，完成硕士学位论文。在论文写作期间：

> 夏老师介绍的两本书：勃鲁克斯的 Modern poetry and Tradition（《近代诗与传统》，笔者按）和 The Well-wrought Urn: Studies in the Structure of Poetry（《精致的瓮：诗歌结构研究》，笔者按）是我经常参看的书，也就是说我用的就是"新批评"的方法。②

叶维廉用新批评派的研究方法研究新批评派大诗人艾略特的诗歌作品，这事听着就很有意思。

当然，叶维廉在港台生活、学习期间，与新批评接触的机会还有很多，比如海外学者陈世骧教授 1958 年前后来台湾大学文学院的几次重要讲演和在《文学杂志》上发表的几篇重要文章，比如《中国诗之分析与鉴赏示例》、《中国诗歌中的自然》等，都是将新批评的观念与方法应用到中国古典诗歌分析中的经典案例；再比如在叶维廉的周围，台港的不少诗论家也都专注在新批评的阐述上，比如吴鲁芹、季红、李英豪等人。

叶维廉在港台时期对新批评的接触，深刻影响了他的文学研究与诗学建构，以致他后来离开台湾，来到美国普林斯顿大学攻读博士学位时，其博士论文的选题，也仍然与新批评有关，他的博士论文选题是谈庞德《华夏集》对中国古典诗歌的翻译。埃兹拉·庞德，这一带有传奇色彩的美国诗人，现在一般被追认为新批评派的远祖，"他对美国诗

---

① 叶维廉：《为友情系舟》，《叶维廉文集》（第 9 卷），安徽教育出版社 2002 年版，第 62 页。
② 叶维廉：《回忆那些克难而丰满的日子——怀念夏济安老师》，载柯庆明主编《台大八十，我的青春梦》，台湾大学出版中心 2008 年版。

歌语言技巧的极端关注和自称取法自中国的'象形文字论',呼应了现代文论对语言研究的重视"。①

二 叶维廉对新批评的译介

夏济安曾在1957年发表在《文学杂志》里的一篇文章中说,把英、美现代文学批评介绍到中国来,不是一件容易的事情:

> 二十世纪英美批评家的一大贡献,可以说是对于诗本身的研究……研究诗的文字……批评家重要的方法是"字句的剖析"(explication of texts)。批评家孜孜不倦的企图从几个字或几行诗里找寻出诗人的魔法和诗的艺术的奥秘。……这种介绍工作是困难的……要介绍英美的新批评,需要一位精通中英两文,他同时对于写诗和批评理论都有修养,这样的人才是难得的。②

夏济安对精通中英两文人才的呼吁,以及因叶维廉对三四十年代诗人、理论家诗风余绪的寻索和在诗歌创作与翻译上的追求而对他青睐有加,并在对叶维廉"庭训"中流露出的殷切希望,大大启发与激动了叶维廉年轻的心。于是,他开始立志做新批评的译介者了,他选择的诗歌翻译与文学研究对象,就是新批评的直接开拓者与诗人T. S. 艾略特。叶维廉精研艾略特诗歌与诗论的成果,是他的硕士论文《艾略特方法论》(T. S. Eliot: A Study of His Method, 1960),原文是用英文写成的,后来经作者用中文改写,而成如下几篇文章《〈艾略特方法论〉序说》、《艾略特的批评》、《静止的中国花瓶——艾略特与中国诗的意象》、《〈荒原〉与神话的应用》等,同时,叶维廉还将《荒原》翻译成中文,于1961年发表在诗

---

① 赵毅衡:《重访新批评》,四川出版集团四川文艺出版社2013年版,第8页。
② 夏济安:《两首坏诗》,《夏济安选集》,辽宁教育出版社2001年版,第89页。

刊《创世纪》第 16 期上。

叶维廉对艾略特的译介与研究，可以从两个方面来看：第一，是叶维廉对艾略特文学批评观点的介绍与研究，第二，是叶维廉对艾略特诗歌的翻译与运用新批评的方法对其诗歌的研读与批评。

叶维廉对艾略特批评理论的介绍，是分成诗人论、批评家论两个部分进行的。根据上述叶维廉的几篇研究文章，概括复述如下：

在诗人论方面，第一，是诗人之成长为诗人，必须要经历的过程。"这个过程是对于宇宙之'原'，对于'永久的'、'超脱时间的'、'属于精神的'事物之深探与浅出。这些事物的'真质'即存在于传统的过去，亦存在于因袭的现在。"① 第二，是对艺术家使命的界定。"艺术家的使命并不在于留恋过往，他的使命是以新的秩序重行建设与调整那'真实'的过去。换言之：艺术家必须以不断比对过去与现在的办法去获得对现代世界的意识。"② 第三，是对诗人个人才华个性的抹杀。作为一个诗人，"他必须在旧传统中的所有材料中创造一个新的传统；他必须活用所有的个人经验来表达人类经验中的共通的基本真质。""每一个诗人必须挣扎努力去'促使其个人私心的痛楚化作丰富的、奇异的、具有共通性的和泯灭个性的东西'。"③ 第四，是强调"艺术的组合"为诗之尺度。诗心之唯一的工作是："使原来是混沌不整、片段的各种分歧的经验混为一些新的组合"，"找出一个能包罗其所感应的分歧多样的经验综合之统一基形，一个能'保运极大变化及繁复性'的骨骼"，从而促成"一切情绪作有秩序的展露"。④ 第五，是诗之意义与诗之音乐的不分性。"一首'音乐性'的诗必具'声音'之'音乐模式'以及'意义'之'音乐模式'，而往往二者是合一不分的。"⑤ 诗之音乐性，不能仅关注诗之字的声律之悦耳，而且还要能够通过字之声

---

① 叶维廉：《艾略特的批评》，《叶维廉文集》（第 3 卷），安徽教育出版社 2002 年版，第 49 页。
② 同上书，第 50 页。
③ 同上书，第 52 页。
④ 同上书，第 42 页。
⑤ 同上书，第 57 页。

律将隐藏于意识之下的事象提升到表面，从而使每一个字都更丰富更有力。第六，是诗之语言。一个民族的诗应从日用语中取得生命而同时能因此赋予日用语新的生机。一个单字或一个片语之是否能美并不依靠该字该语所包含的意义，而要视其应用是否得当，是否能使整首诗产生暗示力量。第七，是诗之体式。艾略特说诗中无自由。在艾氏看来，最自由的诗都有某种"简单节奏的魔灵"在其帷幕后面活动。韵文的生命应存于"对规则的不断逃避与不断认可之间"，艾氏的自由诗就是在这样的努力下产生的，一种中和的风格，不太现代亦不太古旧。第八，是关于诗之难懂。"为了求得暗示力量，诗中省去某些读者常见或预期的事物"①，是叶维廉特别强调的艾氏对诗之难懂的看法之一。这种被艾氏称为"压缩的方法"的诗歌表达策略，也正是他诗之方法的注脚。这种方法会使诗歌产生强大的暗示力。叶维廉认为，这种"压缩的方法"，与中国古典诗歌的运思与创作极为相似。

在批评家论方面，第一，是对其之前的批评家的批判。批判他们或过于抽象，或过于印象化，或太注重私人生活，或太过博学，或太狭义地注重道德观念的批评理论与方法。第二，宣明文学批评的目的。"每一种真正的批评必指向创造"，"它设法在艺术家的努力中求得与创造的一种结合"。"它的目的是以比较或分析的方法对作品的阐述与趣味的修正"②。第三，完美批评家的准则。"批评家因其有用而变得重要，因他'能吸收现代艺术所引起的问题，并设法用过去的力量将之加以解决'。""对过去的文学重新审视、估定，并使之安排在一个新的秩序中"，"使读者更加熟知他们所知道的，使他们更能以新的感受去了解过去的经验"③。

叶维廉对艾略特诗歌的解读与阐述，也是在两个方面展开的：

其一，就像叶维廉在《艾略特的批评》一文的开头所说的：

  许多诗人曾写下不少颇具规模的文学理论，成为他们自己的诗

---

① 叶维廉：《艾略特的批评》，《叶维廉文集》（第3卷），安徽教育出版社2002年版，第57页

② 同上书，第63页。

③ 同上。

最好的辩解；艾略特就是这么一个诗文并著的诗人。因而，我们要衡定他的诗的价值，可以深入到他的批评文字中，找出他对诗的一些基本观念。①

叶维廉在《〈荒原〉与神话的应用》一文中，显然是运用艾略特自己的诗学理论和方法对《荒原》进行了解读。艾略特在《论但丁》一文中，强调对诗歌的解读，必须"从诗之原委及结果中，发掘出一个架构来——亦即是促成'一切情绪作有秩序的展露'的方法"。② 而在《论乔伊斯的〈尤利西斯〉》的文章中，艾略特提出了用"神话的方法"——把现代生活的事件与古代神话的事件相连或并置——做构架来组合现代零碎复杂的经验，从而在同时解决了结构和意义问题后，把原是琐碎的受时空限制的现代事件呈现出永久的意义。叶维廉也正是运用神话的方法，"把和《荒原》一诗有关的主要神话架构分条简述，然后再把诗中现代生活事件联着印证看"③，从而破解了《荒原》难读难懂的神话。无独有偶，叶维廉在《静止的中国花瓶——艾略特与中国诗的意象》一种，也同样运用了艾略特提出的"压缩的方法"对艾氏的诗进行了读解，并获致了独特的审美体验。

其二，是叶维廉引入了平行研究的方法，对艾略特的诗歌与中国诗中的相似点进行比较研究。在叶维廉看来，作为世界文学主流之一的中国诗，其实就是艾略特理想中的诗：

那种使"可解"与"不可解"的事物融会，能"延长静观的一刻"使"一连串的意象重叠或集中成一个深刻的印象"的诗，"真诗的暗示性是包围着一个熠亮、明澈的中心之灵气，那个中心

---

① 叶维廉：《艾略特的批评》，《叶维廉文集》（第3卷），安徽教育出版社2002年版，第48页。
② 叶维廉：《〈艾略特方法论〉序说》，《叶维廉文集》（第3卷），安徽教育出版社2002年版，第40页。
③ 叶维廉：《〈荒原〉与神话的应用》，《叶维廉文集》（第3卷），安徽教育出版社2002年版，第82页。

与灵气是不可分的"。①

艾略特在玄学派诗人那里找到了达致上述理想诗的办法：压缩的方法——隐藏诗中的"链环"或说明的联系的文字，使一连串的意象重叠或集中成一个深刻的印象。受此启发，叶维廉联想到了中国古典诗歌拒绝一般逻辑思维及文法分析，省略联结媒介，以使诗歌意象并置的特点，从而在艾略特诗与中国古典诗之间展开了平行研究。两相烛照之下，中国古典诗歌的特质更加清晰，而艾略特诗歌为达致理想诗的意象独立，以及由此而来的诗歌含义的多义性、暗示性及纯粹性效果而采用的语言策略也更加明晰：使惯用文法的某些联结媒介变得含糊或使之压隐不显和使联结媒介变成过渡语，消解这些媒介的建设作用。通过这样的平行研究，叶维廉将新批评"文字的剖析"的诗歌解读策略进行了充分的运用，在诗的艺术的发掘与诗人魔法奥秘的找寻中，增加了对诗本身的智识。

叶维廉对艾略特诗学的译介及对其诗歌的阐释，在给港台文学研究带来重要影响的同时，也丰富了自身的理论知识，并使其明确了自身的诗学追求。

三 叶维廉对新批评理论的发展

艾略特对完美批评家准则的界定，夏济安先生对新批评家的热切寻求，使得"如何成为一个称职批评家"的问题久久萦绕在叶维廉的心间。艾略特说：

> 批评就必须有明确的目的；这种目的，笼统来说，是解说艺术作品，纠正读者的鉴赏能力……批评活动只有在艺术家的劳动中，与艺术家的创作相结合才能获得它最高的、真正的实现。……比较

---

① 叶维廉：《静止的中国花瓶——艾略特与中国诗的意象》，《叶维廉文集》（第3卷），安徽教育出版社2002年版，第65页。

和分析是批评家的主要工具……但必须谨慎使用……比较和分析只要把尸体放到解剖台上就成；而阐释则始终必须从容器内取出身体的各种部分并按原位把他们拼装。①

夏济安说：

大凡批评家须具备两条件，一曰见识，二曰说理的功夫，而学问还在其次。……见识是知觉趣味的问题，说理的功夫则是把经验转化为文字的问题。中国过去的批评家中，眼光锐利、见解卓绝的人不少，但是条分缕析，把道理一步一步说清楚的很少。②

就此问题，叶维廉在夏济安的启发下，在精研艾略特诗论的基础上，研究并批评了以 I. A. 瑞恰慈和威廉·K. 维姆萨特为代表的新批评派代表人物的理论之后，提出了自己的理论主张。

在叶维廉看来，在新批评之前，批评一首诗或一篇小说大略有两种处理方法：

其一为 Author-psychology，即所谓的 intentional fallacy，即从诗人的用心、背景、历史、思想、哲学、技巧、心理……来推断及鉴定而同时供出标准……其二为 Reader-psychology，即所谓的 Affective fallacy，从读者的反应来归纳出一些标准。最代表此种批评的是 I. A. Richards，William Empson……③

这两种批评均受到新批评派的批评，维姆萨特与比尔兹利合作，分别在1946年和1948年，发表题为"意图谬见"和"感受谬见"的学术文章，对此进行清算。在维姆萨特看来，以上两类文学批评，无论是从作品与作者的关系之间做探讨，还是从作品与读者之间的关系上做探讨，都离开了艺术作品本身的存在性，都是在艺术品之外做功夫。叶维

---

① T. S. 艾略特：《批评的功能》，载托·斯·艾略特、陆建德主编《传统与个人才能：艾略特文集·论文》，卞之琳、李赋宁等译，上海译文出版社2012年版。
② 夏济安：《两首坏诗》，《夏济安选集》，辽宁教育出版社2001年版，第97页。
③ 叶维廉：《叶维廉致李英豪信（1963）》，《东华汉学》2014年第19期。

廉指出，在大力推翻了上述两种文学批评方法之后，新批评派理论家提出了第三种研究方法："主张诗（艺术）的本体论，要求确立'艺术的对象'，美学的核心"，"确立诗的独立主格"，眼光关注作品，切断作品与作者、读者的关系，做"本体论批评"，对一部作品中文字和修辞成分间复杂的相互关系和歧义（多重含义）做细致的分析、解说与阐释，或曰细读。

台湾学者郑蕾著文指出，"叶维廉……对新批评亦非仅引入或奠基，而是具有建设性的借鉴和发展"①，笔者同意她的观点，他对新批评理论的借鉴和发展，明显地体现在他对新批评派"本体论批评"的批评方面：

>　　认为诗有一个 Art-object，是诗的本体论，原是颇有可为的一个开始，但诗的本体为何物？没有一个人说的上来，Wimsatt 用了 concrete universal，substantive level 诸名词，也只知道有那么一个东西，究竟诗是用文字写的，但 Wimsatt 已将洋葱层层剥去（包括上述 intentional 及 affective 的一切外在因素）……②

在叶维廉看来：

>　　持第一第二种方法论的人，其误在未把最终的现实（在中国的语汇中即"自然"）与人之间，其与各现象之间的互为持续的真义，所以把艺术品的对象及其涉及的因素都未能做到"各得其所"的处理，是故才有待用价值之误立（譬如以作者的人格取代艺术品的本身评价，以作者的社会观取代艺术品的构成意味等等）。持第三种方法论的人，其误在二元论的二分法，把自然与诗，人与诗，情感与思想，刺激与理智等都截然二分，才会产生许多至上主

---

① 郑蕾：《叶维廉与香港现代主义文学思潮》，《东华汉学》2014 年第 19 期。
② 叶维廉：《叶维廉致李英豪信（1963）》，《东华汉学》2014 年第 19 期。

义，所以无法将艺术很顺序的置诸自然之中。①

既然第一第二种以及新批评派提供的第三种批评方法，都不是完美的批评方法论，那么完美的批评方法应该往何处寻呢？如何才能建构出既取三种批评之长，而又能避其短的完美批评呢？叶维廉应是从20世纪三四十年代的诗论家如朱自清等人那里找到了灵感。据研究，当年朱自清先生进入新诗文本批评领域的实践时，已经开拓出一条中西批评理论相结合，并融会出新的批评方法的路子：

> 当朱自清进入新诗文本批评领域的实践，接受瑞恰慈、燕卜荪理论的影响，并与古典诗歌批评观念相呼应，酝酿并产生了一个系统的中国现代解诗学的理论与实践，其结出的理论果实，就是我们所熟知……的《新诗杂话》一书中那些富有创造性的"解诗"学文章。②

而对《新诗杂话》，当时的叶维廉是非常熟稔的。于是，叶维廉也将自己的眼光投向中国传统的诗话、诗论。带着新批评的理论视角与批评眼光，叶维廉很快发现由于中国古典诗论家因往往带有"艺术是自然的一部分，生自自然而后归自然，成为一个不可分割的个体"的观念，所以，

> 在理论上，很少用细分法，而要一语道出诗与自然之互相成长与重合，反而直截了当对艺术（诗）的本身而发……内容与技巧之间的一种探讨，完全在艺术品的本身，不在艺术品以外无关连的事物之上，而应该涉及的事物，只要"各得其所"，毫不放过。③

---

① 叶维廉：《批评的职守》，《东华汉学》2014年第19期。
② 孙玉石：《朱自清现代解诗学思想的理论资源——四谈重建中国现代解诗学思想》，《中国现代文学研究丛刊》2005年第2期。
③ 叶维廉：《批评的职守》，《东华汉学》2014年第19期。

而这应该正是叶维廉苦苦寻找的最理想的批评方法！但正如夏济安所说，中国的古典批评家眼光锐利，但却诗论零散，语焉不详。叶维廉应如何处理这多少已触及批评的核心，但因所言过简而给人带来遗憾的古典文学批评呢？他又应该如何确立自己理想的文学批评方法论？

叶维廉在分析了中国古典诗论的优长与缺憾之后，提出了自己的诗论主张：

> 一个称职的批评家，如果要对作者的匠心有公正的印证，对艺术品有适当的确立，对读者有激发的启悟，我以为，自然会逃避了上述的弊端。换句话说：在确立艺术品的存在性时，绝不能在对二分的概念下处理，不扫除诗的外在因素，但在引用时，必要"各得其所，各安其位"。①

叶维廉说：

> 诗是一种生长，固有其独存性（本体），亦有其外在性（如树之有枝有叶），其气势、幅度、格调……及至自然，往往在其组织上见之。②

所以，理想的批评家，不能只做美的欣赏者或思想的惊叹者，他还应该在对美与思想做适量的分析之后，做出适度的传达。

> 他起码应该说："诗人如何如何利用了什么什么使其独有的美（还需说明如何的独有）和气势（还需说明是怎样不同的气势）……而获得了最佳、最适当、最自然的展露和生长。"在适当的地方应该用到的外在因素，毫不放口（但一定要"各得其所"，

---

① 叶维廉：《批评的职守》，《东华汉学》2014 年第 19 期。
② 同上。

不可强求与附会）。①

很显然，叶维廉的文学批评方法论，是在充分分析西方批评方法与中国传统诗论的优劣的基础上，总结提取出来的。这种既关注艺术品（诗）本体，又不忽略相关的外在因素，既能获致艺术品（诗）的弦外之音，又始终不离艺术品（诗）本身，既带有新批评理论印记，又蕴含中国传统诗话特色的文学批评方法论的提出，对叶维廉日后的文学批评研究，产生了深远的影响。可以说，他后来在文学批评、比较诗学以及中国诗学诸领域所取得成果中，都深深打上了这种文学批评方法的烙印。

结　语

新批评理论是叶维廉较早接触的西方现代文学批评之一。因为叶维廉与1930、1940年代文学的血缘关系，我们可以将这种接触追溯到叶维廉在香港读诗、写诗期间，而此时的叶维廉只有十六七岁的年纪。叶维廉与新批评有意识的接触和对他们作品的研读，是在他1955年进入台湾大学外文系之后，这期间有夏济安老师的指点与引导，有他自身强烈的学术研究兴趣的内驱。这两个时期，叶维廉对新批评理论的接触与研究，为叶维廉赴美之后的文学研究与诗学建构奠定了扎实的理论基础。当然，对诗学研究与诗学理论建构有着强烈动机和兴趣的叶维廉，在之后的漫长的研究岁月里，由于又接触与吸收了其他的批评大师与批评理论的影响，如艾布拉姆斯的四要素说，海德格尔的现象学哲学，伽达默尔的诠释学思想等等，并有意识地将这些理论资源吸收到自己的诗学理论体系之中，从而使得他的诗学理论体系更具特色、更丰满，更有成就，但通过我们的分析，也可以明显的发现，新批评的理论与方法，已经化入叶维廉诗学理论体系之中，并已成为他诗学体系的牢固支撑和

---

① 叶维廉：《批评的职守》，《东华汉学》2014年第19期。

有机组成部分。

主要参考文献：

1. I.A. 瑞恰慈等：《现代诗论》，曹葆华译，商务印书馆 1937 年版。
2. 夏济安：《夏济安选集》，辽宁教育出版社 2001 年版。
3. 叶维廉：《叶维廉文集》（1—9 卷），安徽教育出版社 2002 年版。
4. T.S. 艾略特：《传统与个人才能：艾略特文集·论文》，卞之琳、李赋宁等译，陆建德主编，上海译文出版社 2012 年版。
5. 赵毅衡：《重访新批评》，四川出版集团、四川文艺出版社 2013 年版。

朗费罗《人生颂》传播到中国的追问与思考[*]

柳士军[**]

Abstract *A psalm of life* written by Longfellow is the earliest poem translated in China. According to QIAN Zhongshu views and QIAN Niansun ideas, we put forward to a new study vision that is "understanding of sympathy" to interpret *a psalm of life*, and the paper argues that it is dispersed in China is not an accident but the inevitable result because *a psalm of life* contains rich philosophical thoughts, and religious feelings and elegant aesthetic charm.

Keywords *A psalm of life*; Longfellow; philosophical thoughts; religious feelings; elegant aesthetic charm

引言

钱锺书先生在《汉译第一首英语诗〈人生颂〉及有关二三事》中提出：西洋的大诗人很多，第一个介绍到中国来的偏偏是朗费罗。朗费

---

[*] 本文属于国家社会科学基金重点项目"'世界文学史新建构'的中国化阐释"（12AZD090）和江苏省普通研究生科研创新计划资助项目（CXZZ12-0794）的阶段性成果。

[**] 柳士军，信阳师范学院副教授，文学博士，主要研究方向为西方文艺理论与中西诗歌比较。

罗的好诗或较好的诗也不少,第一首译为中文的偏偏是《人生颂》,那可算是文学交流史对文学教授和批评家们的小小嘲讽或挑衅了!历史上很多——现在就也不少——这种不很合理的事例,更确切地说,很不合学者们的理想和理论的事例。这些都显示休谟所指出的,"是这样"(is)和"应该怎样"(ought)两者老合不拢。钱先生的观点至少有两个含义:《人生颂》未必是一首上乘诗歌;其次,朗费罗不应该是第一个译介到中国的英语诗人。钱念孙先生也在《文学交流的盲目性和自觉性》中指出:"在不同民族文学开始接触时,多半互相不摸底细,常常是某个掌握两种语言的人,随便碰到一部作品翻译出来,这部作品也就在彼此文学互输中扮演先行者的角色了。就我国输入西方文学而言,如前面说的美国作家郎费罗的《人生颂》是第一首汉译英语诗。"① 我们认为无论是钱锺书还是钱念孙先生的观点都有可商榷之处,以"拿到篮里便是菜"的思想来解释《人生颂》在中国的撒播与流传特别值得追问、思考。文学作品的流传不是在街道上偶遇别人丢失的一个物件,拾起来之后洋洋得意的鼓吹就能张扬开来的,每一篇能广为流传的作品都是作者的呕心沥血之作。

《人生颂》的译者最初是一位传教士英吉利驻华公使威妥玛翻译成汉语,董恂根据威妥玛的译文再次翻译。随后,在中国翻译界先后有杨德豫、穆旦、黄新渠、黄杲炘、屠岸、施颖洲(菲律宾人)、苏仲翔、江冰华、刘守兰、周永启、李云起、秦希廉、朱孝愚、顾子欣、张梦井、杨传纬、王晋华等翻译家与英美文学研究学者积极翻译此诗,拓展了该诗歌的流布。从读者接受美学视野考察朗费罗的《人生颂》,它确实满足了读者的"期待视野",文本中留下了足够的空白处和不确定性,具有召唤性,也具备了一部经典诗歌所具有的哲学情思、宗教情怀、美学情韵,而不是"在当时可能只是威氏的一次无心之作,权当是一个外国人在当时闭关锁国、沟通匮乏的清政府中尝了尝鲜"②那么简单。

---

① 钱念孙:《文学交流的盲目性和自觉性》,《江汉论坛》1988年第10期,第45—49页。

② 孙莹:从《人生礼赞》译本看经典之流变,《齐齐哈尔大学学报》(哲学社会科学版),2011年第8期,第141—145页。

一 《人生颂》蕴含的哲学情思

诗歌与哲学作为意识形态在本质上是相通的，都是以语言作为交流媒介的人类思想的升华。我们谈到诗歌的哲学情思更多强调的是哲理，是人生的感悟，不是体系的哲学思想。朗费罗的《人生颂》蕴含的哲学情思是在诗歌创作活动中将生活的"真"理传递给他的读者，给予读者启迪和愉悦："不要在哀伤的诗句里告诉我：'人生不过是一场幻梦！'灵魂睡着了，就等于死了，事物的真相与外表不同。"朗费罗用简单的语言，以对话的方式告诉我们最基本的道理：灵魂的高贵远胜于躯体的存在。在判断事物的时候，不要被外表迷住了双眼，要用智慧的眼睛将这个世界看个明明白白，真真切切。"文学研究者不必去思索像历史的哲学和文明最终成为一体之类的大问题，而应该把注意力转向尚未解决或尚未展开充分讨论的具体问题：思想在实际上是怎样进入文学的……只有当这些思想与文学作品的肌理真正交织在一起，成为其组织的'基本要素'，质言之，只有当这些思想不再是通常意义和概念上的思想而成为象征甚至神话时，才会出现文学作品中的思想问题。"[①] 朗费罗诗歌关注人生、社会和命运，通过诗歌真与美的旋律，传递自己人生感悟的哲学情思。

诗歌与哲学是近邻，这一深刻的认识体现在尼采、叔本华、克尔凯郭尔的作品中，他们都在自己的哲学思想中赋予诗歌至高的地位。但是反对诗歌中蕴含哲学的诗人依然很多：朗费罗时代的爱伦·坡认为："诗歌的终极目的是真理"是值得怀疑的；"调和诗歌的浓油和真理的清水"是令人难以置信。[②] 英国的济慈也反对诗歌中的哲学："那种一望而知的旨在对我们发生作用的诗歌"，声称"我们不愿被人强行灌输

---

① [美] 韦勒克、沃伦：《文学理论》，刘象愚等译，生活·读书·新知三联书店1984年版，第128页。

② [美] 雷纳·威勒克：《近代文学批评史》（第三卷），杨自伍译，上海译文出版社1997年版，第188页。

某种哲学。"① 朗费罗《人生颂》坚持哲学入诗的探索是因为作为浪漫主义诗歌的创作者，有更多的精神导师在支持他：华兹华斯在《〈抒情歌谣集〉第二版序言》中声称"诗歌是一切知识的起源与终结——它像人的心灵一样不朽"。他提出诗歌是哲理的情思的闪现，而且"不是个别的和局部的真理，而是普遍的和有效的真理"。② 柯勒律治认为诗歌天才在于"思想的深度和活力"："从未有哪个伟大的诗人，不是同时也是一个渊博的哲学家。因为诗歌就是人类的全部知识、思想、激情、情感、语言的花朵和芳香。"③ 雪莱的《为诗辩护》进一步肯定诗歌的哲学性：诗歌"既是知识的圆心又是它的圆周；它包含一切科学，一切科学也必须溯源到它"。④ 朗费罗在创作时蹈袭英国诗歌的伟大传统，充满哲学情思的《人生颂》面世即获得读者的喜爱，具体的哲学思想如下：(1) 人生是真切的！人生是实在的！人生的归宿绝不是荒坟。(2) 我们命定的目标和道路是行动，超越今天，跨出新步。(3) 这颗心，勇敢坚强。(4) 人生如世界是一片辽阔的战场，做一个威武善战的英雄了。(5) 行动吧——趁着活生生的现在。(6) 伟人的生平启示我们：我们能够生活得高尚。(7) 任何命运要敢于担待。(8) 不断地进取，不断地追求。(9) 要善于劳动，善于等待。

对生命的哲学思考是朗费罗诗歌创作的动力，《人生颂》蕴含了朗费罗的人文情怀与充满理性的哲学思考。"朗费罗为他的世界带来了生的快乐和勇气。他的诗充满了一种乐观向上的精神。他生活在美国蓬勃向上的发展时代，坚忍不拔，知难勇进，成为他的诗作的主旋律……哲理性强，语言浅易轻灵而富了情韵，因而具有永恒魅力。"⑤ 朗费罗诗歌具有鲜明的时代烙印，它再现了特定时代的特殊心理：生命意识。

---

① [美]雷纳·威勒克：《近代文学批评史》（第三卷），杨自伍译上海译文出版社 1997 年版，第 257 页。
② W. Wordsworth, "Preface to the Second Edition of Lyrical Ballads", in W. J. B. Owen ed., *Wordsworth's Literary Criticism*, London: Routledge & Kegan Paul, Ltd., 1974, p. 81.
③ S. T. Coleridge, *Biographia Literaria*, London: J. M. Dent, 1906, p. 171.
④ [英]雪莱：《为诗辩护》，缪灵珠译，见《十九世纪英国诗人论诗》，人民文学出版社 1984 年版，第 153 页。
⑤ 常耀信：《精编美国文学教程》（中文版），南开大学出版社 2005 年版，第 102 页。

《人生颂》表现出来的执着的人生态度也能够给人哲理的启发，哲理情思渗透在字里行间。有学者认为没有哲学意蕴和哲学情思的艺术形象的画图，只能是音乐中的口号、绘画中的招贴、舞蹈时的解说词、书法中的美术字、文学作品中的主题直白，不能称其为艺术。这便是我们呼吁艺术不要"席勒化"要"莎士比亚化"的初衷。[①] 正是朗费罗诗歌中的哲学情思蕴含的生命意识挽救了一个孩子的生命：朗费罗传记中记载一个美国学生悲观厌世，想自杀，读了《人生颂》后，热爱生命，重新燃起生命的激情；钱锺书先生指出传说歌德《少年维特的烦恼》导致了好多人自杀，不知道是否有批评家从这个角度去衡量两位诗人的优劣。而今思之，是朗费罗《人生颂》中的生命意识挽救了那位美国学生，少年维特并没有意识到没有生命的爱情是虚无的，自杀本来就是荒谬的选择。由此看来，《人生颂》在朗费罗生前译成汉语传到中国获得中国读者的重视，并非是阴差阳错。

哲学问题思考较多的就是人生的问题。朗费罗在《人生颂》中对人生给予了尽可能的想象：如"也只如擎鼓，闷声擂动着，一下又一下，向坟地送丧"。既然我们每个人都要死亡，那就勇敢地面对，乐观地接受它，无所畏惧，保持人性的高贵。如"也许我们有一个弟兄航行在庄严的人生大海上，我们的事迹将会是鼓舞他们的榜样"。朗费罗积极的人生态度，奋发有为的进取精神和百折不挠的昂扬斗志塑造一个朝气蓬勃、积极向上的青年人形象。《人生颂》里包含了19世纪美国人乐观务实的思想，崇尚荣誉与英雄行为的个人主义精神。惠蒂埃所说的"这九节简单的诗的价值超过了雪莱、济慈和华兹华斯的全部梦想"，有些夸张了，但是，《人生颂》宣扬人的奋斗情思，却有普遍的持久的意义。从宏观的视野来思考，诗歌的乐观精神对美国人性格的塑造起到一个巨大推进作用。

"大哲学家与大诗人往往心灵相通，他们受同一种痛苦驱逼，寻求着同一个谜的谜底。庄子、柏拉图、卢梭、尼采的哲学著作放射着经久不散的诗的光辉……在西方文化史上，我们可以发现一些极富有诗人气

[①] 朱广贤：《文艺创造三位一体论》，中国文联出版社2007年版，第248页。

质的大哲学家，也可以发现一些极富有哲人气质的大诗人，他们的存在似乎显示了诗与哲学一体的源远流长的传统。"① 朗费罗告诉我们生活的魅力是永恒的，人生的哲学精神应该充满希望。"朗费罗诗歌的最大的虚构的失败在于它不能探索生活的黑暗面以及生活肮脏的一面。失败的原因部分在于他的性情。天生的严谨的性格往往是朗费罗与生活的身体的心灵的丑陋达成妥协，尽管这些丑陋的东西让他很痛苦。虽然他曾经有过神经沮丧的一段时间，但是他认为这些只是过渡现象，不可能引起人的本性、命运发生理智问题。人生经历是不能弥补的，信仰是不能提供的。"② 我们认为这些观点都是对朗费罗的误读而产生的。不能探索人性的阴暗和丑陋，不书写人性的异化也许正是作为贵族的朗费罗要回避的。当朗费罗在创作这首《人生颂》时，妻子去世不久，他自己仍在与忧郁症作顽强搏斗。《人生颂》是美国理性主义、理想主义的产物，它塑造了朗费罗自己，也表达了美国人的人生哲学思想。"他还写过许多在任何时代、任何国家都可以传唱的歌谣和抒情诗，其中最著名的是《生命礼赞》，虽然描写的是一些平常生活中所发生的平常事，但作者却赋予了它深刻的思想和优美的旋律，因而生命礼赞成为了一部传世之作。"③ 朗费罗以隽永的诗的形式创造了美国人共同的文化遗产，并在这个过程中培育一代诗歌读者。

二 《人生颂》萦绕的宗教情怀

我们在朗费罗的诗歌理论中重点讨论了朗费罗诗歌中的宗教诗学的建构。这里我们仅仅讨论《人生颂》的宗教情怀。所谓宗教情怀，就是"在终极需要激发下所产生的一种超越世俗的、追寻精神境界的普

---

① 周国平：《诗人哲学家》，上海人民出版社1998年版，第5页。
② Hirsch, Edward L. *Henry Wadsworth Longfellow*, Minneapolis: University of Minnesota Press, 1964. p. 21.
③ [美] 约翰·阿尔伯特·梅西：《文学史纲》，孙青玥等译，陕西师范大学出版社2006年版，第337页。

泛情怀"①。我们认为宗教情怀不是宗教的情怀，而是宗教般的情怀，"深沉的宗教情怀更多的是意味着对人性、人生、生命以及人类共享的精神价值理念怀有一种敬畏感、神圣感"②。人生拥有宗教的情怀并不是要求我们做一个宗教徒，而是说我们要有如宗教般的虔诚来生活。"此一自由不是任意专断，也不是随心所欲，而是终极必然……那远古显示给我们的暗示，正是神祇的语言。诗人的话语就是倾耳听得神祇的暗示，再把它们传达给自己的民众……神思存在就这样与神祇的足迹联系起来……诗人才能断定人是什么，人在何处安置自己的此在，才能诗意地栖居于这片大地。"③ 海德格尔认为宗教是人类孤独灵魂的栖息地，它既容纳了我们的疲惫心灵，也塑造了我们的一代文学艺术。那些处在宗教情怀之中的人，何尝不是处在审美境界中的高人雅士？

朗费罗《人生颂》的宗教情怀从字面上看是他引用了《圣经》的语句，如：你来自尘土，归于尘土（Dust thou art, to dust returnest）；结合原诗语境，朗费罗认为人的躯体迟早会腐化，而人的灵魂不会。天堂、地狱都是自己的选择，在您离开人世的时候，一切都已判断。那些相信上帝的人非常热爱自己的生命，不会选择死亡来逃避人世间的孤独，因为生命是上帝所赐予的，他们心中憧憬的天堂往往就是他们继续生存的理由。这让我想起西方人在葬礼上的祈祷：无所不能的主耶稣基督，我们将这去世的姊妹的灵魂交托主，把她的身体葬在地里，叫土归土、尘归尘。我们靠主耶稣基督，确信圣徒必要荣耀复活，享受永生。愿主赐福与她、保全她。愿主面上的荣光普照她，赐恩典与她。愿主看顾她。赐平安与她，从现在直到永远。阿门！在这里我们感悟的是对生命的厚爱与坚守，不必计较得失，坦然面对生活。诗歌中"胸中有赤心，头上有上帝！"（Heart within, and God o'er head!）这一诗行告诉读者生命回归本原，做事公正之意。借助圣经的语言对诗歌的传播既是一

---

① 贺绍俊：《从宗教情怀看当代长篇小说的精神内涵》，《文艺研究》2004年第4期。
② 同上。
③ 伍蠡甫、胡经之编：《西方文艺理论名著选编》，北京大学出版社1985年版，第586页。

个推动力，也是诗歌本身的要求，在朗费罗的时代是最好的一种创作方式。

《人生颂》的宗教情怀还是一种蕴含在字里行间人性的终极关怀，它是神圣的，是一种宗教体验，"是个人觉得一定要对之作严肃的、庄重的反映，而不诅咒或嘲弄的这么一种原始的实在"。① 朗费罗同时代的叔本华在其说学中提出人的最大罪恶就是：他诞生了。不管我们认为人生是悲剧还是喜剧，朗费罗认为人生都是值得一活的，因为只要活着，我们就能够感知这个世界，这就是为什么我们生存的意义。加缪说世界、人、人的自由是荒谬的，荒谬的人追求着荒谬的自由。然而，活着就是对荒谬的反抗，生命的意义就存在于此。这是对生命的一种负责任的行为，是一种宗教般的情怀。这种情怀需要两个条件：第一：对生命的激情，这种激情是内在的。第二：对生命的敬畏；人永远是渺小的，知道自己的渺小，才知道敬畏。人的生命仅有一次，它有不可复制的美，因敬畏而更加热爱，因热爱更加珍惜。《人生颂》蕴含的宗教情怀也正是如此：博爱、悲天悯人、终极关怀，一个国家，一个民族，乃至整个人类，倘无宗教情怀，是很难维系生存的。人类的灵魂已经受到无数次理论的震撼与打击：无论是哥白尼的日心说，达尔文的进化论，还是尼采的"上帝已经死亡"，弗洛伊德的性力说都导致一切建立在尊严、高尚、向上的哲学、道德观发出了断裂之声。无论是艺术家还是山野匹夫，一旦踏进宗教的大门，他们都将变得伟大、崇高、完全、神圣起来。"艺术与宗教一牵手，便生出了人类最崇高、最伟大、最神圣、最完全的艺术宗教情绪。宗教与艺术如孪生，紧紧携手于人类生命的母体。宗教期待着艺术的滋润，艺术更渴望宗教的营养；宗教从诞生之日起就打着与艺术同生共死的恋母情结。"② 也许，艺术家只有怀有对艺术的朝圣的情怀和使命才能获得高山仰止的名声吧。

---

① [美]威廉·詹姆士：《宗教经验种种——人性之研究》，唐钺译，商务印书馆 2002 年版，第 31—36 页。

② 朱广贤：《文艺创造三位一体论》，中国文联出版社 2007 年版，第 305 页。

三 《人生颂》流溢的美学情韵

所谓的美学情韵就是诗人在创作活动中美的因子的显现。《人生颂》的美学情韵通过其乐感和修辞来表现。

英国批评家佩特在《文艺复兴论》中提出一切艺术都以逼近音乐为指归。克罗齐说："一切艺术都是音乐。"① 在中国《毛诗序》中记载："情动于中而形于言，言之不足故嗟叹之，嗟叹之不足故咏歌之，咏歌之不足，不知手之舞之足之蹈之也"。由此观之，诗歌与音乐、舞蹈最初是三位一体的混合艺术。相对而言，诗歌与音乐最亲近。钱谷融先生说："诗绝不是与音乐无关之物。任何不重视，甚或否定诗的音乐性的意见，都是错误的，都将不断地碰壁。"② 那些只能靠号叫与呼喊、自白的句子，我们可以称其为诗，绝不可划为歌的范畴。我们认为诗歌一词所要具备的两个因素：既可吟诵，也可歌唱。朗费罗《人生颂》就是这些特色的典范。

朱光潜说过诗是具有音律的纯文学。韵是"诗歌中的一种语音上的回声，更确切地说，是一种音位上的匹配。尾韵是英语中最常见的一种押韵：两个单位（通常是两个单音节词）匹配原音音位（通常是重读音节），词尾的辅音音位都相同，只有起始音位不相同，……这种押韵形式往往出现在格律诗诗行的末尾，出现在诗行中间的则称为行间韵。"③ 由此可知，尾韵与行间韵是最为重要的韵律形式。《人生颂》用四步扬抑格写成，以两音为单位，两音中第一音强，第二音弱，韵律工整，全部呈"ABAB"型。每节四行，共九节，三十六行，诗句长短适中，无突兀变化。扬抑格体现诗人情感跳跃，愉悦，快速、深刻、勇

---

① 吕进：论诗的文体可能，《吕进诗论选》，西南师范大学出版社1995年版，第115—116页。
② 钱谷融：《谈戴望舒——〈戴诗解读〉序》，《文艺理论研究》1995年第3期，第40页。
③ 胡壮麟、刘世生：《西方文体学词典》，清华大学出版社2004年版，第281页。

敢。朗费罗主要运用的尾韵中韵脚的单数行用阴韵，宽厚凝重，委婉平和；双数行用阳韵，音韵清灵，短促有力，如第一小节中第一、第三行的"numbers"、"slumbers"，第二、第四行的"dream"、"seem"。头韵也在《人生颂》中得到了淋漓尽致的使用：第1行；第3行；第4行；第6行；第8行；第17行；头韵的运用使全诗节奏感强，音韵美与意境美达到了和谐。行间韵在诗的第15行"muffled drums"；第22行"Let the dead past bury its dead"；第25行"Lives of great men all remind us"；第26行"We make our lives sublime"；第32行"take heart again"等多次使用，使诗行之间意义相连，语气连贯，富有节奏感。

朗费罗除了利用韵律之外，还采用了修辞增强诗歌美的情感。诗人在形象地感受、形象地思考之余，形象地表达诗情画意是不可或缺的。朗费罗在此诗歌中运用的修辞主要如下：

排比：在行文之中构成排比增强了气势和渲染力，增强节奏感、旋律美。如第5行、第9行；其他如第17、18行，第19、20行，第35行。

比喻：古人所谓"状埋则理趣浑然，状事则事情昭然，状物则物态宛然"。[陆九渊：《敞寻稿略》（二）]这就是比喻的修辞作用。诗人在第4节中运用明喻And our hearts...like muffled drums, are beating? 第5节中使用隐喻的手法把世界比作战场，把人生比作临时的营站，劝人们要在奋斗中做英雄好汉，打好人生这场仗。同时又用明喻告诫人们别像默默的牛羊任驱赶，不要在人生路上没有方向。

典故："明理引乎成辞，征义举乎人事，乃圣贤之鸿漠，经籍之通矩也。"（《文心雕龙·事类》）典故证明某一意义引用有关事例，是圣贤的大文章、经书的通用规范。朗费罗在诗歌的第2节 Dust thou art, to dust returnest（你来自尘土，归于尘土），具体地说，它出自《圣经·创世纪》第三章。第4节中 And our hearts, though stout and brave? Still, like muffled drums, are beating? Funeral marches to the grave 与博蒙特的《幽默的中尉》中第3幕第5场的 Our lives are but our marches to the grave.（人生不过是走向坟墓的进行曲）相同。而在第3节中 Art is long, and time is fleeting（学艺需日久，时光飞如箭）出自希腊希波克拉底的《格言集》第一章:"The life so short, the craft so long to learn"(生命如此短促,学艺却如此久长)。这些典故的运用言简意赅,文约旨丰,增强了诗歌的语言艺术效果:精炼、形象、生动。

结 语

英国诗人柯勒律治说:"Prose is words in their best order, poetry the best words in the best order."笔者认为朗费罗的诗歌除了符合柯勒律治这两个条件之外,还有以上我们讨论的宗教情怀、哲学情思、美学情韵。所有的艺术形式,几乎都是由第一要素的"哲学情思"的"道"之理,第二要素的"宗教情怀"的"学"之理,第三要素的"美学情韵"的"术"之理,这样一种客体、主体、载体三位一体的"情"与"理"的相互交融状态构成的。没有哲学的"真"理,就没有艺术的"美"理;没有艺术的"美"理,就没有宗教的"善"理;哲学的"真"理、宗教的"善"理、艺术的"美"理层递循环互为因果的三位一体关系,构成了艺术家之所以确定进行艺术创造活动的全部理由。[①]《人生颂》作为经典不仅是文学层面上的一种变化,更是关乎于民族文化的一种变革。当然在此文中仅就《人生颂》这一具体的经典译本进行分析,尚属浅显。而真正从形而上的文化战略高度来探讨经典的译介与流变还有待更深入、更系统的研究。

朗费罗的佳作昂扬感奋,强调人的进取精神和自我完善的潜能。他告诉我们,人生旅途犹如攀登高峰,重重险阻就在眼前;但人生值得去探索,只有不怕惊险,知难勇进,才能领悟它的神奇。[②] 朗费罗的诗歌对传统的关注、对大我的拥抱、对内外两面的重视等,貌似"以不变应万变",潜意识中却不失为一种持守、一种既向前又向后的追寻。我们期待朗费罗研究的回归如同期待文学的变化趋势回转一样的重要。

---

① 朱广贤:《文艺创造三位一体论》,中国文联出版社2007年版,第243页。
② 聂珍钊:《外国文学史》,华中师范大学出版社2010年版,第254页。

历史已化作过眼烟云，钱先生在20世纪80年代的论文观点没有获得及时的回应，也许是历史的缘故吧。1930年，陈寅恪先生在对冯友兰《中国哲学史》（上册）的审查报告中，提出了"了解之同情"观念："凡著中国古代哲学史者，其对于古人之学说，应具了解之同情，方可下笔。"所谓"了解"，即研究者"对其持论所以不得不如是之苦心孤诣，表一种之同情，始能批评其学说之是非得失，而无隔阂肤廓之论"。我们正是按照陈先生的思想重新阐释朗费罗《人生颂》，结论发现《人生颂》蕴含丰赡的哲学情思、博大的宗教情怀以及高雅的美学情韵，在中国的流布不是偶然而是必然的结果。本文也权作是对钱锺书先生提出问题的思考。荷尔德林说："让诗人像燕子一样自由高飞吧。"那就让我们的思绪伴随诗人的翅膀一起翱翔在思维的天空中，追寻诗人智慧的倩影。

附：朗费罗《人生颂》原作

Tell me not, in mournful numbers,
Life is but an empty dream!
For the soul is dead that slumbers,
And things are not what they seem.
Life is real—life is earnest—
And the grave is not its goal:
Dust thou art, to dust returnest,
Was not spoken of the soul.

Not enjoyment, and not sorrow,
Is our destin'd end or way;
But to act, that each to-morrow
Find us farther than to-day.

Art is long, and time is fleeting,
And our hearts, though stout and brave,
Still, like muffled drums, are beating
Funeral marches to the grave.

In the world's broad field of battle,
In the bivouac of Life,
Be not like dumb, driven cattle!
Be a hero in the strife!

Trust no Future, howe'er pleasant!
Let the dead Past bury its dead:
Act-act in the glorious present!
Heart within, and God o'er head!

Lives of great men all remind us
We can make our lives sublime,
And, departing, leave behind us
Footsteps on the sands of time.

Footsteps, that, perhaps another,
Sailing o'er life's solemn main,
A forlorn and shipwreck'd brother,
Seeing, shall take heart again.

Let us then be up and doing,
With a heart for any fate;

Still achieving, still pursuing,   Learn to labor and to wait.

主要参考文献：

1. [美] 韦勒克、沃伦：《文学理论》，刘象愚等译，生活·读书·新知三联书店 1984 年版。
2. [美] 雷纳·威勒克：《近代文学批评史·第三卷》，杨自伍译，上海译文出版社 1997 年版。
3. [美] 威廉·詹姆士：《宗教经验种种——人性之研究》，唐钺译，商务印书馆 2002 年版。
4. [美] 约翰·阿尔伯特·梅西：《文学史纲》，孙青玥等译，陕西师范大学出版社 2006 年版。
5. 朱广贤：《文艺创造三位一体论》，中国文联出版社 2007 年版。
6. 聂珍钊：《外国文学史》，华中师范大学出版社 2010 年版。

世界文学视野中的性别写作研究:以凌叔华、曼斯菲尔德和伍尔夫为例

林晓霞[*]

Abstract Interpreting the relationship between female writers and world literature, this paper mainly discusses about how the author's gender may influence the form of narration. The author is exploring the system by comparing a Chinese female writer, Ling Shuhua, with the British, Katherine Mansfield and Virginia Woolf.

Keywords World Literature; Feminism; Woolf; Mansfield; Ling Shuhua

在全球化时代的世界文学语境下,"文学遭到解构之后形成的空白,由文学理论提供的经典填补了进来。假如我们不再把我们的大部分关注焦点集中在小说、诗歌和戏剧经典上,也不再要求我们的学生研究这些经典、不再期望我们的读者了解这些经典,那么,我们就得另谋他就。所以,人们说,我们需要像朱迪斯·巴特勒(Judith Butler)、米歇尔·福柯(Michel Foucault)、爱德华·W. 萨义德(Edward W. Said)、佳亚特里·斯皮瓦克(Gayatri Spivak)这样的理论家们为我们提供一个共同的对话基础,来取代莎士比亚、华兹华斯、普鲁斯特和乔伊斯在我

---

[*] 林晓霞,福建师范大学副教授,文学博士,主要研究领域为女性主义批评和世界文学。

们头脑中占据的位置"。① 当今著名的世界文学学者大卫·达姆罗什（David Damrosch）以上提到的这几位理论家中，有女权主义者或是在性别研究方面颇有建树的，所以这也使得性别研究在当今的世界文学中占有一席之地。受此启发，笔者在此想以凌叔华、曼斯菲尔德和伍尔夫为例，探讨性别写作与世界文学之间的关系。

一 伍尔夫与女性主义

女性主义理论家巴特勒认为，"女性主义理论假设存在有某种身份，它要从妇女这个范畴来理解，它不仅在话语里倡议女性主义的利益和目标，也构成了一个主体，为了这个主体追求政治上的再现。"②在英国小说的版图里，女性的领土通常被描述为是包围沙漠四周的山，即：奥斯汀的山峰、勃朗特的峭壁、艾略特的山脉、伍尔夫的丘陵。"英国女性主义主要包括三个派别：自由女性主义、社会主义女性主义（亦称马克思主义女性主义）、激进女性主义。""在20世纪的语境中，激进女性主义者对于女同性恋主义（lesbianism）推崇备至，她们指出，女同性恋主义不仅仅是一种自由选择，它还是女性主义最基本的政治实践。"③ 在涉及性别写作时，我们就不可避免地要去关注女性的社会地位。在斯皮瓦克看来，"妇女与其他无权的阶层一样，在公民社会里从未获得过完全的公民权和个体独立存在的权利：换句话说，从未成为过国家的一等公民。"④ 创建女性文学的"文学性"，这样的企图或被视为现代性的压迫症状显现，这样的压力从20世纪初就加诸中西方女性作

---

① David Damrosch, "Would literature in a Postcanonical, Hypercanonical Age", in Haun Saussy ed., *Comparative Literature in an Age of Globalization*, Baltimore: The John Hopkins University Press, 2006, p. 44.
② 朱迪斯·巴特勒：《性别麻烦》，宋素凤译，上海三联书店2009年版，第1—2页。
③ 王卫新等：《英国文学批评史》，上海外语教育出版社2012年版，第250页。
④ 佳亚特里·斯皮瓦克：《流散之新与旧：跨国世界中的女女》，载佳亚特里·斯皮瓦克《从解构到全球化批判：斯皮瓦克读本》，陈永国等主编，北京大学出版社2007年版，第286页。

家身上。女性的视角更为特殊，不管是东方还是西方的。"传统的'经典'绝大多数出自那些已经过世的、欧洲的、男性的、白人（Dead White European Man，常常缩写为 DWEM）作家之手，而许多非欧洲的、非白人的、女性的作家却常常被排除在这个名单之外"，"这种激进的经典观大多是从女性主义、后殖民主义、西方马克思主义立场出发的，其政治和意识形态的意味相当强烈。"[①] 达姆罗什则有意识地扭转男性中心主义这一局面，他在给哈佛大学比较文学系博士研究生上的"世界文学教学大纲"这节课，讲到"文选目录表选及介绍"时强调，《朗文世界文学选》（*Longman Anthology of World Literature*，2004）F 卷收入 90 位作家的作品，其中 20 位是女性，包括收录了弗吉尼亚·伍尔夫的《一间自己的房间》（*A Room of One's Own*）等作品，并把她视为现代主义的代表；把张爱玲的《老搭子》（*Stale Mates*）列在性别这一栏。[②] 由此可见，这两位现代女性作家在世界文学中的重要地位，伍尔夫以"自己的力量、失败及困惑成为女性主义批评的主要建筑师与设计者"，[③] 是无可争议的女性主义和现代主义的表率。

尽管 20 世纪英国女性主义运动风起云涌，和欧洲大陆以及美国分庭抗礼，但在女性主义批评方面，英国则要远远落后于美国和法国，[④]而在 20 世纪英国女性主义批评的论坛上，除了伍尔夫之外，其他批评家鲜有人知。作为一个世界级的作家，伍尔夫的著作和一年一度的伍尔

---

① 刘象愚：《经典、经典性与关于"经典"的论争》，载《中国比较文学》2006 年第 2 期，第 55 页。

② 引自笔者在 2013 年 4 月 22 日聆听戴姆拉什在哈佛大学给比较文学系博士研究生上的"世界文学教学大纲"（World Literature on the Syllabus）这节课，讲到"文选目录表选及其介绍"（Selected Anthology Tables of Contents and Introductions）的授课内容。

③ 拉尔夫·科恩编：《文学理论的未来》，中国社会科学出版社 1993 年版，第 153 页。

④ 女性主义批评家，美国有肖尔瓦特（Elaine Showalter, 1941—）、吉尔伯特（Sandra Gilbert, 1936—）、古芭（Susan Gubar, 1944—）、雅各布斯（Mary Jacobus）、米列特（Kate Millet, 1934—）、莫伊（Toril Moi, 1953—）、斯皮瓦克（Gayatri Chakravorty Spivak, 1942—）等一批杰出的女性主义批评家，法国有波伏娃（Simone de Beauvoir, 1908—1986）、克里斯蒂娃（Julia Kristeva, 1941—）、西苏（Helen Cixous, 1937—）、伊里格里（Luce Irigary, 1932—）等女性批评的领军人物。参见王卫新等著《英国文学批评史》，上海教育出版社 2012 年版，第 250—251 页。

夫研讨会证明了有如此多的不同文化和不同语言背景的国外读者深深地喜欢她。作为一个生活在有教养、讲文明的社会里的作家典范，伍尔夫为民族主义和世界主义之间的对立指出了解决方案：一个作家要小心翼翼地去跨越一道宽大的，也许是不可逾越的鸿沟，这道鸿沟分割着这里和那里、分割着已知世界与未知世界、分割着国内和国外、分割着我们的语言和文化的关系与他们的语言和文化的关系。伍尔夫在《三枚金币》中宣称："作为一个女人，我没有国家；作为一个女人，我不想有国家；作为一个女人，我的国家就是整个世界。"① 作为一位敏锐、深刻、个性独特和富有远见的作家，伍尔夫曾经在关于小说的一篇随笔中写道："在1910年10月或左右，人的性情变了。"那个月，伍尔夫"观看了主要在伦敦展览的印象派艺术的开幕式，印象派艺术的特点使伍尔夫认为艺术有能力改变人性"。② 作为一个在维多利亚时代受过良好教育的并有着专业的先锋艺术家意识的作家，伍尔夫努力消除人们对非正统文学文体的偏见，让日记体、书信体写作走向文学殿堂，并通过书信指导中国作家凌叔华撰写英文自传《古韵》。显然，伍尔夫跨越狭隘的民族主义的宽大的胸襟和作为作家的睿智、前瞻性、现代性，也是当今全球化的世界文学所需要的品质。著名的艺术家克莱夫·贝尔认为伍尔夫的思想是世界性的，"没有几个达到了伍尔夫身上那种世界性和世界大同主义"。③ 在全球化的时代，"由于民族—国家疆界的模糊，民族/国别文学的研究也不可能像过去那样壁垒森严，它常常自觉或不自觉地'越过边界'，进入到比较文学的疆域，或在理论上上升到总体文学的高度，或从民族/国别文学的案例出发讨论具有普遍意义的总体文学和世界文学问题"。④ 若要明确民族作家与世界文学的关系，则必须

---

① Virginia Woolf, *Three Guineas*, New York: A Harvest Book · Harcourt' Inc., 1966, p. 109.

② David Damrosch, general ed., *Longman Anthology of World Literature*, New York: Longman, 2009, p. 172.

③ Jane Marcus, *Art and Anger: Reading Like a Woman*, Columbus: Ohio State Universitiy Press, 1988, p. 76.

④ 王宁：《民族主义、世界主义与翻译的文化协调作用》，载《中国翻译》2012年第3期。第5页。

从民族作家与世界作家的关系入手，既要找到共性，也要从不同立场审视其差异性，这也是我们当今审视中国作家凌叔华和英国作家曼斯菲尔德、伍尔夫的意义所在。

二 在世界文学中互相交织的女性作家：凌叔华、曼斯菲尔德和伍尔夫

全球化语境下的世界文学经典是一种流动的经典建构，其"典范"作品是在一种动态的民族文化理解中铸就的。美国当代三大权威选集《朗文世界文学选集》（*Longman Anthology of World Literature*）、《诺顿世界文学选集》（*Norton Anthology of World Literature*）、《贝德福世界文学选集》（*Bedford Anthology of World Literature*）分别增加收入女性作家作品的比例。以20世纪为例，朗文（F卷）收入20位女作家作品（共90位作家）；诺顿（F卷）收入17位女作家作品（共70位作家）；贝德福（6卷）收入18位女作家作品（共88位作家），这是前所未有的。特别值得一提的是，伍尔夫的作品"不仅重叠出现在美国世界文学的三个权威选集（朗文、诺顿、贝德福）里"，同时也是"唯一一位出现在主要的同性恋/女同性恋文集"，[①] 使她成为世界文学中关于性和性别研究的主要作者。

伍尔夫和曼斯菲尔德都是女同性恋的推崇者和实践者。克里斯蒂娃认为，中国"第一批女性激进分子自然是那些出身于有闲阶级、受过日本和欧洲教育的年轻小姐们"。[②] 凌叔华虽不是女同性恋的实践者，但作为"五四"时期的精英女子，其思想受到20世纪初西方的女性主义的冲击和影响也在情理之中，她以女同性恋为主题创作的短篇小说《说有这么回事》就能很好地说明这一点。

[①] Debra A. Castillo, "Gender and Sexuality in World Literature", in Theo d'haen, David Damrosch and Djelal Kadir eds., *The Routledge Comparion to World Literature*, London and New York: Routledge, 2012, p. 393.

[②] 朱丽娅·克里斯蒂娃：《中国妇女》，赵靓译，同济大学出版社2010年版，第94页。

伊莱恩·肖瓦尔特在《她们的文学》一书中，用夏洛特·勃朗特（Charlotte Bront）、乔治·艾略特（George Eliot），弗吉尼亚·伍尔夫、凯瑟琳·曼斯菲尔德，玛格丽特·德拉布尔（Margaret Drabble）、多丽丝·莱辛（Doris Lessing）这三对作家来代表女性作家在英国近代小说、现代小说和当代小说的发展历程中所起到的重要作用。肖瓦尔特把弗吉尼亚·伍尔夫和凯瑟琳·曼斯菲尔德这两个同时代的、现代主义的女性作家捆绑在一起，把她们俩之间的关系视为"一种奇怪的友谊"，或在私人交往和工作这两个层面维系这样关系的"一对不安分的姐妹"。伍尔夫和曼斯菲尔德是经历了一个经典化的过程的作家，她们同是英国20世纪初文学领域的探路人、革新者，"他们以不同的方式，拓展了短篇小说的形式，从而体现和表达了个人经验的社会结构之间互动的一种复杂的观点"[1]，她们为现代小说创作技巧的形成做出了不可磨灭的贡献。伍尔夫"像亨利·詹姆斯和约瑟夫·拉康德一样，刻意追求艺术形式的完美。她是本世纪（20世纪）英国文学中最杰出的一位女作家"[2]。在小说艺术领域，曼斯菲尔德和伍尔夫都是独树一帜的人物，但曼斯菲尔德的名气和在文学史上的地位远远不如伍尔夫。作为短篇小说创作的革新者，曼斯菲尔德以其独特的写作风格蜚声文坛。她的现代主义创作技巧对现代短篇小说的形成起到了很重要的作用，为短篇小说的发展做出了杰出的贡献。

"曼斯菲尔德的时间安排和内心独白的运用，在英语短篇小说的实验改革中不能不说起了开拓的作用"，她的"《已故中校的女儿》写成于1920年，乔伊斯的《尤利西斯》要到两年之后的1922年才问世，沃尔夫的《达罗卫夫人》要到1925年才出现"[3]。"1924年伍尔夫的短篇小说《新衣》（*The New Dress*）在主题上，甚至在语言上都是《极乐》的回响。《戴洛维夫人》是最接近曼斯菲尔德风格和主旨的作品，伍尔

---

[1] Head D., *The Modernist Short Story: A Study in Theroy and Pratice*, Cambridge: Cmabridge University Press, 1992, p. 139.
[2] 侯维瑞主编：《英国文学通史》，上海外语教育出版社1999年版，第629页。
[3] 侯维瑞：《现代英国小说史》，上海外语教育出版社1985年版，第427页。

夫不过是用出神凝思代替了顿悟。"① 曼斯菲尔德于 1923 年 1 月 9 日客死于法国后,伍尔夫在 28 日的日记中承认:凯瑟琳的作品是"我曾忌妒过的唯一的作品"。② 过了几年,伍尔夫写了《一个非常敏感的头脑》(载 1927 年 9 月 18 日《纽约先驱报》)一文,深深佩服曼斯菲尔德灵敏的头脑。"在她的日记里,令我们感兴趣的并不是她作品的性质或者她名声的高低,而是一个头脑的奇观——一个非常敏感的头脑……这是凯瑟琳·曼斯菲尔德讲述凯瑟琳·曼斯菲尔德。"③ 耐人寻味的是,曼斯菲尔德独具慧眼,很早就看出了乔伊斯的意识流开山之作《尤利西斯》的价值。乔伊斯于 1941 年 1 月 13 日去世后,伍尔夫在 15 日的日记中回顾了 1918 年 4 月 18 日哈丽特·维沃尔(这位英国女士曾在经济上资助乔伊斯一家多年)把《尤利西斯》打字稿送到她家的往事。当时弗吉尼亚觉得此作文字粗鄙,不值得印成书,就顺手把它放进抽屉里。伍尔夫在 15 日的日记中写道:

  有一天,凯瑟琳·曼斯菲尔德来了,我拿出手稿,她开始读了起来,边读边哭落着,突然她说道,只是这本书有点意思,有个情节我想会在文学史上赫赫有名的。④

  曼斯菲尔德与乔伊斯有一面之缘。由于凯瑟琳的丈夫约翰·米德尔顿·默里(John Middleton Murry)在《国民》杂志上发表了一篇关于《尤利西斯》的书评,乔伊斯于 1922 年 3 月底登门拜访默里夫妇。安东尼·阿尔珀斯(Antony Alpers)在他所著的《凯瑟琳·曼斯菲尔德的一生》(The life of Katherine Mansfield)传记中,写了曼斯菲尔德和弗吉

---

  ① 伊莱恩·肖瓦尔特:《她们自己的文学》,韩敏中译,浙江大学出版社 2012 年版,第 231 页。
  ② 《弗吉尼亚·伍尔夫日记》第 2 卷,转引自凯瑟琳·曼斯菲尔德著《一个已婚男人的自述》,萧乾等译,上海三联书店 2012 年版,修订版序。
  ③ 弗吉尼亚·伍尔芙:《伍尔芙随笔全集》,王义国等译,中国社会科学出版社 2001 年版,第 1623 页。
  ④ 弗吉尼亚·伍尔芙:《伍尔芙日记选》,戴红珍、宋炳辉译,百花文艺出版社 2012 年版,第 251 页。

尼亚之间长达七年的交往。"凯瑟琳只羡慕弗吉尼亚所拥有的一切（她的家庭，丈夫给她带来的安全感）。弗吉尼亚所妒忌的则是凯瑟琳有可能取得的成就。"① 弗吉尼亚·伍尔夫1918年在《英文评论》（*English Reviews*）上读到《极乐》，很是反感。曼斯菲尔德却坚执地认为伍尔夫认出了她俩的关系："我们在做同样的事情，弗吉尼亚，"她在两人第一次见面后写道，"这真是很奇怪很让人激动的，我们两个竟然……一直在做差不多同样的事情。我们就是这样，你知道；否认没有用。"② 曼斯菲尔德的丈夫默里是"布鲁姆斯伯里"的成员，曼斯菲尔德的一些短篇小说就是在伍尔夫夫妇创办的"霍加斯出版社"出版的。

伍尔夫是引导女性运动的先驱者，《一间自己的房间》被定为西方女性主义思想史上七部指导性文献之一。③《三枚金币》则是她向男权社会意识发出的公开挑战和抗议。《泰晤士报文学副刊》在此文发表当天就登出了两个专栏和一篇社论，赞扬伍尔夫是"英国最杰出的小册子作家，这本书只要认真对待，会成为划时代的作品"。④ 因此，伍尔夫在世界文学史上的重要地位还是体现在其女性思想和意识、女性写作等方面。正如E. M. 福斯特所言："在她的全部作品中，都可以看到女权主义的影子，女权主义始终占据着她的心灵。"⑤ 和伍尔夫不同，曼斯菲尔德一生从未研究过女权主义理论，在写作中也没有把女权主义当作一种理论来公开讨论，但是她的女性意识潜藏在每一部作品中。正如凯特·富伯鲁克（Kate Fullbrook）所说的，"凯瑟琳·曼斯菲尔德的女性主义思想来之自然，这是毫无疑问的。正如政治观点在她文中无所体

---

① 凯瑟琳·曼斯菲尔德：《一个已婚男人的自述》，修订版序。
② 伊莱恩·肖瓦尔特：《她们自己的文学》，第230—231页。
③ 其他的六部著作分别为：皮桑（Christine de Pizan）的《妇女之城》（*The Book of the City Ladies*, 1405）、沃尔斯通克拉夫特（Mary Wollstonecraft）的《女权辩护》（*A Vindication of the Rights of Woman*, 1791）、西蒙·波伏娃（Simone de Beauvoir）的《第二性》（*The Second Sex*, 1949）、弗里丹（Betty Friedan）《女性的奥秘》（*The Feminine Mystique*, 1963）、米利特（Kate Millett）《性政治》（*Sexual Politics*, 1970）、格尔（Germaine Greer）的《女太监》（*The Female Eunuch*, 1970）。
④ 弗吉尼亚·伍尔芙：《伍尔芙日记选》，第220页。
⑤ 瞿世镜编：《伍尔夫研究》，上海文艺出版社1988年版，第18页。

现，但却无处不在一样"。①曼斯菲尔德和伍尔夫在各自的写作中都娴熟地运用意识流艺术手法，旨在唤醒女性自身的觉悟和觉醒。作为男权中心主义的"他者"，颠覆、解构传统的霸权写作模式，显示女性写作的现代主义。她们是把意识流文学推向世界，并极大影响了世界范围内传统的写作手法的两位伟大女性。

"在 19 世纪和 20 世纪，文学越来越和民族建构的话题联系在一起，而国际主义则扮演着一个模糊的角色。在这一期间，世界文学往往被视为是一种入侵的力量，有时直接通过帝国总督抑制当地文化，如英属印度总督、法属印度支那总督和日属朝鲜总督。世界主义则是从狭隘的地方主义解放出来的代表，它也可以被视为是提升文化价值、政治野心和霸权权力的代表。"② 对于伍尔夫而言，她善于协调她所处那个特殊年代作家本土根深蒂固的文化和世界主义之间的紧张关系。伍尔夫身上"那种世界性和世界大同主义"，才使得她指导凌叔华进行英文自传小说《古韵》的创作。1953 年，英国霍加斯出版社（Hogarth Press Ltd.）出版了《古韵》，并在西方世界引起了巨大的反响。《古韵》的成功也使得"中国的曼斯菲尔德"凌叔华、伍尔夫和曼斯菲尔德这三位同时代的女作家相互交织在文学的世界里。

凌叔华和伍尔夫同样出身于书香门第，且两人自幼就博览群书。凌叔华生长在一个有儒学教养的典型中国式大家庭，凌叔华六岁左右就由私塾先生教授古典诗词，七岁时候，就由名家指点、启蒙绘画；伍尔夫的父亲莱斯利·斯提芬（Leslie Stephen，1832—1904）是英国 19 世纪后半期"维多利亚时代"剑桥出身的一位赫赫有名的编辑、著名评论家和传记作家，曾主编《国家名人传记大辞典》，与托马斯·哈代（Thomas Hardy）、乔治·梅瑞狄斯（George Meredith）、亨利·詹姆斯

---

① Kate Fullbrook, *Kahterine Mansfield*, Brighton, Sussex: Harvester Press, 1986, p. 233. 中文见徐晗的翻译。

② David Damrosch, "World Literature and Nation-building." Ed. School of Chinese Language and Literature Beijing Normal University. *Ideas and Methods: What is World Literature? Tension between the Local and the Universal（Conference Manual）*. Beijing: Beijing Normal University, 2015. 3.

（Henry James）等当时许多著名学者、作家都有来往。这是两位中西方的"大家闺秀"能持续以书信的形式进行沟通、交流的重要原因，当然，深厚扎实的国学基础使得凌叔华能够以东方女性的风范面对西方文学的博学鸿儒。凌叔华和伍尔夫在战火纷飞的年代通过书信搭建起来的"师生关系"，其时的信件至今还留存在《弗吉尼亚·伍尔夫书信集》（第六卷）中，这些书信见证了《古韵》的构思和写作过程。她们之间的神交，最早大概要追溯到伍尔夫的外甥朱利安·贝尔的中国之行。这位布鲁姆斯文伯里文化圈的年轻人曾是武汉大学的教授，和凌叔华交往密切，且有过一段婚外情。朱利安在武汉大学任教期间，凌叔华听了他的课，并在他的指导下，阅读伍尔夫的《到灯塔去》等作品。作为"五四"现代文学思潮的接受体，凌叔华是有世界文学的知识和开放性的眼光的，凌叔华在20世纪20、30年代的小说创作中，模仿曼斯菲尔德的写作，那是外在的、形式和技巧上的，非常想得到伍尔夫"内在真实性"的写作指导。凌叔华与弗吉尼亚·伍尔夫维持了一年多的通信联系。伍尔夫在给凌叔华的回信中，开导她以写作来排解战争带来的苦痛，建议凌叔华用英文写自传，因为她"觉得自传比小说好得多"。在发展中国家，个人只能"通过将个人生活镌刻入民族叙述……才能表现个人生活的历史"。[①] 民族文学与世界文学之间的动态关系可以通过国家和本国的文学（每个国家）之间的对抗和竞争来解释，因为这种关系是始于民族概念及构建民族概念的论点。"为了寻求更大的写作空间的那些作家是那些懂得世界文学写作方法的人，他们试图利用这些写作手法来颠覆他们本国占主导地位的写作模式。"[②] "五四"新文学运动中对个性解放的张扬，对"自我"、妇女、儿童的发现为女性自传体小说的出现做好了铺垫。"五四"前后的女作家们不仅用白话文写作，而且也尝试着用自传体小说的创作形式书写女性主义，向以男权为中心的社会发起挑战并试图解构。20世纪三、四十年代出现了大量女性自

[①]《国家及其碎片》，转引自帕特丽卡·劳伦斯《丽莉·布瑞斯珂的中国眼睛》，万江波等译，上海书店出版社2008年版，第430页。

[②] Pascale Casanova, *The World Republic of Letters*, trans. by M. B. Devoise, Cambridge: Harvard University Press, 2007, p. 109.

传体小说，凌叔华《古韵》、谢冰莹《一个女兵的自传》、白薇《悲剧生涯》、丁玲《母亲》、萧红《呼兰河传》、苏青《结婚十年》等作品，这些女作家想通过新文体的尝试，向世界文学看齐，因为包括中国在内的亚洲国家渴望在世界文学中寻求本土文学的合法性和存在感。"现代小说的兴起最初并不是自主发展，而是西方的形式影响（通常是法国和英国的形式）与地方原料折中的结果。"① 女性作家对自传体传记小说这一文体的选择，试图挣脱传统的枷锁，向男权世界发起宣战，更是中国女性写作现代性的重要组成部分，对中国现代文学特别是中国现代小说文体的丰富、突破和创新都有着重要的意义。

三 互文性：凌叔华、曼斯菲尔德和伍尔夫的女同性恋小说比较研究

在当今的全球化时代，世界文学的概念在民族主义和世界主义的相互作用中演变、形成，在这一过程中，中国现代文学所起的作用尤其不能忽视。中国"五四"时期的小说，尤其是"五四"前后写的，近几年被认为是让西方更好地了解中国的潜在的、可行的通道。在这一时期，中国小说从20世纪20年代初的浪漫主义、以自我为中心、自传体作品到30年代以社会和政治为导向的文学，事实上，其中一些作品可与同时期西方的上乘之作相媲美。凌叔华是新月派的重要人物，曼斯菲尔德和伍尔夫是布鲁姆斯伯里的关键人物。虽然语言、风格上中国作家和英国作家由于自身的生活背景不同而造成各自的关注点的不同，但连接她们三者之间的纽带是她们永恒不变的女性写作。达姆罗什在《什么是世界文学》中建议研究者"应从跨文化的不同的文学群体中寻找优秀的作品"，而不是从文学的流派中寻找。因为"今天世界文学的主

---

① 弗朗哥·莫莱蒂：《世界文学猜想》，载大卫·达姆罗什等主编《世界文学理论读本》，北京大学出版社2013年版，第127页。

要特征是它的多变性：不同的读者会着迷于不同文化背景的文本"。①同样地，我们也可以通过对凌叔华、曼斯菲尔德和伍尔夫这三位具有共性的、有典型意义的东西方作者关于女同性恋作品的比较，探讨民族文学与世界文学之间的相互交织的关系，以此进一步说明作者在世界文学体系中所起到的能动作用。

在女同性恋互文性的作品中，以教室为背景是"莎孚式"的女同性恋作品中的一个重要的模式。具体说来，即以教室为背景，女校中一个诱人的女教师在唤醒她一个"无辜"的学生对女同性恋的性趣；或一位年轻的女学生的心理和性的骚动唤醒了对女同性恋的渴望，她与她的老师（或与另一名学生）的关系促成了这种欲望的可能性。伍尔夫的《存在的瞬间：斯莱特的针没有针尖》（Moments of Being："Slater's Pins Have No Points"）描写的是学生范妮·威尔莫特（Fanny Wilmot）和老师朱莉娅·克雷小姐（Miss Julia Braye）之间的女同性恋；而曼斯菲尔德《康乃馨》（Carnation）和凌叔华《说有这么一回事》描写的则是两对女学生之间的恋情：伊芙和凯蒂（Eve and Katie）、影曼和云罗。

有批评家认为伍尔夫的短篇小说创作是受到曼斯菲尔德的影响的。"弗吉尼亚的名作《达洛威夫人》（1925）就是在曼斯菲尔德的《园会》影响下写成的。"② 曼斯菲尔德《康乃馨》写于1918年（这在完成《园会》后的几个月写成）。1927年，伍尔夫发表她的"莎孚式"的短篇小说（"little Sapphist story"）③《存在的瞬间：斯莱特的针没有针尖》。伍尔夫和曼斯菲尔德从她们熟悉的女同性恋主题④来审视师生关系或同窗关系。尽管是以不同视角来描述女同性恋的激情，但是叙述

---

① David Damrosch, *What is World Literature*? Princeton: Princeton University, 2003, p. 281.
② 凯瑟琳·曼斯菲尔德：《一个已婚男人的自述》，萧乾等译，上海三联书店2012年版，前言。
③ 此词来自希腊女诗人莎孚（"Sappho"）的名字。据传，莎孚是女同性恋者，即西语中"lesbian"一词，因此她的名字就演变为"女同性恋"之义。1976年，第三版诺顿文学选集收入了古希腊女诗人莎孚（也译为萨福）的作品，就性别而言，她的作品是第一位被诺顿文学选集收入的女性作品。
④ 弗吉尼亚·伍尔夫有维塔等同性恋人；凯瑟琳·曼斯菲尔德对年长她9岁的女友埃蒂斯·本达尔也充满着既爱又恨的复杂感情。

故事的模式是一样的：课堂环境、教师和学生之间（或学生之间）女性魅力的吸引；利用自然意象来象征同性恋的欲望、基督教的依赖，通过古希腊的"莎孚"模型来加强或拒绝这样的意愿。正如伍尔夫阅读曼斯菲尔德的同性恋短篇小说可能影响到她自己的写作，其实从伍尔夫作品的人物原型可以看到她们自己的影子。众多评论家和传记作家从伍尔夫和曼斯菲尔德的信件、日记、小说来挖掘这两位作家的友谊。她们彼此之间既相互竞争和嫉妒、相互批评对方的作品和生活，又相互影响、相互尊重和钦佩。一些评论家认为，一个女人有激情，依恋对方，是因为有"情"和"色"方面的因素；另外一些则认为是她们机智敏锐的观察力让她们能够很好地沟通交流。我认为，她们在一起是带有"情"和"色"方面的原因。例如，就在曼斯菲尔德去世后一周，伍尔夫梦见"凯瑟琳带着一个花环，离开我们到另一个世界去了；她走得有尊严，有选择"。① 五年半后，伍尔夫又写道：

> 昨晚，我整夜梦见凯瑟琳·曼斯菲尔德而不知道自己做了什么梦；往往在梦里唤起的感情比平常想的要多——仿佛她回来了，强烈地让人感觉到，而不是虚构与回忆。②

这次梦见曼斯菲尔德后，过了三年，伍尔夫又梦见她。"我们如何能超越死亡相见与握手，说一些关于释怀和友谊的话。"③ 事实上，在给维塔的信中，伍尔夫暗示，她和曼斯菲尔德实际上并没有性的实践，她这一说法并不是毫无根据的。"至于凯瑟琳，我想你知道得差不多。我们从来就没有成为一体，但我迷恋她，她尊重我，只是我觉得她廉价，她觉得我一本正经；然而我们俩不得不为了谈论写作见面……我经常梦见她……"④ 伍尔夫与多位女性之间的浪漫情谊主要停留在精神层

---

① Virginia Woolf, *The Diary of Virginia Woolf*, Vol 2, Anne Olivier Bell ed., London: Hongarth Press, 1980, p. 226.
② Virginia Woolf, *The Diary of Virginia Woolf*, Vol 3, p. 187.
③ Virginia Woolf, *The Diary of Virginia Woolf*, Vol 4, p. 29.
④ Virginia Woolf, *The Diary of Virginia Woolf*, Vol 4, p. 366.

面。伍尔夫在中年的时候遇到她一生最重要的情人维塔。维塔年轻漂亮、性格大胆豪放，使伍尔夫陷入热恋之中。伍尔夫在给维塔的信中说："告诉你一个秘密，我等不及要我的女士跟我私奔。"① 维塔曾向自己的丈夫承认与伍尔夫"同床共枕过两次"。② 维塔与伍尔夫的情人关系只维持了几年，但她们的友谊是维系了终身。伍尔夫《存在的瞬间：斯莱特的针没有针尖》就是她们感情最热烈时写的。小说中许多细节的描写和伍尔夫给维塔的信中所提到的女同性恋（Sapphist）之间的微妙、暧昧的情感是相似的。如在小说的最后一段的描述：

> 范妮·威尔莫特的手颤抖地、用花压住克雷小姐的乳房时，克雷小姐说，"斯莱特的针没有针尖，"她一边说，一边怪诞地笑着，并放松着自己的双臂。③

伍尔夫《存在的瞬间：斯莱特的针没有针尖》选择的是音乐课，因为伍尔夫在故事中重点要强调她的女权主义意图。小说中女教师的原型朱莉娅·克雷小姐是伍尔夫的第一位希腊语和拉丁语老师。故事是这样开头的：

> "斯莱特的针没有针尖——你不是总在找它？"克雷小姐转身说道，玫瑰从范妮的裙上丢了下来。范妮弯下腰找丢在地上的针，满耳充斥着的是音乐。④

范妮·威尔莫特沿着一朵玫瑰找落在地上的针，没有在意老师的话。促使范妮改变看法的是：阳具的发现使范妮在无意中知道自己的老师是个同性恋者。范妮态度的转变，也让我们看到了在故事的结尾处范

---

① Virginia Woolf, *The Letters of Virginia Woolf*, Vol 3, p. 156.
② Hermione Lee, *Virginia Woolf*, London: Vintage. 1997, p. 503.
③ Virginia Woolf, *The Complete Shorter Fiction of Virginia Woolf*, San Diego: A Harvest/HBJ Book, 1989, p. 220.
④ Virginia Woolf, *The Complete Shorter Fiction of Virginia Woolf*, p. 215.

妮的大胆举动。伍尔夫把"针"和"紫色的斗篷"作为女同性恋的象征。相比之下，曼斯菲尔德的女同性恋短篇小说常常表现出女性之间情欲的肉体，她们是奇特的、鲁莽的，而且来势汹汹。① 曼斯菲尔德的《康乃馨》是女子学院的一堂法语课的缩影。老师给学生朗读诗，而其中一位女学生伊芙在玩康乃馨。伊芙无聊且烦躁，房间闷热，康乃馨的香味从一个女生飘向另外一个。

曼斯菲尔德用"康乃馨"作为引诱物，象征着女同性恋。故事是这样开头的，

> 在那些火热的日子，伊芙——脾气古怪的伊芙——总是拿着一朵花。她闻了又闻，捻在指间旋转着，贴在颊上，举到嘴边，用它来挠凯蒂的脖子。最后，她把花瓣扯碎，一瓣瓣地吃掉。②

故事发生的当天，伊芙带着"深红色的康乃馨"到课堂上，她试图以其醉人的香味引诱凯蒂，而凯蒂一开始就表现出抵制。

> 唔，好看！芳香一直飘到凯蒂这儿，太浓郁了。凯蒂掉过身去，朝着窗外耀眼的阳光。③

曼斯菲尔德在故事的开始就暗示，一旦伊芙捕捉到猎物，她就会把花瓣扯碎，一瓣瓣地吃掉。故事结尾处，伊芙表现出很轻浮的姿态，"随即把康乃馨插在凯蒂的上衣前襟了"。这也表明了伊芙的诱惑以失败告终。曼斯菲尔德在文中也表现出自己女权主义的观点，女同性恋有时是在精神层面上的，并不一定要有身体上的接触。正如她和伍尔夫之间，"彼此有相当多的猜疑和保留；不过在一起时，她都无拘无束，意

---

① 文如其人，在伍尔夫看来，曼斯菲尔德"是个不讨人喜欢但强有力、绝对肆无忌惮的人"。昆汀·贝尔：《伍尔夫传》，萧易译，江苏教育出版社2005年版，第239页。
② 凯瑟琳·曼斯菲尔德：《康乃馨》，载凯瑟琳·曼斯菲尔德《一个已婚男人的自述》，第111页。
③ 同上书，第113页。

识到彼此是同行"。① 曼斯菲尔德的《康乃馨》写于 1918 年，曼斯菲尔德和伍尔夫相识是 1917 年 1 月前后，② 到了 1917 年 2 月，她们有了这样的交情，以致弗吉尼亚会写信跟瓦奈萨说："我和凯瑟琳·曼斯菲尔德还算和睦。"③ 伍尔夫认为曼斯菲尔德是"被赞美和可怜的对象。她有趣、易受攻击、才华横溢、充满魅力，可她也穿得像个妓女，举步像个婊子"。在某种程度上，伍尔夫以同样的方式赞美曼斯菲尔德的短篇小说，"观察得那么仔细入微，有时是那么富有悲剧性，然而其他时候却那么低劣和浅白"。④ 曼斯菲尔德的《康乃馨》就是对这种赞赏和敌视做出的反应，凯蒂拒绝了伊芙的引诱。因为曼斯菲尔德知道自己不但能给伍尔夫带来欢乐，还能给她带来痛苦，对此她感到挺满足的。况且，曼斯菲尔德清楚，伍尔夫很了解她的写作天赋，这一点足以让她和伍尔夫保留在精神层面的往来，与伍尔夫"同床共枕过两次"的同性恋人维塔有着根本的不同。

凌叔华《说有这么一回事》是应杨振声之约而写的一篇短篇小说，1926 年发表在《晨报副刊》上。女校的女学生云罗与影曼是在排演戏剧《罗密欧与朱丽叶》时认识的，由此演绎着一段如幻似真的同性恋爱。故事结尾以云罗已经做了别人的新娘，给这场同性恋画上句号。与《存在的瞬间：斯莱特的针没有针尖》、《康乃馨》仅仅以教室为背景不同的是，凌叔华对校园中的其他同学着墨较多。云罗与影曼身处封闭的女校，与女性朝夕相对，"情境性的同性恋"很容易发生。演话剧则给予她们恋上彼此的良机，云罗在影曼那里，找到了如同戏剧中的罗密欧一样的白马王子。

影曼把脸贴近云罗，低声笑道："你是我的眷属，听见没有？"

---

① 昆汀·贝尔：《伍尔夫传》，萧易译，江苏教育出版社 2005 年版，第 240 页。
② 昆汀·贝尔在《伍尔夫传》一书的脚注中标注道："1917 年 1 月 12 日，伦纳德第一次在日记里提到他们：'凯瑟琳·曼斯菲尔德、默里和 S. 沃特路来吃了饭。'"昆汀·贝尔：《伍尔夫传》，第 239 页。
③ 昆汀·贝尔：《伍尔夫传》，第 239 页。
④ 同上书，第 240 页。

"又说便宜话，我不同你睡了。"云罗推她一下，就势把头贴伏在她的胸前。①

凌叔华把"手帕"作为女同性恋的象征。故事一开始，影曼来找云罗排练，云罗将手帕"一甩"。故事接近尾声，云罗告诉影曼家里为她安排好了婚事，二人抱成一团，痛哭流泪，此时，再一次出现了手帕擦伤泪的场景。影曼和云罗的恋情还是难逃封建父权机制的厄运，以失败告终。影曼在这段夭折的恋情中扮演的男性角色是对传统性别秩序的质疑，是西蒙娜·德·波伏娃所说"男性化抗议"的一种表现。女同性恋的写作首先是一种对封建礼教、男权中心进行抗争的女权主义写作；其次也表现出作者本人对封建包办婚姻的厌恶和抗争。凌叔华和陈西滢是师生关系，她本人的婚姻就是自由恋爱结成的硕果。凌叔华之前的包办婚姻是，"幼年在日本时，家父与赵秉钧（他们二人是结拜兄弟）口头上曾说及此事，但他（赵秉钧）一死之后此事已如春风过耳，久不成问题，赵氏之母人实明慧，故亦不作此无谓之提议矣"。② 总而言之，对于凌叔华生活的时代而言，女同性恋写作的主题是大胆的，又是富有挑战性的，它必将导致人们对整个经验世界的颠覆和重新认识，这正是"五四"小说的独特之处，也是它的文化价值和现实意义所在。

结　语

在《现代文学的总体精神》一文中，最早的女权主义者之一史达尔夫人从口才和道德这两个方面来比较古代作家和现代作家，提出了最早的女权主义论断：小说到了现代才得以发展，随着现代对女性越来

---

① 凌叔华：《凌叔华文存》（上），陈学勇编，四川文艺出版社1998年版，第121页。
② 凌叔华：《中国儿女——凌叔华佚作·年谱》，陈学勇编，上海书店出版社2008年版，第184页。

尊重使得众多小说的主题转向关注女性生活的私密空间成为可能。① 总之，无论中西方的女性，对同性恋的描写和刻画就是赤裸裸地对男权中心主义性别歧视的挑战和宣战。"拒绝成为（或者拒绝继续成为）一个异性恋者，通常意味着自觉或不自觉地拒绝成为一个男人或一个女人。对于一个同性恋者来说，这样做比拒绝'女人'角色走得更远，是对男人的经济、意识形态和政治权力的拒绝。"② 伍尔夫的《存在的瞬间：斯莱特的针没有针尖》、曼斯菲尔德的《康乃馨》和凌叔华的《说有这么一回事》同是以女同性恋为主题，《存在的瞬间：斯莱特的针没有针尖》中学生范妮·威尔莫特（Fanny Wilmot）和老师朱莉娅·克雷小姐（Miss Julia Braye）之间的女同性恋是有实践的；而曼斯菲尔德《康乃馨》，是凯蒂拒绝了伊芙的诱捕；《说有这么一回事》中影曼和云罗之间的恋情最终是夭折了，以云罗嫁人告终。伍尔夫《存在的瞬间：斯莱特的针没有针尖》的"莎孚性质"（Sapphistry）写作风格具有颠覆性、解构性、多重性和隐喻性，她的写作就是诱惑行动。伍尔夫的这种大胆的女权主义写作风格，使她成为无可争议的世界级的女权主义作家。她所膜拜的古希腊女诗人莎孚，是第一位被诺顿文学选集收入作品的女性作家。伍尔夫"莎孚式"写作风格的形成，与她的女同性恋女诗人维塔有很大的关系，尽管维塔不喜欢伍尔夫的女性主义思想，③ 维塔不是才华横溢的"一个作家"。④ "自从结婚以来，除了凯瑟琳·曼斯菲尔德，从没有人打动过她的心灵，凯瑟琳也只不过是稍微触动了一下。她仍旧爱着伦纳德。可假使如今，年届中旬，她将爱上另外一个

---

① David Damrosch, Natalie Melas, et al. eds. *The Princeton Sourcebook in Comparative Literature: From the European Enlightenment to the Global Present*, p. 11.
② 莫尼克·威蒂格《女人不是天生的》，载葛尔·罗宾等编《酷儿理论——西方90年代性思潮》，时事出版社2000年版，第356页。
③ 维塔特别不喜欢伍尔夫的女性主义思想，《一间自己的房间》在一定程度上是想转变维塔的政治观点，让其接受自己的女性主义思想。
④ 昆汀·贝尔在《伍尔夫传》一书中写道："照弗吉尼娅的说法，她'靠十足的本事和一只黄钢笔'来写作，她在她（维塔）的小说和诗歌中寻找能够加以赞美的东西，不过她从没放任自己到不顾良心的地步，就像她总是乐于为伦纳德做的那样。"昆汀·贝尔《伍尔夫传》，萧易译，第327页。

人。"① 不管怎样，"在这段时间和随后的数年里，她是弗吉尼亚生活中最重要的人——除了伦纳德和瓦奈萨之外"。② 维塔与伍尔夫之间除了友谊之外的同性恋情缘，也是维塔在伍尔夫去世后竭尽全力帮助凌叔华的主要原因。维塔无意中结识了凌叔华，并得知伍尔夫通过书信指导凌进行《古韵》的创作，并积极、主动地请伦纳德帮忙找到《古韵》的手稿、写书的导言、做广告包装等，以至最终促使《古韵》成功问世。这一切，都让我们领略到了世界文学中女权主义的力量和魅力。

凌叔华，一位非欧美国家的女作家，在自己的特定的文学和文化背景下谈论着女同性恋主题。正如达姆拉什所言，在世界文学里，一个"有价值的生命"主题，无论何时何地，都能够在文学体系的框架内活跃在其原有的文化之外。③ 承载和弘扬世界文学史的形成和发展的是中西方共同的文学创作的主题和流派，而不是文本本身。文学创作的主题和流派使我们看到了文学的发展变化，具体说来，就是从文本与文本之间、从一个年度到另一个年度之间，来衡量、考察文学的变化性和复杂性，这就是"参照"在世界文学中的能动作用。通过把凌叔华的《说有这么一回事》与英国作家伍尔夫的《存在的瞬间：斯莱特的针没有针尖》、曼斯菲尔德的《康乃馨》比较，使我们清楚看到了女权主义创作在中国现代文坛的尝试和崛起；同时，也丰富了在世界文学语境下，关于性别研究的文本。"五四"女作家以女同性恋作为创作主题的还有：庐隐的《丽石的日记》、《海滨故人》和丁玲的《岁暮》、《暑假中》等，她们纷纷把笔锋转向了"女性生活的私密空间"。

主要参考文献：

1. Virginia Woolf, *The Complete Shorter Fiction of Virginia Woolf*, San Diego: A Harvest/HBJ Book, 1989.
2. 凌叔华：《凌叔华文存》（上），陈学勇编，四川文艺出版社 1998 年版。

---

① 昆汀·贝尔：《伍尔夫传》，萧易译，第 324 页。
② 同上书，第 323 页。
③ David Damrosch, *What is World Literature*? Princeton: Princeton University, p. 4.

3. David Damrosch, *What is World Literature?* Princeton：Princeton University，2003.
4. 昆汀·贝尔：《伍尔夫传》，萧易译，江苏教育出版社 2005 年版。
5. 凌叔华：《中国儿女——凌叔华佚作·年谱》，陈学勇编，上海书店出版社 2008 年版。
6. 凯瑟琳·曼斯菲尔德：《一个已婚男人的自述》，萧乾等译，上海三联书店 2012 年版。

翻译的"恐怖"以及"恐怖"的翻译:但丁《神曲·地狱篇》翻译三题

乐安东[*]

Abstract "La Divina Commedia", Dante Alighieri's magnum opus, has been read, translated and analysed in China since the early years of the 20th century. Following the first attempts at translation during the first half of the century, and a considerable amount of silence lasting until the nineties, three new Chinese versions appeared almost simultaneously after the year 2000, thus confirming the Chinese readers' renovated interest in the work. Through the close reading of one passage per edition, namely the stories of Paolo and Francesca (by Hong Kong professor Huang Guobin), Pier della Vigna (by Chinese italianist Huang Wenjie) and Count Ugolino (by Chinese poet Zhang Shuguang), all taken from the "Inferno", this text aims to expound and interpret the strategies adopted by the translators of the aforementioned three new versions, ultimately attempting to confirm each version's worth to the Chinese reading public.

Keywords Divina Commedia; literary translation; comparative poetics

---

[*] 乐安东,意大利人,北京语言大学比较文学与世界文学专业博士研究生。

阿根廷作家博尔赫斯认为，但丁的代表作《神曲》是全世界唯一不能模仿的作品。在某种程度上，可说言之有理，在内容方面，《神曲》肯定不仅仅是一部文学作品，因为它所涉及的学科范围（古典文学、神学、哲学、社会学只不过是最表面的而已），它就不愧为一部欧洲中世纪的百科全书；它所讲的故事不仅是一位朝圣者从迷失了方向的状态寻求拯救的旅行，而且因为凡有宗教信仰的人或早或晚均会扪心自问"离开了尘世之后我会往哪儿走"，所以《神曲》所含有的罪人、凡人以及圣人的故事都会拨动世人（无论是有神还是无神）的心弦，使得它早就变成了世界文学的一个经典。而在格局方面，其三韵体以及每一篇的三十三章（加一个序章，共有一百章）的结构也反映了作者对上帝三位一体的信仰，在某种程度上，格局变成了内容的一部分。

19 世纪末到 20 世纪初，由于当时在国外（特别是在日本）的知识分子的贡献，《神曲》终于传入中国，并且有相当大的可能性，当时的中国学者初步接触到的版本是译本。梁启超编昆剧《新罗马》的时候，他把但丁放在剧本的开端；苏曼殊写过"但丁拜伦是我师"，梁氏和苏氏两位运用但丁作为文学模式的时候，还没有人把但丁的任何作品翻译成中文。1921 年，钱稻孙把《神曲·地狱篇》的前三章翻译成中文，并发布在《小说月报》，其标题为《神曲一脔》。这个翻译为什么很重要？因为钱氏把但丁的 14 世纪的意大利语翻译成古文，并且尽量使用了诗体，没有违背原本的格式。这个翻译受到很大的欢迎并到现在还被国内外的学者钦佩。[①] 接着，1939 年，王维克一面参考原著，一面参考法译、德译、英译出版过《神曲》的第一个完整中文译本，把作品原有的诗体改成了散文体；1954 年，朱维基用诗体从英文翻译了《地狱篇》；1990 年，田德望用散文从意大利语翻译了整个作品。

2000 年以来，黄文捷、黄国彬、张曙光三位先生先后发布了《神

[①] 甚至，高利克在《但丁对中国的接受及影响》一文里，引用并提倡浦安迪的看法，认为钱稻孙的《神曲》虽然是不完整的版本，虽然是从日语译的，但是到现在还是最好的翻译。

曲》的三个新译本，这三个版本之间的短时期接连出版会让每个读者怀疑它们是否多余的。我们在这里挑选了《地狱篇》的三个有名的故事情节来对比三位翻译者的策略的异同，通过文本细读来证明每一个版本的不同价值。所选出的片段是黄国彬译的第五章（保罗和芙兰切斯卡的故事）、黄文捷译的第十三章（皮埃尔·德拉·维涅亚的故事）、张曙光译的第三十三章（乌戈利诺伯爵的故事）。这些翻译的分析秩序并不是按照出版时间的顺序，而是以一位既是翻译学家又是意大利语研究者又是诗人（黄国彬）的版本为开头，通过一位纯粹的意大利语研究者（黄文捷），终于到看不懂意大利语的纯粹诗人（张曙光）。再者，三个片段并不是《地狱篇》当中的最可怕的片段，但是它们是最能够引起但丁和读者的同情的故事。以下各章从译本的角度分析上述人物的叙事方式及其跟但丁和读者之间的关系。

黄国彬与第五章——保罗和芙兰切斯卡

《地狱篇》的第五章讲解地狱的第二层，神圣的正义派到这里的是放纵情欲的罪人，他们为一阵吹刮不已的狂风所折磨。领会到了罪人所忍受的惩罚之后，但丁和他的引导者——古罗马诗人维吉尔——碰到了保罗和芙兰切斯卡，此是但丁和一个罪人的第一次交谈，[①] 其结果最后让但丁昏厥过去。

首先二位旅行者一到了第二层地狱就遇到米诺斯——地狱的判官。早在第 2 和第 3 行，我们会领略到地狱恐怖的一面：

……giù nel secondo, che men loco cinghia

e tanto più dolor, che punge a guaio.……

[①] 因为在"幽域"（Limbo）他们所遇到的人物称不上是真正的罪人，而只是没接受过洗礼或出生在耶稣道成肉身之前的人，他们受的刑罚仅仅是他们没法实现看到上帝的欲望。

……第二层环绕的空间较小，
里面的痛苦却大得令人号啕。……

我们能观察到文本的一个很重要的特点：基本上，但丁的史诗至少提供给读者两个层面的诠释，第一个跟文句的内容有关，第二个跟文句的发音及其韵律有关，并且在大部分情况下，它们是同样重要的。这里我们面对一个颇有代表性的例子，便是第三行的最后一个单词 guaio，它既是一个名词（其相对的动词是"guaire"，意思为"呜咽"）又是一个若隐若现的象声词。词尾为四个元音"-uaio"的结构，所以它能够暗示罪人的痛哭、哭声，在某种程度上使得原本的读者听到他们的悲叹。黄国彬怎么解决这个问题？他使用的词是"号啕"，我们一分析这个单词的两个字，就会注意到它们俩都是以"口"字为部首，尤其是"号"因为它是"口"字加"丂"字，所以在地狱的语境下它能够引出一个悲伤声音的形象。甚至，如果我们考虑到它的繁体格式①"號"，它包含着一个"虎"字，更使得读者发挥其想象力。我的推测是：黄国彬成功地借助于另一个官能而建构出同样的形象，因为尽管中国读者没法听到罪人的"guaio"，但是通过"号啕"这个词的构造及其形象，译者让他们看到这些悲叹。为了翻译但丁所创造出的隐现象声词或说简介象声词，接下来，我们看到了米诺斯的"悍然伫立吼叫"（第 4 行），"响哮如大海"（第 29 行），"尖叫、哀号、痛哭"（第 35 行）等。这种巧妙的翻译不完全归因于黄国彬的才能，而汉字本身也扮演了不能忽视的角色，因为包含着口字的象声词为数不少，黄国彬才能够借助于其象形文字的特征将它们用到位。黄文捷和张曙光两个译者都没有用类似的翻译策略，也就是说没有用到汉字的视觉特性，两个都试图复制原本的象声词的发音，黄文捷的译本是"到处都有凄声惨叫"，张曙光的译本是"激起了哭声"。

在米诺斯判官的允许下，但丁和维吉尔继续行走，首先亲眼看到淫欲者所忍受的惩罚：一阵地狱的狂风将他们"疾卷、折磨、向他们攻

---

① 因为黄国彬的译本首先是在港台发布的。

袭"，然后二位旅行者终于碰到了保罗和芙兰切斯卡——第五章的主人公。黄国彬基本上不害怕把一些句子的结构完完全全颠倒过来，但是在少数例子上，他尽量试图复制原有的一些的特点，比方说但丁的一些新颖的比喻按照字面翻译，为的是保持原本的魅力：在原本的第 30 行，"Io venni in loco d'ogne luce muto"，我们看到一个很独特的比喻，但丁使用的是一通感（synesthesia），也就是说把视觉和听觉两个感知结合起来，有关视觉的单词是"luce"，该名词意为"光明"，而有关听觉的单词是"muto"，该形容词意为"无声，哑巴"，表示在地狱的亡魂没法领会到光明。此联觉是但丁创造出的，跟意大利的熟语无关，所以黄国彬成功地将它翻译成"我来到一个众光喑哑的场所"（第 28 行）。尽管此说法在中文的熟语当中根本不存在，可是有助于中文读者体会到原本这个颇有提示性的形象。译者保持了原本的修辞方法和句子结构的例子也不少，但是有时候译者虽然接近于原本，不过没能将其精华传达到译本，这归因于意大利语和汉语两个语言的结构之不同。最难汉译的句子结构是包含着"che"的句子。我们看一个例子，这是芙兰切斯卡初次对但丁说话的一个片段：

>　　……O animal graz？oso e benigno　　　90
>　　che visitando vai per l'aere perso
>　　noi che tignemmo il mondo di sanguigno,
>　　se fosse amico il re de l'universo,　　　93
>　　noi pregheremmo lui de la tua pace……

黄国彬的翻译如下：

>　　……生灵啊，你大方而又充满友爱，
>　　肯穿过黝黑的空间，到这里探访
>　　我们。我们曾用血把世界沾揩，　　　90
>　　如果我们的朋友是宇宙的君王，
>　　我们必定会求他赐你安宁……

原本的第91和92行有两个"che",在意大利语当中,他会替代一个句子的主语以便把一个主要的句子和一个相对的句子结合起来,相当于英文的"that"。相对的句子是以"che"为开头,所以我们看的第一个"che"在译本被翻译成"你"是合适的。问题在于第92行里边的"che",因为这里已经有一个代名词"我们",为了保持原本的词语之顺序,黄国彬放了一个句号,打断了原本的长句,然后重复了这个代名词,但是那边的"che"的功能正好是把这两个短句连接在一起,其字面意义应该是"(你到这里探访)用血着色世界的我们"。这样翻译的好处在于,译本的句子结构让读者重读"我们",有助于强调这个片段的抒情性及其悲剧性效果。另一个问题在于原本的第93行,这里译者又采取了类似的策略,但是犯了一个小错误,也就是说为了紧随原本的字面意义而丢失了其精华。原文是"se fosse amico il re de l'universo",本意是"如果宇宙的君主是我们的朋友",请查看以下各个单词的意义:

Se fosse amico il re de l' universo
假如是朋友（定冠词）王（的）① （定冠词）宇宙

对于一个意大利人来说,我们面对的是一个"动词—宾语—主语"的句子,动词为fosse,宾语为amico,主语为il re de l'universo。大部分情况下,意大利语的句子结构是"主语—动词—宾语",但是像上面例子中这样的句子也相当常见。反过来说,中文的名词没有阴阳性之分类,动词既没有变位也不分现在时、过去时、将来时,所以基本上每句话的每个语素都有自己的定位,以防文句变得模棱两可。对我而言,黄国彬的翻译"如果我们的朋友是宇宙的君主"的有错之处有两层:表面上,是语法的错误,因为译者没发现宾语和主语的位置被倒过来;深入思考的话,这是意识形态的错误,因为哪怕我们在谈的是《地狱篇》,作为有信仰的但丁绝对不会将上帝（宇宙的君王）置于"宾语"

---

① 基本上,中文的"A的B"相当于意大利语的"B de A"或"B di A"。

地位，他肯定是主语。

　　同时，黄国彬的翻译也能够包含一些中文特有的结构来复制但丁的语言技巧。第五章全部盈满了原本没有的感叹词，为的是指出发言者的态度及其感情。我们这里可以分析一些例子：但丁与米诺斯的对话是以"你呀"为开端，这个"呀"字用来替代原有的"O"。但是在第20行，他又对诗人说："啊，别因为进口宽敞而上当！"原本没有"O"，维吉尔却回答："不要阻挡啊"，原本也没有"O"，但丁描述淫欲者的情况，他说他们"得不到希望的安慰；不要说稍息，想减轻痛苦也无望啊，唉！"，原本没有最后的"啊，唉"等。一个问题出现了，它们起什么作用？我推测，译者使用的感叹词是为了反映出发言者的感受，尤其是但丁的两个身份（叙述者和主人公）统一起来的时候，因为看了这些可怜的亡魂，所以就不由得怜悯他们的痛苦。而为了强调此怜悯，黄国彬使得但丁替罪人叹息。到了难受的最高程度，但丁被维吉尔提醒，他的问句用得很到位："在想什么呢？"，那个"呢"也不存在，但是整个问句能够表达出原本的问句"che pense?"。这个问题除了它表面上的意思之外还带着一种言外之意，也就是说维吉尔的警告，他提醒但丁不要怜悯罪人，但是他偏要洗耳恭听两个罪人的悲惨故事。甚至，他用"芙兰切斯卡呀"求她讲他们俩怎么走到死路。

　　与感叹词比起来，用得比较少的是另外一个中文特有的语言技巧：四字词语。与黄文捷和张曙光两位相比，黄国彬把四字词语用得少之又少，但是它们出现的时候，其效果却很可观，一目了然；第一个例子是但丁描写淫欲者的罪过，他先用"他们丧生，都因为让爱欲纵恣"，这里的"爱欲纵恣"虽然不是固定的四字词语，但是能够在四个字之内凝结原本的意义，而不需要字面翻译为"是无限制的爱欲使得他们离开了我们的世界"。

　　现在我们来简单分析一下第五章的结局：当但丁把两个罪人的故事听完的时候，他感动得止不住昏厥下去，跟一个尸体无异。这个片段的结局很突然，这个效果是用什么来引起的？原本的最后一行是"E caddi come corpo morto cade"，这个断然的效果的主要组成部分是

"cade"（意为"掉下"）这个单词被选为整篇的最后一个单词；同样的效果被引入汉译本里，"并且像一具死尸倒卧在地"。主要的因素是，译者用的词是"像"，这个单词之运用使得他不需要加上"一样"或"一般"。而且，这个手段使得第五章的最后三行逐渐减少自己的用字：

> 另一个就哭泣。为此，我哀伤不已，（十三个字）
> 刹那间像死去的人，昏迷不醒，（十二个字）
> 并且像一具死尸倒卧在地。（十一个字）

况且，"在地"的发音（因为是两个四声）也在程度上能够让我们联想到原本的"cade"，断然终止叙述者的声音。

黄文捷与第十三章——皮埃尔·德拉·维涅亚

仅从黄文捷的每一章的标题上，我们就能够发现他是纯粹的意大利语言文学学者：在翻译的过程中他注意到了一些很小的细节，比方说他使用的不是"章"而是"首"，符合原本的 Canto（意为"歌曲"，或者"抒情诗"）。他是第一位使用诗体把"神曲"直接从意大利文翻译成中文的学者。[1]

和大部分但丁的研究者一样，黄文捷的译本依赖于频繁的注释，这并不是说黄国彬和张曙光不用注释，而是若他们俩的译本没有注释的话，读者还能看得懂，但黄文捷的译本只有通过注释才能深入地解释其内容，而且虽然他不试图复制原本的押韵，但是他试图复制其节奏，把

---

[1] 在田德望译本的序里，他写了他不敢把神曲翻译成诗体，因为他不敢背叛但丁文本的精华。这段话被引用于 Alessandra Brezzi, "Il Novecento cinese di Dante", 载于 *Critica del testo*, XIV/3, 2011（Dante, oggi/3）, a cura di R. Antonelli, A. Landolfi, A. Punzi, Roma, Viella, 2011, pp. 415–438。

整个作品分成自由的诗体，① 这样一来他表面上能保持原本的格局，虽然本质上他的译本没有诗律，但是仍然称不上分诗行的散文。这里我们分析第十三首，由自杀的丛林以及名人皮埃尔·德拉·维涅亚而成名，根据西方文学评论家们所进行过的语言研究，这章的语言独立于整个《地狱篇》：自杀者被神圣的正义化成树木和灌木，因为他们在世的时候就拒绝了自己的身体，所以在九泉之下他们的身体跟其他罪人完全不同。这些树木同时是神话恶鸟哈尔比（Arpie）的栖息地，它们的名字被直接从意大利语音译成中文，然后加上了一个注释：

> 哈尔比（Arpie）：希腊神话中陶曼特（Taumante）与海洋女神厄列克特拉（Elettra）所生的人首鸟身女怪，姊妹多人，其中有阿埃洛（Aello）、奥西佩特（Ocipete）、蒂埃洛（Tiello）和塞莲诺（Celeno）等……

面对着这个词，黄文捷和张曙光都决定要把它音译——后者的版本是"哈尔皮"，与此相反，黄国彬的态度与他们不同，他选择把这个词意译成"妖鸟"。其实前者的态度并没有违背中国翻译的传统：玄奘所提倡的"五种不翻"准则之第三便是"……三此无故，若阎浮树，中夏实无此木……"②，意为如果原本的某一个东西在中国不存在，那译者就应该将它音译过来，就像中国原来没有的阎浮树。哈尔比是神话动物，尽管是不存在的，不过其形象在传承古希腊和古罗马的意大利文化中是广泛为人所知的。其音译和上述引用的注释是符合传统的一个选择。反过来说，黄国彬的"妖鸟"宁可迅速传达它们的"人首鸟身"这个形象，也不愿意用它们的名字称呼它们。与此同时，黄国彬译介的版本的每一篇都充满了法国版画家古斯塔夫·多雷（Gustave Doré）的插图，这对读者在阅读时的想象是很有益处的。

---

① Alessandra Brezzi，前面引用的书。
② Jungnok Park："The characteristics of Chinese Buddhist translation"，载于 *How Buddhism Acquired a Soul on the Way to China.*，Equinox publishing Lt，2012，pp. 5 – 37。

翻译的"恐怖"以及"恐怖"的翻译：但丁《神曲·地狱篇》翻译三题 / 231

正如奥地利著名语言学者施皮采尔（Leo Spitzer）早在1942年所指出，第十三章的一大部分词语都带着刺耳的发音，我们看一下他的分析：

> One distinctive feature of the style of this canto consists in the use, to an extent unparalleled elsewhere in the Inferno, of onomatopoeic terms: consider, for example, the following list of harsh-sounding, consonant-ridden words which (often occurring in the rhyme) appear scattered throughout the canto for the purpose of evoking the concepts "trunk, bush" and "cripple, mutilate, dismember". [1]

【第十三首的风格的一个显著特征在于象声词的应用，此用法到达一个全篇无双的程度：例如，请考虑如下的一列刺耳、充满辅音的单词。它们经常押韵，而且稀疏在整个篇章，为的是引到"树干、灌木"和"伤残、切断、肢解"两个概念。】

施皮采尔所观察到的单词以及黄文捷的汉译如下：

Nodosi（多节）　　rosta（枝蔓）　　aspri sterpi（荒凉的荆棘林），
bronchi（荆棘林）　　tronchi（折断）　　nvolti（弯曲），
schiante（折断）　　scerpi（撕裂）　　sterpi（荆棘林）
monchi（全部消失）　　tronco（树干）
scheggia rotta（折断的伤口）　　nocchi（树干）
disvelta（厌弃）　　stizzo（柴）　　cespuglio（丛林）
strazio（伤害）　　tristo cesto（可怕的树丛）

---

[1] Leo Spitzer: "Speech and Language in *Inferno XIII*"，见 Harold Bloom, *Bloom's Major Poets*, Dante, Infobase Publishing, 2001, 第49到第51页。

这个如此入微的细读暴露出来什么？第一，在21个单词之间，原本其中最经常出现的辅音是"s"（15次）、"t"（12次，一次作为双辅音）、"r"（11次）。这些辅音所构成的词语都相当刺耳，而虽然有可能汉文译者无法反映出这些间接的象声词的刺耳特征，但是黄文捷使用的态度比较相似于黄国彬的策略：由于汉字原有的形象文字般的特点，施皮采尔所强调的"树干，灌木"的概念通过"木字旁"和"草字头"两个部首的反反复复的运用而成为可见的意象。至于"伤残、切断、肢解"这个概念，译者不得不将所有的有关"切断"的单词翻译得更加清澈。基本上译者没有很明显的翻译失误，但是我只挑一个案例：维吉尔促使但丁从一棵树上折下来一个小枝，其目的是说服他，让他看这些树木其实是亡魂，他说"li pensier c'hai si faran tutti monchi"（原本第30行），译本"你现有的想法会全部消失"（译本第30行）。基本上译本是没问题的，不过如果把"monchi"译成"全部消失"我们就失去了原词的一个很有效果的暗指和比喻，因为"monco"的字面意义是"缺乏一个或者两个手、胳膊"，也就是说，但丁只要折一根枝蔓，他的所有的想法和成见一下子都会变得残缺不全。显而易见，这个单词不仅仅跟这些被折断的枝蔓有关，而且跟"切断"的概念密切相关。为了达到最佳的效果，应该尽量保留它。

在原本里，皮埃尔想表达的寓意明明是："我是一个受害者，我本来无罪但是被冤枉"[1]。他的言语是以令人怜悯他为目标，下个问题是，译者怎么传递皮埃尔的悲情？我们分析一下皮埃尔的第一句话：但丁刚才从他的身体折断了一个枝蔓，不料皮埃尔发出声音："你为何把我折断？"（第33行）然后继续"你为何把我撕裂？难道你就没有丝毫怜悯之心？"（第35 - 36行）我们可以看见一个重复的格局：其一，为了翻译意大利语的最普遍的疑问副词"perché"，译者两次都宁愿用"为何？"而不用更普遍的"为什么？"我们知道的是"为何？"的语域要比"为什么？"更高一些，所以其含义看来是"我是有文化修养的人，很

---

[1] Lynne Press: "Modes of metamorphoses in the Comedia: The case of InfernoXIII", 载于 Harold Bloom, *Bloom's Modern Critical Views: Dante Alighieri*. 第197到第216页。

优雅的，肯定是无罪的"，而且这肯定不是一个问句，而可能是反问句，含义为"你不要来骚扰我这个受害者"；其二，问句不符合"主语—动词—宾语"的结构，而通过"把"译者就将"我"置于重点。通过何等复杂的结构，译者也能复制皮埃尔的一些弯曲错综的语言，清清楚楚地反映出其弯曲错综的树干、树枝。维吉尔对皮埃尔道歉，然后求他谈自己的故事，这里皮埃尔的答案明明白白地表现出他的态度：

E l tronco:《Sì col dolce dir m'adeschi,
chi' non posso tacere; e voi non gravi
perch'ïo un poco a ragionar m'inveschi.》

树干说道："你的温和话语令我心动，
我不能缄口不语；但你们不至于感到厌烦，
因为我要略费工夫，讲述一番。"

这里有一个值得注意的翻译失误，因为原本的皮埃尔的第一句话带来一种批判性的弦外之音。用比较简单的释义，皮埃尔对维吉尔说："因为你用甘甜的美词来诱惑我，我就不能沉默不语"。皮埃尔在隐含地攻击维吉尔，以为他是一个引诱者，使用甜蜜的词语来欺骗他，潜在的意义总是"我是无罪的，你是一个诱惑者，你想利用我这个罪人"。如果把原本的"adeschi"（引诱）翻译成"令我心动"，那就使皮埃尔的性格突然有了巨大的变化，译本的皮埃尔对维吉尔的要求只不过是表示礼貌而已。在这种变化下，我们能够分析下列的句子，"但你们不至于感到厌烦，因为我要略费工夫，讲述一番"。以皮埃尔的不一样的态度为前提，这句话也包含着不一样的含义：原本道的是，一个非常想要讲述自己的故事的幽灵，为了让别人知道他是受害者。维吉尔的温和要求事实上只代表皮埃尔使用的一个讲自己故事的借口，没有什么大的说服力，甚至他预知其听众会感到厌烦，所以他就提前道歉。译本的皮埃尔是因为接受了维吉尔的邀请而愿意讲述自己的故事，他的道歉就呈现了套话的成分。

最后一方面是黄文捷所运用的中文的特点：他的译本的中文特点比较多，这里我浅谈三个，其实它们都或多或少都跟皮埃尔的语气有关：第一是叠字，尤其是在皮埃尔的片段上，但丁是"稍稍"把一颗枝蔓抓住，皮埃尔说他应该"多多留情"，等等。它们的用法及其在文句中的位置虽然在意义方面没有什么大的作用，但是它们有助于诗体的韵律和可读性，可以推断说，它们对译本的押韵之损失有所弥补，可以使文本更加朗朗上口。第二，四字词语，它们也属于皮埃尔的演说风度，就像他通过美言——这里说的"美言"也包括上述的叠词及"为何"的案例——试图令读者怜悯，证明他是有修养而无罪的亡魂。它讲述自己的故事主要用了两个四字成语："小心翼翼"（第60行）和"信誓旦旦"（第62行），更值得我们关注的是第二个，因为通过它，皮埃尔庄严宣誓他根本没有内疚。第三，趋向补语，在汉语中它们很常见，并且它们分字面上和形象上的意义。但丁是这样描述皮埃尔的伤口的，"既说出话，又流出血"，这句话成功地把趋向补语和排比句结合起来，将皮埃尔的形象弄得极其活泼。再者，当皮埃尔解释自杀者在末日审判之后的情况时，他说"没有一个人能再把它（肉身）披上"而且"在凄惨的丛林中，我们的肉体将一一挂起"。按照一些学者的观点，这个形象的优点在于自杀者和犹大作为自杀者的排比[①]，而我相信，中文的形象由于悬念在句尾的"起"字而显得十分鲜明。

张曙光与第三十三章——乌戈利诺

就《神曲》的翻译而言，张曙光是黄文捷的对立面：他是一个纯粹的诗人，看不懂意大利语，他的翻译主要参考若干英文版本以及其他汉语版本（尤其是田德望的散文体汉译），所以在某一方面我们可以将他的译本称作"语内翻译"。他的译本在表面上保持了原有的诗体，但

---

① 比方说，Lynne Press 在前面引用的书的第212页："……an eternal reminder of their sin and an evocative image of the suicide of Judas."

实际上他的语言有相当突出的口语成分。

《神曲·地狱篇》的第三十三章是因为乌戈利诺伯爵的悲惨故事而成名的。在地狱的第九圈受惩罚的罪人是叛徒，他们的灵魂为神圣的正义埋在冰里；乌戈利诺这个人物的情况很特别，他既是罪人，又是天意的一个工具。罪人，因为他背叛过自己的党派，与卢吉埃里大主教结盟；天意的工具，因为他为卢吉埃里所背叛，与自己的四个孩子们被囚禁在"饿塔"里，接受了几天的饥饿而最后饿死了（其实，按照记载是两个孩子和两个孙子，但是但丁为了增加故事的悲惨效果改变了这个细节）。在地狱，乌戈利诺和卢吉埃里被放在一起，前者应该永恒猛吃后者的头盖骨。张曙光这里用的词暴露出一种黑色幽默特点，说卢吉埃里是乌戈利诺的"邻人"；读者不能不想到耶稣基督的第十一诫，"爱你的所有的邻人，就像爱你自己"，而这两个罪人之间只有痛恨。

本章的原本是以"嘴"这个字（意语是 La bocca）为开端，这样一来但丁确定了整个故事的基调。于此译者碰到了第一个翻译问题，因为原本的"bocca"是"罪人"的宾语，不能将之置于句子的开头，所以张曙光用了"嘴"和"罪人"之间的头韵来开始这一章。完整的第一行如下：

　　　　那个罪人的嘴从可怕的食物上抬起（……）

一个明显的原因是，张曙光很可能参考过田德望的散文体翻译，其第一行如下：

　　　　那个罪人把嘴从野兽般啃着的食物抬起来（……）

"嘴"音的连续运用能够给读者一个接近于原本的形象，但是其有关的官能又变了：意大利读者可以读到"La bocca"作为第一个单词，中国读者在阅读文本的过程中可以在脑子里听到"嘴"音的重复。这个在某种程度上补偿了原有开端的损失。

尽管本版本有着很显著的口语成分，但是译者还能够获得富有诗情的效果，其中之一在于，他使得乌戈利诺的叙述方式变得非常生动，而且与原本比起来，它更有变化。原来，乌戈利诺跟但丁说话的时候，从始至终他的语言都很有诗情，跟整个作品的所有人物无异，他用三韵体来讲述自己的故事，所以因为这个三韵体，但丁考虑到每个词之间的押韵，让文本的风度自然而然显得优雅。但是张曙光的译本，因为没有受到韵律的约束，所以翻译者只要考虑到文本的正确性就好了，然后他应该依赖于其他手段来重新创造出原有的诗意。譬如，让乌戈利诺的表述变得更有波动，他开始用的语言相当平凡，诗意一点也不突出，但是他一回忆自己和他的孩子们怎么忍受了几天的饥饿而终于死了的故事，他的语域突然就升高了。意大利批评家德·桑克蒂斯（Francesco De Sanctis）曾经把这一点指出来，乌戈利诺的叙述风格可以比作一首哀歌①，在张曙光的译本当中，因为这一颇有诗意的哀歌被放在平凡的词汇之后，所以它就可以脱颖而出。从第 4 行到第 21 行，可算是乌戈利诺的故事的绪言，他介绍了自己及其"邻人"卢吉埃里，说他愿意讲他死亡的故事中一些不为人知的细节，为的是让卢吉埃里的臭名传播到人世。所以，到了第 22 行读者便有了耳目一新的感觉，乌戈利诺的叙述突然以"一扇"为开端，这"一扇"的功能既是作窗子的量词又是有比喻意义的，使得读者的想象力另开新门，告诉读者这个部分与上面的部分有隔断。而且因为中文没有从现在时到过去时的时态变化，所以读者会有这种感觉，就像乌戈利诺的故事不是以倒叙的方式来讲述，而是实时发生在他或她的眼下。时态的缺乏实际上把整个故事的背景转到了"饿塔"里面。看起来这是一个故意的选择，特别是因为译本的乌戈利诺用的时间副词是"这时候"而不是"那时候"。再者，时态的缺乏让乌戈利诺的一些旁白显得更有震撼，因为他在评论的不是一个过去发生过的事情，而是在他的面前重新展开的故事。从这个角度来看，他的

---

① Francesco De Sanctis, "L'Ugolino di Dante"（但丁的乌戈利诺），载于 *Nuovi saggi critici*, Morano Editore, 1890，第 51 到第 75 页。

要是想起我的心预见到的，还不
悲伤，那你可真算是残酷了；
而要是此刻不哭，那你什么时候哭？（第 40—42 行）

显得更有感染力，更能令读者体会到乌戈利诺的痛苦。

乌戈利诺的变形在整个故事的过程当中是通过一些手段而指出来的，它们之间的最显而易见的便是上述的旁白，基本上它们是通过一些分号而强调出的，我们看以下的例子：

令人惧怕的塔的大门；没有一句话（第 47 行）

我没有哭；在内心，我变成了石头（第 49 行）

我于是平静下来，为了不使他们更痛苦；
那一天和下面的一天，我们都沉默着；
啊！坚硬的大地，为什么你不裂开？（第 64—66 行）

我们在分号之后所画的线代表什么？它们代表乌戈利诺的一些补充。原本里，它们随着故事的节奏而出现，反过来说在译本里它们和整个故事不是一体了，它们通过分号打断了叙述，与主要的故事隔绝开来了，为了强调乌戈利诺的心情的退化，从沉默到石头心再到最全面的绝望。简单地说，在主要的情节之下有另一个情节在平行发生，便是乌戈利诺的情形之堕落的情节。堕落的最低点一直往下走，直到他的最后一句话（有被分号引入的）："后来，饥饿比悲伤更有力"，虽然他看到所有的儿子们一个接一个死于他眼下，但是他没有痛死，却终于饿死了。我们能够看到的是这个人物的信仰的缺乏，在某种程度上这也算是他的最严重的罪恶。

至于最后一句话，为数不少的批判者提倡过一个更残忍的诠释：对于他们来说"饥饿比悲伤更有力"的言外之意并不是"悲伤没能把我杀死，饥饿能"，而是"我不得不把他们的尸体吃掉"。我们在此应该依赖评论界去解决这个问题：上述的德·桑克蒂斯以及阿根廷文学家博尔赫斯认为，但丁特意使得乌戈利诺的最后一段话显得模棱两可，但丁不想直接让读者幻想到乌戈利诺吃了这些尸体，但是他至少愿意让读者以为这是一个可能性，因为对于博尔赫斯来说，"瞥见乌戈利诺（吃自己的孩子）的这个可怕罪恶，要比否定它或确定它更恐怖"[①]。张曙光了解了乌戈利诺的最后一句话只有保持其含糊特征才能有成效，所以他一字一字地把它翻译成"后来，饥饿比悲伤更有力"。基本上学术界不认可这种字对字的翻译，但是这里张曙光的策略成功了，而且如果我们跟黄文捷的翻译对比起来，其成果更为显著。作为一个纯粹意大利语研究者的黄文捷，主要追求的是准确性、澄清而不是诗意，所以他的翻译是，"后来，饥饿终于比痛苦更有能力把我的性命夺走"；与其说这是翻译，我们还不如称之为释义。作为灵敏诗人的张曙光却特别注意到了这一艺术效果，为艺术性而牺牲了诗句的澄清。

如果我们确认，乌戈利诺是第三十三章的第一部分的绝对主人公，我们却不能不强调其他陪伴者们的任务的重要性。他们虽然在整个故事里只说三句话，可是他们的一举一动及其与主人公的相互作用对故事的气氛做出了不能忽略的贡献。我们参考一下这个描述：饿塔的所有的囚犯在哭泣和沉默之间徘徊，其沉默的表现被张曙光通过省略号和破折号标出，尤其是在第 51 行到第 54 行：

"爸爸，你这样看着我……出了什么事？"
我照样没有流泪——整整一个白天
又通过紧随其后的夜晚——也不说话
直到另一个太阳触摸着世界。

在原本里，第 51 行没有省略号，这里它们之所以被加上，我们推测有两个原因：其一，它们能够放慢叙事的速度，这个与以下的破折号

[①] Jorge Luis Borges, *Il falso problema di Ugolino*（乌戈利诺的假问题），载于 *Nove saggi danteschi*, Adelphi, 2001, 第二章。

并时间副词（白天—夜晚—另一个太阳）的作用无异；其二，它们可以让读者自己去补充乌戈利诺的儿子没有说出的话，这样一来读者不自觉地积极地投入到文本里，按照自己对整个文本的了解去加上自己以为可以加上的词。

在这个文本里，父亲和儿子们互相作用的高潮部分便在于伽多之死；在第68行里，张曙光把原本的"disteso"（伸开、展开）译成"直挺挺"。原本所传达的形象是一个疲惫不堪的身体因为缺乏营养而掉到地上，但（至少对我而言）译本提供给读者的是一个略微不同的形象。这个"直挺挺"因为其所带的叠字，可被看作一个象声词，这个"挺挺"暗示着一种比较机械的、死板的动作。看来，儿子们一个接一个收到了父亲"内心变成了石头"的影响而依次失去了自己的人性，所以在译本上，父亲和儿子们都经过类似的过程，从绝望到沉默再到一种被动的屈从，他们说出的话也透露出其感情的动态：从忧虑和不安（"爸爸……出了什么事？"）到被动的屈从（孩子们要求父亲吃他们的肉，以剥夺他们的痛苦）再到最后的喊救（"爸爸，为什么你不帮我？"）。这样一来，整个叙事都变成了乌戈利诺对卢吉埃里的痛恨的一种辩护：其感情被剥夺了，其心变成了石头，仅仅留下了永恒的痛恨和饥饿。

结　论

当一个外来的作品被另一个文化接受时，它很可能会按照接受者文化的规律被诠释、分析。早在1921年，钱稻孙先生了解到了这一点，这就是为什么他的《神曲一脔》是按照中国古典诗歌的规律重新编排。美国华侨刘若愚在其《中国诗学》一文中强调过，关于中国古典诗歌基本上有四个主流的论说：有教育价值、能够表达出诗人的感情、有创造性、有感知性；现在一些问题突然出现了，因为诚然，但丁的大作或多或少可划入前面三个范围，也就是说我们可以按照前三个论说去解读它，但是它绝对不属于最后一个。在《神曲》上我们不能"忘我"，不能进入"无我"的语境，但丁的史诗的确需要人情的参与，否则的话它就会简化为一个没完没了的罪人、圣人的清单，中国古典诗歌所特有的超然描述会消解《神曲》的诗意。而且，它既是史诗又是小说，所以有一些旧的版本简直把整个作品简化为散文体，但是结果也不是最理想的。甚至，斯洛伐克汉学家高利克在《中国对但丁的接受及其影响》一文中引用并赞同美国教授浦安迪的一句话："（除了钱稻孙之外）……手头所能得到的截止到上世纪末的其他作品，（……）不是没有灵魂的白话文翻译，就是对原文的散文重述"。问题是：中国文学的大传统怎么去对待一个如此棘手的文本？我们以高利克和浦安迪的观点为起点，以上各章都试图证明 2000 年之后的三个译本，无论译者是纯粹的诗人还是纯粹的学者，抑或在两个身份之间徘徊，都在尊敬原本，为了保留其精神及其微妙的地方做出了不能忽略的加工。三位译者的翻译策略共同点只有一两个：其一，至少在表面上保留下来了原有的诗体；其二，他们的参考系并不是中国文学的大传统而是中文语言本身独有的象形文字、语法结构以及语调。他们依赖于中文的特点重新创造但丁的语言技巧，保持归化翻译和异化翻译之间的平衡。

主要参考文献：

1. Francesco DeSanctis, *Nuovi saggi critici*, Morano Editore, Napoli 1890.
2. Francesco DeSanctis, *Saggi critici*, Morano Editore, Napoli 1898.
3. ［美］刘若愚:《中国诗学》，韩铁椿、蒋小雯译，长江文艺出版社 1991 年版。
4. 郑阿宁:《中国古典文学中的风度鬼城与但丁"神曲"的亡魂世界之比较》，载于《重庆师范学院学报》（哲社版），1997 年第四期。
5. Francesco DeSanctis, *Storia della Letteratura Italiana*, Einaudi, 1997.
6. Jorge Luis Borges, *Nove saggi danteschi*, Adelphi, 2001.
7. Harold Bloom（ed.）, *Bloom's Major Poets*: Dante, Infobase Publishing, 2001.
8. 叶维廉:《比较诗学》，载于《叶维廉文集·第一卷》，安徽教育出版社 2002 年版。
9. ［意］但丁:《神曲·地狱篇》，黄文捷译，译林出版社 2005 年版。
10. ［意］但丁:《神曲·地狱篇》，张曙光译，广西大学出版社 2005 年版。
11. ［意］但丁:《神曲·地狱篇》，黄国彬译，外语教学与研究出版社 2009 年版。

12. Alessandra Brezzi, Il Novecento cinese di Dante, 载于 *Critica del testo*, XIV/3, 2011 (Dante, oggi/3), a cura di R. Antonelli, A. Landolfi, A. Punzi, Roma, Viella, 2011。
13. Harold Bloom (ed.), *Bloom's Modern Critical Views*: *Dante Alighieri* (New Edition), Infobase Publishing, 2011.
14. ［斯］玛丽安·高利克：《中国对但丁的接受及其影响》，载于《扬子江评论》，2012年第一期。
15. Jungnok Park, *How Buddhism Acquired a Soul on the Way to China*, Equinox publishing Lt., 2012.

《中美比较文学》稿件体例

　　《中美比较文学》是由中美两国比较文学界合办的人文社会科学综合性学术集刊，旨在集中展示中美比较文学界最新研究成果。为方便作者写作和读者阅读，现将中文投稿注意事项告知如下：

　　1. 来稿以 15,000 字以内为宜。欢迎简明扼要而又论证充分的万字以内文章。所论重大理论问题、重要学术问题的论文允许篇幅稍长一些。正文之前请附中文摘要（300—400 字）、英文摘要（约 200 个英文单词）、关键词（3—5 个）、作者简介（姓名、工作单位、学位、职称）。如果所投稿件是作者承担的科研基金项目，请注明项目名称和项目编号。

　　2. 论文区分注释与参考文献，分别以脚注和主要参考文献形式出现。注释与参考文献著录项目要齐全，不标注文献标识码，具体示例如下：

　　* 专著：主要责任者，文献名，出版地，出版单位，出版年，起止页码。

　　* 译著：原著者，文献名，译者名，出版社，出版单位，出版年，起止页码。

　　* 期刊文章：主要责任者，文献题名，刊名，年，卷（期），起止页码。

　　* 报纸文章：主要责任者，文献题名，报纸名，出版日期（版次）。

　　* 专著中的析出文献：析出文献主要责任者，析出文献题名，专

著主要责任者,专著名,出版地:出版者,出版年,析出文献起止页码。

3. 外文参考文献要用外文原文,作者、书名、杂志名字体一致,书名、杂志名等用斜体,其余采用正体。

4. 来稿请寄送电子文本:sajournal@163.com。稿件末尾请务必注明作者联系方式,详细通讯地址(含街道路名)、邮政编码、联系电话。

5. 来稿一般不退,请作者自留底稿;也不奉告评审意见,敬请海涵;稿件一经录用,编辑部会在三个月内通知作者。

《中美比较文学》编辑部
2016 年 3 月

Call for Papers

Sino-American Journal of Comparative Literatures, an academic journal focusing on Comparative Literature and World Literature. Submissions are welcome based on the following guidelines:

1. Papers should not exceed the length limit of 15,000 words. The Abstract and 3-5 keywords are supposed to be in Chinese and English, and a short biography of the author should be included in the submitted papers with the order of abstract, keywords and biography of the author.

2. Papers written in English should follow the MLA format in their documentation.

3. Submissions should be in electronic form and emailed to SAJCL@gmail.com.